MORE PRAISE FOR *THE HAZ*

"Reading Jessica Shattuck's pitch... the children and grandchildren of John Cheever's Wapshots."
—Mark Rozzo, *Los Angeles Times*

"A witty and promising first novel. . . . [Shattuck's] descriptive brio can leave the reader punchy with surprise and admiration."
—Jennifer Egan, *New York Times Book Review*

"[A] stunning debut novel, Cambridge native Shattuck renders the sad, comic decline of the Dunlap family, mirroring the demise of the Boston Brahmins themselves."
—Greg Lalas, *Boston Magazine*

"[With a] keen understanding of human nature and frailty [Shattuck] often displays a magnetic use of detail that not only makes her scenes come visually alive but also illuminates character."
—David Wiegand, *San Francisco Chronicle*

"*The Hazards of Good Breeding* showcases Shattuck's sophisticated eye and her talent for turning arch observation into words."
—Dan Santow, *Chicago Tribune*

"Shattuck is an observant and graceful writer, and contrives elegant and touching scenes."
—*Publishers Weekly*

"Quiet . . . funny and moving."
—Kristine Huntley, *Booklist*

"[Shattuck] has a real gift for crafting beautiful small moments."
—Leah Greenblatt, *Seattle Weekly*

"[*The Hazards of Good Breeding*] is at once a funny send-up of blue bloods in debauched decline and a profoundly compassionate contemplation of the burdens of inheritance."
—Donna Seaman, *Ruminator Review*

"Shattuck's prose is graceful and unforced, full of unexpected and casually tossed insights, and, like Lorrie Moore, her humor acts both as scourge and salve, to skewer and to deflect."
—Nicola Smith, *Valley News*

"A loopy, tightly wound WASP family in Concord, Massachusetts, unravels with the introduction of alien elements in a generously portrayed and richly appointed debut. . . . Shattuck has done wonders bringing to luminous life her patriotic diorama."
—*Kirkus Reviews*

"Wickedly funny."   —*New York Observer*

"An excellent novel. . . . The author avoids contrivance in presenting sensitive issues experienced by totally credible, thoughtful people and comes up with a new understanding of American life every bit as affecting as Richard Yates's magnificent *Revolutionary Road*."   —Ann Beattie

"Jessica Shattuck has written a thoughtful and elegant first novel, full of insight and humor. It is set in a rarefied world, one that she knows intimately and reveals perceptively; one which, for all its flaws and eccentricities, she loves."
—Roxana Robinson

"With great skill and wisdom Jessica Shattuck weaves an intricate domestic web that highlights the most vulnerable threads in a myriad of relationships: parents, children, friends, and lovers. *The Hazards of Good Breeding* is all that the title promises and more. It is a terrific debut by a talented writer."
—Jill McCorkle

"With her sharp eye for detail and witty, winning prose, Jessica Shattuck takes the familiar story of a high-WASP family's demise and turns it on its head. There are at least fifteen certifiable pleasures in every paragraph of this charming, intelligent, and exceedingly well-crafted debut."
—Helen Shulman

THE HAZARDS OF
GOOD BREEDING

THE HAZARDS OF GOOD BREEDING

Jessica Shattuck

W. W. NORTON & COMPANY

NEW YORK   LONDON

For information about permission to reproduce selections from this
book, write to Permissions, W. W. Norton & Company, Inc., 500 Fifth
Avenue, New York, NY 10110

Manufacturing by Quebecor World, Fairfield
Book design by Mary A. Wirth
Production manager: Amanda Morrison

LIBRARY OF CONGRESS CATALOGING-IN-PUBLICATION DATA

Shattuck, Jessica.
The hazards of good breeding / by Jessica Shattuck.– 1st ed.
p. cm.
ISBN 0-393-05132-3 (hardcover)
1. Young women—Fiction. 2. Children of divorced parents—Fiction.
3. Women college graduates—Fiction. 4. Parent and adult
child—Fiction. 5. Upper class families—Fiction. 6. Boston
(Mass.)—Fiction. 7. Housekeepers—Fiction. I. Title.
PS3619.H357 H39 2003
813'.6—dc21
2002014203

ISBN 0-393-32483-4 pbk.

W. W. Norton & Company, Inc.
500 Fifth Avenue, New York, N.Y. 10110
www.wwnorton.com

W. W. Norton & Company Ltd.
Castle House, 75/76 Wells Street, London W1T 3QT

3 4 5 6 7 8 9 0

To

A. P. J.,

WITHOUT WHOM THERE WOULD BE NO STORY

ACKNOWLEDGMENTS

I OWE HEARTFELT THANKS to Eric Simonoff for his guidance and wisdom, and to Jill Bialosky for her capable direction and understanding. To Bill Buford for his support and Cressida Leyshon for her kindness and advocacy, to Binnie Kirshenbaum and Helen Schulman for their generous encouragement and advice, to Karen Schwartz, Gordon Haber, and Rebecca Donner for their readings and moral support, and to Verlyn Klinkenborg for getting me started on the right foot.

I am also deeply grateful to my father and mother for their values and their belief in my imagination, to my whole family for their enthusiasm and encouragement, and to my husband for his gift of insight, his sense of humor, and his faith in my work. And I am forever indebted to my friends, especially the girls of Lowell House, for sharing their stories and their jokes, and their unfailing recognition of the meaningful and the absurd.

THE HAZARDS OF
GOOD BREEDING

THE DUNLAP HOUSE SITS *on the western slope of the third largest hill in Middlesex County, like a dark spot between the green fields of the Ponkatawset Golf Course and the Marret School for the Blind. It is an austere place, built in 1820, with black shutters, a peaked carpenter's roof, and a slight list to its mahogany-stained clapboards, as if a powerful magnet under the old root cellar is gradually pulling the whole structure back into the earth.*

There has been a house on this spot since 1747, when the first John Forsythe Dunlap turned in his barrister's wig, bought three chickens and two pigs, and moved west from Boston to farm the land. According to the Old Houses of Concord *pamphlet put out by the local chapter of the DAR, the house he built was burnt to the ground by his daughter*

Abigail in protest of his domineering ways. According to the current John Forsythe (known as Jack) Dunlap this is hogwash. He has conducted his own research on the matter and determined that it was the Ponkatawset Indians who set fire to the property in one of their fierce, but little discussed, raids. And while in most things Jack is a private and uncommunicative man, he likes to tell this story. This is in part to set the record straight—he cannot let the truth fall victim to a bunch of gossiping DAR members—and in part because he loves the great American drama of property ownership, which is more vivid in his version of the story.

For the last 254 years, minus a brief interlude Jack thinks of as "the occupation," the house has remained in Dunlap-Whiteside family hands. Jack himself bought the house back from the interloping owners, a Swiss couple named the Neiderbergers, whom he remembers as weak-chinned, soulless-looking people who had the gall to install a Jacuzzi in the two-hundred-year-old butter churn room, carve skylights into the kitchen, and paint the ancient clapboards a cheerful butter yellow. Mr. Neiderberger had made millions selling some marvel of Swiss engineering, which he described at length to Jack during their one conversation, but Jack was thinking of the ancient Franklin stove the man had had melted into ball bearings and heard nothing but white noise.

Jack's ex-wife, Faith, remembers the couple as sweet and sorrowfully childless, and she liked the house the way it looked under their care. She had to stand aside, though, and watch as Jack restored its original gloomy colors and awkward proportions, as he ripped up the comfortable wall-to-wall carpeting and tore out the offending Jacuzzi. The skylights in the breakfast room were her one triumph; Jack couldn't take them out without putting in a whole new roof. On sunny winter days she could find refuge on the sofa beneath them with her favorite plaid throw blanket and a copy of People. *But even there, in her woolly pool of sunlight, the presence of all the dark rooms beyond the doorway made itself felt. She has never, even for a moment, missed one thing about the place, which has, in retrospect, come to seem like the stern and joyless embodiment of her marriage.*

When Jack and Faith's daughter Caroline is at home, she likes to count new cracks in the ceilings, moth holes in the curtains, and dead flies in the window sashes. It has come to seem funny to her—all this opulent decrepitude and self-consciously maintained lack of creature comfort. But at the same time, it is the house she grew up in. Which makes it all she really knows. Over the holidays when she is back from school, she burns candles in her bedroom and listens to weepy female vocalists and Led Zeppelin. This seems to clear the way for the present, which otherwise enters 23 Memorial Road stillborn.

For Eliot Dunlap, the youngest of Jack and Faith's children, the house is not just his home, but his world—a disparate collection of cities and states, geographies and regions, each with its own climate, history, and culture. The dining room, for instance, is a repressive totalitarian state; the pink and white guest room, an inviting, but neglected warm-weather island. His favorite places are outside the house: the dappled clearing in the middle of the rhododendron bushes, and the small wood of red pines, golden beeches, and startling white birch trees that separates the Dunlap's field from the Ponkatawset Golf Course. Eliot calls this Sarajevo; it is a name he has heard somewhere before, which seems as lovely and mysterious as this place is. At dusk, he likes to collect lost golf balls buried here among the pine needles, elephant ear ferns, roots, and fallen branches. In the last reflective light of evening, these glimmer a soft and otherworldly purple. And from above, the wood takes on the look of a sieve—a universe full of tiny, bright, unpatchable holes.

1

CAROLINE DUNLAP HAS ALWAYS been surrounded by crazy men. First of all, there is her father, who wakes at five every morning to build Revolutionary War dioramas and sleeps with his grandfather's ancient nine-gauge pistol under his pillow. Then there are her identical-twin older brothers, who are famous throughout the New England Independent School League for having swung, Flying Wallenda–style, from the St. Stephan's Chapel bell tower into the headmaster's bathroom on a string of knotted dress shirts. There is also Wheelie Barrett, the retired NHL player who mows the Dunlaps' lawn and believes the 747s flying en route to Logan drop gelatinous sewage by-products over the roses and boxwood bushes behind

the house. Then there are the hundreds of salesclerks, bus
passengers, male flight attendants, paper delivery boys, bank
tellers, and lost pedestrians who have a much higher incidence
of insanity in Caroline's life than in anyone else's she knows.
(Just yesterday a man sitting on a park bench beside her got up
and tried to urinate on a pigeon.)

Last on the list, there is Rock Coughlin, who is, at this
moment, sitting cross-legged on the floor at the foot of Caroline's childhood bed.

Caroline blinks to make sure she is awake and pulls herself
up onto one elbow, knocking her shoulder against the head-
board.

"Good morning." Rock grins before she is even fully
upright.

"Rock!" Caroline looks at the ancient E.T. alarm clock on
the bedside table. Seven forty-seven, its eyes blink at her. "What
are you doing here?"

"Welcoming you back." Rock says this as if she has asked
him what color his hair is, or if he is breathing.

"While I was sleeping?" Caroline stares at him.

"You looked so peaceful. I didn't want to wake you."

"Hmm," Caroline says, reaching for the pack of cigarettes
beside her bed. "That's creepy."

"You did the right thing, you know. Coming back here. You
would have hated San Francisco. The whole city is like a fucking telecommunications ad and everyone is into mountain bik-
ing and fleece vests and . . ."

Caroline lights her cigarette and takes a drag. She sweeps
her eyes around the room. From floor to ceiling, it is populated
by the hopeful, temporary objects of her childhood: James
Dean posters, trophies, an empty glass hamster cage, her
ancient dilapidated dollhouse. In the middle of this her duffel
bags and crates of CDs, toiletries, and poster rolls look out of
place, like garbage washed up on some innocent New England
beach.

Within the few minutes it has taken her to fully absorb this,

Rock has launched into a story about a group of monks he met in Harvard Square, an orange T-shirt he was wearing, and the possibility that it—or they? or some combination of circumstances?—represents his calling. Caroline is not really listening, though. She has to figure out how to reclaim her morning from him; Rock has been known to spend hours in the company of those who don't want his. At Quilton, the boarding school he and Caroline both went to, he was famous for following Kirstin Hedrin to a bikini wax during their breakup.

Caroline already has to take her little brother, Eliot, to his school play this morning, which will have its challenges without Rock trailing after her with some dilettantish dilemma about his spiritual future. Her mother is making her first trip back to Concord since she left it last year to be at the play for one thing, which is sure to be traumatic. Faith Dunlap nearly collapses upon contact with her dry cleaner, not to mention the bevy of ex-golf partners and country club pals she is sure to run into at the Barton Country Day School.

". . . I mean, they don't ask everyone to come live with them," Rock is saying. "What if they just saw something, like a halo over my head—some sign invisible to most people?"

"I don't think Buddhists believe in halos," Caroline says.

Rock ignores her. He has begun running his hand along her bookshelf, rocking every third book forward. For the first time, it occurs to her he might be slightly serious. "You're too old to become a monk anyway, Rocky," Caroline sighs. "Those guys practically start training in utero."

"That's the whole point, though. They wanted me to come because there was a link between us, something that would make me able to learn their prayers or meditations or whatever faster than, you know, you or your brothers or any other normal American."

"Oh, right, of course," Caroline says, blowing a cloud of smoke out the open window.

At the moment, Rock actually looks almost childish—he is twenty-four years old, but with his shaggy brown hair flattened and explosive-looking on one side (his pillow? or has he fallen asleep on the beach again?), skinny legs, and bleach-stained green shirt, he could easily still be in high school. He has lost weight over the last year, mulching gardens and breeding asparagus or whatever it is he was doing at the organic farm he worked at.

Caroline herself looks exactly the same, though. She glances at the face reflected in the pink Miss Piggy mirror hanging over Rock's head. She has just graduated from college, broken up with her boyfriend of two years, and, on account of this, thrown any semblance of plans for her immediate future out the window; she would like, at least, to look tired. But the face that stares back out at her is remarkably smooth and calm—hardly different than it was a year ago, or, for that matter, ten years ago when she was twelve: straight blond hair cut to her shoulders, gray eyes, silvery eyebrows, and sharp, straight features that manage, without fail, to give the impression of competence and reserve.

"I mean, what if I just passed up the one thing I was really meant to do in my life—the one really meaningful thing?" Rock continues. "I mean, it's not like I'm stemming the tide here. Like there's even any tide to be stemmed here." His book-rocking has become feverish. "You know what I mean?"

Caroline swings her legs over the side of the bed. "I do, actually." She stubs the cigarette out in the water glass beside the alarm clock. "I don't know if hanging out in a robe and decoding parchment papers or whatever all day is the answer, but"—she stands up and looks down at him—"maybe."

Rock stops harassing the books, leaving his right index finger on her high school copy of *Moby-Dick*. "Hmm." He chews on his bottom lip, flummoxed by her concession. "I guess it might drive me crazy."

Outside on the lawn Caroline can see Wheelie rounding the edge of the garage on his new Gatorade-orange tractor mower. He has a pink linen napkin tied over his head: protection against the sewage.

"It might just do that," Caroline says, standing up. "Rocky?" She pushes a hand through her hair. "I really have to get dressed now."

———————

CAROLINE'S YOUNGER BROTHER, Eliot, the dregs of his parents' conjugal activity, has made it to age ten with a certain degree of grace—virtually unheard of in men of the Dunlap family. He is a slender boy, small for his age, with snowy blond hair and a high-cheekboned, almost Slavic-looking face. There is something secretive, but not dishonest, about his demeanor that comes, maybe, because in his lifetime he has already had so much exposure to silence. He has a birthmark shaped like a Christmas tree on his left shoulder and wide, speckled gray-blue eyes, which are, not without reason, exceptionally wary.

This morning, he is sitting in the kitchen, fully costumed, mouthing the lines he has to recite in his school play, and cutting a banana into his bowl of cornflakes. He has been interrupted once, by a shaggy apparition that turned out to be Rock Coughlin rapping on the front door, but since then he has sat in meditative silence. Occasionally there is a rattling, thumping sound as Brutus, one of his father's beloved blue heelers, throws himself against the wire gate pulled shut between the mudroom and the kitchen. Eliot checks his watch: in twenty minutes Caroline is supposed to drive him to school, but he has not heard the shower turn on upstairs yet.

The play is his drama teacher's musical adaptation of "Paul Revere's Ride," the Longfellow poem, which is one of Eliot's favorites. He loves the acute sense of urgency and fate embedded in the story. He loves the lilt of "One if by land, two if by sea / and I on the opposite shore shall be," and the dark garbled images of phantom ships and huge black hulks, the reflections and silence and eager ears that populate the second verse, which makes him think of fairies. Most of all he likes the phrase "a shape in the moonlight, a bulk in the dark" as if the weight of the man's deed has transformed him into some vague and formidable agent of the future, the way darkness transforms a laundry pile into a body or a hunchback with an evil eye.

The play is not without its challenges, though—the essential role of a horse (not allowed in the theater), the school requirement that drama productions include dance (which is hardly organic to the story), and the varied ages and skills of the actors (from Lucy Poole, who is not yet fully toilet-trained, to Eliot himself, who can recite the whole poem by heart). Eliot has been awake since six this morning with a gnawing premonition of disaster.

Eliot shifts in his seat and his knickers make a synthetic peeling sound on the stool. His costume is something of a sore spot. The knickers are all right—a bright, shiny royal blue—but the tunic is too fussy. It was originally sewn for his drama teacher's son, who was Aladdin for Halloween. Eliot and his teacher have made a pact to keep this quiet. Unlike most of the other Barton Country Day mothers, Eliot's mother no longer lives in the greater Boston area, and would not have the wherewithal to sew her son a costume even if she did. For his head, Eliot and his drama teacher have constructed a tricornered hat from triangles of thick brown felt glued and stapled together in a haphazard heap, which bears a surprising resemblance to a stack of pancakes. Eliot keeps this at school, in a carefully tented paper bag at the bottom of his cubby.

"One if by land, two if by sea," Eliot says bravely into the empty kitchen but the image of himself forming a sweaty-handed bridge with Josh Hopkins intrudes on the rhythm of the language and erases the next verse from his head. It will be his mother's first trip back to Concord in one year. *Will Penny Harley's mother be there? Will Anne Kittridge? And should I wear pants or a skirt or is it a kind of blue jeans thing?* she wanted to know on the phone last night. Eliot did his best to provide answers. The conversation left him with a tight, hard feeling in his stomach, which makes his digesting cornflakes feel like bird food.

When Eliot is done with his cereal, he drops lightly to the floor and pads across the linoleum to the sink, careful not to knock off the cardboard buckles he has taped to his bedroom slippers. He rinses his bowl, places it in the dish rack, and then stands still for a moment, spoon poised in midair, staring out the window. There is a cardinal perched on a branch of the apple tree, not more than five feet from the house. His babysitter, Rosita, always said if you can stare at a bird and count to twenty before it flies away, it will bring you a wish. Eliot counts slowly, spelling *Mississippi* between every number. He knows what he will wish for: Rosita's return. He misses the way she hums when she washes dishes and nods her head when she listens, the way her lips form the words when she is reading recipes or the directions on the back of cleaning supplies. There is something reassuring about the presence of her solid brown body in the house, about the sharp sting of Spanish she speaks into the telephone. She has been gone for almost six months now.

"Hey, if it isn't Rex Harrison," Rock Coughlin's voice shoots through the doorway, frightening the bird away. Eliot has just gotten to nineteen.

"El—what are you doing?" Caroline says from behind him. She has been home for less than a day and already she has taken the bossy, worried tone of someone on the lookout for disaster. "Aren't you supposed to get dressed at school?"

Eliot puts the spoon in the dish rack and turns around without answering.

"What's the part? Aladdin?" Rock asks.

"No." Eliot stiffens.

"You look great," Caroline adds hastily.

Eliot lifts his backpack off the counter and looks straight at her. "Can we go?" he asks.

"I'll stay here and wait for you," Rock announces from the table, where he is noisily rifling through the newspaper.

Caroline and Eliot both turn to stare at him, gape-mouthed. The idea of him here in the house when they are gone and the only sound is the hum of the refrigerator and the tinkle of the wind chime makes Eliot start sweating.

"It'll be a while," Caroline says, frowning. "I have errands to do when it's over."

"No problem—maybe I'll play a little frizz with D.D."

" 'D.D.'?" Caroline raises her eyebrows.

"Daddy Dunlap," Rock says, grinning.

Alarm shoots through Eliot. "He doesn't like Frisbee," he says automatically.

"Oh, sure he does—I'll show him the old over-easy."

"Whatever that is." Caroline glares at the top of his head. "Anyway, I don't think—" she cuts herself off and a strange stricken look comes over her face. "Oh, El—you don't think—do you think he'll come to your play this morning?"

"No," Eliot says firmly. He has had to assure his mother of this fact at least once every phone call for the last six weeks. "He has a meeting."

"Okay," Caroline says uncertainly. The possibility of their mother and father in the same room seems to dull her worry about Rock, who is still sitting, now with the antique chair tipped up on its back legs, at their kitchen table. Eliot does not feel similarly liberated.

Caroline follows his gaze to Rock and shrugs, lifting her hands in a gesture of helplessness. "Don't burn the house down," she says to Rock, jingling her car keys.

"Just the garage," Rock says. "Hey, break a leg," he calls after Eliot, in what seems like a less-than-reassuring send-off.

———

LEFT ALONE IN THE HOUSE, Rock continues shuffling through the paper until it hits him that he is in the house alone. Caroline's house alone. Jack Dunlap's house alone. It is an exciting thought. He could jerk off right here, at their kitchen table.

But the idea is vulgar, unsensual. Rock is after something finer. He closes the paper and pushes his chair back, almost over-turning it. There is a sudden wild barking from the mudroom from one of the Dunlap Devils, Rock's personal nickname for the blue-black beasts Jack Dunlap breeds and raises. "Hey," he says, standing up and walking toward the refrigerator. The dog stops barking and stands very still. "Where's your partner?" Then he realizes the dog is not actually silent—there is an ugly, almost inaudible growl coming from its chest.

Rock opens the refrigerator and closes it quickly—the dog is making him nervous. The kitchen is uninteresting, anyway. The secrets it holds (dietary preferences, cleanliness, brand affiliation) are chaste, feminine, busybody material. Rock is after deeper, more psychological insight.

Rock has known the Dunlaps since he was a boy, and his mother introduced Faith Dunlap to the writings of Deepak Chopra. This has not ceased to amuse Rock since his mother proudly recounted it last Thanksgiving. It proves his theory that reading spiritual self-help books is a harbinger of disaster. Rock has been *by* the Dunlaps' house plenty of times since the divorce—to drive Caroline home from the likes of Adam Lowell's Yankee Swap party or Bee Bee Mender's twenty-first birthday—but it has been a long time since he has been inside it.

He heads through the door to the dining room, which is long and dark and boring—full of framed oil paintings and a grim, precise rubbing of some English ancestor's tombstone. He has a vague memory of dinner here, long ago, when he was still playing PeeWee Hockey with the Dunlap boys. There was something uncomfortable about it, a new pair of shoes, a scratchy shirt collar, maybe a silent pinch fight with Jack Jr. under the table.

The library, which he pokes his head into hoping for some immense, imposing desk to rout through, is dark, spare, and unoriginal, down to the black iron Remington horse and rider on the mantel. No desk.

Rock sprints up the stairs, enjoying the screech of the wood under his feet. The house epitomizes what he loves about this part of Massachusetts—the austerity of design, the carefully maintained modesty of its appointments, and the cultivation of a somber moral framework through household furniture. Where else in America would a man who just spent $2.2 million on an empty plot of land outside Sun Valley have a grubby, moth-eaten hall runner with matching, similarly decrepit drapes depicting tiny scenes of the Boston Tea Party? There is something so perfectly dysfunctional about it, but at the same time so bravely and sincerely hopeful. After all, isn't all this self-denial predicated on the idea that there is some sort of here-after?

At the top of the stairs and to the right is Caroline's room, the only room up here Rock has ever actually been into. He could read her journal, run his hands through her underwear drawer. But this is something anyone would do, and he has already been there once this morning. He continues down the hall and opens a door at the left: a battered wooden bunk bed and *National Geographic* posters of lion cubs, a panda, and a pregnant iguana—Eliot's room. In the middle, on the carpet, is a giant papier-mâché work in progress—a four-by-four-foot landscape with big ugly mounds of unpainted newspaper and clumps of dandruffy-looking trees. What the hell would compel the kid to make something like this? But this doesn't really interest Rock, except insomuch as it reminds him he could get high. He gropes around in his pocket for the half-smoked joint he thinks he remembers—yes, there it is—and pushes the screen open. Then he lights up, sits on the windowsill, and discreetly hangs the joint out the window, stooping to exhale into the fresh summer air. Storybook air—it actually smells sweet, of strawberries and cut grass. There are cicadas revving up in the trees like the disparate parts of some giant engine.

Back out in the hall, Rock is drawn to the door at the end. Mr. Dunlap's room. Rock knows instinctively what it must be. He can feel his heart cluck and ruffle at the threshold.

Inside, it is quite dark. Only one shade to the left of an enormous unmade bed has been partially pulled up. Rock hits the overhead light and floods the room with an ugly greenish yellow fluorescence. There are newspapers, magazines, and white eight-by-twelve institutional reports scattered on an ottoman and the carpet around it. On the right, two framed pictures draped with T-shirts. Rock pads across the carpet to peer at what is beneath these. A photo of Jack and his wife taken at their wedding, and a more recent, painfully posed family portrait. If he hates them so much, why hasn't he just removed them?

Rock kicks his shoes off and scuffles his bare feet over the dark green carpet, feeling it chafe at the delicate, almost sticky skin of his arches. He never walks around without shoes. He worries about worms and tetanus and that his feet are too thin for a man's—or that they are too pale, too hairy. He picks up the magazine lying face down on the bed. *The Economist*— opened to an article about fear as an important motivator among canning industry workers. Rock stretches out on the burgundy sheets—flannel, slightly greasy-feeling. They have a comfortable, bready smell that suggests they haven't been washed for weeks. Rock stares up at the ceiling and imagines he is Jack Dunlap, founder of Amerithon, Inc., terrorizer of the Ponkatawset Club Events Committee and Concord Junior League, father of the most beautiful girl he, Rock Coughlin, knows.

2

FAITH DUNLAP HAS NEVER been good at packing. Looking ahead, planning strategically, incorporating variables (a hurricane? a rash? an unexpected party?) has never been her forte. Once, when she was ten, she went to St. Barth's for two weeks with nothing but corduroys, wool sweaters, plaid skirts, and thick white tights. Her parents had never said it was a warm place, that it was different from Boston, New Hampshire, or the Cape—never mentioned palm trees, or beaches, or gecko lizards, or anything else a ten-year-old would be interested in. That is the kind of parents they were. If they had been different, if they had held her hand on her first airplane trip, or remembered her birthdays, or let her sleep with a night-light, things might have turned out differently. She might still be married and a good mother, someone capable of identifying and filling her own week's worth of needs and packing in a jiffy. This is what she has determined from therapy; it is the simplest answer to the question of how she got to where she is now.

This morning, sitting on the scratchy blue and gray polyester seat cushion of the seven-thirty Delta shuttle she is taking up to Boston from her new home in New York City, Faith is exhausted. She was up until nearly one A.M. packing, sorting through sweaters and blouses, creams and lotions, allergy medications and anti-anxiety pills. At midnight she was still choosing her reading material: the last five issues of *House Beautiful?* or the novel Caroline sent her for her last birthday—something thick, but suspiciously light-looking (does her daughter think she isn't capable of real literature?)? She packed and unpacked a first-aid kit three times and replaced her third pair of sandals with a pair of twelve-year-old, never-used golf shoes. After her son's play, she is going to her old friend Lucy's summer home, and Lucy is so sporty; Faith will surely be roped into stressful rounds of tennis, badminton, golf, and croquet.

Staring out the scratched double-glass window of the airplane, Faith can feel her blood pressure rising. From above, Boston looks just like any other city: an uneven grid of rectangles broken up by more rectangles, looped together by a few sinewy ribbons of road. Last week, Faith had a computer installed in her apartment so she could e-mail with her children—a possibility that seems incredible to her still. The technician pulled out a flat metal panel covered with tiny squares and rectangles, called, what was it? it had such a sad, human-sounding name—the motherboard, that was it. It housed all the information the computer would ever need to carry out its operations, he explained, the mechanical equivalent of DNA. From here, the city looks remarkably like this thing; the shiny channels of highways, the smooth square tops of buildings. It seems almost mystical, this repetition of structure—as if both are reflections of the same archetypal image of order.

When the plane touches down, Boston looks brighter and sunnier than Faith expected. It looks hot, in fact, the way the leaves on the trees sag and the grass is that deep, almost blurry shade of green. The captain makes an elaborate announcement about what gate they will be pulling into in the same falsely enthusiastic, sidewalk-salesman voice he has used throughout the flight to fill passengers in on everything from cruising altitude to obscure geographical features of the Connecticut coastline. "Eighty-eight degrees and rising," he confirms Faith's suspicions. She is certainly wearing all the wrong things. The pink-and-white-striped blouse she has on is long-sleeved and her linen pants are lined! She will sweat through Eliot's performance—through her first visit back to Concord since she left it. The thought sends a shimmery burst of adrenaline from her gut to her heart. She is just going to a play, she tells herself. Just a morning, and then lunch with her children, and then she will be off. At least the twins, who have come to intimidate her with their baseball caps and loud voices and aggressive, uncommunicative way of speaking, are off in Colorado. And most importantly, Jack won't be there; she is lucky, really, to have this opportunity to see the place without him. It could be so much worse.

The fact remains, though, that Faith dreads this morning at the play: all the hugs of sympathetic neighbors, curious glances of familiar strangers, and nosy, condescending "how *are* you's" and "so good to see you *back* here's" of all the Barton Country Day mothers she has not seen since what Dr. Marcus suggests she think of as her "time-out," a term he accompanies with a refereelike gesture.

Faith is a small, slim woman, only five-foot-five. Her limbs and fingers are long and nervous; when she sits down and crosses her legs it is almost impossible to stop the anxious back-and-forth movement of her size-six foot. She is pretty also—her features are delicate, indistinct, and give the impression of being somehow watery, as if, faced with something really shocking or gruesome, they would melt. This is misleading, though. In fact, Faith has been privy to more shocking, gruesome things than many women of her class and age group. When she was nineteen, for example, her older brother was decapitated in an auto accident with Faith seated right beside him. There was an elm tree, a Bloody Mary in his hand, a tremendous sound of smashing machinery. She emerged from the overturned car with two cuts above her right eyebrow and a sprained wrist.

Faith manages to get her own bag out of the overhead compartment, wrestles it down the aisle and into the cool, antiseptic-smelling airport. Then she joins the masses of official, business-suited people streaming down the long gray hall to the taxi line out front. She feels like an impostor, someone who shouldn't be allowed to take such a professional, early morning plane.

"Where you going?" the driver asks when Faith is finally settled in the dark cavern of a yellow cab.

"To BCD," she says. "In Belmont."

"BCD," he repeats. Faith is not sure if it is a question or an affirmation. He is very thin and his skin is so black it is almost bluish. His voice is surprisingly high and sorrowful-sounding.

"Barton Country Day School—do you know where that is?" He shakes his head.

"Oh, dear—I don't know if I remember what street it's on. It's sort of modern-looking. I think—I hope—I have it written down somewhere . . . maybe you can just get started in that direction and I'll try to find—I can always ask directions in Belmont. . . ." She lets her voice trail off.

The driver does not answer but pulls out into the traffic of the terminal. So typical of her, to have forgotten the address! She roots around in her purse for her address book, which she can't find, but then it comes to her. "Bethune Street," she says. Up front the driver nods without turning.

Outside, the familiar raggedy pink brick of Chelsea springs

into view along the water, and in the distance the Bunker Hill
Monument, which has always struck Faith as mean-looking, full
of shabby puritanical delusions of grandeur.

It is strongly air-conditioned in the backseat of the taxi.
Faith leans her head against the slippery black vinyl. There is
an almost overpowering smell of berries—sweet, artificial, but
not at all unpleasant. It strikes her as effeminate, which gives
her a surge of compassion for the driver, who seems vulnerable,
someone so new to this country he has not yet absorbed its
most basic gender prohibitions. Someone who is probably
made fun of behind his back.

"I can't believe I forgot the name of that street," Faith says
aloud, in an excess of warm feeling toward him. "My children
all went there, my husband—actually, my ex-husband. . . . It's
just I guess you don't really think about it, when you go there
every day—drop off, pick up, you just think *school*, not Bethune
Street."

The driver looks at her in the rearview mirror without smiling or nodding, and Faith immediately regrets her words. He
has a gaunt face and bloodshot eyes, as if he has been driving
all night. He is probably from one of those awful, war-torn
countries whose names Faith always confuses. His wife and children are probably halfway across the planet in some shanty
with no toilet, or worse—they are probably dead. And now
Faith has reminded him of them with this frivolous talk about
school—as if he had the opportunity to "drop them off, pick
them up"—her words ring inanely in her ears. His children
probably never had the opportunity to learn to read.

The driver turns the radio on and settles on a classical station, and the soft notes of a cello stream out of the speakers—
not the rock and roll or easy listening or daytime talk show
Faith expected. Maybe he is from somewhere gentler than she
had imagined. Somewhere subtler and more full of longing
than fear. Or maybe . . . maybe—is it possible to be somewhere
both grim and full of longing?

Faith does not know much about classical music, but she

recognizes this piece—the low warble of cello strings and undulating motion that makes her think of someone running across a wide-open expanse of rolling hills in late afternoon sunshine.

"Do you know what this is?" she asks, leaning forward.

The driver looks at her in the rearview mirror. "Music," he says.

"Ah." Faith nods and sits back. She rests her head against the smooth vinyl again and lets the sound take them both somewhere kinder and softer than here.

OVER THE LAST FEW MONTHS, Jack Dunlap has become one of those people who do strange things in their sleep: he wakes up pounding the door to his closet, or sitting upright in his armchair, or slipping the key to the basement door into his left tennis sneaker. It gives him a feeling of shame and incompetence—what kind of man has he become, that he doesn't collapse into the immobilizing embrace of a deep slumber?

This morning, Jack has a crick in his neck from having spent the night with his head propped against the bedside table. He is beginning the day early, because he has two missions to accomplish before he goes to Eliot's performance. He has to swing by Colby Kesson, the poorly managed publishing business his company, Amerithon, is in the process of buying out, and bring his dog Caesar to the breeder's. He has cleared the rest of his appointments before lunch. It is unfair, after all, that just because she divorced him, his ex-wife should be the only one to see their son in his end-of-the-school-year performance.

When they arrive at the breeder's, Caesar waits obediently for Jack to let him out, watching with bright, almost catlike eyes as a squirrel races up the trunk of a maple over Jack's shoulder. He is a good hunter for a blue heeler: he has caught two rabbits and a crow in the last three months—a feat Brutus, the smaller and more timid of Jack's two dogs, could never have accomplished. Jack loves his dogs, who are both descended from the first blue heeler in America, who belonged to Jack's grandfather. Part shepherd, part Border collie, part dingo, there is a real animalness about them that is missing from so many breeds. Jack admires their firmness of intent and purpose. He trained them himself, and they are good dogs—obedient, watchful, and well behaved. He can feed them from the same dish, one at a time, and they won't squabble as they did when they were puppies. Instead they will sit back, licking their chops, waiting their turns with patience.

With Caesar trotting at his heels, Jack crosses the Ridgeways' lawn to the side door of the house, which opens into a small concrete-floored room, off which Jim Ridgeway has several kennels. Jim is the biggest Australian cattle dog breeder in New England and he loves Jack's dogs, whose height and speed and intelligence make their genes an excellent supply for local bloodlines. Jack lets Jim use them free of charge. The favor works both ways; Caesar especially is better behaved when he has mated. *Neuter them, for Christ's sake,* Jack's daughter Caroline says. *Why do they need to be such stallions?* But Jack has no intention of acting on this suggestion.

Jim comes to the door promptly at Jack's knock and takes the leash, pats Caesar on the shoulder. "He limping?" he asks, watching the dog nose along the baseboards of the room. Jack is impressed; the limp is almost gone. He himself can barely see it.

"Stepped on a thorn," he says. Jim pulls his mouth down at the edges. He is a man of few words, which Jack admires. He does not engage in the smarmy innuendos and elbows in the ribs that Jack has found such deals often inspire. Nor does he make small talk about the weather, the price of Science Diet, or the prevalence of hip dysplasia among retrievers. He never offers Jack an obligatory cup of coffee. This morning the whole exchange is complete in less than four minutes.

From the Ridgeways', Jack makes his way to Colby Kesson. Colby Kesson is a company with the kind of New Age, self-actualization bent that makes it exactly the sort of business Jack resents including in the Amerithon umbrella. It sells educational "kits" on-line to disgruntled pharmacy clerks looking to become telephone switchboard operators, overweight secretaries with a yen to practice aromatherapy, Burger King fry boys who've always wanted to be shoe salesmen, and any number of other individuals with lateral-movement career ambitions which the "kits" will take no nearer to fulfillment than they already are.

There was a time when Jack dreamed that Amerithon would be the Tiffany's of American history textbook publishers. That it would build on the dignified reputation of the fusty hundred-year-old textbook publisher he bought twenty years ago as the foundation for his business and become bigger, better, and more widely known. But the demand for top-notch, finely printed, traditional textbooks at the price such books come at was, he found, remarkably low—limited to a few expensive boys' schools in the Northeast. So Amerithon expanded. Jack bought out its lower-priced, lower-quality competitors whose books featured chapters like "The Female Minuteman" and "The American Holocaust: Lost Tribes of the Eastern Seaboard," which make Jack's skin crawl. He bought out humdrum newsletter publishers and esoteric local-interest magazines and eventually altogether non-publishing-related companies like a chain of men's formal wear rentals called The Tasteful Tux and a motorboat detailing business on Cape Cod, all teetering on the edge of bankruptcy. And he has turned the businesses around, made them profitable parts of the Amerithon umbrella. It would be downright un-American to turn his nose up at a business-building opportunity just because it didn't fit his "concept"; he is running a company, not a showroom, after all. But still—still there are times he hates the fact that he has created a well-run, well-oiled conglomerate that produces nothing but garbage. This was not the dream he began with.

Today is Colby Kesson's monthly "Choices Celebration," or simply "Choices," as its organizers affectionately refer to it. "Choices" is a one-day "seminar/retreat" attended by any and all proud purchasers of Colby Kesson kits who wish to make a pilgrimage to Needham, Massachusetts, for some inspirational speaking and heartwarming sharing with their fellow consumers—it is one of the company's many fraudulently life-affirming, profit-cramping extras. It will be the first thing Jack cuts when Amerithon takes the helm. Unless, of course, he spots some hidden upside or untapped revenue-building opportunity today. Which seems unlikely, based on the number of cars (less than forty) in the parking lot.

Jack has timed his arrival so that he will be able to slip into the auditorium without having to identify himself and put up with the ridiculous, nervous kowtowing that accompanies his introduction under circumstances like these. He makes his way up to the balcony of the high school auditorium the event is held in and stands for a moment, letting his eyes adjust to the darkness. Colby Kesson has made some attempt to introduce cheer to this suffocatingly inoffensive cavern: a few insubstantial bouquets of purple balloons teeter in the corners and a gold banner emblazoned with CHOOSE YOUR FUTURE hangs across the central aisle. But rather than fight off the relentless blandness of the space, they seem to feed it; like fresh drops of blood caught in the gaping, all-consuming gullet of mediocrity.

Jack settles into one of the rear seats by the door and pulls out his notepad. Frank Berucci, the moist-eyed, frizzy-haired, ex-football-captain/reformed-cocaine-addict-type leading the event, has opened the mike to the poor, floundering "choosers," as Frank reverentially refers to his constituents (they are "*choosing* happiness, *choosing* change," he has explained to Jack on the phone). In droves they are getting up to make quavering comments about *family* and *meaning* and *opportunity* in the canned language of daytime talk shows. It drives Jack crazy—these people scraping up the rarest marrow of their lives and lofting it for approval or support or whatever it is they are looking for, as if such ephemeral slips of feeling can be hung out to weather the elements like flags. He hates the way Frank and his two assistants urge them on to these exhibitions; when did talking ever bring anyone anything but grief? He hates the Native American poetry the Colby Kessonites co-opt to lend their agenda spiritual clout. He hates the soothing tones they take care to speak in, the loose cottony garments they wear. And he hates the people who are dumb enough to sign on to this program, who haven't the smarts or the mettle to take life by the horns. These, Jack thinks, are the new Americans—the ones who skew the national averages toward ignorance, selfishness, and obesity. Within five minutes of their fraudulent outpourings, Frank Berucci has actually worked up a good tablespoon of tears.

Meanwhile, Jack has worked up Frank's severance package: six months' pay, a strong recommendation, a good-bye page on the company's web site. Colby Kesson has remarkable potential once costly indulgences like "Choices" can be taken out. Jack has a hungry twenty-six-year-old Harvard Business School graduate who is set to turn the place around for ten percent of the equity and three weeks' vacation time.

At the podium, a man in a purple polo shirt is now describing how hard it was to learn bartending with a broken arm—"broke in two places." Jack puts his notebook away. He has seen enough. By the time he has reached the door, a redhead with a pouchy face and battery-operated earrings has commandeered the mike to thank her husband for helping her discover her passion for dog grooming. Jack has to pause, one hand on the door handle, and scan the audience for the dickless wonder who has made his wife realize she wants to spend her days clipping poodle toenails and delousing golden retrievers. Maybe the dark-haired man in a short-sleeved oxford or the breasty baldy in the front row—but then Jack sees something that wipes the man, his wife, and any thought of poodles' nails out of his mind completely.

Sitting two rows behind the rest of the group, where until now she has been obscured from Jack's line of sight by the second-tier balustrade, is Eliot's old babysitter, Rosita. He does not doubt for a moment that it is her—the fiercely pulled-back knot of black hair, the way she is sitting, straight-backed, head tilted slightly to the left, one hand opening and closing over the end of the armrest. The sight of her is familiar and at the same time jarringly foreign, like the sound of his own voice on an answering machine. What is she doing here, among these sad-sack Americans and their vapid secular gurus?

Jack takes a step to the side to see her more clearly. He can see her profile, her neck, her body now—and his own flesh freezes. She is pregnant. Unmistakably. Her belly is a perfectly round protrusion under the white blouse, hard and tight as a basketball. Shock sounds through Jack like the vibration of a tuning fork struck in his head.

Below him, the redheaded woman continues with a litany of thank-you's that Jack can no longer make out. There is just the sound of her voice, oddly clear and monotonous, like that of an acolyte reciting an ancient, incomprehensible prayer.

Staring at Rosita's small form below him, Jack waits for some fragment of information to reach his extremities and remind him how to press down the door handle, how to open the door, how to walk away.

But for what seems like a long time, it doesn't come.

3

CLIMBING THE STEPS to the porch of the Barton Country Day School behind Eliot's tunic-clad body, Caroline feels a swell of relief at having managed to shake Rock this morning.

She has known Rock peripherally since grade school and intimately since her freshman year at Quilton. Rock's father went to Harvard with Caroline's father, worked with him on Wall Street, and lived down the road from him in Concord until he got divorced. Every time Caroline sees him, he gives her a hearty I'm-no-sexist clap on the shoulder and says Jack Dunlap is the ballsiest guy he knows. Jack Dunlap, on the other hand, rolls his eyes at the mention of Rock Coughlin, Sr. "That moron," he says, if anything.

Thanks to her older brothers' pimping, Caroline was the
stand-in for Rock's high school senior prom date—an evening
she remembers with an acute sense of both embarrassment and
injury, but which Rock likes to refer to, even now, as "the first
night of the rest of my life." He is only half sarcastic. Caroline
reminds him that they didn't even kiss. And more importantly,
that weeks later, when they did, it wasn't anything to write
home about. Encounters with Rock (sloppy kisses at John
Hoop's party, an uncomfortably sandy make-out session on the
beach four Fourth of Julys ago, a drunken and aborted attempt
at intercouse last summer) have been mixed, like so many drops
of iodine, into the murky waters of Caroline's teenage life.

But Caroline is twenty-two now, and out of college—of Harvard? (When asked where, she answers as if the question mark
belongs, as if, maybe, it might be unfamiliar, and now the question mark seems intrinsic to the place itself, as if, maybe, if her
father hadn't gone, and his father hadn't gone, and his father's
father before that, she wouldn't have gotten in.) She may have
reneged on the internship at the Film Archive in Berkeley she
had lined up, but she is still a full-fledged participant, however
humble, in the real world now. And while Rock, who graduated
three years ago, seems to have been left untouched by adult-
hood's demand for renunciation, Caroline has embraced it
whole hog. No more drunken nights on Sissy Mender's roof or
meaningless conversations with the whole Alex Pary posse. And
no more Rock ups, as she refers, internally, to her hookups
with Rock.

Through the glass-paneled walls of the lobby, Caroline can
see a host of nonsensically intense mothers, hassled teachers,
and children revved up like a roomful of windup toys. It is
always mothers at these school functions: mothers at school
plays and science fairs and bake sales and open houses and
then suddenly, Caroline realized last week, it becomes all
fathers at graduation. Fathers securing seats and whistling their
college fight songs, carrying lamps and futons and giant Tupperware boxes full of their daughters' papers and shoes and

tampons, taking pictures and being introduced and inspecting classrooms and ancient team photos and dining halls. Proud fathers and no mothers, or invisible mothers—quiet, signed-off mothers wringing their hands and looking helpless now that the hard work is done. But here at BCD elementary and middle school it is still mothers—and already Caroline recognizes a few of them, although her own is nowhere to be seen.

At the front door of the school, Mrs. Corliss, Caroline's old sixth-grade teacher, is handing out programs and barking orders at a group of eighth-grade "helpers" waiting for their charges.

To the right of the porch Caroline can see Denise Meirhoffer, Rock Coughlin, Sr.'s fiancée and BCD board member. Actually, she can hear her before she can see her: "What you don't understand," Denise is saying in the shrilly emphatic voice she reserves for sharing her insights on anything from politics to garbage collection, "is that six years ago everyone *complained* about this." Caroline is about to duck around to the side entrance in the interest of avoiding her when she catches sight of an unusually tall, lanky man with shoulder-length black hair loosely pulled back into a ponytail, standing beside Denise. He looks wholly out of place among the gaggle of middle-aged women in pressed slacks and pleated shorts. He appears actually to be uninvolved in their conversation, fiddling with the viewfinder on a fancy video camera. He has olive skin and a distinctly hawkish nose and is, actually, both startlingly handsome and oddly familiar-looking. With a flick of his wrist he snaps something shut on the camera and looks up, directly at her. Caroline feels the blood rush to her face—he has caught her staring at him. It only heightens her sense that she has seen him before.

"This way," she says to Eliot, more sharply than she intends to.

Eliot looks back at her questioningly, but then shifts direction agreeably. Caroline feels a swell of appreciation for him. He is such an understanding little boy, has never been given to asking obnoxious questions or making scenes. The whole ride over here he sat beside her mouthing his lines with his small hands crossed like an old man's on the front pocket of his backpack. He looked so serious and sincere it sent an almost panicky pang of love through her.

Inside the lobby, there is no sign yet of their mother. Eliot begins to slink off toward the back stairway. "El!" Caroline says. Her voice comes out sounding shrill. "I think we should find Mom first." The bright-blue-painted walls are giving Caroline a headache and the whole place has the sickly smell of Windex, pencil shavings, sweaty children. Eliot stops and looks back at her impassively.

"I mean, she'll be fine," she adds. "I just think you should see her first."

Eliot frowns. "Fine with what?" he asks.

"Oh, whatever—just being back here, all the people, you know. . . ." Caroline lets her voice trail off. She shouldn't have said it. There is maybe no reason to think he expects otherwise. Except, of course, for the fact that he has seen his mother throw herself into the swimming pool in evening clothes and thrash around with great rips and tears of silk and nylon; that he has heard her converse freely and seriously, even respectfully, with her pillow; that he has come in to kiss her good night every night for a whole month in which she lay in bed, shades drawn and ocean sounds crooning at low volume from the tape player.

"She'll be so proud of you," Caroline says, hoping her voice doesn't sound insincere.

And then there *is* her mother, emerging from the theater, swiveling her head, clutching her shiny white purse with both hands. Caroline waves at her and flashes a mincing smile at Eliot.

"Oh, there—I was wondering—I thought maybe I—" her mother is already saying as she approaches, anxious tapping shoes and too much perfume. "Oh, Caroline, I'm so glad you're not off driving across country!" She stops almost hesitantly before them.

"Hi," Caroline says clumsily, giving her a hug; her mother's

ribs and shoulders feel tense and fragile in her arms. "And
Eliot!" Faith says, extricating herself from Caroline's grasp,
"You look just—! What a great costume!" He is not helping her
out, standing absolutely still, the same flat look in his eyes.
Faith extends her arm hesitantly, settling for a hand on his
shoulder as if he is some rare and delicate bird, or a prom
queen—as if she is unsure a real hug is allowed. "Oh, you look
wonderful." Of course, there are already tears springing to
her eyes.

"Was your trip up okay?" Caroline asks. In her mother's
presence she always feels dull and responsible, like an endlessly
competent cruise director. She wishes she had sunglasses. Nice
big ones, like the ones her mother—yes, like this woman beside
her—used to wear. Square, rose-tinted, maximally concealing.

"Oh, fine—fine. I got here early. I helped set up," Faith
says.

"You did?" Caroline asks. Eliot looks alarmed.

"Just the chairs and—nothing, really," Faith's eyes dart
around the room nervously. "So are you ready, Eliot?" she asks,
changing the topic. "Your drama teacher—what a nice lady."

Caroline glances at Eliot, who has pressed his lips together,
turning the skin around his mouth a ghastly bluish white. It is
possible he is about to faint. "You probably have to go get
ready, right, El?" Caroline asks.

Eliot nods.

"Good luck," she says, taking his hand and giving it a
squeeze. "You'll be great."

"Good luck!" Faith echoes as he walks carefully but speedily
to the back stairs. For a moment Faith and Caroline are frozen
in the middle of the lobby's wholesome chaos (running children, fluttering construction paper cutouts, the buzz of
parental instructions) watching Eliot's blue tunic disappear. He
is so small and quiet and focused, the crowd seems to part
around him like floating debris around the prow of a sailboat.

"Well," Caroline says.

"Well." Faith shifts her purse to one hand and slaps the

other one against her side as if she is about to propose something. But then what could she have to propose? She doesn't
even have the confidence to hug her own son. Caroline feels a
dart of anger snap up from her gut. Not only has Faith Dunlap
bowed out of Caroline's own life as a mother, but she has left
her little son to live with his father in a cold, unfriendly house
with no more to offer than endless time to build creepy papier-
mâché projects. Of course, technically this is not her fault: the
various doctors and lawyers involved in the divorce would not
grant Faith even partial custody until next year. But then, she
didn't have to fall apart so completely in the first place.

Caroline can see Mamie Starks emerge from the ladies'
room—can see her catch sight of Faith, touch Gloria Edwards's
elbow, lean to the side, and whisper something in the shorter,
rounder woman's ear. For a moment, Caroline is tempted to
feed her mother to these wolves, but as quickly as the possibility has occurred to her, an equally strong desire to protect
her—to shield her nervous, broken ego and whatever poor
sorry scraps of motherhood she is nurturing—rises in her.

"We better get seats," she says, placing her own hand on
her mother's elbow, pushing her toward the stairs. Out of the
corner of her eye she sees the man with the camera leaning
against the wall, one knee up, filming the crowd as it makes its
way into the theater.

4

ROCK WAKES UP with a start. He is looking into a pair of gray eyes, ringed by bushy eyebrows, also gray, and alarmingly close. There is a tight, vertiginous feeling in his chest as if he can't breathe, which is, he realizes, because he is being held up by the collar of his shirt.

"What the hell is this?" Jack Dunlap says, giving Rock, via the shirt, a surprisingly successful shake.

Rock pats the bed behind him, worried for a moment that—but no, the bed is dry. Mr. Dunlap is simply referring to him, here on the bed. "Mr. Dunlap," he says. "Sorry—I just—"

Jack Dunlap is not an exceptionally tall man, but something about the long, craggy shape of his head makes his height seem

imposing. There is also something wild about his appearance—
his gaunt cheeks and the wiry gray hair that grows in an upward
tangle from his receding hairline and his eyebrows give him
the impression of having recently returned from a harrowing
sailing trip or three weeks without provisions in an African jungle. He does not recognize Rock, that much is clear.

"Rock Coughlin," Rock says, and reflexively begins to
extend his hand but thinks better of it. Jack's fingers still have a
solid grasp on a good few inches of his shirt.

"Oh," Jack says, releasing his grasp. He looks momentarily
confused but no warmer or more welcoming than he did two
minutes ago.

"I was hanging out with Caroline—she told me to wait."
Rock's legs are extended awkwardly before him in the middle
of Jack's messy bed, but he is not sure it is safe yet to slide over
to the edge.

"Here? In my room?" Jack says. His eyebrows quiver slightly
when he speaks. The air in the room is hot and smells close.
Not only are the shades down, but the windows are shut, Rock
realizes. And the air-conditioning isn't working.

"No—no, no, no" Rock repeats vigorously. "I just—I was
looking for something and I got so tired I just—"

But Jack does not appear to be listening. His eyes have nar-
rowed and he is nodding his head almost imperceptibly. "Did
you drive here?"

"Yes, yes, sir," Rock says, finally standing, having scooted
as gracefully as possible to the edge of the bed. He thinks, for
one terrifying moment, that he can see the joint from his
back pocket lying in a coil of greasy burgundy sheeting. And
Jack Dunlap would be just the sort to call the cops. Would be
overjoyed to put Rock on the McCarthy list—but then this
is the new millennium. There is no McCarthy list. Rock is
obsessed with the McCarthy list. He has smoked his joint
already, he remembers suddenly, thrown the butt out the window. Thank God.

"Is that your car out front?" Jack says, flipping a shade up with a snap and rapping on the glass.

"Seven hundred bucks and it's yours," Rock says. "Manual steering and seats of genuine flesh-colored vinyl." The thrill of relief that it is not his joint, that he will not become the victim of some complex capitalist insecurity scapegoating process, makes him take this tone, even though he knows, as soon as he has spoken, it is inappropriate.

Jack doesn't smile.

"I need a ride to BCD," he says.

"Oh," Rock says. He should have seen this coming. "At your service." He taps his hand to an imaginary cap. "Explorer needs a break?"

"The Explorer just died on me. And your friend Caroline took the Jeep." Jack pronounces each word with strenuous precision and enough venom to cover both subject and listener.

"Oh," Rock says, rubbing his shirt collar smooth. "Right." He is about to have to spend twenty minutes in the car with the man who single-handedly prevented the town of Concord from building affordable housing for the elderly and drove his own wife insane. And not as his new friend and confidant, but as his impromptu chauffeur.

———

A PAIR OF SPARKLY drugstore sunglasses, purple, sitting, hot as fired bullets, on the dash. Seven empty Gatorade bottles, a pack of Marlboros, a crumpled *Martha Stewart Living* magazine, CD cases, drugstore receipts, and crumbs. Millions of unidentifiable crumbs on the floor, on the grubby gray seat cushion, in the cracks of the armrest, the ashtray, the leather well of the emergency brake, as if the boy has somehow pulverized three-quarters of anything—animal, vegetable, or mineral—that has passed through the four doors of his car. What kind of person lives like this?

Jack has had a cold, splintery feeling in the pit of his stom-

ach and a strange numbness at the top of his skull since leaving
Colby Kesson this morning. But he is not going to let this interfere with his plans for the day. He has, after all, already canceled all his appointments between eleven and one to be able
to go to his son's performance. And Rosita's life is not his concern. She has gotten herself . . . knocked up? impregnated? . . .
Jack doesn't even have the vocabulary for her state; in this context, the words he knows make him squeamish. In any case, it
does not warrant looking into. He has a play to attend, a company to take over, a conference call at two—he takes four Advils
and erects the list of his responsibilities like a wall of sandbags,
blocking out the image of her dark head, the slim curve of her
neck, the swell of pregnancy beneath her dress.

Rock turns the key in the ignition and an impossible shouting and clanging comes from the car stereo before his hand
darts out to shut it off. He casts a hesitant, apologetic look at
Jack, who makes a point of staring straight ahead. Jack does
not put his seat belt on; sitting in the passenger seat like an old
person, or an incompetent, is bad enough. He can't remember the last time he sat in a passenger seat—when he broke
his arm, maybe. He was subject to Faith's birdbrained efforts at
the wheel until he hired a driver for four weeks. But that was
ages ago.

"So," Rock says, coughing a little, as if the word itself is
another handful of crumbs he has dredged up and tossed out
into the air between them. "You canceled your meeting?"

Jack glances over at the boy. "Meeting?" he repeats.

Rock darts a nervous look at him out of the corner of his
eye. "Eliot said something like you were gone all day—or, I
mean, I thought they said you weren't coming to. . . ." He lets
his voice trail off.

"Hmm," Jack says. He has not really considered his children in his decision to go to BCD. Do they, it occurs to him, not
want him there? The thought stings; this would be on Faith's
behalf.

"Your son is quite a dramatist," Rock says, after a pause.

There is a fine layer of sweat standing out on his brow and he looks a little pale under his tan.

"I wouldn't say that," Jack responds after a few moments. The numbness at the top of his skull is blossoming into a full-fledged headache.

He pulls out his cell phone, flips it open, and punches the autodial button for his secretary, but halfway through its ghostly beeping he remembers she is out today. He lets it finish dialing anyway, listens to her voice mail before stealthily punching the END button, but does not put the phone away. "Jane!" he barks convincingly. He had not planned on doing this, but now that his fingers have gotten ahead of him, he feels actually quite pleased with the ruse. "What's the story with the Lambrecht deal? Papers come through?" He pauses, brows knit. "Read it to me." This is brilliant. He doesn't have to do anything but sit—offer an occasional, "Okay," "Check that," "Hmmmm"—this with a scowl.

They are now driving down Main Street, past Patriot Real Estate, Minuteman Travel, storefronts hung with copper kettles and hand-knit sweaters patterned after the American flag. This is what Concord Center has become—a collection of freshly painted picket fences and quaint "shoppes," immaculate houses, and tourist attraction graveyards. All this commoditizing and cutesifying of the world's purest revolution! On the corner of Heywood Street, there is a new, hand-painted sign that proclaims, HISTORY HAPPENED HERE, as if history were some accident people could gape at and feel pleased to have avoided. It wasn't like this when Jack came here to visit his grandfather as a boy. Or twenty years ago, when he bought the house back. Back then, it was still a simple, small town with no frilly amenities or attractions—"the dullest little nest of puritans you've ever laid eyes on," in the words of Jack's aunt Helen, the self-centered Beacon Hill socialite who raised him after his parents died in a car crash. Which was exactly what Jack loved about it. The pandering cuteness of its new stores and restaurants makes him want to give up on New England

and move out to Idaho or Wyoming, where being American is still a commitment, not just a happenstance.

Rock makes his way onto Route 2, using no blinker, accelerating haphazardly, and braking in short choppy bursts. Jack would like to wrest the wheel from the boy's hands. Instead he continues to frown and nod into the cell phone.

"All right," Jack says into the dead space on the other end of the line. Rock is pulling off Route 2 into Belmont now.

"Put it on my desk for Monday morning. Top of the pile." On the sidewalk, there is a young woman pushing a stroller on the corner, dark-skinned with long black hair lying in a braid down her back, glistening silver-blue in the sun. It stops Jack for a moment—that otherworldly color and the stretch of her brown arm. But she has a broad, placid-looking face and wide hips—she is entirely unfamiliar. "Thanks," he says, and flips the end of the phone back up.

"Important call?" the boy asks. There is a hint of sarcasm to his voice—and something else, maybe a leer. Is he on to the farce? It doesn't really matter. Jack clamps his teeth together and stares out the window.

"Left," he says at the corner of Bethune Street, although the boy obviously knows where he is going—has gotten them this far. "Turn here." He gestures with his chin. Then he reaches for the small pocketknife he has attached to his key chain and begins cleaning his nails. But behind the wall of sandbags his mind has constructed, there is a single white sail rising with the murky waters, forcing his eye.

5

ELIOT IS STANDING in the dimly lit alcove between the stage and the changing room away from the other children with their waving hobbyhorses and Pilgrim's bonnets and exaggerated cases of stage fright. "Eliot." He can hear his name being hissed in Jen Edwards's hysterical little voice. "Where's Eliot?"

He says nothing, but freezes with the photograph he is holding pinched between his thumb and forefinger. The face of the boy staring up at him registers nothing—his eyes remain dark and a little wary, his mouth quiet, possibly suppressing something—an idea or a smile. After all, he is just a photo. He can't hear Jen calling. Eliot almost forgets this sometimes—the boy's eyes are so full of mysterious kinship, it is as though they must be thinking the same thing. "Roberto is a quiet boy like you," Rosita has told him. "This mark you have on your shoulder—he has the same one." Roberto's skin is a pale caramel color and his hair is black and curly, not an Afro, exactly, but thicker and fuller than Eliot's own hair. Eliot does not know many black children. There is a boy named Winston in the grade above him at BCD and there is Dominique on his soccer team. Which makes Roberto different. Eliot imagines Roberto would understand what it is like to be among other children and even in their presence feel apart. *Do black children have as many friends as white children?* Eliot asked his father once, and his father looked at him strangely. *I don't know,* he answered. *It depends on what kind of friends you mean.* Eliot had the feeling this was a question he was not supposed to ask. Maybe because his father feels that in some way Eliot himself is black. Looking at the photograph of Roberto makes Eliot happy. He likes to imagine he goes to school with him—that together they do more interesting things than the other children: build models and read books and create inventions that will someday make them famous. Only this is impossible because Roberto is missing: has disappeared into the jungle of Colombia, where he and Rosita come from, which from what Eliot understands is worse than being dead.

"Eliot," Jen Edwards exclaims, poking her panicky round face around the old lockers that obscure the alcove from view. "You're next! Go! Go!"

"Okay," Eliot says, sliding the photograph into the pocket of his tunic, and pushes past her onto the stage, bumping one cardboard buckle off on the way out.

"The British are coming, the British are coming," he shouts as practiced. It is bright out on the stage; he finds himself squinting, struggling to enter the scene—to become a part of the loud, brash colors and movement. The stillness of Roberto's face sticks to him like a woolly coat thrown over his head.

"The British! The British!" the chorus shouts, jumping up and down. Eliot realizes that he doesn't have the stupid hobbyhorse he is supposed to ride away on. Out of the corner of his eye he can see the man with a video camera. He has almost forgotten about him. If Eliot is good enough, his drama teacher says, he will be famous. The man is making a movie. Eliot would like to start over—would like to get his prop and begin again, the right way. He looks straight into the dark eye of the lens. There is something cruel about its glassy, lidless surface, as if its inability to blink makes it unable to forgive.

"*Our homes will burn / Our luck will turn!*" the children onstage are singing and one on each side of him snatches his hands, draws him into the dance they have been practicing for weeks, but Eliot is not ready yet. This is too fast. Too wild. Across the circle Greta Paley isn't even following the steps, just jumping and flinging about her arms, her mouth wide open in some fleshy, teeth-chattering version of a grin. Whirring around the circle, Eliot is aware of the man with the camera again—there at the corner of the audience, watching and recording, catching all the discordant notes and missteps.

"*It was two by the village clock, / When he came to the bridge in Concord town. / He heard the bleating of the flock, / And the twitter of birds among the trees, / And felt the breath of the morning breeze,*" Jen Edwards begins in her hyperenunciated voice.

Eliot swings his leg over his invisible hobbyhorse and turns to ride toward the audience in the grand semicircle his drama teacher has planned. The door at the back of the theater opens, spilling a triangle of light into the darkness just as Eliot makes it to the apex of his circle, the very front edge of the stage. One form and then another appear in the doorway: his father, followed by Rock Coughlin. Eliot thinks of his mother, out there in the darkness. She will crumple when she sees them, or worse. And it will be his fault—how many times has he told her that his father won't be there? Automatically, his feet come to a complete stop; his hands forget the reins. Around him he can feel the other children slowing down, bumbling into a silent confusion. There is nothing to do but wait, frozen in the spotlight of responsibility, for the thing—whatever it is— that will happen between them, here, now that his parents are together in the same room.

INSIDE THE BCD LADIES' ROOM, it smells of Lysol and diabetic urine. Faith runs her hands over her hair and pats on a little lip gloss—she has stopped wearing the garish pink lipstick in vogue around here. The play is over, and beyond the bathroom door Mamie Starks is surely assembling the masses: Anne Hibbins, or Lady H, as Faith has heard caddies at the club refer to her, and Gloria Edwards must be here because Faith spotted their children up onstage. To think that she and Gloria had their fortieth birthday parties together—a Caribbean-themed evening at the club featuring jerked chicken and piña coladas, a whole coterie of caterers in hula skirts. And that was only five years ago!

She takes a deep breath and tries to focus on what is important. Eliot, her son who looked so small and vulnerable onstage, stumbling through the performance, battling demons unknown to her and coming suddenly to a complete stop. Watching him, for the first time since arriving, Faith felt the full weight of her motherhood. Here was her own son onstage—this sweet blond boy, this delicate faltering creature, grew from her body!

This is not a good time to get emotional, though. She should think of some clever, thoughtful things to say to him— no, to *ask* him. Asking is better than telling. And listening— really, listening is the best of all. A good mother is a good listener. Faith, on the other hand, finds herself almost unable to hear, let alone listen, at least half the time. Her brain is loud with its own frantic flipping through possible things to say. "Relax and it'll come to you," Dr. Marcus says. "What's the

worst thing that could happen—there's a pause? Good conversations are full of thoughtful pauses." But this is not what Faith
was taught. Faith was taught that silence indicates stupidity—or
worse, shyness. Smooth, charming chatter—this was what her
mother raised her to know. "And look what it got you," Dr. Marcus says. "Jack Dunlap." But here Faith and he do not see eye to
eye. Despite all the miserably rugged ski vacations and grim
observances of obscure traditions, the bullying and stoic
silence and lack of affection that dominated her twenty-four
years of marriage, she still sees Jack as having been a catch. Still
feels proud that she, of all the pretty Pine Manor girls—and
she really was just a girl, not even twenty yet—was the one who
snagged him. So perverse but so true!

Faith takes a deep breath and steps out into the buzz and
holler of the lobby, the indistinct sea of madras shorts and yellow polo shirts, children racing through the crowd with the
residue of lemon squares and brownies on their fingers, followed by a lumbering Irish setter, who is trotting after them
obligingly. "He's coming, he's coming, here he comes," one of
the little boys is screaming in a mix of real blood-chilling terror
and excitement. *Stay calm*, Faith tells herself. *Calm*. She lets the
word reverberate in her head. It is a perfect word, really.
Repeating it almost accomplishes the task. It makes her think
of the glassy black puddles that formed in the driveway of the
house she grew up in—the edges of the world, she had imagined them, wormholes that could suck a person through and
out the other side to China, or maybe to another universe completely.

Suddenly someone has hold of her elbow. It is a firm grasp
(not Mamie Starks's, but Caroline's, thankfully), but almost
before Faith has had the chance to appreciate this, her eyes
have found a straight line through the whir of bodies to what
might as well be a ticking bomb, or a dead body: Jack. He is
looking right at her, exploding the word *calm* into four letters
that tumble heavily through her brain, catching and tearing on
the delicate tent of assurance she has attempted to erect.

He wasn't supposed to be here; Eliot said . . . what did Eliot
say? "I'm sorry," Caroline is whispering, "I didn't think he
would . . . " But Faith is hardly listening.

"Faith," Jack says when she is standing in front of him. (Did
Caroline steer her over? Or did she come, like some dumb
magnet, of her own accord?) He is nodding slightly, distantly—
looking over her shoulder as if there is another, more reasonable, more adult Faith there beside her—the mother of Faith
the troublesome, frivolous little girl.

All her words have been knocked flat—even the stumbling,
faltering ones that come to her when she is nervous lie pros-
trate, as indecipherable as colors under a blind woman's hand.

"Poor Eliot," Caroline says. "He really kind of froze up
onstage."

"Hmph," Jack says. Faith has not seen him since he brought
Eliot down to New York to stay with her over Thanksgiving. He
looks both exactly the same as he always has and completely
different.

"Poor Eliot," Faith repeats dumbly.

"He just got shaken up," Caroline says. "I'm sure he was
surprised to see you. We thought—last we heard, you were supposed to be at a meeting. . . ." There is a snap of irritation in
her voice. Caroline has always known how to handle Jack in a
way Faith never learned. Even at Eliot's age she could reprove
him for things Faith wouldn't dream of.

Faith can see Eliot's shiny blue costume across the crowd—
the other minutemen have rushed past him up the stairs and
into the crowd of parents, but Eliot is lingering, hanging back
at the top of the stairs, talking to a tall, striking-looking man
with dark, almost shoulder-length hair and a video camera. He
looks over as Faith stares and catches her eye. The blood rushes
to her cheeks. They have been talking about her. Or about her
and Jack and Caroline standing here in this awkward configu-
ration.

"So how's New York?" Jack says.

"Fine," Faith says. "All right." The words are beginning to return, limping back like injured animals. "And Concord?"

Jack grunts dismissively—as if it is a foolish, inappropriate question.

Behind him, the red setter streaks past, followed by even more yelping children.

"You still see the Delaneys?" Jack lets his eyes touch on Faith, the real Faith, not the one he wants to see beside her. Quickly he redirects them at the ceiling.

"Oh," Faith says. She is surprised that he remembers them—old friends of her family whose Christmas party she used to force Jack to attend with her, long ago, when they were first married. "I do. They still live in that same place with the lions outside and they still have— I went to their Christmas party." She stops, somewhat breathless. It was a sad affair, really—with all the same people, only everyone was so much older.

"Aha," Jack says, with a spark of genuine interest, and for a moment Faith feels something break free from the dark discarded heap their married life has become in her mind—some ragged but still-sparkling streamer. "The De-stingys," he used to call them, on account of their serving nothing but melba toast and sardines with their highballs—and he and Faith would go out to the Oak Bar for steaks and chocolate mousse cake afterward.

"I saw George Burt, actually," Faith offers. George Burt is Jack's lawyer. "It was so strange to see him there. . . ." Faith feels herself coloring again. It was strange because the only context she knows him in is the litigation over their divorce, which Jack is perfectly well aware of. Why has she started down this path?

Jack's expression has frozen over. "Well," he says coolly. "That must have been"—he pauses significantly—"overwhelming."

Faith stares at him. *No*, she would like to say. *No, it was not.* But she can only stand there in tense, terrible silence, looking at the space where only a moment ago she could see this sweet, heartbreaking flutter.

"Coffee, anyone?" Caroline asks, clearing her throat.

Faith shakes her head and looks down, begins working the clasp on her purse open and closed between her pale fingers. It was funny, for a moment, how she had almost forgotten.

———

SITTING AT A WHITE-CLOTHED table in the inventively named Garden Restaurant of Belmont Center with Caroline, Faith, and Eliot Dunlap, Rock has an almost uncontrollable desire to get high. He has gone out to his car twice, under the pretense of needing to use the "gents'," to check whether there might possibly—in the glove compartment, under the passenger-side floor mat, in the first-aid kit in the trunk—be at least some small, mostly smoked joint. But there is nothing. Nothing.

The Garden has a generic, movie-set-like quality, which, Caroline has explained, is exactly why she chose it: it contains nothing familiar, no possibilities of running into anyone. Since her breakdown, Faith Dunlap brings out a fierce, take-charge side of Caroline; in her presence, Caroline is suddenly protector and vigilante, the kind of person who knows how to cure hiccups and steer conversations, whether to treat a spill with salt or soda water. Just watching her is making Rock tired. And the weird blandness of the restaurant makes him feel edgy; the decor looks as if it were assembled by aliens following a set of instructions: *a restaurant must have potted palm trees in the corners, chef's salad on the menu, unremarkable watercolors of beaches and wild animals.* Rock is sure the place is a front for something unorthodox.

"What would we do without you?" Faith says for what must be the thirty-seventh time. "It was so good of you to drive us here." The conversation since they left BCD has been like air traffic control—both tense and incredibly boring.

"Mom," Caroline says. "Okay. We're here."

Faith seems unfazed by her daughter's exasperation.

"No problem," Rock says. He had no choice; Jack took off in the car Caroline drove over.

The day has definitely not gone as Rock planned. Or at least it has not gone as he imagined. He would never have sat through the full hour of manipulative historical docudrama acted out by preadolescents if he had not thought he could lure Caroline out to Singing Beach afterward, or to Somerville to go record shopping. Instead, here he is, three hours later, sitting at the Garden picking at a possibly botulism-ridden tuna salad beamed in from Mars.

In his new role as Dunlap family chauffeur, Rock has subjected the entire family to the gritty seats and sour milk smell of his shit-brown Toyota. He has also made fifteen minutes of awkward conversation with his old sixth-grade teacher and twice been mistaken for one of the Dunlap twins and slapped violently on the back by their thuggish, middle-aged ex-golf partners. Possibly worst of all, he has had to endure being featured in his stepmother-to-be's condescending, ten-minute-long treatise about the modest aspirations of college graduates today, which she delivered to an audience of the pretentious, cool-guy filmmaker "friend" of hers—whom Rock suspects she's sleeping with, Caroline—and a panicked-looking, obviously inattentive Faith Dunlap.

Before Bensen's Organic closed down last week to make room for the expansion of InfoGraphix, its more successful next-door neighbor on Route 2, Rock would be working his shift, heaping dung onto the compost pile or tending to hydroponic tomatoes. While he was never "taken by the possibilities of all this environmentally conscious sustainable agriculture stuff," as his father likes to spin the job to his friends (presumably to validate the four years of liberal arts education and twelve years of private schooling he paid for), Rock has always enjoyed manual labor. And right now he would give his left arm to be doing even the worst of his Bensen's responsibilities—hosing down the petting-zoo pigs or mucking out the duck

pond. Even listening to Linda Bensen go on about the restora-
tive powers of moonstones and bladderwort would be better
than this.

"The rolls?" Caroline is saying, and Rock realizes it is the
second time she has asked him. She looks so pretty sitting there
with her pink T-shirt and shakily parted hair—her thin
browned forearms resting on the table.

"Right-io." It comes out too loud and Rock nearly upsets his
water glass reaching them to her.

"So has Stephan been filming your rehearsals also?" Caroline asks Eliot.

Stephan, pronounced *Ste-fahn* with a pretentious soft *ph* and
long *ah*. Rock notes. So she is on a first-name basis with this
film guy, who, Rock is sure, is already boffing his soon-to-be
stepmother.

Eliot shakes his head. They have been in the restaurant for
fifteen minutes and he has not yet spoken. With the remnants
of his makeup—the fluorescent afterglow of wiped-off lipstick,
eyeliner, and a bluish cloud of whatever was used to darken his
almost invisible eyebrows—he looks like a child porn star.

"What sort of movie is he making?" Faith asks. "Maybe
you'll be famous, Eliot."

Eliot shrugs without looking at his mother.

"*The Last of the WASPS—from Puritans to Preppies,* or something," Caroline quotes. "How does Denise know him anyway?"
she asks Rock.

"From her days as an exotic dancer." Rock puts his fork
down.

"Right." Caroline says giving him a fake smile.

"She . . . ?" Faith looks so genuinely shocked that Rock feels
guilty.

"No, no—I'm just joking. She's his lawyer—or she *was* his
lawyer for the last movie he made or something."

"I didn't *think* that was right," Faith says, folding her napkin
into a triangle on her lap.

"I saw that movie—in my film class. I figured it out when I

was talking to him," Caroline says. "I couldn't figure out why he looked so familiar at first." There is a sort of musing interest in her voice, a change from the beleaguered holding-up-the-conversation tone she has had up until now. Does she have a crush on him? The guy is, Rock has to admit, handsome. Has exactly the sort of exotic, tall-dark-stranger looks girls seem to equate with being smart, sensitive, and soulful. Caroline was chatting with him when Rock came back from his cigarette break; she was laughing and running her hand along her collarbone in, now that Rock thinks about it, a suggestively intimate way. And the guy certainly made a beeline for her—Rock saw him excuse himself from some no-doubt awful conversation with Denise and Mamie Starks and zoom over to her.

"He must be very talented," Faith says, pushing a piece of feta off her salad.

"Why?" Caroline asks.

"Well—I mean, it's very hard to make a movie—or at least, I know it used to be, maybe it's gotten easier, but there's so much behind the scenes, I don't know, talking, and applying . . . Your uncle Merrill wanted so badly to make it in Hollywood and it was so hard, so expensive."

"But Merrill is an idiot, Mom—he wanted to when? In between wanting to start that ridiculous antique business and wanting to be a professional polo player?"

"Well," Faith says, rearranging her fork and knife apologetically on her plate. "He had a lot of dreams."

Looking at her bowed head, the neat, gray-blond part, and her thin fingers, the ropy veins on the backs of her hands, Rock has the sudden hopeless feeling he gets watching those nature shows about baby wildebeests that can't get up and walk in time to keep up with the herd, or mother zebras with broken legs who have to be left at lonely watering holes to die. There is something about Faith that seems so inviting of disaster. Rock wasn't surprised when she ended up in Maclean's last year—in a way it is her presence back in the real world that is surprising.

"I had a dream last night," Eliot says—he is looking at the

corner of the table rather than anyone in particular—"that you were dead."

There is the sound of forks clinking, the wind flapping the awning outside the open window, the waiter calling something over his shoulder as he steps out of the kitchen—missteps, actually—and nearly drops his tray.

"Me?" Faith is more mouthing than saying, sitting back as if she has been slapped.

"That's terrible, El," Caroline says.

Rock's stomach lets out an inappropriate growl.

"Oh, Eliot," Faith says. There are tears welling up in her eyes. The shadow of the American Legion flag flutters up the side of the building next door like a flame.

6

SINCE LEAVING THE PLAY yesterday, Jack has gotten a car wash, closed a deal, chaired a board meeting, talked John Liggat into selling his stake in the Lambrecht venture, and swung by Tarbell's Toys and Models to pick up the miniature Franklin stove, Mason & Tuttle minuteman figures, and new glue gun he needs for the diorama he is finishing. The numbness in his head and splintery feeling in his stomach he had after leaving Colby Kesson has been steamrolled by the familiar combination of frustration and bitterness that seeing his ex-wife inspires in him. It fuels him to get things done, be productive, keep moving.

What happened to the pretty, shy Faith Cartwright he married? What happened to the young woman who used to crew for him on his grandfather's sailboat, or ski down the toughest trails on Whistler Mountain behind him in avalanche season? *That* Faith Dunlap was quiet, sweet, and often uncertain, but not the meek, wounded little bird-woman who trembled her way through the BCD lobby yesterday morning. The present Faith is, perhaps, better than the veritable madwoman who checked herself into Maclean's last year. That Faith believed a carful of Cuban doctors were trying to steal her kidneys. But this Faith—she is *still* so goddamn timid and fragile. And Jack sees this as a personality of her own choosing, the product of her own actions; what was it if not her desire to get divorced that caused the breakdown in the first place? And all the therapy and self-help books and yoga classes he has been forced to foot the bill for have left her exactly where he predicted.

It would be almost vindicating if he didn't know she blamed him. Which is absurd; he never asked for a divorce or told her to go live on her own, five blocks from Harlem, in New York City. He isn't the one who threw the carefully constructed model of her life—no, both of their lives, and the children's— up into the air to watch it rain down in a million irreparable pieces. Jack knows this, but the vision of himself that he sees reflected in her wide, fidgety gray eyes contradicts this. It may be false, but it is clear enough to be persuasive.

On his way home from picking Caesar up from Jim Ridgeway's, Jack pulls off Route 20 to the Keystone Steak House. He does not have to be in the office until noon today and he has called ahead for three orders of French toast, bacon, and sausage in honor of Caroline's second morning home from college. He has always liked Keystone's, with its old-fashioned bowl of mints by the door, its dignified dark green walls and working fireplace. When he was a boy, and then later, when he was newly married, whenever he was in Boston he would come here for Sunday brunches with his grandfather. They would inspect the old hunting prints and cartoons cut from the *Boston Globe*, the *Wall Street Journal*, and *Harper's*. "Pansies," he can hear his grandfather saying about this one that depicts a horde of skinny, long-haired young men, brandishing anti-war signs, climbing the steps of the statehouse. "Thank god you're not one of them." The place has not changed much since then—a new sign outside, a glassed-in addition in the back, but otherwise the same unpretentious, straightforward, *upstanding* feeling.

Jack is pleased to have come up with the plan to come here, to have thought of calling ahead. At home, there is nothing in the refrigerator—maybe some cornflakes or whatever it is Eliot has for breakfast. He is, now that he thinks about it, looking forward to having Caroline home for a while—of course, not for too long, a young person has to make his own way in the world, but for the time being. And she is a young *woman*, after all; the need to go out and make a name for herself is less urgent than it is for the boys, whom Jack finds alarmingly unambitious. Hanging around a ski resort in Colorado is not what he had in mind when he paid for their Harvard educations.

He has more faith in Caroline, though. She has a good head on her shoulders. He has never had to chide her for bad grades or discipline her for the frivolous kind of pranks her brothers pulled off all the way through high school. Once, when she was ten, she was sent home from school early because she had gotten into a fight—a real physical fight in which she kicked a boy in the stomach. She would not say what started it and was silent that night while Faith served chicken and chattered about a neighbor's new swimming pool or some other nonsense to relieve the tension. *He called her a name*, Caroline had said finally when Faith ducked back through the swinging door to get the pie out of the oven. Jack can still remember those steady gray eyes meeting his in challenge across the table. *Hmm*, he had said, and nodded, staring back at her. He did not ask what it was. But neither did he make her go straight upstairs to bed after dinner.

"Here you go, sir," says the chirpy blond who has gone back to the kitchen to see about his order. "Anything else?" the woman asks. "Juice? Coffee?"

"No," Jack says. "Thank you." But then his eyes land on the cheesecake under the glass cake plate on the counter, which stirs some deep, long-forgotten fold of brain tissue. Cheesecake, which is Caroline's favorite. He can't think how he knows this, but he is quite certain. "Actually, yes. Cheesecake—three slices," he says.

"Cheesecake?" the woman says doubtfully. It is too early for cheesecake, Jack realizes.

"Cheesecake," he repeats firmly. It doesn't matter, though. He will surprise his daughter.

There is no sign of activity when Jack walks through the kitchen door, bearing the warm Styrofoam boxes of French toast. There is a skittering sound from the mudroom and then a short burst of half-repressed barking. Brutus. Which is strange, because Jack left him outside last night. Someone has brought him in and penned him up overnight; the poor dog probably has to go to the bathroom. Jack lets him out of the pen and then the front door to join Caesar. He streaks to the middle of the lawn, where he squats and pees like a female. Jack frowns in the doorway.

"Caroline?" he calls, walking through the dining room. "Eliot?"

There is a distant response—Caroline's voice. Jack turns and walks back into the kitchen, trying to repress his irritation. What if he had gone to the office? The dog would have been stuck inside for God knows how long. For all this competence and responsibility he has been reflecting on, Caroline can still be as careless as her older brothers. Jack can't imagine himself, even as a boy, let alone at twenty-two, doing the same thing.

Of course, Jack never really had a *home* in the true sense of the word, to come back to. He was raised, from the age of seven on, by his father's sister, Helen, after his parents were killed in a car crash. And Helen, better known as Lilo, was certainly not much of a maternal figure. He slept in the austere third-floor guest bedroom of her Beacon Hill brownstone and learned early to be circumspect about his presence so as not to invite the attentions of her self-absorbed, alcoholic husbands—there were four of them. When he came back from boarding school to Helen's for holidays or visits, he asked permission to stay however long he planned to, to give Beatrice his laundry to do, even to get himself a glass of water. He didn't interfere with any household habits. Even here in Concord, at his grandfather's, where he felt the most at ease, he was careful to adapt, for instance, to his grandmother's habit of walking *around* the dining room carpet rather than *on* it, or his grandfather's habit of wearing a jacket to dinner. It was a matter of respect, simple as that.

"Dad!" Caroline says, coming through the door from the dining room to the kitchen in some sort of athletic outfit. "You're not working this morning?"

"Not for another hour," Jack says. "Did you bring Brutus in last night?"

"Oh. . . ." Caroline darts a look over at the mudroom. "I did—why? Where is he?"

"I let him out. He needed to go to the bathroom."

"Oh," Caroline says, "sorry." She opens a tin of saltines that have been sitting on the counter for God knows how long, takes out a cracker, and gives him a sidelong glance, leaning against the counter. "So, you really gave Mom a minor heart attack, showing up at the play yesterday."

"Oh?" Jack tries to affect distracted bemusement. An image of the BCD lobby, Faith's trembly face, the oppressive feeling of just *standing around*, his least favorite thing in the world, flashes before him.

"You *saw* her. Jesus—these are disgusting." Caroline tosses the cracker into the garbage. "What made you decide to do that?"

"Do what?" Jack looks back at her. "I would think I could go to my own son's play if my schedule cleared up, without an interrogation."

"Hmm." Caroline cocks her head to the side and brushes

the crumbs off her hands. "Well," she says, noticing Eliot, who has slunk into the kitchen and is walking toward the sink with an empty water glass. She gives an unconvincing, if not slightly hostile, shrug. "Whatever."

Eliot turns on the faucet and lets water splatter into the glass. He is wearing what looks like a pair of long underwear and a huge pale blue T-shirt that says NAKED CO-ED WATER POLO—undoubtedly one of the twins' cast-offs. It hangs all the way down to his knees and makes him look frail and slightly clownish.

"Okay," Caroline says, pushing herself off from the counter. "I'm going for a run. I made Eliot oatmeal and there's some left over if you want it."

"Oh," Jack says. He looks over at the Styrofoam boxes and the little cardboard container of cheesecake.

"What's that . . . ?" Caroline follows his gaze. "Oh, did you get—was that for breakfast?" There is that look Jack dreads on her face—alarm, concern . . . pity even.

"No," Jack grunts dismissively, turning to wash his hands at the sink, which he can do facing out the window. "Leftovers from dinner last night."

"Oh," Caroline says doubtfully. "Okay—well, I'm sorry to be leaving you guys. I just—"

"Caro-line," Eliot sighs.

"Okay, okay, I'm off." And in a moment she has slammed through the screen door out into the driveway.

"'Bye," Eliot calls.

"'Bye," Jack echoes gruffly. He watches her start up the drive and then shortcut the curve over the grass Wheelie has just mowed. He tries to feel annoyed, but feels instead something else, sadder and more piercing, watching her shadow precede her across the grass. Carefully, he dries his hands on the dish towel.

There is a rustle from the table and then a pause. From outside there is once again the sound of Caroline's footsteps, faster now, on the gravel.

"But it's still warm," Jack can hear Eliot saying from behind him.

———————

CAROLINE HAS A VAGUELY guilty feeling as she lets herself out of the house. Is she skipping out on what her father hoped to make some sort of family breakfast? How could she know, though, when he won't even give a straight answer? She bends over to stretch out her calves. Whatever. She is not going to let it put her in a bad mood.

It is beautiful out: hot, but not as humid as yesterday. The sun has the strong but bloodless shine of early morning: white across the bricks of the walkway and silver on the panoply of leaves over the drive. There is the hush of warming air, the smell of sage growing between the bricks, and the feel of evaporating dew—no sign of the brown Toyota. She has beaten Rock this morning.

At the end of the driveway Caroline breaks into a jog. The pavement is surprisingly springy under her feet and she feels spry and sporty in her new running shoes and sports bra: the products of repeated, and often abandoned, resolutions to get in shape. Caroline has never been terribly athletic. Proficient, yes—she can wield a lacrosse stick and tennis racket and can even knock around a hockey puck with some success, thanks to all the sports camps and teams the New England Independent School League deemed essential to a fruitful adolescence. But the drive to make a goal or slam a serve or score a point has always eluded her. This is perhaps not unrelated to her father's relationship to athletics, which bring out a severe and terrifying enthusiasm in him, not dissimilar from greed. He was actually banned from attending her older brothers' Little League games in Lexington because of the time he screamed, "You fat fucking idiot," at a chubby boy who tagged out one of the twins in a controversial double play.

Caroline takes a left onto Liberty Street, past the North

Bridge Visitors' Center. Everywhere she is aware of the scrim of
her childhood obscuring the lines and contours of the present—transforming the trees, the street signs, the telephone
poles and boxwood bushes, the open vistas and stands of wood
into complex forms with double meanings—the overlay of
childhood vision onto the here and now.

Here is the Kittridge house, the Dellars' field, the famous
intersection in which the little Dorchester girl bused in to
Alcott Elementary School was hit by a car. Here is the patch of
woods where Silas Kittridge used to lead violent games of capture the flag and where Clare Whiteside claimed to have lost
her virginity. Here is where her older brothers used to fashion
cruel and elaborate worm factories out of sticks and paper cups
and stones that dropped from mini-parapets to sever worms in
two. Here is the Concord Rod and Gun Club she was afraid of
as a little girl—for good reason, it occurs to her; what kind of
person joins a club dedicated to using *rods* as a hobby?

On the left, the row of weeping cherries and then the neat
white picture-book gazebo in front of the Tooleys' house
emerges. And up ahead, Caroline can see the green oblong of
Concord Circle, complete with its—not two or three—but five
monuments within eyesight. Below the "War of the Rebellion"
obelisk in the center of the pretty green traffic island, there is a
patch of scarred black earth riddled with stones that makes the
rest of the manicured grass look like a hastily unfolded picnic
blanket—not quite big enough to cover up the dirt beneath.

The stitch in Caroline's side has blossomed into a full-
fledged cramp and her lungs hurt now, too. *Keep running or you
will die*, she tells herself. *Keep running or you will be stuck here forever*. The threats are effective. She is a superstitious person.
There is a pain in her chest that might be her heart, although,
of course, statistically it probably isn't. She is unlikely to drop
dead of a heart attack or heat exhaustion. But there are always
those freakish cases: the long-distance runner who jogs every
day and then, rounding his favorite corner one bright, beautiful morning, collapses—dead; the woman who walks out of her

split-level ranch house in the safest town in Iowa, into the arms of a gun-toting madman and off all the charts of sociological probability. Caroline is at the top of the pyramid of data on heart disease and life span, rare viruses and violent deaths; she lives in that slim, coveted triangle of money and health and education where the odds are always in your favor. She is young and white and female. She uses birth control and takes vitamins and has health insurance. She eats vegetables and wears sunscreen and does not work with heavy objects or chemical products. She lives in a Western country with calcium in the orange juice and fluoride in the water. And even so, she feels unsafe! What if she were at the long, squat bottom of this same pyramid? What if she woke up every morning knowing she was twice as likely to have a heart attack or get AIDS or die in her sleep or be the victim of a violent crime? She would probably be bedridden by the sheer horror of anticipation. But then, if she *was* on the bottom, would she even know the pyramid existed? Isn't it the people on top who are aware of statistical probabilities and sociological predictions? The thought is absurd though—if she were on the bottom, surely she wouldn't need a pyramid to tell her so. The whole train of thought actually succeeds in making her feel three times as certain she is having a heat stroke.

"Hey," comes a voice from behind her, startling enough to make her leap off the pavement. She hasn't even heard the battered blue Buick Skylark approach.

She sees first the long black hair, and then the man leaning across the seat to the passenger side. Stephan—the moviemaker she talked to at the play yesterday. "Oh," she says, from the ditch she has skipped off the road into. "You gave me a heart attack."

"Sorry. I thought you heard me behind you." He extends his hand through the open window.

Caroline has to scrabble up out of the ditch to accept it. Her own hand looks sweaty and bloated from running. "Hi," she says stupidly. He is wearing a snug light gray T-shirt—she can see the long wiry muscles in his upper arms extend and retract as he pulls his hand away. Something about this makes her think of beef jerky. Makes her think of sex, actually. According to Rock, the guy is screwing Denise. Caroline can feel her face getting hotter, standing there, mud soaking through one sneaker. The fact that she has determined the nature of his familiarity does not add to her composure; he was the filmmaker she and her best friend Abby referred to as "Roman Polcute-ski" after seeing his movie in their senior film class.

"I don't want to interrupt your run. I gave your wallet to your little brother—you left it on the bench where we were talking yesterday."

"I did? I didn't even notice—that's so nice of you to have brought it out here."

"No problem. I had to come out here anyway." He has a very intense gaze and almost yellowy green eyes.

"Oh, for your—for the movie?"

"Yeah. . . ." He sighs and shifts his weight against the flesh-colored vinyl car seat, which makes a wheezing, crackling sound. "Trying to rustle up some interviews. You know Mamie Starks?"

"She—yeah—she was a friend of my mother's." Caroline regrets this as soon as it is out of her mouth. She does not want to have to try to explain the *was*, and more importantly she doesn't want to be implicated by her acquaintance with Mamie Starks, a woman whose burning ambition is to make sure the Boston Cotillion stops its slippery slide toward becoming *open to just anyone.*

"Oh, yeah?" he nods his head in a thoughtful way—but as if he is thinking about something else, actually.

"Not really good friends," Caroline adds.

Stephan stops nodding and looks right at her. "So now that you've graduated, you have something lined up for the summer?"

"Something? No. I mean, I did—I was going to move to San Francisco, but I didn't."

"And you like film—that class you were telling me about

yesterday, you learned something about production and all that?"

"Some." Caroline feels herself blushing again.

"Well, how about working for me in sort of a production assistant/liaison position? I mean, you know this place, you like film, I need a little help with the material. I can't pay you, but it would be good experience and I know some people in the field I could connect you with."

"Oh," Caroline has finally stopped feeling her heart beating in her face. "That's nice of you. . . ."

"Think about it," Stephan says, giving the car door his arm has been resting on a final-sounding pat. "We'll talk later—you'll be there tomorrow, right? At this wedding?"

"What wed— Skip Krasdale's?"

Stephan pulls a scrap of paper from his back pocket. "Is that the same as Matthew Krasdale's?" he says.

Caroline nods, although Skip has certainly never been called Matthew in his life.

"That's the one, then."

"How do you know him? Or is this also for your movie?"

"You got it." Stephan grins. It is a slightly practiced-looking, sheepish grin, but handsome anyway. "My camera makes friends."

"Oh," Caroline says. "Well, Skip is definitely a character."

Stephan's eyes stay on her expectantly. "Is that a yes, you'll be there?"

"Ye-es," Caroline says, despite the fact that she is certainly not expected—that in fact she turned down the invitation ages ago, kept her ex-boyfriend Dan up laughing the night she got it with imitations of Skip's stilted speaking manner. "I'll be there," she adds, as if sounding authoritative will somehow change this.

"All right, then. I'll find you."

As the car pulls away, Caroline catches sight of her reflection in the rear window. Her head looks about five times too large for her body. She didn't even put on deodorant this morning. And how is she supposed to just show up at Skip's wedding? She no longer feels like running.

It is a thought, certainly, to have a role helping this guy with his movie. How often has she told people that what she wants to do when she graduates is go into documentary film? Of course, it would mean she would have to stay in Concord for a while, which was not what she had in mind. But then, it's not like she has any offers anywhere else. And with this on her résumé and some money saved up—she could waitress somewhere maybe, since her father surely won't lend her a penny—she could go somewhere really great, Italy or Australia or Costa Rica or something, and work on some *National Geographic* documentary. The idea sends a dart of excitement through her for what feels like the first time in weeks. Plus, of course, she would be spending an awful lot of time with a handsome young documentary filmmaker. And what would Dan think about that?

Caroline walks over to the roadside and stretches her stiff legs against the split-rail fence that runs along it. A faint breeze lifts her hair and cools the sweat on her scalp. In front of her, there is the fluorescent green of the Ponkatawset Golf Course—the carefully manicured rise and fall of hills and dells and neat white sand pits, a pond covered with blossoming Chinese lily pads.

As she looks out at this, a pair of early morning riders appear at the crest of the hill, their helmeted heads round and hard as insects'. They are staring at her, she thinks for a moment, and lifts a hand uncertainly to wave. But then, they are looking the other way, she realizes, down at the flag on the ninth hole below them. Slowly—imperiously even—one of them nods his head and together they move in on it like explorers at the cusp of a new, and still colonizable, world.

ONCE, WHEN ELIOT WAS SIX, he planted a tulip garden with his mother. Three rows of yellow, two of white, one red, then yellow again. He remembers the order still, and the feel of the soil, cool and soft, with white crystalline fertilizer stones that seemed somehow good enough to eat—crisp, nourishing cereal for the plants. *All right, good night, little guy,* his mother had said, pushing earth back over a naked bulb he had placed in one of the holes. *He needs his beauty sleep—in the spring he'll pop his head back out and we'll watch him grow.*

But in the spring his mother was "sick" and had forgotten all about the tulips. They pushed out sturdy and strong as she had predicted, but then froze in an unexpected May snowstorm, became brittle and weak before they blossomed. This is a memory Eliot cannot quite find a place for—the assured singsong of his mother's prediction, and the feel of her hands, cool and capable, guiding his clumsy fingers through the dirt. It seems to feature a different person than the woman sitting across the table at lunch yesterday, whose hands fidget like a liar's, whose eyes are paler and more nervous, the opposite of reassuring.

What made her sick? Eliot asked his father once, knowing that the word did not really accurately speak to her condition but having no other at his disposal. *Too many questions,* his father answered. Eliot has never understood whether these were questions that she asked, or that were asked of her. But it was enough to make him stop questioning.

There is the sound of the screen door slamming downstairs and Eliot freezes where he is kneeling, clutching the photo of Roberto he was about to replace in his desk drawer when he was struck by the thought of his mother and the flowers, and now he is stuck with it in plain sight in the middle of his room. The footsteps have reached the stairs now: Caroline's—he recognizes the groan and squeak of floorboards under her feet. He glances at his watch—there are ten minutes before he is supposed to meet Forester outside to make arrangements. Caroline is in the hall now and here he is, still holding the picture. In a moment of inspiration, Eliot slips the photo under the wooden baseboard of the papier-mâché replica of Concord he is building just in time for her footsteps to reach his door.

But to Eliot's surprise she passes his room and continues, at a rapid pace, down the hall. This is almost unheard of. He is expecting her to come in, plomp herself down on the bed, and ask him whether he has had breakfast yet, whether he slept all right, what he is thinking about. To fall back on the bed and stare at the ceiling, sit up suddenly, and look at him with those concerned, searching eyes as if he is a leak she is trying to patch.

Instead of relief, Eliot feels an unexpected pang of disappointment. It isn't that he needs Caroline the way she thinks he does. He can cook eggs and toast and cream of wheat, and microwave the dinners his father buys in bulk at Costco. He does his homework. He keeps his room neat. He never sits for hours in front of the TV. But still. There is something he likes about having Caroline back at home. She is too anxious to make him feel taken care of, but there is some kinship in her presence, some comfort in the fact of another person in the house now that Rosita is gone.

He looks at his watch again—he has to be outside to meet Forester in seven minutes now anyway. It is for the best that Caroline didn't come in and settle down. He will attach the little replica of Old North Bridge he has created—it is a little out of proportion with the rest of the landscape, but Eliot doesn't mind so much; this way it will not be overlooked, which seems important to him. He places it carefully over the curve in the Concord River, which he has painted a shiny navy blue, and then secures it with two dollops of rubber cement.

"Hello?"

Eliot has not heard the screen door bang shut this time. "Hello?" the voice comes again, starting up the stairs. It is familiar, but not yet distinct. Eliot remains planted on his knees beside his papier-mâché sculpture, eyes fixed on the doorway as the footsteps approach. Suddenly Rock Coughlin appears in it.

"Hey!" he says. "What are you kneeling like that for? You scared me."

Eliot stares at him.

"Your sister around?"

"I don't know," Eliot lies, getting to his feet, but Rock is already out of sight—down the hall to Caroline's room. Eliot hears him knock on the door, turn the knob, open it. The shower is not running and he has not heard Caroline go back downstairs. But there is no sound from her. Rock's footsteps return.

"Know where she is?" Rock asks.

Eliot shakes his head. He is about to insist that she must be here, he has just heard her come in, but something stops him. He is not sure what to make of Rock Coughlin. He is his brothers' age, but is not as big and loud and altogether incomprehensible to him as they are. Around them, Eliot feels like another species; around Rock, he feels merely different.

To his dismay, Rock takes a few steps into the room, begins looking around with interest. It is only at this renewed threat to his privacy that Eliot spies the corner of Roberto's photograph sticking out from under the corner of the papier-mâché project.

"What's this?" Rock asks, making Eliot jump. But he is not pointing at the picture, just at the bridge Eliot has secured, which does, he realizes, *really* look out of proportion.

"A project."

"But what *is* it?"

"Boston. That"—Eliot gestures at the offending addition—"is Old North Bridge."

"Oh-ho," Rock says, as if he understands something more complicated and profound than the identity of what he is looking at. "You like it down there?"

"Down where?"

"Under the bridge—we used to hang down there, too. You just have to watch out for the park police—they called my folks once."

"Oh," Eliot says. He has never been under Old North Bridge. He has only walked over it, hundreds of times. Eliot looks at his watch; it is time to go outside.

"I had my first smoke down there, my first kiss. . . ." Rock lets out a little snort of delight. "I even put up my first tag—I used to . . ."

But Eliot is no longer listening. Caroline's face has emerged in his doorway, with her finger raised to her lips. She is gesturing frantically, pointing at herself and making a decisive slash with her hand. *Not here*, Eliot finally realizes she is mouthing.

Rock has wandered over to the window in his reminiscence, his back turned toward the door. He is playing with the wind chime made of flattened silver spoons and little disks of glass that Eliot's mother hung up there when he was a baby. Pretty, fragile sounds bounce around the room while he speaks.

"Okay," Eliot says, and Caroline's head disappears immediately.

"Okay, what?" Rock says, interrupting his own monologue. He backs toward the center of the room and stares into Eliot's face and then, rapidly, to the now-empty door. "Who are you talking to?"

"You," Eliot says.

"Okay to get grounded for four weeks?" Rock looks skeptical.

"Yes," Eliot says gravely. "I mean, okay I have to clean up my room now."

"Says who?" Rock walks out into the hallway and looks around.

"Me," Eliot says.

Rock lifts his eyebrows. "Okay," he says finally, and shrugs. "But I think what you need to do is loosen up—have a little more fun. Not clean your room."

Eliot says nothing.

"Well, all right, then—tell your sister I stopped by." And then Rock is gone, footsteps banging down the stairs in a sloppy haphazard order. Eliot checks his watch once more—it will take Rock another minute or two to get into his car and be gone, which will make Eliot late. He stands in the middle of the room for another moment and then walks over to the window to monitor Rock's leaving. Above him the wind chime is still tinkling faintly, a sad, leftover sound.

———————

IN HIS HURRY to see Caroline, Rock has left his car parked in the middle of the driveway under the bright glare of the sun. When he opens the door, the sour milk smell accosts him with unusual intensity. There is junk all over the floor and some stupid dirty baseball has ended up, God knows how, right smack in the middle of the driver's seat. A fucking pigsty. A dart of irritation stabs up through Rock—at the car, which is old and putrid-smelling, at the day, which has started all wrong, at himself, for things too vast and vague to itemize. He picks up the ball and hurls it into the rhododendron bushes on the other side of the circular drive, where he hears it drop through the leaves with a satisfying ripping sound. But then as he turns the ignition on he remembers: it is the ball his mother dug out of some box of his childhood possessions and gave him at the surprise party she threw for his mildly retarded cousin Betsy last Thursday night. Possibly the ball he caught from right field during the '86 playoffs. Why does his mother have to purge her household of his childhood belongings as if they are carriers of the plague? And why does she dump them on him at weird events when he is in between apartments? And why did he just chuck what might possibly be one of the greatest mementos of his adolescence into a fucking king-sized rhododendron bush?

Rock slams the car door and jogs across the gravel to what is actually a mini-forest of rhododendrons, an ungainly ring of them stretching up the bottom of the hill to the road, each bush sturdy and tough enough to be a small tree. Fighting through the big glossy leaves and springy branches, he feels a sharp pain on his forehead and, when he reaches his hand up to touch it, comes away with blood. "Fuck," he swears, standing bent with one leg over a low branch and the other twisted awkwardly behind him. He sweeps his eyes over the ground ahead of him—there is a small clearing in the middle of the bushes and to the right side of this is a grayish object that appears to be his ball. Except it isn't his ball. It is a sneaker, and above the sneaker a leg. Rock raises his eyes and finds himself looking straight at a person—a blond, pink-polo-shirt-wearing boy, to be exact. "What the fuck?" Rock hears himself saying aloud, still frozen in his awkward semi-crouch.

"Hi," the boy says in a scared, robotic voice. It is Forester Kittridge, Rock recognizes him now. Rock steps over the branch and works his way into the clearing, where he can now actually see his ball.

"What are you doing in here?" Rock asks.

"Looking for something." Forester is tall and long-headed, oddly unmarked by the gawkiness of adolescence, which gives him the uncanny appearance of a mini-adult. Or a mini-version of his mother, who Rock knows well from his caddying days: an aggressive, slightly cross-eyed woman, notorious for never tipping.

"Oh, yeah?" Rock casts his eyes around the clearing. Dirt and stones and fallen branches—nothing out of the ordinary.

"Yeah."

"You planning on camping out in here?" Rock asks, gesturing at the kid's backpack, which is substantial.

"No." Forester glowers at Rock.

"Mr. Dunlap know you're poking around his bushes for buried treasure or whatever?" Rock asks. He is enjoying himself now. The kid is an asshole, that much is written across his face. One of those boys who like to goad weaker, younger children into eating chalk or raw hamburger, or making shit sculptures with their own feces. He is probably blackmailing Eliot into giving him his allowance, or forcing him to buy cigarettes at a dollar a pop.

Forester shrugs again. But he looks more anxious now. There is sweat beading on his forehead.

"Well, maybe you and I should go in there and have a little chat with him, just, you know, let him know what you're after."

"Gimme a break," Forester says. Mr. Dunlap is almost a cult figure in the community—known for his rudeness, for his refusal to let the Higginses' wedding guests park in his driveway, for having made his own sons clean litter off Route 2 as a punishment for having mooned someone at a drive-through. Rock allows silence to fill the space around them with tension. "I'm just waiting for Eliot," Forester says finally.

"Well, why don't you do your waiting out in the open?" Rock says, stooping to pick up the ball. He cocks his head in the direction of the ragged tunnel through which he came, and Forester follows him with a certain degree of reluctance.

Once out in the open, Rock glances over at the house and, sure enough, there is Eliot's little face in the window. Rock raises his arm in an exaggeratedly cheery wave. He has certainly stumbled on to something. Behind him, Forester is looking over his shoulder to the road in what is either an attempt to seem nonchalant or a bona fide calculation of whether he should bolt.

"So, Forester," Rock says over his shoulder as he approaches his car, "say hello to your mother—tell her to give me a call about that produce garden she wants to set up."

"Whatever," Forester mutters, and Rock climbs into his stinky car, with the painstakingly retrieved baseball beside him on the seat. He can see the kid glowering after him in the rearview mirror.

7

IT IS EMBARRASSING to have slept through breakfast. This is what teenagers do after long nights of drinking and necking and staying awake to watch the sun rise, not middle-aged mothers visiting old family friends. Faith has a vague recollection of Lucy poking her face around the narrow wooden door, smiling, head bobbing vigorously in explanation—breakfast, it must have been—breakfast is in half an hour, or ten minutes, or whatever it was. Faith must have gone promptly back to sleep. She is now pulling a comb through her flattened hair at ten forty-five. *She's not completely well,* she imagines Lucy's sweet but tactless husband Pete would have explained to the other guests. *She's been through a lot.* A whole tableful of healthy, stable individuals who've been out running and swimming and playing tennis since dawn turn sympathetic but smug, generic faces at her.

No. This is not the right way to start the day. Faith replaces the image with that of a pretty harbor scene, quiet, a single red boat with a white sail. Picture something soothing when you feel yourself getting anxious, Dr. Marcus says. Something that makes you feel relaxed. She had thought it was her own invention—a unique and individuated image of safety generated by her peace-seeking soul. It was a shock to recognize it, months later, in the December page of Marcus's own hanging calendar—Monet's *Red Sail Boat*. A regurgitated projection of some more articulate, more capable inner eye. It is almost tragic that it works.

"Faithey." There is a gentle rapping at the door. Faith shoves the comb into her toilet kit, checks to see that her blouse is buttoned. Lucy's face peers back around the door, a reality-based déjà vu. Except this time Faith is dressed, standing at the sink, not lolling like some teenage slut on her bed.

"You're awake! I saved you some breakfast," Lucy says, coming through the door like a brisk, reassuring puff of oxygen—a safety line thrown out into the dense, gravityless orbit Faith has been floating in. Faith has known Lucy for thirty-six years now. Together they used to sneak cigarettes at cotillion events, lie out on silver reflective blankets slathered in baby oil, take the bus in to Harvard to sit on the steps of Widener Library smiling at the handsome young men. Lucy is a short woman with an athletic-looking body, compact and tanned, with firm round muscles on the backs of her calves, the swell of her forearms, even the curve of her neck. For ten years in a row she has won her country club tennis tournament in the energetic, good-spirited way tennis tournaments are supposed to be won, not with the sort of catty desperation that scared Faith off the Ponkatawset Club courts. With her sensible brown bobbed hair and clean pink polo shirt, Lucy looks as strong and sturdy as a little rocking horse. Faith would like, for a moment, to fall at

Lucy's feet, hug her competent round knees in an excess of relief. "Oh, you didn't have to—I'm so embarrassed—so silly of me to sleep so long," she says instead, lifting a hand to her hair.

"Can it," Lucy says. She is a fan of wholesome 1950s expressions—*fiddlesticks, blow off steam, okeydoke.* Coming from her, they sound exactly right. "Rest and relaxation—that's what this place is all about. What do you think Pete and I come here for? Now—let's bring this out to the porch and then I'll give you the tour. There's a tennis tournament at four and . . ." Faith finds herself listening instead to the energy crackling from Lucy's body. What a wonderful mother she must be! If only her own mother had sounded like this. Obediently—carelessly, even— she follows Lucy down the flights of stairs, through the dark cool common rooms, and out into the sunshine.

From the beginning, Faith did not want to go on this trip to Pea Island. It was Lucy's idea that she come—that they have some time to rest and catch up and reminisce together. Faith didn't realize when she agreed that this plan included six of Lucy and Pete's closest friends from Greenwich and her own former neighbor, Rock Coughlin, who was Pete's college room-mate. Faith has spent the last few weeks worrying that she will be the outsider among this sampling of hearty couples who have weathered marital storms and raised kids together, have cried on each other's shoulders and flirted with each other's spouses. Who will probably finish each other's sentences, speak in code, and like to play charades. In their presence, Faith will be the intruder—the lonely divorcée. The word, at least, is pleasantly exotic. She hopes Lucy has referred to her in such terms—*my friend Faith, the divorcée.*

When she has eaten enough of the cinnamon buns and fruit salad to appease Lucy, they begin a walk through the house and around the island, which Faith is amazed to find she remembers quite distinctly. She visited it several times as a teenager, but has not been back for almost twenty-five years. It is a small hump of land, thickly wooded and bean-shaped. There are three rambling, weather-beaten houses owned by

Lucy's family and built by her great-great-grandfather in 1909 for throwing rustic weekend parties and luring the Vanderbilts up from Newport. Each of these has ten to twelve bedrooms, now occupied by a motley crew of cousins and their guests, great-aunts, grandnieces older than Lucy, cousins-in-law, and one mildly deranged uncle who lives in the unwinterized "honeymoon cottage" year-round. Most of whom Lucy cannot explain her exact relationship to. All of whom trace their heritage back to the early days of the Republic. Lucy herself is a great-great-great-grandniece of Betsy Ross; Faith can never remember if this is the one who was married to George Washington or the one who sewed the first Star-Spangled Banner, despite the fact that Lucy has clarified the matter more than once for her. There is an old-fashioned sauna perched precariously on a rocky cliff over the ocean and the remnants of a lovely sculpted garden that has sunk beneath the surface of the sea. There are fluffy, unprickly-looking pine trees that shed long rust-colored needles all over the paths, and, of course, there are no cars.

Crossing a narrow path that leads to the wild part of the island, Faith has a vague recollection of being groped by Lucy's drunken father there, against that giant boulder—the picnic stone. He was a sweet man, really—not hard or bullyish, just desperately, desperately—what? lost? Strange, she has never, till this moment, even thought of his advances as anything but sad. Dr. Marcus would certainly think otherwise.

Faith came here only once with Jack, shortly after they were married, and it was not a fun trip, as she remembers it. Lucy and Jack never liked each other and Jack found the place stifling— not enough space and not enough to do and all these blue-haired old aunts and uncles in your face morning, noon, and night. This was Jack's criticism. There was some sort of disastrous picnic on the headlands in which Jack did something truly boorish that resulted in, what was it? some sort of accident with a food item, a pie he stepped in or sat on or otherwise ruined.

Around the corner from the last house, Lucy's husband,

Pete, is practicing his golf swing, hitting balls off an almost trim lawn into the woods. "Faithey!" he calls, dropping the nine iron in his hand. The ease with which he has picked up Lucy's girlish pet name for her has always struck Faith as endearing. On his tongue it has such an absurd and surprising sound to it, like a frilly nightgown on a football player. Pete is the manliest man Faith knows, except maybe for Jack, who is manly in a quieter, more intense, and, Faith thinks, crueler way. Where Jack likes to drink bourbon straight and climb mountains in torrential downpours without complaining, Pete likes to drink beer and watch football and slap other men on the back in the hearty, comradely way of men in Budweiser commercials. Pete grew up in Yonkers, the son of Irish immigrants, and made millions selling his family car rental business to the Japanese. Lucy's parents did not approve of him, which has always struck Faith as romantic, suggestive of a great, otherwise hidden, passion.

"There's someone I want you to meet," Pete says, flinging his arm out toward a man taking spastic swings at the ball with a putter. "John John—what are you doing with that toothpick back there? Get over here!" Pete barks. The man grins and tosses his club after Pete's iron and walks toward them. He is wearing what looks like a safari outfit—a beige fishing hat and short-sleeved beige oxford shirt and khakis. He has olive skin and an almost pretty face, flat as an Eskimo's.

"Faith, this is Lucy's cousin Jean Pierre—flew all the way from France just to meet you."

The delicate balloon of Faith's confidence, which has been floating along on the breeze of Lucy's comfortable certainty, bumps and sags, punctured by the terrifying possibility that, in fact, they have lured her here to set her up—to force her into the desperate and intimidating world of adult dating. And with a Frenchman! A man who probably believes in mistresses and puts garlic in his eggs.

"No, no—stop it, Pete," Lucy says. "Jean Pierre is visiting on his way to California." Behind Jean Pierre's back, Lucy is rolling her eyes, lifting her hands in helplessness. "We didn't even know he would be here."

"An unexpected vis-i-tor." Jean Pierre bows slightly, extending his hand. The word sounds scientific the way he says it, like an extinct species.

"Nice to meet you," Faith says. "I'm sorry I don't speak French." She takes care to speak loudly and slowly.

"No problems." Jean Pierre smiles. "I speak English."

"And I can always *parlez*," Pete says, at which both he and Jean Pierre laugh.

"Well—*parlez* away," Lucy says.

Faith lifts a hand in a tentative wave.

Once they have rounded the bend and are again on one of the soft cool paths through the trees, Faith pulls out the paper she has been nervously folding and unfolding in her jacket pocket and unfolds it, idly, as they are walking—something for her anxious fingers to do. Lucy is talking about the golf tournament she and Pete just played in—Marvin Dobbs and Cee Cee McCormac, did Faith remember them from the old days? Faith's eyes meet the words *Property of Eliot Dunlap—Do Not Open!!!!!* in careful, elongated script on the inside fold of the paper. The sight of her son's handwriting gives Faith a start. There is a skull and crossbones below the letters—slightly shaky, as if drawn with great care. What is this? And why is it in her pocket? He must have stuck it in when he borrowed her jacket after the play. Carefully she unfolds it with a flutter in her stomach, half expecting some tirade against her, or frightening confession of self-hatred. But what it is, is almost more surprising—a xeroxed map of Concord and Lexington with a route outlined in black running through it. What does it mean for such a simple thing to be marked with such dire threats?

"... it was that paddle tennis court with the broken fence, wasn't it?" Lucy is saying. The needles hiss gently beneath their feet.

"I'm sorry," Faith says. "I just . . ."

Lucy turns around and looks back at Faith quizzically. "Are you okay, Faithey?"

"Oh, yes, I just . . ." suddenly Faith realizes she does not want to share her discovery. "I forgot my bathing suit," she says, holding the paper down at the bottom of her pocket as if, left to its own devices, it might spring out into the air between them. The blood has rushed to her face and her heart is beating quite fast.

"Hmm." Lucy frowns. She has reminded Faith about her swimsuit at the end of every phone conversation they have had for the last two weeks. "I have an extra one—it'll be a little big, but it should do the trick," she says.

What a stupid lie it was—now, after all that careful searching for an appropriate new suit, she will have to wear one of Lucy's! But it is only a brief thought, barely registered over the clatter in her mind set off by the piece of paper. Which is probably silly. He is just a little boy coming up with silly boy-pranks. But somehow this is not convincing to her. What sort of route is her son tracing? After all, what sort of mother has she been?

———————

ROCK IS SURE HE HAS STUMBLED on to something. Has actually been on to it all morning—Forester in the rhododendrons is just the final piece of evidence. There is a certain trapped way Eliot acts, a passive sneakiness that Rock knows from darker moments of his own life. He's got something. Cigarettes, maybe, but bigger, Rock thinks. Pot, probably. Maybe even stashed away in that "project" of his. It's a shame because he's just the sort of kid to get fucked by that kind of thing—pensive, cynical—if he's smoking up, it's his own trip, not some joiner's attempt to be cool. A few more years and he'll be off at Holderness, popping whippets in Saturday morning study hall, stealing turpentine from the wood shop. It's almost tragic, considering how much Caroline loves the kid. Maybe he should tell her, but there's really nothing to be done—the master plan is in motion.

Rock is a firm believer in destiny. Caroline, on the other hand, is one of those responsibility-takers. She will chastise herself for Eliot's downfall no matter what, but the self-chastisement will reach catastrophic proportions if she has foreknowledge and a sense that she could have saved him. She'll end up waitressing at some ski resort in Utah, practicing holistic medicine, and listening to Phish bootlegs and Mickey Hart drum solos, talking incessantly about the wisdom of the Anasazi. She will become as tentative and self-despising as her mother. For a moment this image of her—stringy-haired, stunned-looking, and wearing some blowsy South American getup—is so immediate that it blurs the contours of here and now: Caroline as clear-eyed and sharp-tongued, a girl who, even when she first wakes up, succeeds in looking somehow streamlined.

Rock parks the car across the street from his father's post-divorce dwelling in Brookline. He has been living here nearly a year now—since the apartment he shared with two of his friends from Wesleyan was repossessed by the landlord. A year in this place! Fucking incredible! The house itself has a crippled, incomplete feeling to Rock—a parody of a home. It is a "duplex," according to his father, but Rock is certain the word means something more specific than Rock Sr. intends it to. Stretching haphazardly up the right side of a beautiful old Victorian that, for a short period of time, the Kennedy family lived in, it has the feeling of something left over. It is as if the "duplex" is the remainder of some intricate living space equation worked out by the Pforzheimer family, who own the main part of the house—the superfluous rooms they have lopped off like extra piecrust. That his father doesn't see the indignity of this seems emblematic of a deeper, possibly incurable problem, which Rock cannot name but is afraid he has inherited.

The "duplex" was decorated by a painfully shy, sad-eyed young interior decorator named Thelma, who was dating Rock Sr. at the time he moved in. Everything in the living room, dining room, and front hall—from the mirror frames to the coffee table—is made of variously stained wicker, which gives the place the feel of a moderately priced hotel winter garden. It took Rock only a few days after moving back in to recognize the brittle, twisted ropes of wicker as the manifestation of psychic distress.

Rock drops his keys and wallet on the coffee table (wildly tangled, rust-colored wicker with a glass top) and walks around the corner. There is time for lunch and a nap before he has to meet Jimmy Sorrens. He is halfway to the kitchen when a voice assaults him from behind. "Don't do anything embarrassing," it says, "because I'm sitting right here."

Rock whirls around, knocking into a delicately positioned wicker service cart and nearly losing his balance. It is Denise, who has recently given up her partnership at a prestigious entertainment law firm in Los Angeles to become an advocate for welfare mothers and domestic workers, and is liable to be hanging around the house at odd hours—something Rock has yet to get used to. Denise has never been injured or tricked by Rock, but she speaks to him in a suspicious, sarcastic voice as if she is on to inappropriate double meanings in everything he says—as if he, Rock, cannot get away with his usual degree of nonsense with her around.

"Denise," Rock says. "Hi."

She cocks her head to the side and gives him the kind of mincing, cut-the-crap smile Rock imagines she uses on trial witnesses to compel them into long, terrified revelations of the truth. She is not unattractive, but has a roundish face with a certain inexactness to the placement of its features that gives the constant impression she is wearing faded, sloppily applied makeup.

"Dad home?"

"No, he is not," Denise says as if Rock has been asking gratuitous questions of her all day.

"At the office?" he says, involuntarily compelled to fulfill the role she has carved out for him.

"That's where he usually is on Fridays, isn't it?" she says.

"Right," he says.

"Is there anything else I can help you with?"

Rock attempts a laugh, even if it is supposed to be at his own expense. It comes out sounding like he has a frog in his throat. "All set," he says stupidly, and backs into the kitchen.

He suspects the reason Denise is marrying his father is because he is pliant and tolerant, that because of his extreme blandness, they are able to have an elaborately choreographed sex life. He imagines there is lots of role-playing—that Denise spends her time on the StairMaster in the basement developing plans and comes upstairs to Rock Sr. with orders. *This time I will be the lion tamer*, she says, *you'll be the baby*. According to a *Cosmo* article Rock read at the dentist's, these are the two most popular American role-playing games. Rock loves reading *Cosmo*. In his mind he has equated the two roles into one imbalanced scenario: Denise in leather, hissing, flicking an imaginary whip— his father a pasty mass of middle-aged flesh protruding from an enormous diaper.

Now that Rock has actually met this filmmaker friend of Denise's she has been talking up for the last two months, he has to admit he is less convinced that she is sleeping with him. She's too old for the guy, for one thing, and too unhip. But then . . . there *is* something oddly sexy about Denise, in a frightening, bloaty kind of way; she has one of those disproportionately large asses that looks downright buoyant, but her breasts are quite round and firm-looking, just the right size. Letting the thought cross his mind as he rifles through the sorry contents of the refrigerator makes Rock feel creepy. It is high time to start looking for his own place, a revelation he has had at least once a day for the last twelve months. Or else take those monks up on their invitation. He tries to conjure up a picture of getting off a plane in Tibet, some narrow runway in between two massive Himalayan peaks. It is a captivating image: Rock the adventure traveler, whittling clever objects out of yak bones or wood or whatever, developing previously unknown talents.

He pulls out a bottle of Coke and a Tupperware canister full of garlic soup cooked by a woman Rock Sr. pays to keep his refrigerator full of low-fat, low-sodium, easily reheatable foods. Then he sneaks up the back stairs so he won't have to face any more of Denise's condescending remarks and settles down on his unmade, wicker-frame bed. The soup tastes like salad dressing. The room smells of old socks. Through the wall he can hear one of the Pforzheimers' eight-year-old twins screaming for toilet paper.

IT IS NOT EXACTLY RESPECT that is the cornerstone of Jack Dunlap's relationship to Wheelie Barrett, although he certainly respects the man. Anyone who could play for the Bruins and weigh in at five-foot-six, 160 pounds, has a hell of a lot of balls. It is more what goes unspoken between them—the amount of small talk and boring, considerate questioning he and Wheelie do *not* partake in—that defines their friendship. "How'd you do this week?" Jack will ask. Wheelie is always in on at least one high-stakes sports pool per season, in which he employs complex and fascinating strategies, which are almost always successful. "How's Quantex?" Wheelie will ask in turn. Jack supplies Wheelie with high-risk, high-return investment tips. Neither of them asks out of politeness—they share the directness that accompanies self-interest. They have never spoken of Wheelie's son, who is in a school for deaf teenagers, of Jack's own children, or, for that matter, of Jack's divorce.

Wheelie belongs to the oldest branch of the Barrett family, whose length of residency in Carlisle, Massachusetts, exceeds even that of the Dunlaps here in Concord. He is descended not only from Dr. Jonathan Wheeler Barrett, the first surgeon to use ether in Boston, but also, on his mother's side, from Alexander Hamilton. The Wheeler Barrett homestead sits on one of the finest pieces of land in the area, in a still wild-looking corner of Carlisle. But it is owned by a fat stockbroker from Connecticut now; Wheelie and his wife live in a trailer on the edge of the property, from which his wife runs some sort of industrious but, Jack has always felt, crass pancake-mix-making business. Wheelie himself is the last of the great Wheeler Barretts, who are famous for their stubbornness, understated conviction, and laconic speech; Wheelie's brother is a fat drunk who works the night watch shift at the Ponkatawset Club and his two sisters have moved to Rhode Island with loutish, deadbeat husbands. Wheelie carries with him the air of extinction, the whiff of inevitable endings.

This evening he hoists his gardening shears as Jack drives in on his way back from work.

"Right rear tire needs air," Wheelie says by way of greeting as Jack stops and rolls down his window.

"Hmm," Jack says. "Caroline's been driving."

There is a round of barking and the dogs streak past the boxwood bushes down toward the golf course in the twilight. Both Jack and Wheelie follow them with their eyes. "Looks like his limp is gone," Wheelie says, looking after Caesar. He is standing right beside the car window now.

"It is," Jack says. Like Jim Ridgeway, Wheelie is uncannily observant. Only, unlike Jim Ridgeway, his observations are not limited to the animal kingdom. Wheelie probably knows more about the life of the Dunlap household than any single one of its members does. He used to take the twins to Bruins games when they were teenagers and he often gives Eliot rides to school. He is also the person who drove Faith to Maclean's after the kidney-kidnapping episode. Jack can only imagine the conversation they had on the way into Boston. Despite Wheelie's silent, unfailingly discreet demeanor, all this gives Jack a certain cautious, occasionally awed feeling around him.

Wheelie rocks forward on his toes slightly. "Some guy came by here asking for Caroline this morning when she was jogging." He looks off to the side, almost as if in embarrassment.

"Oh?"

"Long-haired guy."

Jack waits to see if there is more.

"He asked how long you lived here. How old the house was.

Where your wife was." Here Wheelie meets Jack's eyes for a quick moment. "Some other questions."

"Hmm." Jack frowns. "I'll ask Caroline who he was."

Wheelie shrugs. This seems to be all he has to say on the matter.

"All right," Jack says.

Wheelie nods and hefts the pair of gardening shears back up to shoulder level. There seems to be a subtext to his statement—something important that he would like to transmit without saying. A man here, looking for Caroline, asking questions.

Jack blows on the invisible noise whistle he wears around his neck and the dogs streak out from the little wood at the far corner of the back meadow. He lifts his hand to Wheelie in a parting gesture and starts down the driveway to his two obedient dogs, who dash up the hill to greet him.

At the top of the steps to the kitchen door, Jack stops for a moment and looks through the screen into the kitchen. Inside, he can see Eliot sitting at the kitchen counter, carefully arranging sliced bananas on a piece of bread smeared with peanut butter. Caroline is hunched over on the love seat painting her toenails a violent shade of lavender, humming along to something on the radio. There is a warm, comfortable feeling to the room that makes Jack pause on the threshold, stopped for a moment by the quiet sense of intimacy he knows will be disturbed the moment he walks in.

"Here," Eliot says, placing the top slice of bread on one of the sandwiches and holding it out to Caroline. Neither of them have noticed Jack on the other side of the screen door. He could be a kidnapper or rapist or psychopath on a serial killing rampage, just standing there waiting for the right moment to explode this delicate domesticity. The thought makes him feel huge and menacing, even to himself. He swings through the screen, which slams shut behind him. Eliot's sandwich drops from his extended hand and lands face up on the floor.

"Jesus," Caroline says, looking up. "I didn't hear the car."

"Hello," Jack says, shifting his gaze to Eliot, who is stooping to pick up the sandwich he dropped, inspecting it for dirt. He is so careful and particular in a considerate, womanly way. It is, maybe, a result of the name. From the start, Jack was against "Eliot." A name for a pansy. A bookworm. A redhead. But Faith insisted. It was her brother's name. Her dead brother. There was no persuading her out of it. "A little dirt puts hair on your chest," Jack says.

Eliot looks up at him and then back at the sandwich he is blowing on. "It's for Caroline."

"Hmm." Jack loosens his necktie.

"Dad," Caroline says, stretching her feet with their newly painted toenails out in front of her. "Do you think I can go to Skip Krasdale's wedding with you tomorrow, now that I'm home for it?"

"That's tomorrow?" Jack rifles through the mail. "I'm not going."

"You're his *godfather*."

Jack shrugs.

"You *anointed* him."

"Maybe I'll stick my head in."

"I would *think* so." Caroline wiggles her toes. "So do you think you could call and see if it would be okay if I went, too?" There is something rehearsed about her tone, as if she has been practicing sounding casual.

"Sure." Jack turns to look at her. "I didn't realize you'd become such a fan of old Skipper."

"I'm not," Caroline blushes. "I just—I think it'll be good to see who's around and whatever."

"Oh?" Jack raises his eyebrows. "You mean all the personalityless drones?" Jack enjoys the fact this is what Caroline called her brothers' childhood acquaintances during a fight she had with Jack Jr. at Christmas.

"I didn't really *mean* that. Oh, El—you're so sweet!" she says, accepting the plate Eliot is handing her with a carefully quartered sandwich. "Thank you."

"You're welcome," Eliot says, turning his attention to a new slice of bread.

"Is that okay, El, if Dad and I are both out tomorrow night?" Caroline says, switching into her concerned voice. "Do you mind being here by yourself?"

Jack does not want to be a part of some new wave of concern Caroline is brewing up. She has the uncanny ability to make him feel irresponsible as a father—like someone around whom the world is about to fall. "I'll be in my study," he says, picking his briefcase back up. "If the phone rings."

"You don't mind old Sir Percy?" Jack can hear Caroline saying, and Eliot murmurs something in response that elicits laughter from his sister. Jack has no idea what they are talking about. And he has forgotten to ask Caroline about this man who came by asking for her this morning.

8

SATURDAY LUNCH ON PEA ISLAND consists of cold lemon
chicken, baby spinach salad with caraway seed vinaigrette,
ropelike loaves of whole wheat sourdough bread, and three
kinds of fresh chutney. For dessert there is mixed-berry tart and
rice pudding. Lucy has employed an impossibly thin, under-
nourished-looking young Czech culinary student from the
Cambridge Culinary Institute to assist/take charge of Pete and
Lucy's Cantonese housekeeper, Margaret, while they are on
Pea Island.

"He not wash potatoes enough," Margaret complains to
Faith, who has volunteered to help set the table. "Chicken too
uncook—soft like for old lady."

"What's that?" Faith says. She has been watching a spindly, antique-looking yacht drift across the dining room windows under power of one black sail. What does this signify? The fact of it out there on the calm blue water is unsettling.

"Chicken too uncook," Margaret repeats, dumping a pile of forks on the table for Faith to distribute. She is a short woman, built like a bulldog, given to wearing skin-tight polyester stretch pants. Most of the time she lets the muscles of her face remain completely slack, which has the effect of making her seem permanently nonplussed, even hostile.

"In his country," Margaret says, lowering her voice conspiratorially, "they not wash hands before cook."

"Well, I'm sure he knows, from his school—" Faith begins uncertainly.

"Europe people not know how is clean," Margaret cuts her off. "Like in India." Her voice seems to be rising somewhat incautiously and Faith darts a glance at the swinging door to the kitchen. "They eat meat not even wash hands from go to bathroom."

Faith shakes her head sympathetically, feeling somewhat less enthusiastic about the delicious smells emanating from the kitchen.

"You know Denny?" Margaret says after a pause.

"Denny?" Faith repeats, hoping she is not one of the Eintopfs—but no, she is quite sure they are Wendy, Sue, Whistler, and Bee—or is it Fee?

"She make mess also."

"Oh," Faith says. "Too bad."

"She make cook all over kitchen mess and with dirty fingernail. Always talk talk," here she slips into a mimicking tone. "'Margaret, you know my friend . . .'"

Faith loses track of what Margaret is saying. But it is clear Denny does not meet with Margaret's approval. Unlike Felice, who helps take care of Faith's New York apartment (this is how Faith likes to think of it—"helps take care," like something a friend or concerned relation would do), there is a moral force that emanates from Margaret. Even in silence, at the edges of the situation, she is constantly making judgments. Faith is never quite sure how Margaret feels about her. In a way, they are friends after all these years of visits—Faith has always taken the time to inquire about Margaret's bad back and nieces in Shanghai, and always offers to help in the kitchen. Margaret, in turn, sends Faith Christmas cards and enlists her in long complaining conversations over Lucy and Pete's daughter, the price of fresh vegetables, the priest in her church, sex on television. But within this, Faith senses a note of personal reproval, as if each of the wrongdoings Margaret catalogues has been carefully selected to mirror some wrongdoing of Faith's own—some harm Faith has inflicted upon Margaret, caused by the mere, but irrevocable, fact of her existence.

"She ask about you, too, sometime."

"Me?" Faith exclaims in genuine surprise, stopping her napkin folding. "I don't know Denny."

"She ask, 'you know Faith husband? He used work with Rock.'"

"With Rock!" Faith says, and then realizes they are talking about Rock Coughlin, Sr.'s fiancée. "Oh—*Denise*," she says involuntarily.

"'You know Faith husband?'" Margaret continues. "'He ever make bother you?'" Margaret stops her hands for a moment in the bristly pile of silverware she is sorting and for a split second looks Faith directly in the eye. "I told her no," she says in an angry voice. "He not my business."

"Oh," Faith says again. She has not followed the story. How would Jack have bothered Margaret? But there is something in Margaret's tone that makes her feel indebted to her—makes her feel that she has been protected or stood up for. "Thank you," she finds herself saying.

Margaret shrugs. "I not like gossip."

Despite Margaret's hygienic suspicions, the lunch turns out to be delicious. "Get out here and take a bow," Pete bellows into

the kitchen at Jiri, the Czech culinary student, after sampling
each dish. "Best damn chicken I've ever had—Lucy, get this
recipe in that book of yours." After all these years, Pete still has
Yonkers in his voice. Jiri, who looks all of thirteen years old,
with his scrawny neck coming out of a too-large white cooking
smock, shuffles in and out of the kitchen unsmilingly. Margaret is nowhere to be seen.

Faith has spent the meal hearing Emmett, Lucy's uninvited
stepbrother, recount the adventures of starting two now-failed
ski resorts in Steamboat Springs. "Who wants all that root vegetable stew and arugala salad they serve at Taos or Sun Valley?"
he is saying. "I said, 'Let people pick a nice piece of beef and
slap it on the grill themselves.'" He has an oddly clear, addled
voice that gives the impression of a great pressure building
against his diaphragm from the inside. Faith remembers him
from her debutante days as a handsome, reckless playboy most
famous for having gotten some girl from Philadelphia pregnant
and getting into frequent fistfights. He has, since then, thick-
ened and gone bald, or shaved his head, or some combination
of both, which gives him the fuzzy, half-cocked appearance of a
newborn eagle. He has also, according to Lucy, squandered his
inheritance and abandoned two hotel enterprises, three marriages, and countless fix-it projects around Pea Island.

Faith has given up nodding understandingly, which doesn't
affect Emmett's monologue in the slightest. The crinkly map
with Eliot's violent warning is now resting under her mattress
upstairs, having been unfolded, refolded, and unfolded again,
at least six times. The paper itself is irrelevant at this point, having been replicated, with exacting precision, in Faith's mind.
She can peruse the map at leisure while she sits pushing a
stringy piece of mango through the creamy sauce on her plate.

She should, she tells herself, stop being silly. She should be
relieved that the paper was a map, not some dreadful confession. But the map seems frightening in its surprising neutrality
—what is a map, after all, but a recording? An unbiased look at
the most stolid and feelingless of elements—the ground itself.

For Eliot to have guarded it with such sinister threats seems to hint at a deeper, darker, more disturbing secret, like one of those scary movies in which the murderer is a beautiful woman who turns out to be a man.

Under the table Emmett's bare knee has found Faith's and is pressing insistently against it. "He's a great guy," he is saying. "A real ass-kicker. A lot like Jack, actually." His knuckles graze her knee.

Faith nearly drops her coffee cup.

"Who's this?" one of the Eintopfs, an affable, round-faced man with squinty eyes and a Bahamas T-shirt that says WE BE JAMMIN', under a colorful cutout of a Rastafarian, interjects. Faith has no idea and no desire to hear the answer. Excusing herself before Emmett can direct more nonsense at her, she makes her way around a chatty knot of Eintopfs to Lucy's end of the table, where Lucy and a leathery-faced woman with a square chin and tennis whites on are discussing—could it be?—Handi Wipes.

"Luce—" Faith whispers, "I'm going to go lie down   "

"My oldest friend, Faith Dunlap," Lucy says, clapping an arm around Faith's waist. "Did you know Wendy's parents knew your parents?"

"Yes," Faith says politely. "We were talking about that this morning."

"Faith and I have known each other since, when? Ninth grade, is it, Faithey?" Lucy says for the benefit of the near half of the table, which is now smiling up at her with benevolent interest, as if she is a child who has been called in to say good night to her parents' dinner party.

"Right," Faith says, forcing a smile. It occurs to Faith that Lucy has described her to these people as a recently released mental patient. At the far end of the table she can still hear Emmett jabbering at least five decibels louder than necessary. The French cousin, she realizes idly, does not seem to be present.

"Wonderful," one of the Eintopf's says.

"Our access to embarrassing Lucy stories!" another quips.

Faith's smile feels as if it is made of heavy, crumbling plaster of paris.

"I'm going upstairs to take a little rest," she whispers to Lucy when the group's thirst for entertainment has redirected itself to a college friend of Pete's, who is offering up imitations of Pete as a Harvard sophomore. "Okay, Faithey," Lucy says distractedly. "You do that."

Faith wakes up with the image of the bike trail spread out before her. She can tell from the light that she has slept longer than she intended to—the bright strip of sunshine on the green-painted floorboards has yellowed and lengthened into a rectangle the size of a gravestone. The thought of the map transports her seamlessly from sleep to waking, and before anything else has had the chance to enter her mind, she is sitting up on the cot, looking out over the overgrown flagstone terrace at the water, seeing instead the dark path, marked roads, and the paler, thicker line of the Charles River.

There is a movement below—a hand waving from the terrace that jars Faith from this train of thought. She realizes that she has been staring, gape-mouthed out at the sea, her forehead resting on the glass windowpane.

Someone—Jean Pierre—is now motioning with his arms for her to open the window. Obediently, but not without resentment, Faith complies.

"You are looking sad," he says. "Come have a cocktail." He is still wearing the fishing hat, but has changed into a short-sleeved navy blue shirt and olive green trousers. Twice this morning, Faith bumped into him speed-walking around the island in a tiny pair of nylon shorts and no shirt. His chest was startlingly *there*—round and firm and brown with a gold cross nestled in the symmetrical covering of dark curly hair like a dropped coin. He has showered and shaved and looks much milder and less intimidating now that he is fully clothed.

"Oh, no," Faith says. "I mean—I have to change and get

ready and I'll come down—aren't we having cocktails on the front porch?"

Jean Pierre smiles and shrugs. "Maybe these Eintopfs" (he says the word with a certain degree of derision) "are on the porch. I thought you were not in such a mood—yet."

"Oh, no—yes—well, I've got to get changed," Faith says lamely.

"And I will bring you a cocktail here. Which one?" Jean Pierre is still sitting, arm draped confidently over the bench, smiling up at her.

"Which cocktail?"

"Exactly."

"Well, all right—gin—no, a glass of wine would be fine. Thank you." Faith pulls down the shade. How does one refuse such an offer without being impolite? This is exactly the sort of thing she needs to remember. Say what you mean, Dr. Marcus says. Think of your own wants—not what other people want from you. But the more Faith ventures out into the world beyond her apartment, the more she cannot imagine Dr. Marcus in it. Does he have friends? Acquaintances? Does he go away for weekends? Or to cocktail parties? In her mind's eye he stands out among a crowd of people—a bright-colored Lego man whose feelings are as solid and uncomplicated as plastic bath toys. It would make her giggle if she didn't see the map on the cracking gray backside of the shade she is pulling down— insistent in its offering of information as incomprehensible as writing on some ancient cave wall.

9

THE LAST TIME Caroline saw Skip Krasdale, he was coming out of the Harvard Club wearing a yellow V-neck sweater with a pink-collared shirt tucked into it like a pair of pig's ears. Other than the extra pounds he has put on, he looks exactly like he did when he was fourteen: blank-eyed, blond, stoop-shouldered, and vaguely sneering. He has the pale, translucent sort of face that gives the impression his nose is always running. When Caroline was twelve, he "accidentally" used his BB gun to shoot her guinea pig, Dora. That was when he was friends with her brothers. Now he disapproves of their "party-boy" lifestyle, according to Jack Jr. who in turn thinks Skip has become a priggish, overworked bore. Caroline thinks both sides are right about each other.

There will be so many boys like Skip at his wedding, boys Caroline grew up with who are in their mid-twenties now, well launched into inevitable futures of gradual hair loss, back problems, and knee surgery; of cool, polite marriages to blond girls whose health and athletic prowess had everyone fooled, for a brief window of time, into calling them pretty; of desperate, distraction-seeking love affairs with golf, paddle tennis, squash, and backgammon; of memberships at the Ponkatawset Club and coat-and-tie thirtieth birthday parties; of having the same conversations with the same people in the same mind-numbingly dull places forever. Their very existence feels stifling to her— what do people like Skip Krasdale or Pete Duffey or her brothers, for that matter, think about driving alone at twilight, or leaning on an empty porch rail at sunset? Their weekend plans? Their bank accounts? Do they ever feel the overwhelming presence of all the other people who have stared, or are staring simultaneously into the growing dark?

They are certainly fine subjects for Stephan's movie, these strange last adherents to a thoroughly disproven way of living— the children of bystanders of the sixties, of parents whose whole generation passed them by while they stood on the sidelines scratching their heads and staring into stiff drinks, hampered by their own wealth and good breeding. They are already two steps removed from the dynamic center of the species. Which makes their blind, self-satisfied preservation of their grandparents' ways all the more absurd and at the same time desperate.

It is exciting, actually, to imagine capturing this on camera. It has not taken much for Caroline to decide to be Stephan's production assistant or whatever title he's going to come up with for her. Not only because she has nothing else lined up, either. The more she has thought about it, the more the idea of actually making something of all the ridiculous bits and pieces of experience she has collected growing up here appeals to her. How wonderful would it be, for instance, to capture Honey Walter talking about that ridiculous girls final club she started at Harvard? Or to interview Welty Reed about his gun collection? Why didn't she think of making a movie like this herself? There were grants she could have applied for and film department resources she could have made use of if she had just been organized, had just taken advantage of the opportunities laid out before her.

Of course, Caroline is not different from all these people herself, in all manner of background and upbringing—a fact that is abundantly apparent as she rifles through her formal dresses for something interesting and unpreppy to mark her as apart from Stephan's subjects. Her reflection in the mirror is neat, clean, and all-American—not all that different from the little blond no-makeup-wearing girls who get married to people like Skip Krasdale and Pete Duffey. But she has a different future in store for herself, one in which she will read good books and visit exotic places and meet thoughtful, eccentric, and interesting people. She can go abroad if she saves enough money—live with her friend Miriam in her mud hut in Bali, an adventure her father would certainly never underwrite. Or apply to film school, or move to Paris and write some witty, insightful article about this antiquated corner of the world she comes from.

Caroline decides on a gray strapless dress and puts it down on the bed beside her black sweater. It is getting late—they will need to get going in fifteen minutes to make it to the wedding. Her father has not even changed yet. She can see him out the window right now: a solitary figure on the back lawn, dark against the gold grass in the evening sunlight. He is throwing what looks like some sort of baton for the dogs to chase after: picking it up, bringing his arm back, hurling it toward the woods with the two dogs close behind it. He stands for a moment watching them, in a pose half defiant, half unsure, as if he is not certain they will actually come back to him with it.

Caroline leans toward the window, which is open, to call out to him. But something stops her and she stays quiet instead, one hand on the peeling sill, watching him stoop, draw back, throw again, and then stand still in the odd, uncertain posture. His shadow stretches like a long thin minute hand across the gleaming gold grass.

When she is dressed and ready, Caroline goes downstairs and sits down at the kitchen table. Her father has finally gone upstairs to get ready. They will be late, as usual, which ordinarily she wouldn't mind, but which, in light of her already precarious position as unexpected guest, she doesn't relish. Caroline reaches into the drawer under the table for one of the silver lobster skewering implements she used to put up her hair with in high school. But just as she is sliding this into a slippery, makeshift bun she has created, the telephone rings.

"Just a minute, I told you I'm phoning," an impatient, gravelly voice is saying on the other end of the line when she lifts the receiver.

"Lilo," Caroline says, wishing she hadn't picked up.

"To whom am I speaking?" Lilo demands haughtily.

"Caroline," Caroline sighs. Lilo, or Helen Whittier Dunlap, as she is formally known, is for all intents and purposes her grandmother, the aunt who raised Jack after his parents' car wreck—a job she carried out with, from what Caroline can tell, all the love and good feeling of one of those Harlow wire monkeys.

"Caroline *Dunlap*?"

"Lilo, its me, Caroline. How are you?"

"I have been better." There is a significant pause on the other end of the line. Caroline does not rush to fill it. "I have something here I think you might be interested in."

"Oh, really?" Caroline slides the lobster skewer back out of her hair, which falls in a swish around her shoulders. The implement smells faintly of the sea and unpolished silver.

"It's not something I take any pleasure in telling you about—you know I don't like to involve myself in family dramas

and you can imagine my discomfort at being the person . . ."
Caroline rolls her eyes. Lilo is, contrary to her assertions, the
primary chronicler, purveyor, and producer of family drama
for the Dunlaps. ". . . and so I thought, 'Well, what is this motley getup lying on my wing chair and how can I get rid of it?' "
Lilo is saying. The punch line, Caroline has guessed long ago,
is that her father has—God forbid—left his jacket on some visit
to her. "So I picked it up and . . ." But Caroline is not listening
anymore.

Her father has emerged in the doorway, wearing a battered
green cap of his grandfather's that looks, to Caroline, like
something a cartoon character would wear. *Lilo*, she mouths at
him. "I'm not here," he says, loud enough to express disregard
for the fact that Lilo can quite possibly hear him.

"Lilo?" Caroline says. "Dad isn't home and I'm running out
the door now to a wedding. Can I call you tomorrow?"

"Well," Lilo says, "you *can* and you *may* also—I do think you
should come by—"

"Okay, I'll call you tomorrow," Caroline says brightly. "Bye-
bye." She replaces the receiver.

In the car, Jack Dunlap pulls the invitation out of his breast
pocket and lays it against the windshield, as if without it he
would have no idea how to find First Parish Church or the
Ponkatawset Club. As if he didn't know Concord like the back
of his hand or belong to the club for eighteen years and go
there as a boy every Sunday with his grandfather. Since he with-
drew his membership, Jack has become a virtual denier of the
club's existence. "The Ponkatawset Club!" he'll say scornfully.
"Oh, you mean Disneyland." This is, as far as Caroline can tell,
in reference to the new spa facilities in the locker rooms, the
expanded membership, the renovated dining area, which
includes a whole wall of tinted floor-to-ceiling windows. Unlike
most successful men of his generation, her father has an almost
violent distaste for anything, other than cars and property, that

smacks of luxury. Caroline is all for his new disgust with the place, albeit for different reasons. It has had two nonwhite members in its entire history, costs $30,000 a year to belong to, and seems to lower the threshold for acceptable conversation topics to include blow-by-blow recounts of golf plays and car-buying searches. God forbid anyone bring up, for instance, Bosnia. Not that Caroline herself is anything but hopelessly uninformed on the matter, but at least—well, at least she is ashamed of her ignorance.

"So," her father says, startling Caroline out of her thoughts. They have passed the last five minutes of the drive in silence, having covered the bulk of accessible conversation topics (the Red Sox, the new addition to the Hibberts' house, rumors of the recent fall from grace of Jack's old undergraduate men's club) already. "You had a good visit with your mother?"

"Mm-hmm," Caroline nods.

"She seemed"—he pauses—"well to you?"

"Fine." Caroline is suspicious of this line of questioning. Her father loves to try to draw her into conversations that allow him the opportunity to make condescending or wry comments about everything from her mother's propensity for being star-tled to her famously poor cooking abilities. These are not the whole story, though, which makes such conversations especially uncomfortable. There was the night shortly after Faith moved out, for instance, that Caroline found him organizing the old shoe box of photos that Faith had for years bemoaned not hav-ing enough time or energy, or whatever it was, to sort through. He was pasting them into a beautiful leather-bound album with black pages, and labeling each with a special white pencil he had bought for the occasion. It was late—maybe two A.M., the night black and hard with the bite of coming winter, when Car-oline came home to find him surrounded by neat piles of stiff-backed, formal-looking photos of his courtship and early years of marriage. It was nothing, he had said gruffly, just a little nec-essary cleanup. But she had seen his face, in that moment of turning when she walked in. And the address of Lucy's home in

Greenwich where Faith was staying, neatly penciled in his hand on a piece of paper clipped to the inside cover. There had been the awkward moment of pure silence—no wind outside or clank of radiators or scuffling of the dogs (where were they?) to diffuse the intensity of his absolute aloneness here at the kitchen table, reconstructing his failed marriage in the early hours of the morning. *Well,* Caroline had said finally—she was a little drunk—*it's getting really cold out.* His denial was fierce enough to be contagious.

"Did she mention anything about Eliot visiting?" her father asks.

"Sometime before camp," Caroline says.

"Well—if she can figure out—"

"I think it's a good idea," Caroline interrupts. "I mean, she's going to have him for all his vacations next year anyway, right? So he might as well get used to visiting." She pauses. "What else does he have to do? He has three weeks before camp and no school, and it does seem so lonely that he's just—like right now—going to be all by himself at home. I don't understand, I guess, why he never got a new babysitter after Rosita moved away—you don't really think he's too old—"

Her father pulls up directly behind the van in front of them and flashes his brights. "He's almost eleven," he says.

"Okay—but at least a housekeeper, or someone who's home sometimes. I could find out about my friend Sarah's old housekeeper," Caroline begins again. "She might be able to work, since she doesn't work for her family anymore—"

"You know, Caroline," her father says in his chilliest voice, "Eliot and I *have* been okay for the last year without your assistance."

Caroline feels the blood rush to her ears. "Right," she says, surprised to find her throat has constricted. "I didn't realize it was such a touchy subject."

"It is not a 'touchy subject.' " He flashes his lights again, three times fast now, and the van that has been lurching along in front of them pulls over. BILLERICA SENIOR CENTER is printed on the side of it in navy lettering. Above this, a series of pale faces stare back through the glass squares of their windows at her like a sort of woeful, reproving chorus. As Jack accelerates past it, the driver glares out his window at Caroline.

"I could," her father says after a while, clearing his throat, "take Eliot down with me next week."

"To New York?" Caroline says.

He nods, stiff-jawed, and flicks on the blinker to turn onto Main Street.

"Okay." She shrugs and looks back out the window. There is an Indian tour group climbing off a bus, blinking their eyes in the slanted evening sunlight.

"If you wanted, you could come, too," he says without looking at her. "I could get the three of us tickets to something before Eliot goes to your mother's."

Caroline turns to see if he is joking. But he looks absolutely serious, if uncomfortable. Her father, it occurs to her as almost wondrous, is trying to make some sort of amends for being such an asshole. "That's nice of you," she says, almost to see if he will retract it. Niceness is not a quality that he has respect for.

They are now in view of First Parish Church, the steps of which are dotted with latecomers. Her father pulls into a parking place on the other side of the street from it. "Well," he says brusquely, opening his door. "Just a thought."

Caroline pauses for a moment before opening her own door and watches him making his way around the front of the car to her side. He has a very upright stride, which seems suddenly, as he navigates the narrow space between his front fender and the back of the station wagon ahead of it, fragile in its rigidity. She can count on half a hand the times she has ever seen him offer anything approximating a gesture of contrition. It should make her angry, but as he turns to wait for her, eyebrows raised, she feels instead a swell of compassion. He is a man who knows so little about affection that he can't even invite his children to New York without feeling embarrassed. "Coming," she says, opening the door and climbing out into the humid air of evening.

Rock is going to Skip Krasdale's wedding for two reasons: (a) Caroline will be there and (b) staying home while Denise "helps" his father pack for Pea Island will possibly kill him. Until last week, Denise was to accompany her fiancé on the trip and Rock Jr. was to have the "duplex" to himself for a blissful six days. But Denise has decided she has "too much work" and that Rock Sr. needs "alone time" with his old friends before they get married. Rock Jr. suspects there are other factors at work here—namely Stephan Dartman, a.k.a. Denise's boy toy.

Through the closed door to his father's bedroom, Rock has already started to hear things like: "You're bringing your tennis racket? God help us," and "You don't need that old sweater—Jesus, what would you do without me? Walk around looking like Archie Bunker?" Rock Sr., as portrayed by his fiancée, is a bumbling idiot barely capable of dressing himself, let alone interacting in social situations. "You're hopeless, Coughlin," is one of Denise's favorite ways to punctuate cocktail party stories. "Can you believe this guy?" Rock Sr. will just stand there, looking tired and slightly distracted, but accepting the pathetic vision of himself Denise proffers as if it were no less fair than a parking ticket or a jury duty summons. Rock is in no mood to play audience to this show.

By the time Rock arrives at the white clapboard church on Thorough Street he has had ample time to remember the two distinct reasons why he was *not* going to go in the first place: (a) he will have to see his mother and (b) he hates the groom. Skip Krasdale is Rock's third cousin. A solemn, self-proclaimed moralist, Skip is comfortable making pronouncements about politics, culture, and members of the Coughlin family with the kind of authority generally reserved for veterans of foreign wars and ancient southern matriarchs—not twenty-eight-year-olds with a Harvard education and six years of institutional investment work under their belts. Rock has never heard the guy laugh at anything other than the kind of joke that can be written up in the minutes of a men's club. Neither, for that matter, has Rock ever seen Skip wear a pair of jeans.

It isn't until the reception that Rock even catches sight of Caroline. He has, as expected, been cornered by his mother, who is attempting to explain the essential nature of a daily yoga routine to him. "You'll have so much more energy, Rock," she is saying. "You need to care for your body first and the rest will follow. Really. I can see everything so much more clearly now that I'm working with Ravi. He's so *grounded*. He would be really good for you."

Since her divorce she has become an avid consumer of new dietary strategies, meditational techniques, and homeopathy workshops. Her body has been kickboxed, treadmilled, stepped, and yogaed into a stringy fat-free mass of muscle and sharp jutting bones, wrapped in a mysterious year-round nut-brown tan. Even her eyes have acquired an intense, stripped-down way of looking at things, as if everything they take in has, like her body, been honed to its bare essentials. To Rock, she looks about twenty times older than she did when she was an unhappy, out-of-shape drunk. But she feels good—she feels great, in fact. This is what she is trying to explain to Rock. "Right," Rock says intermittently. He has heard enough New Age rhetoric at Bensen's Organic to last a lifetime. "Excellent."

Out of the corner of his eye he is watching Caroline talk to some tall European guy with slicked-back hair pulled into a little ponytail—no American would have hair like that. Caroline is talking quite seriously, nodding her head and standing with one hand cradling the other elbow. She has one of those thin, extra-naked-looking bodies, all long bones and bright eyes, no padding to speak of, and a certain condensed quietness about her that attracts attention in a roomful of people, like a gap in a mouthful of teeth. Talking to this guy, she looks so focused and interested, nodding her head and asking questions. When she talks to Rock, there is always something faintly distracted about her, as if some secret but essential part of her is missing—off sitting on a windowsill, staring into the dusk somewhere.

As Rock watches, the European turns and reveals himself to be Stephan—*Ste-fan,* who has shed his ripped T-shirt in favor of a smartly fitted tuxedo. Did Caroline invite him here? Rock stares at the two of them, or at Caroline, more precisely, until he realizes he is waiting—with the muscle-tight tension of someone watching a child learn how to bike-ride—for the slippery S curve of Caroline's hair draped over her shoulder to fall straight. Jesus! As if this would be a fucking tragedy! The whole joyless high church ceremony, with its stark readings from the King James Bible, cautionary homily, and silent, floorboard-creaking, dress-rustling exchanging of rings has really wound him up. His cummerbund feels too tight to draw a good deep breath. And the air in the tent smells musky—twice breathed.

Rock downs the rest of his Manhattan and heads back to the bar. When his glass is replenished (his third drink already), he makes his way toward Caroline, who is still talking to Stephan. "The European" is how Rock prefers to think of him. It would make a good name for a contender of Stone Cold Steve Austin or The Undertaker on late-night wrestling.

When Rock gets to the spot where Caroline and he should be, though, they are nowhere in sight. He has been delayed by a forced exchange of hand slaps with the groom's brothers—a triumvirate of blond fraternity boys with beefy necks and bad hearing, whom Rock hates even more than he did five minutes ago. The band has struck up a tepid re-creation of Sinatra's "The Best Is Yet to Come," and on the raised platform the bride and groom are making their way, workman-like, around the floor: Skip with his usual stiff, constipated look and his wan little bride dragging slightly, like a deflating blow-up doll. In the far right corner of the tent a bird has gotten in under the billowy canvas and is fluttering frantically against it, gathering a crowd at least as large as that collected around the dance floor. In the middle of all this, Rock spots Caroline—*still* talking to Stephan!—now closer to the seafood bar. They have been joined by a hefty, pouf-haired girl in a dress that makes her look like Nancy Reagan. And Stephan has whipped out his video camera.

"Carol," Rock calls from a little too far away, and all three turn to look at him as if he is possibly dangerous. Calling Caroline Carol gives Rock a particularly satisfying kind of amusement. "Hey."

"Hi, Rock," Caroline says graciously. "You remember Stephan—and you know Mindy, don't you? We all went to dancing school together," she offers by way of explanation, putting her hand on the girl's purple shoulder in that giggly, expansive way that she gets when she is drinking. There is a faint dart of white skin running up from the top of her strapless dress to the nape of her neck, the ghost of some impossibly thin bathing suit tie.

"Sure," Rock says, extending his hand. "I think you know my father's fiancée, Denise Meirhoffer, don't you?" He has donned his Bob Hope voice despite his best intentions not to.

"Oh." Stephan looks genuinely startled. "Of course."

"I remember you," Nancy Reagan interrupts, turning to Rock. "You were suspended with Sam Daedalus, weren't you? For smoking or something—or for sending an obscene fax? Or letter? What was it?" She has a rapid, aggressive way of speaking and a slight nostril flare that accompanies her vowel sounds.

"That wasn't me," Rock lies.

"Of course it was," Caroline pats his arm. "Rocky the rebel. Do any of you need a drink?"

Rock looks at her in dismay. She is going to use him as her out, leave him to steer this motley conversation crew. Rock gulps at the drink in his hand, but can't really make enough headway to justify tagging along. Anyway, he has already been zeroed in on by Mindy, who is asking, nostrils aflare: Where does he live now? What does he do? How does he know Skip?

Rock keeps his answers to a minimum. Stephan seems to be checking the fit of his tuxedo, looking surreptitiously over his shoulder toward his ass.

"So Denise says you're from Cambridge." Rock turns to Stephan, cutting Mindy off in midquestion.

"What's that?" Stephan asks.

"So you're from Cambridge?" Rock immediately regrets the *so*, which there was no good reason to repeat. Standing across from him, Mindy looks wounded.

"Not really. I lived there for a few years during high school."

"Hmm," Rock says. "And now you live in LA?"

"Actually"—Stephan is unzipping his camera bag now, casting an eye around the room—for good scenes to film, presumably—"I just spent a year in Europe."

"*Really.* I was just thinking you looked kind of European," Rock is saying before he can stop himself. "The 'do or something."

Stephan raises his eyebrows.

"I was thinking it would be a good name for a WWF character—you know, 'The European,'" he says in a cheesy announcers voice. "And he'd be all tall and blond and wearing assless leather pants and a scarf or something." His voice, he realizes, is rising inappropriately.

"Riiiii-iiiight," Mindy says. The girl is a real pill. She probably balances her checkbook on-line and reads the wedding section of the *Globe* and sends theme cards to people on their birthdays and when they're in the hospital. She probably loves the Steve Miller Band.

Stephan smiles benevolently and lifts the camera to his eye.

"So how do you know Caroline again?" he asks, panning around the room.

"School, growing up, family." Stephan's smile strikes him as condescending.

"And you said you're Denise's boyfriend's son?"

"Fiancé's."

"Right." Stephan is now focusing his camera on some older couple standing by the wedding cake, but there is something phony about his show of casual distraction. Rock senses a certain real interest in his voice—as if he is trying to determine something. "And where was school again?" Stephan asks in the same tone.

Rock is beginning to feel like he is being interviewed. "Quilton. And how about yourself, you went to . . . ?"

"Rindge and Latin—public school, in Cambridge." He says it hastily.

There is a sharp intake of breath at the far side of the tent as the poor bird, which has been batted at with a whole retinue of white linen napkins and caterers' serving tongs, is swatted onto the ground and then, apparently (Rock sees its body fly up from the ground in an odd, closed-winged, not exactly aerodynamic trajectory), *kicked* out into the night air by a wiry gray-haired man in a tuxedo. There are a few nervous, halfhearted cheers from the crowd, most of whom seem undecided on this radical final solution to the bird problem. The man presses out from between them, brushing his hands off as if he has done no more than pick up a fallen roll or uncork a bottle of champagne. It is, of course, Jack Dunlap. Rock finds himself grinning. The guy is a true weirdo. People are looking after him with the kind of hostile, awe-filled consternation that always seems to follow Spider-Man in the Sunday morning comics.

"Excuse me," Rock says, and turns to find Stephan has already moved a few yards away to get a better angle on Mr. D's exit. The guy's intentions are hard to get a read on, but whatever they are, Rock doesn't like him: too smug and a little sneaky somehow. He makes his own rapid zigzagging path around the tables toward the side of the tent Jack Dunlap has retreated to. The vodka tonics have Rock seeing in sharp, abrupt chunks—a slick black helmet of hair, a heave of too much goose-bumpy cleavage, a half-eaten platter of bacon-wrapped scallops. "And they had a jukebox, and spiked punch, and everyone wore saddle shoes! It was a riot," a woman with a ridiculous UFO-like hat is saying as Rock pushes past.

When he reaches Caroline's father, he is out of breath and he can feel his heart beating in his left middle toe from having been ground under the leg of someone's chair. "Mr. Dunlap," Rock says when he is within range. He is panting slightly.

Jack turns around with a blank look on his face and then narrows his eyes with recognition. "Ron," he says warily.

"Rock." Rock nods encouragingly.

Jack does not correct himself. They are at the side of the tent that looks out onto the rolling swells of the golf course, blanketed in a soft moonlit darkness. Beside them a table of elderly people (five chatty women and three fairly subdued men, one of whom is staring directly at Rock with an incredulous expression and a bit of cheese stuck to the corner of his mouth) is still working on plates of roast beef, potatoes au gratin, string beans, and wilty-looking salad with pomegranate seeds, which must be murder on their dentures. It occurs to Rock, now that he has made a beeline over, that he has nothing to say.

"Quite a play the other day," he finally says, and coughs.

Jack nods his head in perfunctory, distracted consent. His eyes are sweeping the tent in search of—who would he be looking for? Rock follows his glance and finds it stops on Caroline. There she is, in line for the buffet with two older women and Adam Lowell, a tall spindly boy a few years younger than Rock, with the kind of neck and shoulders that seem to taper into, rather than balance, his head. A human penis with little wire-rimmed glasses and enough goofy good spirits to float the *Hindenburg*. On the other side of the table the European, which is what Stephan has become in Rock's mind now, is standing at one of the tent posts filming them, his video camera protruding from between the puffy white flowers the post is wrapped with.

"You know anything about that guy?" Jack asks.

"Who, Adam Lowell? He went to—"

"With the camera."

Rock darts a look at Jack, who is standing impassively, arms folded across his chest.

"Oh—he's making some kind of movie. . . ." Rock pauses.

In line, Adam throws his head back and laughs at something Caroline has said. Adam is always worming his way into girls' hearts, taking the unmenacing, androgynous, best-friend back door to their affections, and, once within the general parameters, making weaselly, whiny, desperate dashes at their hearts. Rock almost feels sorry for him for the first time ever; everything from his body language to his stupid bow tie presents a perfect, obnoxious vision of boisterous phoniness that Stephan must be lapping up.

Jack seems to be waiting for Rock to continue, although he really has nothing else to say. "It's about Concord," Rock continues. "Some kind of documentary—I don't know, social commentary or something."

Jack cocks his head to look at Rock directly for the first time. It is not exactly an encouraging look, but the alcohol begins pulling words out of Rock's mouth like one of those trick streamers under a clown's tongue.

"He's made a few already—about prominent places, you know, and their seamy undersides. . . . He's got a degree in women's studies from Sarah Lawrence, I think, and I guess he used to be a harpist for some New Age choir, but it was too hard on his fingers or his back or something—he'd been training since he was a kid. He's still in therapy about it—he's"— Rock makes the quotation gesture with his fingers—" 'working through it' in his films."

Jack is still staring at Rock, but frowning now.

Jesus—how did he get started on this? Dunlap probably thinks he's friends with the guy or something—some kind of harp music fanatic or art film buff.

"Bullshit," Jack says, looking back across the room at Stephan, who is now talking to Adam and Caroline, who looks somewhat disconcerted to have found herself being filmed.

"Well . . ." Rock shrugs himself lower into his jacket and looks into the bottom of his empty glass. There is a wet cocktail napkin stuck to it that he hasn't even noticed—it seems suddenly equivalent to walking around with a piece of toilet paper on the bottom of his shoe.

Jack makes a sharp sudden sound, which at first Rock thinks is an outraged yelp, but it isn't. It's laughter. Jack Dunlap is laughing. A triumphant gloating feeling pushes up from Rock's abdomen. A salty breeze blows through the tent from the ocean. It is turning out to be an all right night after all. Rock and Jack stand side by side, staring across the room.

Almost at the front of the buffet line now, Adam is demonstrating something with his hands, describing points in the air with emphatic gestures while Caroline and Stephan look on. His right hand sweeps from his shoulder toward the table and knocks the neat roll of silverware out of Caroline's hand. "Sorry, sorry," his voice carries all the way across to where Jack and Rock are standing as he leans over to pick up the dropped pieces. Caroline leans to help, but before she disappears behind the table she smiles at Stephan—a sort of gentle, amused smile accompanied by a little helpless shrug. There is something sweet about it, almost childish—and more than that—something intimate.

The triumphant feeling washes out of Rock completely and in its wake he can feel the foolish smile he has been wearing fall from his lips. Beside him Jack has shifted his gaze up at the pointed roof of the tent, as if maybe he is hoping for another bird in need of disposing. Across the tent, Stephan has lifted his camera and pointed it directly at them. Rock considers giving him the finger, but somehow, even in his drunkenness, he has a clear sense that this would be exactly what Stephan is looking for. Except, it dawns on him, that it would be him, and not Jack Dunlap. And judging from where the camera has been all night, Jack Dunlap seems to be at the heart of what the guy is after.

JACK IS NOT INITIALLY PLANNING to make this little tromp out onto the golf course his exit from the Krasdale wedding. He just needs fresh air. And silence—the Coughlin kid has talked his car off. The band is honking away at some frantic swing tune he recognizes vaguely from every other wedding he has ever been to. Lots of sliding horns and quick twists—the kind of music that made him feel like a lumbering idiot when he was a boy in dancing school. Jack has never been a fan of dancing, or, for that matter, of music. There is always something intrusive about it; something about the composition of notes and melodies that makes him feel manipulated. He knows nothing of them except that they are constructed, put together with the same cunning and precision that goes into building a house or a legal argument.

When he was a young man, he discovered a collection of dusty old records that had belonged to his mother, who had been, at this point, reduced in his mind to an ethereal black and white image, the smell of her perfume, and the click of heels across polished marble. Rhapsodies by Dvorak, the Mozart *Requiem*, some violin songs by a composer named Kreisler. He played these one afternoon in his Harvard dorm room and was sucked away into some other time and place where he did not have to keep his hands busy or his brain active, but could just sit, for hours in the brown-paneled room, watching the dust motes catch the afternoon sunlight and the snow outside be enveloped, slowly but surely, in icy blue shadow.

And it made him feel what can only be described as real sorrow—unlike anything he had ever felt before: filled with not just visions, but whole pieces of himself as the little boy climbing the creaky, mothball-smelling back steps to bed in Helen's empty house alone, or building, secretly, a model airplane in the damp basement; spending Thanksgiving by himself in the cold, abandoned dormitory of his boy's school. His whole person was taken over and filled up with this great, oppressive sense—of all despicable things—of self-pity! He had been swept away by this unfathomable substance of arranged sounds into a deep state of melancholy. It was a profound manipulation; he has been suspicious of music ever since.

The wedding tent is set up away from the main building of the Ponkatawset Club, at the low end of the back lawn, where ordinarily parties are not allowed but which Skip's father, Hank Krasdale, having financed the club dining room renovation, has been given special permission to occupy. On one side of the tent there is a small wood—a carefully planted stand of fast-growing pine trees—and on the other, there is the golf course, glistening faintly in the moonlight. Here, beyond the throng of bodies and moist wine-scented air of the tent, the temperature drops pleasantly and there is a cool, damp breeze rushing out of the pines across the dark grass. Jack takes a deep breath and starts out toward the rise of the third hole; here he is one man, distinguished from the earth around him by his bones and blood and movement, not the color of his tuxedo jacket, the way he stands, the meaningless words coming out of his mouth. This is how he likes it. Why did he even come to this ridiculous event? The only reason he is even Skip's godfather is because when Skip was born, Hank wanted to buy the field Jack owns across the street from him, which Jack told him, even at the time, he would never sell. The man is a smarmy numbskull known for going through extravagant, high-profile divorces—Jack would have refused to become the boy's godfather if Faith hadn't thrown such a fit about the impropriety of such a thing.

Walking up the small rise of the third hole, Jack makes out what looks like a person—a small person, a child, actually, stretched out on his back on the close-cropped putting green. It makes him stop short, sloshing bourbon over the side of his hand—he has forgotten he is still holding his glass. "Who's that?" he says, and the figure scrabbles up to a sitting position. Jack can make out a squarish head and pudgy T-shirt-clad upper body—Joe Barrett. It sends an odd chill of recoil through him, enough that he has to stop himself from stepping backward.

"Joe?" he says, squinting through the darkness.

"Yeah." The response is faint—too soft to sound as tough as it is obviously meant to.

"What are you doing out here?" Jack says.

"Nothing." Joe is standing up now, looking down at his feet, one of which is scuffing back and forth over the short grass.

Joe is the son of the night watchman at the club, Jack's gardener Wheelie Barrett's brother. Jack would not know this if he hadn't helped save the boy's life last winter. The kid had been thrown from a snowmobile going, it was later noted, over thirty miles an hour on a winding path through the wildlife refuge that lies in the lowland between Monument and Bedford streets. He had cleared a good four feet in the air and landed on an old, half-snow-covered threshing machine, which sent one of its spikes straight through the soft flesh of his upper arm. Which was how Jack and Rosita found him—a small body, two corduroy-clad legs, a beige parka, and a lot of livid blood soaking out into the snow around him. They had been en route to the commuter train that Rosita was going to take back to her sister's for the weekend when a small, hysterical woman in a dirty-looking down vest and rubber boots came waving and screaming out of the brush along the road. An ugly little thing, with scraggly hair, no hat, barely intelligible, she had led them over the crunchy, ice-encrusted snow to an unkempt trail obscured from the road by a stand of trees. And in the middle

of this—the overturned snowmobile with an unconscious man
(Joe's drunken father) trapped beneath it, and the surreally
spiked body of the boy. Eleven years old, and improbably skew-
ered by the rusty spike of an ancient piece of farm machinery.
He was screaming—a high, weak, inhuman sound that seemed
as much a cause as a result of his trauma.

Out on the golf course there is a rush of wind through the
pines. "Why aren't you home in bed? It must be past your bed-
time." Jack is surprised to find his voice has taken on a thick,
gruff quality.

"Waiting for Pop." The boy shrugs. "He works until midnight."

Jack nods and stares at him. A distinct strain of music separates itself from the general buzz of voices emanating from the
tent and floats across through the night air toward them.

On that afternoon, in the snow, Jack had stood there,
stunned for a moment, before snapping into action. He told
the wailing, screaming woman (who turned out later to be Joe's
father's girlfriend, the owner of the snowmobile) to shut up
and go back to the road to call an ambulance. As if through
some unspoken agreement, he and Rosita had moved toward
the terrifying hump of dingy corduroys and blood-slickened
parka. The spike had gone straight through the boy's arm,
about two inches below his shoulder—a half inch to the right
and it would have been his lung; the boy would be dead now,
Jack was told later. Rosita wrapped her hands around the boy's
arm and shoulder, steadying it, while Jack slid one hand under
his back and one just below the spike, then wrenched upward
in one smooth motion. There was the slick feeling of the nylon
parka, like a wet sail, and the impossible sucking that must have
been the boy's flesh. And there was the sound of Rosita's voice,
strangely calm and low, speaking to the boy, stopping his
wheezy screaming.

"You don't want to wait inside?" Jack asks. "Or in there?" He
motions at the tent.

"Un-unh." The boy shakes his head emphatically.

"Hmm." Jack nods and glances back at the bright squares of yellow light that compose the tent from here. It looks frivolous and impenetrable, like something on a television screen. He does not, he realizes, particularly want to go back there, either.

"Look," the boy says, approaching him shyly. He is holding his arm out, pulling the T-shirt sleeve back with his other hand. Jack looks at the pale appendage being proffered. It is marked with a deep, indented purple scar that spiders its way along the bone for about four inches between his elbow and shoulder.

"No more bandage," Jack says heavily.

"I'm taking Spanish in school," the boy offers, kicking at the ground again.

"Oh?" For a moment Jack can't think what this is supposed to mean. But then he remembers: *uno, dos, tres*, was what Rosita was saying. *This is how you count in my language*, holding this boy's hand and speaking as if they were sitting snugly on some living room sofa, her eyes unflinching.

"Aha." Jack stiffens. A shriek of laughter from inside the tent hurtles through the darkness. The boy is looking up at him, waiting for something with a guarded but insistent expression on his face. Jack can almost feel this more than he can see it in the moonlight. "Well, take care of yourself," he says, stepping backward and then turning to walk away from the tent toward the parking lot across the grass.

Behind him, he can feel the boy's presence like a distant banging that works its way into a dream.

10

THE DRIVEWAY SHINES white and chalky in the moonlight, a wide bright path that narrows and darkens under the scraggly, intertwined limbs of the beech trees as it nears the road. There is no one home, no one around to hear, but Eliot walks softly anyway, measuring his footfalls so that the crunch of gravel beneath his feet is no louder than a sigh. On his back, his backpack sits snug and heavy, like a parachute. The night is sticky, heavier than the day, and full of the wet, decaying smells of summer.

Eliot is not actually scared out here in the night. It is scarier to be in the house, with its distant, darkened rooms and creaky sounds, its feeling of live emptiness. Inside, there are all those portraits of stern, unhappy-looking ancestors and the constant, unacknowledged presence of the attic overhead. Eliot is afraid to walk through the dining room, with its framed brass rubbing óf Sir Percival in a full suit of armor, lifted from the knight's own Westminster Abbey grave. People were smaller back then, according to Eliot's mother. He has always taken this to mean the reproduction is Sir Percival's actual size. Eliot is already two inches taller than the dark, skeletal form in the rubbing, and the image of its ghost walking around eye level with the sideboard is unnerving.

On the road, he switches his flashlight on and shines it up into the canopy of leaves above him. Their dusky underbellies rustle like a mass of scurrying animals, alive in the wind. He shines the light ahead of him, illuminating a round spot of purplish pavement, a scattering of wet leaves and twigs, two fat orange slugs. The night is full of the gentle crackling sounds of summer: peeping crickets, rustling bushes, and the soft trickle of water in the ditch.

Eliot walks a quarter of a mile down Memorial Road and then turns right on the narrow path that horses take from the stable to the road. It is darker and closer here in the woods and he can feel his heart speed up inside his rib cage. He has had this nervous, wound-up feeling for the last few days and it has only gotten more extreme as his plan nears completion. Yesterday, he realized the map he printed out from the Internet was missing. It doesn't really matter, he has built the route into his papier-mâché project and memorized all its forks and turns already. But still, he doesn't like the idea of it at large in the world.

The other end of a twig he has stepped on scratches against a stone and Eliot jumps at the sound it makes. His brothers once told him a young girl was murdered in this wood a hundred years ago and that at night her spirit walks around in the patent-leather shoes she was wearing. He pictures the path as it is in the daylight to drive out this image. Pictures the light falling in moving pieces on the rotting leaves under his feet, the stretch of Memorial Road visible below them through the trees. He is almost at the place where he and Rosita would scrabble down the bank of the hill to sit on the flat rocks that jut out over the river here. *How do you call this?* he remembers Rosita asking of the furry moss here under the trees. *How do you call this?* of the bird's nest at the top of the apple tree. Hearing her voice in his head is comforting—it makes Eliot feel brave navigating this darkness. *Brave,* Rosita's voice pops into his mind suddenly, *like your father.* She had rested the vocabulary book on her knee for a moment with an unfamiliar, almost self-conscious expression on her face. *Arrojado,* she pronounced musingly. Eliot has never thought of his father as particularly brave.

At the end of the path, the Sunny Gables Stable meadow appears, a bright moonlit plain punctuated by the dense black form of the stable at the far end. The manicured grass, neatly cornered field, and clean bright fences that inhabit this place by day have become an inky watercolor version of themselves—the absolute distinctions between wood and grass, sky and tree rendered insignificant.

Crouching down slightly, Eliot starts across the meadow. Forester said there would be no one there after eight, but Eliot is not sure he truly believes him. He has paid Forester a good four months' worth of allowance, which should be enough to ensure veracity, but Forester is not a boy who inspires trust. Better to be careful, which is why he is here in the first place: this is his trial run. He needs to be sure there is no night watchman, that he can find everything, that the key Forester handed him is the right one.

When Eliot is twenty feet from the stable, he turns his flashlight off and skirts the perimeter, letting his eyes adjust to the darkness. A complete loop reveals nothing but grass and air and darkness. At the door he can hear soft creaking, sighing sounds from inside, the almost imperceptible hum of animal breaths. He props his backpack against the wall and tries the keys in the rusty padlock. The first one doesn't fit, but the sec-

ond, with some fiddling, opens it. The heavy door swings open
and the warm pungent smell of horses and soiled straw sweeps
over him. It is almost completely black.

Eliot turns on his flashlight and walks gingerly toward
Blacksmith, who dips his head and nudges the half door. Seeing this is strangely affecting—Eliot has spent so little time with
him since he was sold, but yet somehow the horse seems to recognize him, perking his ears forward and then back and then
forward again, and then coming closer, nudging his velvety face
against Eliot's chest. Eliot digs into his pocket and pulls out an
apple he has brought, holds it out for Blacksmith to flutter his
big silly-looking lips around—blubberingly at first, and then
with a sudden fierceness that pulls the whole fruit between his
snapping teeth.

Blacksmith is a beautiful, delicately constructed black thor-
oughbred. He used to belong to Eliot's mother, who is an
accomplished equestrian and would ride him in amateur com-
petitions and steeplechases. When she was first "away" at
Maclean's, Blacksmith became Eliot's responsibility. He
brushed and groomed the horse himself and rode him at least
twice a week. But while Eliot has his mother's slight build, light
bones, and natural affinity for the saddle, he lacks the passion
to be a true equestrian. He likes Blacksmith's hugeness and
patience—the way he holds his sturdy hoof up to be scraped
with a pick. He likes the solid, muscular bulk of him, and his
generous obedience. But he has never liked all the rigid fussi-
ness of riding as a sport, the jumping and posting and keeping
his hands down and wrists straight and winning silly garish-
colored ribbons. He was not crushed when his father sold
Blacksmith to Anne Kittridge.

But now, watching the horse chew the apple almost shyly,
standing back a few paces in his stall, Eliot feels a pang of
sorrow that this beautiful creature no longer belongs to his
mother. That now he belongs, really, to Forester. When Eliot
was little, Faith read him countless horse stories—*The Black
Stallion, My Friend Flicka,* even the ancient Blaze series she had

read as a girl. The stories themselves were boring to Eliot; there was something overwhelmingly tragic, but at the same time tedious about the trials and tribulations of the animal kingdom. But Eliot loved the smooth, gentle tones his mother's voice took on when reading them. Reading these tales of mute suffering and ultimate, costly triumph, she became wise and competent and even-keeled, a woman who could be counted on not to lose her head.

Blacksmith has not seen Faith for almost two years now. Watching him, Eliot wonders if he misses her. Certainly if he were Blaze, or the Black, or even Flicka, he would be getting thin with worry and plotting ways to escape and track his mistress down. But he does not look that smart to Eliot. He looks soulful, perplexed sometimes, inquisitive even, but not really intelligent.

"Hold on a minute," Eliot says, gathering his backpack up. The jarring sound of his voice makes him more aware of the silence and darkness he is surrounded by. *Be right back*, he thinks, but this time he doesn't say it out loud.

The tack room is even darker than the main part of the stable, but Eliot does not want to turn on the overhead light. His flashlight passes over stacks of saddles piled high on posts along the far wall, and at the front, a desk messy with paperwork, candy bar wrappers, and little bowls of paper clips, thumbtacks, and bottle caps. There is something spooky about its untidiness—the chair pushed back as if someone has just risen from it, the feeling of interrupted activity. It is as if he has walked in on the ghost of the day.

He hurries to the back of the room according to Forester's instructions and looks for the Kittridges' saddle on the third post where Forester has assured him it will be, finds it, and lifts it off. It is surprisingly heavy. He carries this back to Blacksmith's stall and approaches him slowly. "Good boy," he murmurs, patting the hot flank and then awkwardly throwing the saddle up over him, straightening it, fumbling under his stomach with the buckles. It is important to have tried all this, that he know how to get into the stable, find the equipment, and get Blacksmith ready. Blacksmith is a little tense, but patient. He lets Eliot feed him the bit and bows enough to let him loop the halter over his ears, and Eliot feels a swell of gratitude to this great big, considerate creature who could just as easily kick him aside, or rear his head upward and refuse to be mounted by a boy who, for all intents and purposes, abandoned him to Forester. He rests one hand on Blacksmith's shoulder and presses his forehead against the smooth short hair just below his mane. Beneath this he can feel the powerful beating of his heart.

When Eliot has let himself back out of the stable into the night, he feels almost nauseous with the excitement of anticipation. It is nearly impossible to fasten the padlock with his jumpy fingers; when he has finally managed to jam the metal prong into the body of the lock, turn the key, and extract it, he breaks into a run.

The wind is damp against his face and whistles softly in his ears. Under his feet the ground is springy and uneven. He spreads his arms and hands and the air separates around them with the soft solidity of Jell-O. He is aware of the faint trace of webbing between his fingers, the remnant of a time before America, before Sir Percival, before human beings could stand up. As he runs he imagines himself underwater, a vague shadow rising toward the surface, defining himself slowly but surely against the particles he is surrounded by.

———————

Caroline has been to the bathroom twice already since the wedding reception started, but the hall looks different this time. Is it the planters along the wall that have moved? Or the silly little Louis XIV sofa with its splayed toes and bristly purple velvet that is different? Only once Caroline is faced with Mr.

Holden's flaccid penis does she realize she has opened the door to the men's room. And she doesn't even feel drunk, really.

In the women's room, Caroline dabs on some lipstick, a dark mauvey shade she picked out last spring. But once it's on, it feels vulgar, as if she has painted *over*, rather than *on* her lips. As if she is wearing a mask. She stares at herself in the mirror and lets her face go slack, relaxing all the little muscles that keep it halfway to an expression. The face that stares back at her looks terribly sad.

Hello, she thinks, shaping the full word in her mind—the *h*, the *e*, the double *l*, the *o*. *Hello*. It sounds formal and absurd, but the face in front of her remains frighteningly impassive. Does one normally have to tell oneself to laugh? Caroline blinks. There is an unfamiliar freckle on the line of her jaw and a faint premonition of two wrinkles between her brows. She can see exactly what she will look like when she is old.

She has spent most of the night talking to Stephan, not quite so much about what he will expect of her as his production liaison as about everyone at the wedding: where the Chatman children go to school and how John Hollsworth smashed his own son's car up driving home after the Murtins' Christmas party last year, and the time the Wallers were robbed by their handyman last summer. And about her family: about the time her brothers thought it would be funny to steal a goat from Drumlin Farm and let it loose in their lacrosse coach's house, where it promptly chewed up a family heirloom, about how Jack Jr. thought Bulgaria, Lithuania, and Romania were in South America until he was eighteen, and about her father's diorama-building. She feels a twinge of guilt thinking about this—not because the dioramas are secret or anything, but because Stephan seemed so very interested in them, he must have seen this as some appalling act of WASP-hood. She even— here is the real twinge of guilt—mentioned the time her mother signed up for a year's worth of vitamins and a set of breathing crystals, which she actually thinks is very sad and not that funny. Particularly because of its proximity to her nervous breakdown. Which Caroline did not mention. Which, for that matter, Caroline never mentions. Drinking has made her loose-lipped. And talking to Stephan seems to have trotted all the old family skeletons out of the closet.

There is a shriek of laughter from outside the bathroom door and the sound of someone practically throwing herself against it. Caroline rearranges her features into a half smile and slips out as a gaggle of bridesmaids enter.

In the hall, the lights are dim, brownish, and almost insti-tutional. Someone is sitting hunched over on the little spindly-legged sofa now, head resting on his upturned palms. Caroline almost walks past, but then—it's Rock sitting there with his head in his hands.

"Rock," Caroline exclaims. "What are you doing?"

"What?" His face, on lifting, looks tired and somehow unfa-miliar. "Oh. Waiting."

"Ugh," Caroline says, sinking down next to him. "I have to get out of here." She lets her shoes fall off, wiggles her toes appreciatively. Her feet feel swollen from standing around all night. "Maybe I should go work on one of those cannery ships in Alaska."

"Sure—who really needs fingers?"

"Mm. That's not very encouraging." There is the sound of Jenny Banks's laughter coming out of the bathroom. "Who're you waiting for?"

"Jimmy Sorrens—I told him I'd give him a ride. He's chat-ting up some girl over there." Rock gestures at the corner where a tall, good-looking guy from Rock's class at Quilton is leaning over a pretty little redhead who looks no older than six-teen. He has the pendant hanging around her neck in his hand and seems, from the girl's giddy laughter, to be saying some-thing funny about it. "Isn't she a little young for him?"

"No such thing for Jimmy."

Caroline rests her head against the back of the sofa and looks up at the ceiling. There is a delicate brown water stain in the corner, shaped like a butterfly. It has an ancient, out-of-place look here in the newly renovated foyer. "Do you ever think about what you'll be like when you're old?"

"Oh, probably mean-spirited and deaf and wearing leaky Depends that make my grandchildren not want to hug me."

Caroline rolls her head in Rock's direction and looks up at his face, which from this angle, looks once again less familiar— a little weary, older, and sharper. She can see the stubble along his jaw line. "No, you won't," she says, brushing a piece of lint off his tuxedo jacket. "You'll be cool."

"Ready to roll?" Jimmy Sorrens's shadow falls over them and Caroline sits back upright, straightening her dress.

"Right," Rock says, getting to his feet.

"You're looking awfully lovely, Miss Dunlap," Jimmy says.

Caroline smiles politely and slips her feet back into her shoes.

"See you, Carol," Rock says softly, touching the top of her head as they turn to go.

Caroline stares after them. "No way," she can hear Jimmy say, "not without the works." It has a sinister ring to it. In a moment there is the turning over of an engine, the squeal of a car spinning around the curve of the drive and out onto the street. The redhead has been joined by two cronies—equally young, although not as pretty, little cousins of the Krasdales. ". . . for my *number*, silly," the redhead is saying in a tizzy of excitement, her little freckled cheeks all flushed. Poor kid—she's really in for it. Caroline was hospitalized once, when she was that age, for the poison ivy she caught while being mauled by her own generation's equivalent of Jimmy Sorrens, who happened to be the BCD swim instructor the summer she was a junior counselor at the day camp. At the time, it seemed fair enough—the price you paid for making out with a twenty-six-year-old dreamboat. In retrospect she remembers him as having breath that smelled like baby shit and a yellow Speedo swimsuit.

Remembering this, Caroline feels older than she is and sorry for her former self. She considers crossing the room and telling the girls to watch out, telling them not to be too impressed by the likes of Jimmy Sorrens. But they would probably just think she was some sort of crazy spinster with a religious agenda. She pulls herself up off the little sofa and walks unsteadily back down the hall, feeling her body weave and bob above her feet.

Back in the tent, the band is packing up long coils of electrical wire and the empty parquet dance floor shines like a bald spot. White linen napkins are scattered on the grass and over the seats of chairs and the remaining guests are huddled in small vicious-looking groups around the bar, or intimate drunken conversations at the edges of the tent. It is nearly two A.M., after all. How can she possibly have stayed this late? She wasn't even on the A list, wasn't even supposed to be here in the first place.

And how will she get home now? She should have asked Rock for a ride. Her father is certainly long gone, although she does not remember saying good-bye. Maybe the Forlinghams will give her a ride if she can find them—the Holdens are no longer an option now that she has gaped at Frank's penis. And Anne Radley left in the middle of the dinner. Which leaves her stranded.

"Dunstable," a voice says. Adam Lowell's hand snakes around her waist from behind. He is a master of stupid nicknames. Caroline can't think of one person under the age of thirty whom she has heard Adam address by his or her real name within the last four years.

"Wanna get out of here?" he says, holding her arm out and moving his hips as if they are doing the cha-cha front to back. It makes Caroline feel like an ungainly rag doll.

"Adam," she says, moving out of his grasp. "I've got to get to bed."

"But the night is young! Bee Bee Menders is having people over to her sister's house, all the old gang—it'll be a blast." Adam is the kind of person who insists on boxing the past into a neater, cheerier version of itself in which groups of awkward, surly adolescents thrown together on country club swim teams and neighborhood Christmas parties become a "gang" and gatherings hosted by Bee Bee Menders become a "blast." Adam drives a black BMW he got from his grandfather for his twenty-first birthday, and which was, at one point during college, spray-painted with the words COME OUT YOU FAGG with two *g*'s. Caroline knows this only through Rock, who thinks the two *g*'s are hysterical—a true expression of Middlebury College's para-noiac isolation from the real world.

"Not for me," Caroline says, moving away. "I've got to get to bed."

"Sweet Car-o-line," Adam begins singing—something he is not alone in feeling the need to do at least once every two hours he is in her presence.

"Oh, Adam, come on—could you just give me a ride home?" Caroline asks.

"Via Bee Bee's, sure!" Adam says brightly.

"You need a ride?" comes a voice from over Caroline's shoulder. And there is Stephan at the table behind her, packing up his camera and mike. He has taken his hair out of its slicked-back ponytail—a style Caroline found not so appeal-ing—and it hangs into his face as he bends over. Through it, she can see his grin.

"Oh, that would be great," Caroline says, and Adam's face falls.

"No problem." Stephan straightens up and swings his cam-era bag over his shoulder.

Out in the parking lot Caroline feels suddenly jittery and dumb. Stephan is at least a full head taller than her, which she is not used to, and he is really very sexy, and here she is, drunk and tired and all talked out. There must be other things, besides this place, they could discuss. It occurs to her he has not asked her much of anything about herself, really, and has given witty, evasive answers to anything vaguely personal she has asked him. What do he and Denise talk about? She really can't imagine. Maybe, if Rock's theory is right, they don't talk. Maybe they just have sex.

"So Denise was your lawyer?" she asks, and then blushes, afraid she has somehow given away her train of thought. It is dark, though, thankfully. She looks down at the asphalt, which is slightly glittery, full of tiny bits of mica.

"Yeah." He shrugs. "There was this whole thing about my last movie—the studio was freaking out about the content and liability, blah blah blah. I get a kick out of her—she's such a powerhouse, take-no-prisoners kind of gal."

Caroline has never thought of Denise as a "gal" before. "She's nice," she finds herself offering inanely.

Stephan laughs. "It's not the first word that comes to mind." He unlocks the door for her. The front seat is one long vinyl bench, roomy enough to be where he and Denise have their rendezvous. She settles herself against the cool, slightly sticky vinyl and watches the aces suspended from the rearview mirror bounce gently as Stephan backs the car out of its spot and onto the driveway.

"Was it—did you get good footage in there?"

"Eh." Stephan shrugs. "All right. Nothing spectacular."

"What would be spectacular?"

Caroline can see Adam Lowell and Bee Bee Menders coming out on the porch of the Ponkatawset Club. Adam is still doing the cha-cha.

"I don't know—the usual—anything surprising, or unexpected, or, you know"—he glances at her evaluatively—"ugly." There is a pause. "I mean, I'm looking for some kind of a story."

Caroline rests her head against the seat back. "Oh."

"How did you come up with—here? I mean, the whole Old Boston idea or whatever?" she asks after a pause.

"In a fit of insanity." Stephan laughs. "No, I don't know—I guess it was actually Denise who got me excited about it, all her stories about living here and stuff. She's got a natural sense for what plays well on camera, what people will want to see."

"Hunh." Caroline shifts and the bare skin of her back makes a peeling sound against the vinyl. "And what if you don't find it?"

"Find what?"

"What people will want to see."

"Why?" Stephan looks over at her sharply. "Why wouldn't I?"

"I don't know—no reason. Just what if it wasn't how you pictured it or whatever?"

Stephan shrugs. There is a pause and Adam Lowell's black BMW passes them, trailing "Sweet Home Alabama." "I guess that's never happened to me. If I see it some way, then that's what comes out in the picture. You just have to be careful not to overcomplicate, you know? You have to have a distinct vision of the thing and it comes through."

"Mmm." Caroline nods, although she is not sure she agrees with his answer. What if it isn't really distinct? What if, once you're in the middle of your subject, you can see it in more ways than one? What if, for instance, you can find Adam Lowell's nicknames as stupid and annoying and full of small-minded reverence of all things insular, but also as pitiable attempts to stand in for an intimacy he has no idea how to create? Or what if you can decry your father's insistence on raising aggressive, overbred jackal-dogs, but be moved nearly to tears watching him throw a stick for them across the grass? Outside, trees toss gently in the wind like obscure, restless creatures. She leans her head back again. When she closes her eyes, she is surprised to find the window, the dashboard, the world outside are spinning against her eyelids.

"Caroline," Stephan is saying. "Hey, Caroline." There is a warm pressure of his hand on her knee.

She has been sleeping. When she opens her eyes, she can see Stephan's face in front of hers. For a moment she thinks they are in bed together—has the slight skip of panic that she doesn't remember what has happened, but then, of course, they are in her father's driveway, in the front seat of his car.

"Sorry," she says, straightening her neck. "I don't know how I got so sleepy."

"No problem," he says, keeping his eyes on her.

"Thank you so much for the ride home—I don't know what I would have done."

"I have a feeling you had some other willing drivers." Outside, there is the sound of tree limbs creaking in the wind and the gentle hiss of blowing leaves. Caroline wonders suddenly if they are about to kiss. Is this how it happens? After two years of going out with Dan, she has forgotten.

"So listen," Stephan says, his tone changing. "I'd love to meet your grandmother—or aunt or whatever—the one you were telling me about in the . . . what did you call it? The Monte Carlo of the North Shore? Think she'd let me interview her?"

"Oh," Caroline says. She sits up straighter against the slippery vinyl. "I don't know. I mean, I can ask her." This is what she gets for blabbering on about Lilo. "She's difficult, though," she adds lamely.

"Why don't I give you a call tomorrow? If she'd let me, I'd love to go over there with you. And anyway"—Stephan fixes his eyes on her again—"maybe we could go out for coffee or something."

Caroline is glad it's dark out. She feels a blush rising to her cheeks. "Okay." Her father is probably awake up in his bedroom wondering what the hell is going on in his driveway. She opens the door and puts one foot out on the gravel. "Thanks again for the ride."

"Hey," Stephan says, and leans across to give her a kiss on the cheek. Just a light brush of lips, no different from that an uncle or cousin would give, but he holds his hand on her shoulder for a second longer than usual, flat of thumb pressing against the smooth round of her bone. It feels hot and dry and pressureful and intensely foreign to her. "Good night."

Crossing in front of the headlights, Caroline tries to walk gracefully despite the fact that it is very dark and she feels unsteady with her high heels catching on the loose stones. She can feel Stephan's thumbprint on her skin. Did she get out of the car too quickly? Behind her the car is shifted into gear and there is the crackle of gravel under the wheels.

Inside the house, it is dark and silent. Not even the porch light is on.

In the mudroom, Caesar is up on his hind legs barking, front paws rattling the metal gate in the doorway. "Shush," Caroline says, and, surprisingly, he stops. "Here." She thrusts her hand into the box of milk bones Jack keeps on the counter and walks over to the gate. The dogs are sitting at attention now, a shaggy, panting mass in the darkness. Caroline has not turned on any lights. She pauses for a moment, holding the milk bones up in front of them, on her side of the gate. Their eyes glitter in the darkness. "Fucking morons," she says finally, and throws in her handful. There is a thudding of weight and scrabbling of nails on the floor as they grapple silently for the bones.

Caroline is kicking her shoes off when the telephone rings—a sharp, startling sound in the dark house. It is nearly three A.M. She rushes across the kitchen, banging her hip into the corner of the table—Rock, probably, she thinks in a panic, or Adam. And her father will pick up the phone and make a scene.

"Hello?" she pants, pressing her bruised hip.

A stream of angry-sounding Spanish accosts her from the other end of the line.

"Rock?" Caroline says stupidly.

There is a click and then the buzz of a dial tone in her ear.

Why is some angry Spanish man calling in the middle of the night? A prank call. Or a wrong number.

Carefully, Caroline replaces the receiver. There is a cold, heavy feeling in her gut that makes her sit down. She feels hungover already—a great sloshy sea of gin and white wine churns dangerously in her stomach.

Without thinking, she puts one hand to her shoulder—the shoulder Stephan's fingers touched—and lets her fingertips rest on her collarbone. It is quite thin, considering. Nothing a falling branch or a thrown stone wouldn't break. She can see it in the hands of an archaeologist, some tall, terrifyingly evolved version of a human, a thousand years from now. *A female,* he would say, running his hand along it, *about five-eight, a hundred and sixteen pounds, Bostonus erectus.*

Caroline drops her hand to her lap and stares at the telephone, which slips upward again and again like an image at the end of a loosened roll of film.

11

FAITH DOES NOT WANT to be sitting around all morning waiting for Jean Pierre to ask her to go bird-watching. It is not that
she wants to bird-watch, or that she doesn't want to bird-watch,
just that she doesn't want to be waiting all morning to find out
if she is going to go bird-watching or not. He didn't say he was
definitely going, after all, did he? And of course it doesn't really
matter. Pete and Lucy and the Eintopfs would all think it was
very funny (*Oh, poor Faith*, Lucy would say, *don't let him bully
you*), and anyway Faith would have nothing to say to him. He is
so silly, with his pith helmet or whatever it is and gold necklace
and questions about why she taps her foot so much and how
she can stand the Eintopfs. She is, in retrospect, embarrassed

that she answered all these with such earnestness yesterday evening. It was a cocktail party, for God's sake. He was probably expecting sly, witty responses; a Frenchwoman would certainly have been sarcastic and smart, not hopelessly, drunkenly sincere.

Pushing at the eggs on her plate and pretending to read the paper, Faith decides she will go back up to her room after breakfast so that she doesn't have to wait. She will read and write letters; she will write to Eliot. The egg stops in its greasy, crumb-absorbing track. Should she call him and ask him about the map? Faith puts down her fork. What would she say? *Eliot, I found your map.* But then he would know she opened it despite his dire warning labels on the cover. And anyway it sounds so sinister. What about, *Eliot, I found this paper in my pocket, is it yours?* This is ridiculous because it says *Property of Eliot Dunlap* on the cover. Picturing it gives Faith a gray, sorrowful feeling. She imagines his little freckled hand holding the pencil, drawing the skull and crossbones on the cover. His writing still has that rounded childishness—he is, after all, still really a baby. And she has left him all alone—he doesn't even have that sweet girl Rosita to take care of him any longer! What does he do all day? How does he fall asleep at night? These are things a mother should know. She can feel the quiet, familiar panic begin to engulf her.

Outside the windows, the sky is overcast and the water reflects back a cold pale gray. A ring of seagulls rises, squawking, from the marshy grass below. Well, Faith will go up to her room anyway. That was the point, even if she no longer feels like writing letters.

Walking across the porch to the stairway, Faith nearly trips over Jean Pierre, who is sitting, still as a cat, among the pillows of the wicker sofa.

"You have breakfasted," he says, looking up at her.

"Yes," Faith says uncertainly, lifting a hand to her mouth to check for crumbs or a remnant of egg.

"Then we can go."

"Go?" Faith asks, as blankly as possible.

"To see the yellow-belly," Jean Pierre says, unruffled, standing and holding his binoculars aloft. It is possible he is shorter than she is.

"Oh." Faith feels herself blushing. The yellow-bellied sapsucker, whose name she offered up in some *National Geographic* story she was retelling last night. She should remember not to drink gin and tonics.

"We will *portage*?" Jean Pierre says.

"Oh—I'm not sure—isn't it too gray out?" Faith begins.

"Too gray for canoeing?" He pronounces it exotically, as if there is an umlaut over the *o.*

"Well, I have some letters I have to write, too, and I thought since it isn't—"

Jean Pierre raises his eyebrows. "It is your holiday," he says, looking hurt. Out on the water, the ferry's horn blows.

"Oh, all right," Faith says. "But I'll have to put on different shoes."

As they lower the canoe off the dock, Faith's despondence has been replaced by a feeling of jittery recklessness. What is she doing, going out on the water with this man? Such an intimate thing, really, to be snugged up in a canoe. She will have to steer because Jean Pierre has never even been in a canoe before. And when was the last time she steered? Camp Kyoda for Girls, 1967? Jack would have died before putting her in charge of anything that floated.

On the other side of the dock, Emmett is making a science out of selecting the right-sized life vest for a bouncy sixteen-year-old cousin who is going out on the catamaran with him. ("Can't be too careful—you get hit on the head, you'll want something that floats you," he is saying in a brisk, official-sounding voice.) Just watching him hold life vests up and measure them, squint-eyed, against the girl's breasts makes Faith's skin crawl.

"Where will you like to sit?" Jean Pierre asks over Emmett's voice. In contrast, he seems suddenly kind and sophisticated and reasonable.

Once they are in position, Faith takes a few tentative strokes, which zigzag the canoe out into the cove unevenly. It is one of those noisy aluminum boats, which clang and pop when you shift weight or knock the oars into it, which Faith has done three times already, once splashing Jean Pierre's right side.

"I'm sorry—I don't know—I haven't steered a canoe in forever," Faith apologizes, giggling nervously.

"It is wonderful," Jean Pierre says, ignoring her. "Like sitting directly on the water."

It is, actually, quite nice, now that Faith thinks about it. The water makes gentle lapping sounds at the helm as they glide toward the marshy far side of the cove. Beach grass sprouts up, a startling yellow-green color against the gray of the water, sky, and pebbly sand, like a reminder of Christmas, or vacation, or the possibility of God. The steering is coming back to Faith when she doesn't think too hard about it. A J-stroke here on the left and then a straight stroke on the right. The terms present themselves in working order, along with a whole list of names of girls, women now (so strange! even little Kibby McCormac must be at least thirty-nine) who went to camp with her. Along with the image of herself, at fifteen, racing down the Saco River trying to get to the campsite first. It is like remembering another person, another girl, with a familiar name.

"Your children are in Boston?" Jean Pierre says. They have not spoken for a while.

"Yes—well, not right now. I mean, two of them are not right now, but the younger two . . ." Faith says, feeling again the twinge of, what is it—remorse? Or worry? The canoe is rounding the uninhabited part of the island, where low scrub pines and rose-hip bushes grow along the headland and large peach-colored boulders rise out of the water like knees from a bathtub.

"But you do not get to see them so often." It is more of a statement than a question.

"Well," Faith begins, "actually I just . . ." but then, of course, it is true. The girl racing down the Saco River, excited to get back to the campsite, to grow up and get married, to have babies and a husband and host big Thanksgiving dinners, has become a mother who does not see her children often—a mother who scares her children, even. A mother who lives carefully contained in a small apartment in a big city 230 miles away from her ten-year-old son. But the other, anticipated life of motherhood exists in her mind with such vivid specificity it seems almost more real than this. She has, after all, imagined it so carefully, so often, with such attention to the details, it is as if it actually *is*. As if, at this moment, separated not by time or space, but by half a million small decisions and indecisions, inadequacies and mistakes, she is unpacking a homemade beach picnic for her family, rubbing sunblock on Eliot's freckled back, giving Caroline advice on her love life, watching Tom and Jack Jr. throw a football in the low-breaking waves.

But right here, in this canoe, Faith does not actually *want* to fight her way back through the thicket of her failings to this other life. The realization hits her like a plunge into cold water. For a moment she forgets to paddle.

"Aha!" Jean Pierre says softly, his back tensing in front of her. "You see?" he whispers. Faith lifts her paddle out of the water. On the far side of one of the larger boulders there is a blue heron, standing absolutely still, staring at them. Silently, Jean Pierre reaches back to hand Faith the binoculars. As Faith lifts them to her eyes, the heron begins to flap its wings; it is close enough for them to hear its bones. There is something frighteningly unstable about its slow, effortful transition into flight. But the precarious breach of gravity is over in a moment—the bird airborne, soaring smoothly heavenward. Pressed against Faith's eye sockets, the binoculars feel warm from Jean Pierre's face.

It is almost an hour before they are docked again at Pea Island. Faith's arms are tired and stiff—this is more exercise than they have gotten in months. Even years, maybe. She and Jean Pierre have seen three cormorants, four egrets, a blue jay, and three drab little birds with elegant French names that seemed much too grand for their dowdy New England plumage. Climbing out of the canoe, Faith realizes her legs are pale and covered with goose bumps, and her hair—yes, it feels frizzy when she reaches up to touch it—must look like a pom-pom. It has started to rain.

A collection of snug-looking Eintopfs struggle to top each other's aggressive salutations from the porch. "Happy canoeing?" "Catch anything?" "Louis and Clark ahoy!" She and Jean Pierre have become a spectacle. Faith's Keds squish water out onto the dock.

"*Merde*," Jean Pierre says under his breath.

Together they drag the canoe up onto the dock, out of the water.

Lucy emerges from the house and shoulders through the Eintopfs with a concerned look on her face. "Faith!" she calls, hurrying toward her. "Come on in out of the rain—did Jean Pierre hijack you for one of his bird hunts?" Lucy says this last bit for Jean Pierre's appreciation, turning an exaggerated scowl at him. It is embarrassing, really, as if Faith is a child to be watched out for. "You'll catch a cold," Lucy exclaims as Faith straightens, nearly dropping her end of the canoe on her toes.

"I will finish here," Jean Pierre says, looking amused by the fuss. Lucy takes Faith's arm before she can protest and pulls her toward the house. Faith looks over her shoulder to say— what should she say? Well, to smile anyway, but he is bent over the canoe, gathering up the seat cushions.

"I'm sorry," Lucy says, as they climb the steps to the porch. "I hope he didn't strong-arm you."

"It was fine," Faith says. "I like bird-watching."

"You do?" Lucy makes a face.

Inside, there is a delicious-looking fire burning in the living room and a sweet, chocolaty smell wafts out of the kitchen. It is actually, Faith realizes with surprise, quite pleasant here. She does not need to go out and make conversation with the Eintopfs or hide in her room. She can sit here by the fire and read, or play cards—maybe Pete will want to play bridge. Maybe Jean Pierre likes to play bridge. This seems doubtful. He has very quick hands though, brown and lean and artful-looking. No wedding ring. What would it be like to kiss him? The thought sends color racing to her cheeks. She has not kissed anyone other than Jack in, what, twenty-three years? She has probably forgotten how.

". . . and then cocktails at six," Lucy is saying, when Faith catches sight of Rock Coughlin's bald pate across the room. She has almost forgotten he is coming.

"Rock," she says. She is genuinely happy to see him. He is such a sweet man and Jack was always so unkind to him. Faith has always felt a strong unspoken kinship to him.

"Faith!" he says, lighting up. "I heard you would be here." He crosses the room in his usual graceless stride and gives her an awkward hug in which she ends up kissing his neck by accident instead of his cheek as intended. Oh, well—it is only Rock Coughlin.

"How are you?" he says, stepping back and grinning, but still holding on to her shoulder.

"Good," Faith says, smiling back. He reminds her of one of those big, clumsy, cuddly-looking bears that eats nothing but nuts and berries. "I'm fine. I just saw your fiancée at Eliot's play."

"Denise? Oh, yes—right." Suddenly his expression changes—the smile drops and an odd, uncertain look comes over his face. "You were in Concord before this; she said she saw you."

Faith nods and Rock shifts his weight. Faith feels her own smile disappearing. Why does he suddenly seem so uncomfortable? Has Denise said something about her? But what could she have said? Faith barely even spoke with her.

"All right—" Lucy says, reentering the conversation from the across-room argument about cribbage rules she has been engaged in. "Faith has to get upstairs and out of these wet clothes, Rock," she says scoldingly. "You'll have plenty of time to catch up later." And already she is steering Faith off toward the stairs by the elbow.

Faith gives Rock a little half wave. Red splotches have sprung up on the surface of his bald head and he is still standing there staring after her with this strange undecided expression.

"Rocco!" There is a voice from the door. "Come on out here!"

She is probably just imagining that he looks strange, Faith tells herself. What could Rock Jr. or Denise, even, have said to make him look so discomfited? But all the same, it gives her an unsettled feeling.

When Faith reaches the landing, she stops for a moment to look back over the room. The prettiest of the Eintopf women is standing talking to Jean Pierre in the doorway, a Bloody Mary in hand. "Do I know Paris?" she is saying. "I lived on the Rue de Racine for three years." It makes Faith think of her own frizzy hair and wet sneakers. She turns quickly and continues upstairs. After all, she does not want to be seen standing on the landing, staring out over the party.

————————

SINCE SEVEN A.M. Rock has been lying in bed awake—or at least not asleep—with his brain whirring drunken nonsense: last night's conversation with Jack Dunlap at the wedding running on a loop and infused with a slightly frantic quality, as if he can't quite hear him, or has a pressing question he can't figure out how to introduce. No amount of sitting up and taking sips of water, ordering himself to think of sheep or numbers or the names of his sixth-grade classmates, can keep his brain from retracing this circle—half real, half dreamed—like a hobbled windup toy.

Outside the window, the world is gray and abandoned-looking. It has been raining and the sky has a concave weight to it like the underbelly of some giant fish. In the Pforzheimers' backyard, the children have left a collection of stuffed animals, now soaked, on the patio table. Staring out at this, Rock feels gloom stiffen over him like a brittle lichen. And his stomach feels queasy—for all his watching the buffet line last night, he never actually got any dinner to wash down his Manhattans.

What he needs is a joint to settle his stomach and turn his brain off. He gets up and pats through the pockets of the shorts he had on yesterday and the drawer of his desk for the little cigar box he keeps his stash in. But it is nowhere. Which is irritating, because he just spent fifty bucks on some quality Humboldt County.

He pulls on his shorts and pads downstairs to the kitchen. All the gleaming new appliances Denise has put in make the place look like a hospital—coldly white, shiny, and sterilized. It reeks of Lysol. Rock searches through the refrigerator, the cupboards, the pantry, and the electric brisker. There is nothing but Weight Watchers cereal, no milk, SnackWell's, and a shelf of canned soups. He wants something greasy and satisfying: a plate of eggs and bacon, hot biscuits, and a big fat brown joint. It is enough to propel him out the door. He will swing by Don Hammond's for something to tide him over until the cigar box turns back up and then go to Denny's for the Hungry Man Platter, after which he can crawl back into bed. There was some reason he wanted to go see Don Hammond anyway, wasn't there? Unfortunately, his brain won't supply it to him.

Outside, the rain has not cooled the air off much and it smells earthy, as if the ground has released some cloud of sediment into the lighter matter above, like the bottom of a pond disturbed by footsteps. Rock winds his way through the streets of Brookline, across to 28, and into Roxbury, where he makes a right off of Blue Hill onto Center. He likes going to see Don here; Don moved out of Somerville last year when Starbucks set up shop on the corner. Rock appreciates the sentiment. And there is a certain gratifying clichéd quality to buying drugs on a street like this, which Davis Square certainly didn't offer.

Rock parks the car across from number 37 and climbs the stairs to its ramshackle, tarpaper-floored porch.

"Ya-oh," Don's voice comes over the scratchy intercom. It

sounds farther away than usual. Don is a chemistry Ph.D. student at Harvard and a legendary figure in the greater, preppier Boston area—famous for having tripped his way through high school AP classes and into Harvard, and for having operated the most successful side business ever run out of Emack and Bolio's. Which is how Rock knows him; even Quilton kids came into town on weekends to score from Don, who was about as intimidating as Greg Brady.

"It's Rock."

There is a pause, and for a moment Rock regrets having come. He feels tired now anyway. He won't need to get stoned to fall asleep.

"Okay." Don sounds disappointed.

Rock shifts his weight and shoves his hands deeper in his pockets. Despite their long-standing friendship, Rock can, at times like this, be convinced that secretly Don thinks he is a sheltered buffoon. The shy, nondescript teenager who sold dime bags to prep school kids was, after all, just a convenient mantle; Don is one of the most aggressively sharp, sarcastic people Rock knows. He has already made monumental breakthroughs in the study of polymer networks in his Ph.D. program and frequently turns down invitations to speak at conferences run by the American *and* Royal Societies of Chemistry.

When Don opens the door he is wearing a brown and orange terry cloth bathrobe, which his body sticks out of like a collection of uncooked chicken wings. "What's up?" he asks unencouragingly. The apartment smells sour, like ramen noodle broth and wet cardboard.

"I'm sorry to get here so early—I just—shit, I forgot how early it is." Rock shifts his weight and the boards let out a resounding shriek.

Don stares at him for a moment, narrowing his eyes. Then, to Rock's relief, he breaks into a grin. "What can I do you for?" he says in a twangy, high-pitched voice. He and Rock have a joke about expressions like this. "What's the matter, pookie, cat got your tongue?" Don puts one hand on his hip and sticks out his thin lower lip.

"I'm out already," Rock says, stepping over three days' worth of newspapers and sinking onto the brown velour sofa, which lets out a satisfying creak. "I don't know how—I haven't even been smoking much."

"Right," Don says, heading into the kitchen. "Just like I haven't been rogering the world's leading manifold theory geometer. Hang on." Rock laughs. He is not sure if Don is kidding or if there is actually a woman in his bedroom.

The apartment is nicer than the outside would lead one to believe—spacious and light and not neat, but pleasantly empty. No fuss, no wicker, no carpeting. There is an upright piano in one corner with brownish keys like tobacco-stained teeth, a halogen lamp, and the sofa. The only decoration is a row of photos and postcards propped on the mantel: a woman with hippie hair and bell-bottoms, a MARYLAND IS FOR CRABS postcard, two pictures of Don with a blond Afro, wearing some sort of sackcloth getup, standing between two Tibetan monks. Rock gets up to have a closer look at this. Don was the one who brought him to hear the monks in Harvard Square last week. He lived at their monastery for—what was it? six months? a year?—before graduate school, and has been, for the last year, trying to get Rock to follow in his footsteps. He looks happy in the picture—a little rounder and more straightforward, devoid of his usual shrewdness. The monks themselves look sincere and pleased, entirely unironic. Behind them there are four crumbly pillars that look too perfect to be anything but the backdrop for some kind of mobile communications ad.

"Come to us—come to us, little one," Don whispers from behind Rock.

"Jesus," Rock says. "You scared me."

"Buddha, my friend—always Buddha." Don places the metal toolbox and scale he has brought in on top of the piano and begins sifting through its contents.

"Do you . . . ?" Rock begins, turning back to the pictures on the mantel. "You really weren't bored over there?"

"I had the best time of my life," Don says, speaking in his own normal voice for the first time since Rock walked in.

"It wasn't creepy or cultish?"

"Well, it's the oldest fucking cult on the planet, so—"

"No, I mean, you know, like David Koresh or Baba whatever, that guy who ruined the Beatles."

Don turns to look at Rock, head cocked to the side. "Not like Baba Whatever," he says sharply. "You going?" he asks after a pause, his head still at an odd angle, staring at Rock.

"Nahhhh—I mean, it looks cool. It looks great. But I have shit I have to—"

"You should go," Don says. "I'm telling you—I can feel it. You should get on the next plane and get out of here." With this pronouncement, he whisks the buds off the scale and into a little zip-lock bag.

Rock tries to make out if he is being sarcastic, but he looks remarkably sincere.

Over Don's shoulder, there is a movement in the doorway to the bedroom and a naked Asian woman slips out wrapped in a dingy crocheted afghan. She has an astonished expression on her face and long fluffy, but straight bangs that make her look like a bassist in a heavy metal band. "Sakura," Don says, turning and looking surprised himself, as if he has forgotten she is there. "This is Rock."

"Nice to meet you," Rock says. The astonished expression remains plastered to her face.

"Sakura doesn't speak English," Don says cheerfully.

Sakura looks from Rock to Don questioningly and Don says something in a mock stern voice that sounds like "Hickie fish feet." This elicits a hearty pound on his arm from Sakura, who then disappears into the bathroom in a fit of incredulous giggles, blanket collecting a fine cloud of dust bunnies as it trails over the floor.

"The world's leading manifold theory geometer," Don says, rubbing his arm.

"Aha." Rock is not sure whether to look amused or impressed and opts instead to stare distractedly after her. An ancient Cambridge Rindge and Latin basketball team poster rustles against the wall as she passes it. Which reminds Rock, in a flash, why he wanted to come see Don even before his pot was missing.

"Hey, did you know someone named Stephan Dartman in high school?"

"Stephan?" Don asks, handing Rock the bag and dropping into his armchair. "Mmm . . ." He shakes his head, but then stops and starts laughing. "Stephan," he says once, and then repeats it in a schmaltzy, lowered voice raising one eyebrow.

"Yeah—him. He's—"

"Right," Don cuts him off. "Filming a movie—he told me about it—Boston society, the last Yankees or whatever. He said there was"—here Don slips into his imitation of Stephan's fluid baritone—"'some pretty interesting stuff brewing—a couple of good rumors to follow up on.'"

"Good rumors . . . ?" Rock begins.

"Stephan's not his real name."

"What?"

"Wendel."

Rock lets out a shout of laughter. "No way."

"Wendel," Don repeats.

"You friends with him?"

Don cocks his eyebrows. "He permed his hair and auditioned for Calvin Klein ads in high school."

Rock begins laughing again.

"He called me up a few weeks ago, though," Don says. "To see if I had any prep school contacts from around here from my Emack days that I could hook him up with. I could have offered you up," Don says, eyeing Rock as if it is just occurring to him. "I forget you went to prep school."

Rock crosses himself. Outside it has begun to rain again, there is a patter of drops against the glass.

"I don't know why *he* didn't have any—I guess he didn't make any friends at the prep school he went to—I mean, can't say I'm *surprised*."

"What do you mean, prep school—I thought—"

"Oh, he just went to Rindge for a year because he got kicked out of some other school and then his folks shipped him off somewhere down South—I forget where—they have, you know . . ." He rubs his thumb and forefingers together and makes a kissing gesture. "Oil money."

"*Real*ly," Rock begins, "because I thought—"

"Listen," Don interrupts, standing up abruptly and looking at Rock. "I don't really know shit about him, but you got to get out of Concord or Lexington or wherever the hell it is before you wind up in some crapped-out documentary about lifestyles of the rich and WASPy or whatever. Are you still living at your dad's house?"

"Yeah," Rock sighs, pulling a twenty out of his back pocket. "Go to Tibet."

There is a tuneless, high-pitched humming coming from the bathroom, over the sound of running tap water. "Singing don't a songbird make." Don grins, snapping out of the intense stare he has been leveling at Rock.

The humming does have a tune, Rock realizes—or an off-tune anyway: "We Are the Champions" by Queen. Or is he imagining that? "Thanks," he says, handing Don the cash and patting the bag into his pocket. "I'll think about it."

Crossing the room ahead of Rock, Don's skinny brown-robed figure looks not altogether unmonklike itself. "Thinking is one thing, doing is another." Don grins at Rock. "And meanwhile your Pop is probably stealing your shit."

"Yeah, right," Rock says, heading into the hallway. "So long."

Outside, the warm rain feels good on Rock's bare arms and

head. In the distance there is a siren wailing. It's almost too
much, really, that the guy's name would be Wendel. And that
he went to prep school, which he certainly did not offer up in
conversation. It explains the handy tailored tuxedo. Wendel
the oil money brat turned documentarian following up on a
few good rumors, whatever that means. *Hello, Wendel,* he imagines saying in a voice lowered an octave. He will have to tell
Caroline. Although she's so smitten by him she probably won't
even care that of all the things the guy could have *chosen* to call
himself he picked Ste-fhan.

JACK'S BASEMENT WORKROOM is cool and bunkerlike, dark
around the edges and bright in the middle—like an operating
room. He has trained two powerful dish lights on the Formica
drafting table at the center and covered the walls with black
metal cabinets full of his diorama-making supplies. He likes the
feeling of focus this affords him: no clutter, no distractions, just
light and darkness. There is something primeval about it. Pressing an X-acto knife into plywood, mixing suitably drab New
England colors, and painting tree limbs, stone walls, and
wooden fences—these activities are for him like lapsing into a
native tongue. Only this morning the language doesn't come.

The scene he is working on is different from his usual
projects, which involve re-creating battles and skirmishes—it
was not his idea to begin with. "Why does it always have to be
battlefields?" Caroline had said of his dioramas last Christmas,
"You have all those old pictures and stuff—why don't you make
one of Ye Olde Dunlap family?" She said it facetiously, of
course, but Jack took it as a sort of challenge. He put in hours
researching Dunlap family stories, corroborating ancient journal entries, clarifying names and dates. The scene he settled
on was one from a story his grandfather used to tell him, of
Ruth Westly Dunlap, who at age eighty-four employed enough

wily and seductive rhetoric to dissuade a whole squadron of British soldiers from searching the attic and uncovering the town's munitions store. There is a certain charm to the story. Rosita, who was helping him with piecework, liked the idea of a domestic setting. She fashioned a tiny rug and painted the kitchen, turned a thread spool into a convincing table for the tiny figures to eat at.

Until this afternoon, the diorama has been collecting dust on a shelf in the corner. Jack was too parsimonious to throw it away, but at the same time unable to finish. But the abandoned husk of it has begun to strike him as a reproach or sign of failure. He is not, after all, the sort of man to leave unfinished business.

The work left to be done is more challenging than he expected. Without Rosita's help, Jack is stuck with the task of crafting a likeness of Ruth Westly and he has no idea how to make a woman. In all his years of model-building Jack has built only one other indoor scene—the marriage of Mary, Queen of Scots, which was a wedding present for Faith. And even that, which was more stylized (he could go out and buy, for instance, a porcelain Mary, Queen of Scots, figure) took him weeks to finish. Faith, who is a lover of all tragic elements of British royal history, particularly tales about anyone who was beheaded, cried when he gave it to her. But Jack suspects this was because she was disturbed rather than moved by the meticulously constructed lintels, pews, and tiny stained-glass windows he had put together. She was never a great fan of his hobby. She worried that the glue he used might contain dangerous chemicals, that the sharp knives would somehow find their way into the children's hands, that something about the concentration it required betrayed a certain mental depravation.

Jack picks up the permanent black Magic Marker from the table and begins drawing, in bold strokes, over one of the minutemen's brown caps. He will turn this into a knot of hair, wrap a piece of material around his waist, and stand him at the miniature Franklin stove stirring a pot of porridge. Jack's fingers are clumsy with the pen, though, and despite the fact that it is unnecessary—foolish, a waste of time, really—his mind keeps serving up the fact of Rosita: pregnant. Running into the kid on the golf course last night jarred him—seems to have started long-submerged things bobbing back up to the surface of his mind.

It has been nearly six months now since he fired Rosita—not so much by design as by sudden clarity of vision. It was a fiercely cold Saturday full of new snow as fine and dry as dust. The back lawn looked like some white dune-filled Saharan desert, with Eliot traipsing around its edges—a small figure in a dark jacket and bright red hat. Ordinarily Jack would be driving Rosita to the station for the train back to Boston, where she stayed until her return on Sunday evenings. But she was getting picked up by her brother-in-law, who was to drive her to Revere for a family event of some sort—a christening of a niece or nephew? A wedding? She had on a new dress: cheap-looking and bright orange, and, Jack thought, too tight and low-cut to be respectable. Hank Krasdale was at the house, dropping off some idiotic edible bribe baked by his wife, and trying, once again, to yak Jack into selling the field across from his stables.

The brother-in-law was not what Jack expected. He pulled his pickup truck nearly onto the front steps, driving over the snow-covered flower border and walking through the snow in his ridiculous shiny—could they have been patent leather?—dress shoes, not to ring the bell, but to rap arrogantly on the glass like someone intimately acquainted with the house and its inhabitants. He was short and heavy, wearing a flashy, expensive-looking suit and dark shirt and reeking of cigarettes and aftershave. He looked smug and pretentious, taking in the house, the kitchen, Jack, and Hank Krasdale with wry, unapologetic interest. And he spoke no English, just nodded curtly at Jack and talked in sharp dictatorial bursts of Spanish to Rosita, who to Jack's surprise became meek and placating, as if, in fact, she was impressed by this obnoxious little man. As the door shut behind her—Rosita in her sensible boots with her shoes in a plastic bag in her hand and the man ruining his fancy footwear—Hank elbowed Jack in the ribs. "That's a hot number you've got, here," he said with an enthusiastic leer.

It was as though Jack had been sleepwalking and had wakened with a start to find himself out on a narrow ledge with a sharp dropoff. *You know a nice girl by her body,* Jack's grandfather always said, *the less you see of it, the better she is.* Rosita was gone by the start of the next week, vanished as quietly and completely as a pile of snow in the first spring sun. At Jack's request, Wheelie delivered a letter and check to her—a generous severance package: three months' pay and health insurance. He is responsible, after all, for the environment his son grows up in. Rosita had to move away, Jack told Eliot. And Jack has not spoken with her since then. There was a letter from her about a month afterward, which he didn't open, didn't even hold on to. He is a believer in absolutes. A closed door should not be reopened. Jack has not even thought of her since. Not really. Until, of course, Colby Kesson. The now-familiar electric prickle runs through his mind at the words.

Jack scribbles the marker viciously over the little plastic figure. His efforts have made the man ridiculous—the black ink looks more like a giant cockroach than a neat knot of womanly hair. In his hand, the minuteman-cum-Ruth Westly stares up at him balefully. There is something shameful and perverted about his efforts. Jack tosses the little figure across the room into the garbage can. It makes a satisfying pinging sound when it hits. Then he stands up, flicks the lights off in his studio, and makes his way through the darkness of the basement, tripping over boxes and old shelving in the dark.

When he comes back up to the kitchen, there are no lights on and the sink is overflowing with dirty dishes. It is a gray day, cool from the rain this morning. Eliot is hunched over a book at the table.

Jack flicks the overhead light on. "You want to go blind?" he says.

Eliot stares at him, blinking. "You can't go blind from reading."

"In the dark," Jack says. He takes a carton of milk out of the refrigerator and pours cornflakes into a bowl. There is a loud pattering as what is left of the night's rain blows off the trees and against the side of the house. Jack leans on the counter and takes a spoonful of cereal; the milk has gone sour. "Shit," he says, spitting into the sink.

"The milk is bad," Eliot volunteers in a calm voice.

"Well, thanks for telling me." Jack dumps the rest of the carton over the dirty dishes in the sink. The refrigerator offers little else by way of breakfast: a half loaf of wheat bread and no butter, three greasy white boxes of Chinese food leftovers, an empty pizza box, a bag of mini-carrots, ketchup, mustard, and chutney. The vegetable drawer is full of peppers and broccoli and mushrooms, which Caroline buys and steams for herself to eat in the place of normal food. "What did you eat?" he asks Eliot, who glances at the clock. It is nearly one, Jack realizes. He has been down there for hours.

"Toast."

"With . . . ?"

Eliot shrugs and turns back to his book. "Plain."

A sour milk smell is now rising from the sink. A surge of disgust shoots through Jack's gut. He throws the empty milk carton into the trash, which is full to the top. It bounces back out and falls to the floor. "I'll go get donuts," he says without picking it up. "What kind do you want?"

"I don't want any," Eliot says without looking up this time.

Jack stares at the crown of his blond head bent over the book. What kind of boy does not want donuts? What kind of boy likes to read in the dark all morning? His son has become unknown to him over the last seven months. It is as though he is staging some sort of strike or protest.

"Okay," Jack says.

"Has Rosita sent you her new address yet?" Eliot's voice accosts Jack as the screen door screeches open under his hand. It is not a question, but a demand Eliot makes at least once a month.

Jack straightens and looks back at his son. "No," he says evenly. "She hasn't."

12

THE WEST LOBBY of the Fair Oaks Retirement Home is a gallery of time's masterpieces—a room littered with bodies from whom all distinguishing marks of sex, experience, and personality have been exchanged for the uniform gray wash of old age. It smells of Lubriderm, air freshener, mucus, and sloughed cells.

Waiting just inside the sliding door while Stephan parks, Caroline wishes she were at home sorting through her college photos, or organizing her papers, or, for that matter, staring at the ceiling—just not being here. She should have told Stephan to come straight to Lilo's "Comfort Cottage," which in comparison to the west wing is a cheerful hub of sprightly, sentient activity. Or actually, she should have told Stephan not to come at all. Instead, she has been almost overly helpful and conscientious in securing him permission to film what Rock refers to as "the aging heart of the blue blood gene pool." She has gotten not only Lilo's go-ahead, but the misguided endorsement of the nursing home administration, which, she realized only *after* she made the call, she had been hoping would bar the whole endeavor. Which is not exactly the mark of an ace production "liaison," the title Stephan has informed her over breakfast will be most appropriate to put on her résumé. It can hardly come as a surprise that it is her connections rather than her production skills he is after, but somehow it felt like a betrayal all the same.

Behind Caroline, an orderly is rounding up bodies, pushing wheelchairs back to their rooms, and speaking in kind, reassuring tones about medication, the weather, the carpeting. "This way, Mrs. Sitwell," a willowy young black nurse is saying to a shriveled woman in a checked Chanel suit who is clinging to her hand like a small child. "Just a few more steps," the young woman says, and the older one's eyes fall on Caroline with a look of surprise and recognition followed immediately by confusion, as if maybe, for a moment, she thought Caroline was someone else—or actually that she *herself* was someone else, and then looked down and saw her tiny withered hand pressed against this firm, capable palm. How is it possible that she, a grown woman, is walking through a set of sliding doors into a roomful of people, holding hands?

Caroline ducks her head apologetically, but the woman is now caught up completely in her own private world of bewilderment, casting big watery eyes around her like a newborn. "Come on, now," the black woman says gently, and gives Caroline a sympathetic shrug. There is something that seems significant about the exchange—that reinforces Caroline's feeling that she is a menace here. And then there is Stephan starting across the driveway with his camera case and tripod hanging at his side. Caroline starts toward him with a sudden, inexplicable

urge to stop him from entering the lobby and further unsettling poor . . . what was it? Mrs. Sitwell? She hurries out into the
hot air of the drive through the automatic glass doors, which
swish closed behind her.

"Hey," Stephan says, and Caroline realizes she has been
nearly jogging toward him in her haste. "Nice digs your grandma
has." He grins.

"Let's go," Caroline says. From behind the plate-glass walls,
she can feel the old woman's eyes looking after her as one
might look after a thief.

Harriet, Lilo's faithful, long-suffering attendant, comes to
the door of the cottage full of apologies—for the weather (too
hot), the entrance hall (undusted), Lilo's appearance (not
dressed yet). "I told her the blue suit would be lovely, but she
thinks *you* should tell her what to wear." This Harriet says with a
shy glance at Stephan, avoiding eye contact. She is a sweet,
mild-mannered Irish woman, no more than ten years younger
than Lilo herself, who has somehow put up with Lilo's extravagant tantrums and mean-spirited manipulations for the last
twenty-five years.

"Stop monopolizing the visitors," Lilo bellows from the sitting room. "They're here to see *me*, Harriet."

"*And* you, Harriet," Caroline apologizes. "This is Stephan."

Harriet accepts Stephan's hand hastily, as if it is an illicit
gesture to be carried out quickly and discreetly, and then hus-
tles them into the sitting room—a sunny, cluttered chamber
that feels like a bomb shelter outfitted by the DAR. In it, Lilo is
seated on her favorite wing chair, surrounded by all her most
special, most favorite possessions from the four-floor brownstone she lived in on Beacon Hill: a grim portrait of Lilo's godfather Grover Cleveland ("dear dear Grover—such a rare breed
of man"), a set of stiff-backed candy-striped chairs that once
belonged to Lady Astor, a corner cupboard filled with Revere silver, two life-sized china dogs with red eyes and horrific inbred
grins. And a collection of nearly a hundred antique clowns.

"There you are," Lilo says, flashing her widest smile. "Let

me look at you," she says as Caroline bends to kiss her cheek. "Haven't you just wasted away!" She holds Caroline at arm's length. "You know"—she gestures at the braid hanging down Caroline's back—"this almost makes you look like a Jewess."

Caroline can see Stephan's face light up at this. He is already unzipping his camera bag.

"Let me meet the young man." Lilo claps her hands together before Caroline can even respond. "I've been in the movies already," she says, turning a wide, insincere smile on Stephan. "I was interviewed last year for a Smithsonian film about early American china. They wanted me to show my collection—a charming young man, really, who they hired to make it—he explained all the fundamentals of screen presence."

"Great," Stephan says, extending his hand. "You look like a natural."

"Well." Lilo inclines her substantial head in a display of false modesty.

Lilo, Helen Whittier Dunlap, is a handsome woman, in an impressive, almost manly way. She has remained lean and tall with age—the only part of her body to take on weight as she has gotten older seems to be her head. This is fleshy and square, haloed by a great many durable-looking iron gray curls.

"Bring out my lavender gown to show him," Lilo barks at Harriet. "And the green silk—unless they pressed it wrong again. They're always ruining things here—" She lowers her voice conspiratorially. "All the laundry people are *Spanish* and they have no idea about nice things. You tell me what to put on." She smiles coyly at Stephan. "I'll be your humble subject."

She is really pulling out the stops for him; Caroline can tell by the extra tinkly quality her voice has taken on that she has decided he is someone to impress. Which makes Caroline nervous. Lilo is at her worst when she is trying to be impressive. But this will be good for Stephan's film, which, in turn, will be good for her now that she is his production liaison, she reassures herself. Which has the effect of making her feel even hotter and more out of sorts.

"I'd love to start filming now, if that would be all right," Stephan says. "And then you could go change and I'd get you in whatever you—in the green silk let's start with, we'll see how everything plays on film."

Lilo's face, which had fallen at the first suggestion of immediate filming, brightens again at this logical explanation for starting prewardrobe. Caroline suspects it is more for the spectacle than for color analysis that Stephan would like to start filming pronto. And Lilo *is* a spectacle, which is, of course, why Caroline even mentioned her to Stephan to begin with. She is truly an absurd and self-obsessed woman, shaped by the worst possible influences of every time period she has lived through. She has the stinginess engendered by having come of age during the Depression, the moral righteousness of the 1940s, and the stark, unapologetic prejudice of the 1950s. Around her there is always the possibility something truly terrible will be said—some deep and disgusting sentiment unearthed and tossed out as carelessly as a handkerchief.

"This is . . . ?" Stephan says, standing in front of a photo of Caroline's older brothers in their Harvard hockey gear when Lilo has disappeared back into her room for another costume change.

"Oh—my brothers."

Stephan raises his eyebrows. "The ones who stole the goat—"

Caroline nods. "They're crazy." She offers this almost as an apology.

"Aha." He steps back and focuses his camera on it. He is just moving on to the portrait of Grover Cleveland when Lilo comes out in what looks like a giant, multilayered kimono. "Now, how shall we do this?" she emerges saying. "You want to ask me questions or shall I just begin at what my mother always referred to as the 'original sin'—the beginning."

"Perfect," Stephan says, focusing the camera. "The 'original sin.' "

"Well, when I was very young—oh, we'll skip my babyhood

and all that dreary stuff—James LaFond, of the Ohio LaFonds, claimed he had lost his heart to me and everyone thought it was such a lark until he actually proposed. I was all of fourteen and as the story goes I looked him right in the eye and said, 'don't you think you're a little old for me?' And of course it would have been a fine match—I don't half wonder if Mother and Father didn't just hate the fact it wasn't four years later. He wasn't a bad-looking man and he had the finest manners—really top-quality. It's not something I suppose you would appreciate even today, since no one gives a hoot whether a man tucks his shirt in or holds the door open for a lady or . . ."

Caroline has heard this story, complete with its segue into the lament on the loss of common politeness, at least ten times. Behind the camera, she imagines, Stephan is probably delighted. So why should she have this sinking feeling? This is the woman who told her at age thirteen that she was lucky she wasn't fat because she certainly wasn't going to be a beauty. But still—there is something that makes her feel a twinge of guilt at having served her up, practically shrink-wrapped, for the camera.

". . . and it's hard for you to appreciate, but it didn't used to be this way," Lilo is now saying. "Of course, if you look far enough back, everyone in America has someone in their family who was once a social climber, so I try to keep that in mind. But it wasn't like this—these people just thinking enough money can buy them right up to the top of the waiting list."

Caroline has a sudden memory of visiting Lilo, when she was much younger, maybe fifteen years ago, or even longer than that, and Lilo still lived on Beacon Hill in the house with the long churchlike windows and old-fashioned iron boot-scrape at the door. There had a been a lunch of some kind—all Lilo's best silver and china out on the table and some sort of molded fish pudding, little sandwiches with the crusts cut off, and Harriet's brittle, crumbly brownies. And a minister? Or a diplomat? Some old bowlegged Roosevelt whom Lilo wanted desperately to impress. And she had seated everyone around the table and made some sort of toast about how sad it was that

this distinguished guest had come back to Boston to find the
Somerset Club, like so many of Boston's most venerable orga-
nizations, so *changed* in its membership. Lilo had been smug
with self-satisfaction at having been, even as a woman (and
therefore not a member), so intimately acquainted with the
club's workings and so devastated by its apparent degenera-
tion—the whole of her remarks addressed like a loving serenade to this bowlegged bald man. And then, after she had
seated herself back at the head of the table, he had stood and
begun his own speech with a casual remark that actually the
club had needed a good shake-up—that it was in danger of
becoming downright provincial. Caroline had happened to
look at Lilo at that moment and her face had been completely
distorted by dismay and uncertainty, as if suddenly the earth
had heaved under her feet or the moon had bounced in its
orbit. It was the same shocked, almost childish bewilderment
that had registered on the old woman's face in the lobby of the
west wing this afternoon.

". . . clown collection."

"What?" Caroline asks, startled out of her train of thought.

"That's quite a clown collection," Stephan repeats. Caroline is once again in the room alone with him.

"I know." Caroline grimaces. "No one's told her clowns
have turned into the exclusive property of serial killers, polter-
geists, and child molesters." Her voice comes out sounding
more sorrowful than she intended.

"The fall of the clown." Stephan laughs anyway. "There's a
good documentary subject."

It is hot in the cluttered room—the sunlight cuts a woolly
swath across the pink sofa on which Caroline is sitting. "It's
funny to think clowns used to just be, you know, cheerful," she
says distractedly. She is trying to come up with a casual way to
ask if Lilo's full name will be used in the movie (why on earth
didn't she ask him to begin with?), when Lilo herself calls Caroline's name from the bedroom.

"Coming," she says automatically, and pulls herself up off the stuffy embrace of the sofa.

In the bedroom, Lilo is sitting at her dressing table in a shocking state of undress—baggy pizza-dough-like white flab hanging over the top of some impossible flesh-colored girdle and stiff white brassiere. There are about twenty-five colorful dresses spread out on the bed in front of a dismayed-looking Harriet.

"You are a woman now, so I am turning to you," Lilo begins with an elaborate, theatrically knowing look. Caroline has a sudden fear she is about to describe some awful age-related feminine problem. "There is something I really think you should see."

"Right now?" Caroline asks, thinking of Stephan sitting on the other side of the wall, but Lilo is already reaching behind a row of china boxes along the top of her windowsill.

"Here," she says, straightening up and holding something small and square in her hand. Her eyes are gleaming. "A phi-latic." She pronounces the word with a breathy sense of victory.

"A—" Caroline begins, and then realizes that it is a wrapped condom—a prophylactic. She stifles the burst of laughter that has risen in her throat.

"Far be it from me to tell your father what he should or should not do in the privacy of your home, but I find it humiliating to have him leaving this sort of paraphernalia in his wake like a common gigolo."

The laughter freezes in Caroline's throat and she can only stare at the shiny plastic perched incongruously between Lilo's fingers. "What did he—? You mean he gave this to you?" she can only stammer. She has a sudden horrific image of her father as some sort of nursing home marauder, intentionally shocking the woman who raised him—and who else? Has he gone completely insane?

"Gave it to me!" Lilo snorts dramatically. "Well, you could say so, although I don't think he intended to."

"Well, how—"

"*As I told you on the telephone,* he left his golf jacket here a few months ago, and since he didn't seem to care to pick it up I thought I'd let Terrence Reed have it," Lilo says, settling herself into high storytelling mode, "and I wanted to have it pressed and cleaned—it looked decrepit, you know, your mother never keeps you all even halfway neat and tidy." She looks reprovingly at Caroline here—they have reached a stalemate on the matter of Jack and Faith's divorce, which Lilo refuses to acknowledge. "So I made Harriet help me go through the pockets to make sure we wouldn't lose any of his personal belongings down there in the laundry room—they'll just pocket any extras, you know, they stole four of my lipsticks that way and Mary Daimler's gold pin . . ." Lilo's voice trails away. "And," she resumes, returning to the story. But she seems stuck here. "And . . ."

"And when you went through the pockets of the jacket you found . . . ?"

"Yes!" Lilo snaps. "Right there, for everyone to see. Imagine! Imagine my having to look Harriet in the face after such a thing. My own nephew, a common gigolo."

Harriet, who is helping Lilo step into her lavender gown, looks unimpressed by this revelation of Lilo's scruples.

It is possible that this is all an invention. But then, Lilo is holding a condom in her hand. To the best of Caroline's knowledge her father has not dated, not even flirted with, anyone since he has been divorced. After all, what sort of woman would be able to hold a decent conversation, let alone a romance, with a man who refers to Oprah Winfrey as "that fat black woman with a big mouth"? Just picturing him on a date is impossible. An image of him soliciting a prostitute—some thick red-lipped drag queen—rears up in Caroline's mind and gives her a violent head rush. The backs of her knees have begun to sweat.

"Well, I don't know—" she begins.

"You will have to tell your mother to manage this—it really looks terrible for her reputation," Lilo says, standing. "Wish me well, my dear." She adjusts the collar of her dress and sweeps out into the sitting room. "If this is too bold, I have plenty of other softer colors," Caroline can hear her saying.

She sits down on the chair Lilo has just vacated and looks out the window. The idea of sitting through another five outfit changes, or whatever else Lilo has planned, seems almost excruciating. She is a truly crazy woman and now Caroline has opened the door for her to be truly crazy on film, possibly in front of a national audience. What if, for instance, he wins Sundance? She will forever be known as the great-niece of an offensive snob, and in addition—her palms begin to sweat—her father will probably disown her.

As she watches, the same orderly she saw earlier is parking a row of wheelchairs in the bright sun along a narrow rose garden. From here, the old people in them could be sacks of laundry. It makes Caroline anxious—all this gleamingly white skin out under the hot sun.

"I suppose you want to hear about my brief and tragic marriage to Cy Gifford," she can hear Lilo saying. In front of her, the condom in its bright blue package is still sitting, like a visitor from another planet, on Lilo's shaker dressing table.

———

WAITING FOR CAROLINE to come back from Lilo's and pick him up from gathering up the contents of his cubby at school, Eliot stares at the bright display of second-grade paintings of *The Midnight Messenger*, artistic compliments to Friday's performance. In one brilliant interpretation directly across from him, "Foriners Get Out" is printed in a speech bubble coming from Paul Revere's lips. It is giving Eliot a headache; he can see the scraggly letters even with his eyes closed.

He is trying to avoid Jen Edwards, who is here with her mother, at the other side of the lobby. Jen is an anxious girl, one year younger than Eliot is, and overly excitable. The school has her under constant food surveillance because she is missing the gene that makes people stop eating when they are full. Eliot imagines it like a little rubber plug that has slipped down into Jen's gullet, leaving her throat and stomach to gape wide, pink, and glistening with greed. It makes him feel unsafe around her, as if she is that much more likely to turn cannibal.

Eliot is also trying to avoid Forester's mother, Anne Kittridge, who is yakking away with his drama teacher at the opposite side of the room. Especially after Forester's run-in with Rock yesterday, Eliot does not want to invite her attention. Who knows what Forester might have said to Rock, what Rock might have said to the Mrs. "Mrs. Big Nose," Rosita always called Mrs. Kittridge, who, in turn, always referred to Rosita as "your maid," as in "Eliot, shouldn't your maid be here by now to get you?"

Eliot could make Rosita laugh until she was practically weeping by imitating Mrs. Kittridge's intense stare, always leveled at the bridge of your nose, and her brisk, determined stride. A pang of missing Rosita sweeps up from his abdomen. He has not gotten a postcard from her for a long time now. He does not believe she has forgotten about him, but he is afraid she has maybe moved in with another family. That there is maybe another boy she has become friends with. Or worse, that she is in trouble or danger, or has gone missing like Roberto. He pushes this out of his mind—he cannot allow himself to think it.

When Caroline finally shows up, the lobby is nearly empty. She seems distracted and a little discombobulated—so sorry she is late—Lilo was being difficult, so sorry he has been waiting, how was getting all his stuff? Is he happy to be leaving the place for a whole summer? Eliot answers her questions minimally with an exaggerated calm. Her face looks flushed and her hair is messy. She has picked up sandwiches though, and iced tea and a bag of Pepperidge Farm cookies. Eliot isn't really in the mood to go for a picnic but she will certainly be crushed if he says so, and worse yet, she will launch into her million and one questions mode: why doesn't he want to go? Is something wrong? Why doesn't he want to talk about it?

In the car, Caroline sings along to the radio, slightly off-key. *Love is a rose but you better not pick it, it only grows when it's on the vine.* Her voice sounds small and childish, one beat behind the lyrics. It is hot out and Eliot would like to turn on the air-conditioning, but Caroline insists on driving with the windows rolled down, the hot wind rustling the pages of the newspaper on the back dashboard.

"Do you know, El," Caroline says, breaking off her singing, "when Dad last visited Lilo?"

"I don't know." Eliot keeps his eyes on the world flying past outside his window.

There is a ripping sound as one of the sheets of paper slaps up against the back window.

"He was mad at her because she gave his jacket away," Eliot adds.

Caroline frowns. Eliot could ask why she wants to know, why she is using that voice, but he has more important things to think about. And anyway, he hates to visit Lilo. The stuffy smell of gravy and mothballs, the clowns on the wall, the way Lilo always confuses him with his brothers. The last time he was there, Lilo told a story about a little boy who died because his mother forgot him in the backseat of her car with the windows rolled up.

The slope of Old Burial Ground and the shady ridge of the hill are, at least, a little cooler than the hot pavement; there is a sort of temperate bunkerlike climate created by the ancient gravestones. No one has been buried here for over a hundred years and the stones jut out of the earth at haphazard angles, as if every fifty years or so they have been upset by some massive, irritable, earthly shrug. Eliot came here once with Rosita last fall. *Prudence, Ezekial, Rebeka,* and *Jedediah,* she had sounded out the unfamiliar names, in a way that transformed the stern, humorless syllables into lighter, more interesting sounds.

Today, the area behind the maintenance shed is blocked off by yellow plastic CAUTION streamers, behind which there is a fresh pile of earth mounded almost five feet high and a stack of plastic-wrapped gravestones leaning against a tree. Restoration of some sort. Eliot averts his eyes from this and climbs farther up, with Caroline huffing and puffing behind him with the brown paper bag of goodies. At the top he sits down against a dark slate stone that protrudes from the earth at a perfect comfortable angle for reclining. At the top of this, a chiseled wreath of roses and a skull are barely visible and the name is worn away almost entirely. Eliot is pleased to have rediscovered it; it is exactly where he sat when he came with Rosita.

"I don't think you should sit there," Caroline says, dropping to the ground at the base of a wide oak tree beside it.

"Why not?"

"It's so old—it might fall over." There is a note of urgency in her voice.

"No, it won't. It's been like this for hundreds of years."

"Well, it's disrespectful."

"Why?"

"It just is—you wouldn't like someone sitting on your grave, would you?"

Eliot considers this. On his grave. He would be below the earth. Dead. "I wouldn't mind," he says, feeling the cold of the slate rise through the thin cotton of his T-shirt.

Caroline frowns and takes their sandwiches out of the bag, puts them on the napkin she has spread on the ground in front of her.

"I would be dead anyway," he adds. "I wouldn't be watching."

"Well, of course, but—I don't know." A gust of wind blows through the leaves overhead. "I just think it's sort of creepy."

Eliot closes his eyes. Leans the bulb of his own skull against the stone. Caroline is spoiling this place—making it as if all these graves are actually full of unforgiving, hawklike observers. As if the dead don't have better things to do than criticize the living. It's just a place—a quiet, peaceful place of . . . how did Rosita say it? *A home for finished people.* He and Caroline should never have come here.

"Here." Caroline hands him a sandwich. "Whatever—I'm probably just being silly." Below them, an ambulance wails its way around Monument Square and a small group of tourists stops at the base of the cemetery to read the ubiquitous round blue informational sign. One of them glares reprovingly up at them and Eliot has the urge to stick his tongue out.

"So what should we do this weekend, El?" Caroline says in a forcedly cheerful, change-the-topic tone of voice. "Let's make fun plans now that I'm back."

"Okay." Eliot takes a bite of the sandwich.

"We could go to the beach or to Canobie Lake Park." Above their heads another burst of warm wind sweeps through the oak tree, tossing the leaves into a papery frenzy. Eliot closes his eyes and lets the insides of his eyelids flicker from orange to black, orange to black, in time with the sunlight filtering through the leaves.

"Or we could just go on a real picnic, with a basket and everything," Caroline adds. "Somewhere interesting."

"Okay," Eliot says.

"We could go somewhere outside of Concord, like, I don't know, Gloucester, or Manchester, or Marblehead."

"We could go to Roxbury." He says it without really thinking and clamps his mouth shut as soon as it is out.

"To Roxbury?" Caroline looks over at him. "Why do you want to go there?"

"No reason," he says into his bottle of iced tea.

"Well, I don't know if it's really a good place for a picnic. I mean—" Caroline lowers the sandwich she has been holding.

Eliot shrugs and presses his shoulders more firmly against the cold gravestone.

"What made you think of it?" Caroline gives him a long, evaluative look, with her head tilted to one side. In her lap her fingers have twisted themselves into an anxious knot. They are long and thin, but strong-looking, with short, half-moon-arched nails—like their mother's, actually. Eliot lifts his eyes and finds she is still looking at him, the exasperation replaced with a puzzled, searching look.

"Nothing," he says. "Really."

Below them, the tourists are regrouping, pushing on to the next historical site with their cameras and backpacks and flimsy sun visors. They move as a whole, one or two lagging behind or getting ahead, but all within a certain set perimeter like the cells of some gelatinous see-through sea creature.

"Well," Caroline says, reaching out and smoothing a lock of hair behind Eliot's ear. "We'll go somewhere fun anyway. I think we need to." There is a red splotch of prickly heat standing out on her collarbone. She looks tired.

Eliot feels a flash of love and something like pity for her. "It's all right here," he says. "It's not so bad, Car."

WHEN JACK LEAVES the house, he is planning on getting an oil change and possibly a haircut. He has not looked up Rosita's address with the intention of going to find it, but simply because Eliot's question about whether she has sent him her new address has reminded him that he could find it if he was so inclined. He has never, after all, seen where she came from—or, more to the point, where he sent her back to. It was Wheelie who delivered the letter and check Jack wrote terminating her employment. Which, in retrospect, makes Jack uncomfortable. He should have done it himself, really.

Jack flips the radio on and tunes in to the news. A fire in Belmont, a suicide gunman in Jerusalem, a new development in prostate cancer research. He is not really listening. Instead of exiting Route 2 in Lexington, though, he finds himself going on to 128, which will take him south toward Roxbury, Dorchester, and Mattapan. He flips the radio back off and without it, the car seems exceptionally quiet. There is the hum of air-conditioning, the faint crinkle of leather when Jack shifts gears, and, indistinctly, the sound of his own breathing.

The change in scenery as he enters Mattapan is abrupt: as soon as Jack has crossed the Neponset River, the squat, working-class suburban houses with window awnings and boxwood bushes give way to concrete and cheap pink bricks, auto repair shops, and metal-grate-covered storefronts. As he nears the border between Dorchester and Roxbury, Jack begins reading the street signs. Route 28 is Blue Hill Avenue here—which is where that woman was pulled out of the car last year and brutally murdered. He hits his automatic door lock, but slows down to take in his surroundings. Everywhere there are convenience stores advertising beer and spirits, wire fences and empty lots fluttering with newspaper, broken plastic bags, wind-worn candy wrappers. Ahead of him, the Hancock Building, with his office in it, swings into view on the horizon—a solitary glass rectangle that looks, from this unfamiliar angle, like the only building in the Boston skyline.

Tennis, Hiawatha, Dorset. The street names become increasingly incongruous. It is a ridiculous thing to be doing—driving through Roxbury searching for—what? What does he even expect to do when he finds Rosita's house? He has seen the neighborhood. He should turn around right here. But his foot stays on the accelerator, firm and accurate. It crosses his mind that this disconnect between brain and body might be what it is to go insane. But the thought is like a tiny, irrelevant pair of arms waving in the rearview mirror. And then suddenly there it is, an ordinary green sign marked CENTER. It is both strange and familiar, like a note in his own handwriting he has found lying on the sidewalk.

The street is lined, on either side, by classic Boston triple-deckers with bars on the windows and saggy, derelict-looking porches, barren yards lined with chain-link fences or, occasionally, low, arched garden wire. It is unnaturally silent. There are only a few cars parked, and the shades in many windows are down. At the far end of the block there is a low, gray brick housing project with the words FOUR PLAY spray-painted over the doorway. Jack drives slowly, peering through security bars to make out door numbers. Thirty-seven is about halfway down on the left—a white aluminum-fronted triple-decker with dark, wormy-looking shingles along the side. Instead of a porch, there is a concrete stoop covered with plastic tubs, metal trays, and soggy spattered canvas cloths. In the first-floor window, a cardboard ghost from some long-gone Halloween is pressed between the pulled shade and the glass, as if it has been flattened in the process of escaping.

Jack puts the engine into idle, just for a moment, and keeps his hands firmly planted on the steering wheel. There is a spindly row of tomato plants along the back of the small yard, supported by neat green stakes and covered with a film of dust, and in the middle of the house, on the second floor, a blank, out-of-place-looking picture window. So this is the house. Funny that it has never occurred to him before to go find it. It feels hot even with the air-conditioning blasting and there is an odd, airless feeling in Jack's lungs as if they have forgotten how to absorb oxygen.

He is not sure how long he has been sitting, staring out at nothing, really, when he becomes aware that a van has pulled up behind him and a young man—a boy, really—has jumped out the passenger-side door and gone around to open the back doors. Jack has no idea how to account for his thoughts; it is as if they have been running through some subterranean obstacle course, from which he can hear only a distant thumping and clicking. He squeezes his eyes shut to bring things back into focus. He has work to take care of, papers he wants to look over before work tomorrow. When he opens his eyes again, he is aware of a man in overalls standing in the middle of the street with a bucket in each hand. Jack puts the car into reverse to edge out and looks over his shoulder. The man is standing absolutely still, staring. He is stocky and brown skinned and— Jack realizes with a jolt—absolutely familiar. Rosita's brother-in-law. At what seems to be the same moment the man takes a step closer and swears in Spanish. For the first time in years, since he was a boy, really, Jack experiences a kind of physical panic— his palms sweat and his mouth is dry and there is an explosive rattling feeling in his head, which can only think, *Get out, get out, get out.* As he pulls away from the curb, he can see the man in the rearview mirror—can hear him, actually, before he can see him. "Now you come," he is calling, in heavily accented English. "*Now* you come!"

Inside Jack, under the dry, terrifying rattle of his brain, there is the rumbling, tectonic shifting of whole bodies of experience he has submerged, and below this, the profound ring of recognition.

13

THE MOMENT ROCK WALKS in the door he can smell the pot smoke. His pot smoke. Or rather the smoke from his pot which he is not smoking. He is quite sure it's his. That distinctive wet leaf, almost mud smell that comes from the crop Don just got in.

As Rock closes the door behind him there is a loud gaspy laugh from the kitchen—Denise. Is Denise smoking his pot? With his keys dangling above the key dish, Rock freezes.

"Hello . . . ?" comes a male voice and Rock hesitates for a moment. Ste-fahn, a.k.a. Wendel. The guy *is* sleeping with Denise. Rock considers opening the door up again and backing out silently, shutting it softly behind him. But he can't do this—he'd probably end up knocking over the umbrella stand or slipping on the doormat; they would certainly hear him. "Anyone out there?" the voice comes again, followed by more hysterical, wheezy Denise laughter.

"It's Rock," Rock says.

"Oh, shit," Stephan says under his breath, but loud enough that Rock can hear him.

"Hi, Rock!" Denise calls brightly, and breaks into more laughter.

Rock drops his keys into the bowl and stands for a moment, staring at his own face inanely in the mirror above the mail table. He looks, quite visibly, panicked.

"How was your day?" Denise calls in the same bright, giggly voice. "Come in here and tell us."

There is nothing to do but follow orders. Rock arranges his features into a casual but somewhat haughty expression and makes his way around the wicker obstacle course into the kitchen. Stephan is sitting next to the microwave on the counter and Denise is at the table with a pint of ice cream in front of her and her glasses propped up on her head, her eyes red and tearing with laughter. "Want some?" she offers, holding up the ice cream. "You know Stephan, right?"

"Right," Rock says. And again Denise starts laughing.

"I'm sorry," Denise says, fanning her face. "Stephan was just saying—he was just—" She is laughing too hard to finish.

"What are you smoking?" Rock says, walking over to the window and lifting it a few more inches.

"Oh, what do you think?" Denise says, wiping her eyes. "We're all adults here."

"I'll replace it, man," Stephan says. "I just didn't have any shit with me today."

Rock stares at Denise. Can this be real? He was actually right? His future stepmother and this guy, *Wendel,* are sitting in his father's kitchen smoking his, Rock's, pot? "You went through my stuff?" he asks.

"*Please,*" Denise says, gesturing across the room. "You left your little cigar box sitting on the counter."

Rock tries to think if this is possible. Would he have brought it downstairs? Is that why he couldn't find it?

Denise sighs melodramatically and puts the lid back on the pint of ice cream. But then, before she can stand up to put it back in the freezer, she is doubled over again, snorting with laughter. "I just keep picturing—I keep picturing—"

Stephan looks alarmed sitting on the counter.

"A little Dunlap monster baby." She makes a terrifyingly stupid facial expression and holds her two pointer fingers above her head like horns or antennae.

"A Dunlap what?" Rock asks.

"Because Jack Dunlap's such a monster," she gasps out.

"Should we order some pizza?" Stephan asks.

"He's having a baby?" Rock says at the same time.

Denise sits back in her chair and stops laughing. The refrigerator chooses this moment to stop humming. "Oh, what the hell," she says, looking more like the usual, pissed-off, no-nonsense Denise again. "Yes. With Esmerelda's sister."

For a moment Rock has no idea who this is, but then it hits him. She was here two days ago. Denise and his father's cleaning lady. He finds he actually has to back up, lean against the sink for support.

"It's all my fault," Denise says, straightening up, finally, still holding the ice cream. "I introduced them when I found out he needed a babysitter, but, I mean, I didn't really *know* him, I knew from the BCD board he could be an asshole, but I didn't *know*—I just figured I'd be a Good Samaritan! I had no idea I was sending that poor girl off to be, God knows, maybe even raped, who knows what circumstances she got pregnant in. He fired her, after all . . ."

Rock is finding it very difficult to absorb this information. He is picturing chubby Esmerelda, who must be nearly fifty, in the forest-green housedress she changes into to clean in, and her black high-top Reebok sneakers. But not her. Esmerelda's sister. Another picture comes into his head—less defined. A slimmer woman with black hair pulled back tightly. Painted nails. A striped T-shirt. Whom he has not seen since last Christmas.

"Their old babysitter?" he says. The edge of the sink is pressing painfully into his lower back. "How do you know?"

Denise closes the ice cream into the freezer and turns back around to face him. "Get with the program, Rock—how do you think I know?" she says. "She's Esmerelda's sister. I *do* actually communicate with my employees."

The whole time, Rock realizes, Stephan has been sitting absolutely still with a frozen, dismayed expression on his face, feet dangling against the cereal cabinet. He is wearing, of all impossible things, a SAVE THE WHALES T-shirt.

"Oh, I see," Rock says, turning to him. "This is one of the 'rumors you're following'—I guess it would make for pretty interesting material."

"Hunh?" Stephan says, blanching, but then shrugging and recovering his expression. "Whatever. I'm just after good footage, not behind-the-scenes intrigue."

"Mmmm," Rock says. He feels suddenly almost physically angry. Denise and this whole childish stoned act, sitting here with another man, slandering Jack Dunlap, a man she couldn't possibly understand if he came with a manual, while her fiancé, Rock's father, is off on some miserable solo vacation! She is so goddamn righteous and self-satisfied and convinced of her own great sense of justice and morality in the world when she can't even figure out how to have a normal, uncondescending conversation! Of course she is blind to the emotional import of this rumor she is spreading. She sees the world in bright, uninteresting, politically correct Technicolor. And here is this poser idiot just lapping up her bullshit with his ass parked on her fiancé's kitchen counter.

"Well, I'll let you two get on with your fun and games here," Rock says, trying to keep his voice from shaking. "Help yourself to whatever's left in my box. I know, Denise, you're always so generous."

"Oh, Jesus," Rock can hear Denise saying. There is the scraping of a chair across the floor as if she is getting up to follow him. "Rock—"

But Rock has already grabbed his keys from the dish in the front hall and is out the door, beyond the wicker, and into the night.

ON PEA ISLAND, Jiri, the Czech culinary student, has set up a barbecue on the square of lawn between the house and the south dock at Lucy's request—an operation which he and Margaret are both fairly put out by: Margaret, because it means carrying the food all the way from the kitchen out to the grill, and Jiri, because he has not gotten to the grilling unit of the Cambridge Culinary Institute's training program yet. Pete has stepped in to supervise as barbecue-expert-in-residence. This is less to get things moving in the right direction than it is to entertain the Eintopfs, who are working on a pitcher of homemade margaritas and calling Pete "Roy Rogers" and, more mysteriously, "Cowboy Bob."

Faith has been delegated to cut tomatoes for the hamburgers, which she is actually enjoying because it allows her to stand inside, at the kitchen window, looking out along the nubbly coast of the island to the bright orange yoke of the sinking sun. The water is calm tonight. One of those giant, low-slung tankers from China or Taiwan, or some other exotic, industrial place, is inching south along the horizon. Watching the dark, surely rust- and barnacle-stained bulk of it making its slow, almost imperceptible progress gives Faith a lonely feeling, as if she is out there on it, a speck of life on a flake of metal, over miles and miles of ancient, sluggish sea.

To the west, far in the distance, a sliver of purple mainland is visible beyond the tip of the island. Massachusetts. Somewhere in its smooth contours, Concord and the track of land her son had mapped with such meticulous precision lies waiting like a riddle. Above this, the sky is turning a delicate, forgetful shade of lavender.

"Soup's on," Faith hears Pete calling, and someone else begins ringing the little dinner bell that hangs beside the porch door. It makes a stifled, tinny little sound that elicits peels of laughter from the lawn. The smell of barbecue smoke wafts in through the open window and, to Faith's surprise, her stomach grumbles.

"Hi ho, hi ho," one of the Eintopfs begins singing on the lawn, "it's off to our deaths we go." More laughter, especially from Pete. A buoy clangs in lonely, accidental answer to the dinner bell. They will come looking for the tomatoes soon. Faith cuts the last one into sloppy slices and drops them on the plate. She pats her hands off on the dishtowel and runs one through her hair, gathers her face into an alert, hopefully enthusiastic look, and swings, bearing tomatoes, through the kitchen door.

By the time the last of the charred burgers have been enjoyed and everyone has said good night to a chagrined-looking Jiri, whom Pete has been calling "Tonto," having, presumably, turned Cowboy Bob into the Lone Ranger, a relieving lull falls over the night. The Eintopfs are sitting around in small groups on the porch and the flat rocks that jut out over the water, nursing red wine and lukewarm glasses of bourbon. The icy, youthful taste of margaritas is already a thing of the past; over the course of the evening everyone seems to have settled creakily back into the ambiguous embrace of middle age. Their time on Pea Island is half over. Faith can feel them groping anxiously for the thoughtful, probing conversations, shared confessions, and soulful moments they have promised themselves to have—that they are counting on carrying through the winter like private torches they can light while raking the leaves or driving their sons to soccer practice or lying, sleepless, in their beds.

Twice in the last forty minutes Faith has had to excuse herself from conversations that seem about to take the plunge into territory that will require long supportive embraces followed by sensitive searching looks at breakfast, tender good-byes tempered with wry but insightful comments, possibly even letters and cards to "check in," none of which are Faith's specialty. Plus the sharing of their woes would have to be reciprocated by sharing of her own. And what would she say—*I have a ten-year-old son I barely know anymore? Who, along with my ex-husband and daughter, possibly hates me? Who, if I'm lucky, I will get custody of on* vacations *next year?* It sends a shiver through her even though she intended it to sound, in her own mind, comical and melodramatic.

Having detached herself from Lucy and two of the more vulnerable-looking Eintopf women, she looks around for Jean Pierre or Rock Coughlin, neither of whom is anywhere to be seen. From the rocks there is a burst of hard, cynical-sounding laughter; the kind that starts with a bang and then trickles down an octave, like a spilled drink.

The kerosene lantern sends flickery orange light and dark shadows out over the lawn and the wind is surprisingly warm and soft; it is a lovely night to be outside. Faith walks back out the side door of the house and down the sloping lawn to the dock, which is nearly invisible in the dark. There is no moon out, just a scattering of distant stars, half hidden by low cloud cover. From here the Eintopfs are obscured by the highest part of the rock ledge and their voices are almost inaudible. The loudest sound is that of the ocean lapping at the dock and the gentle creaking of planks.

Faith is almost on the dock before she realizes there is a form at the end of it, lying flat across its width, knees bent over the edge and feet dangling into the water.

"Oh," she says aloud, catching her breath.

The form struggles up on one elbow and then waves. "Faith-ey" it says, the *ey* like a distinction—Faith E., as opposed to, for instance, Faith *F.* It is Jean Pierre.

"You scared me," Faith says.

"I scared you!" he laughs. "You are the one walking like a ghost—poof—here you are."

"Well, I didn't know anyone was down here," Faith says, still standing at the end of the dock.

"Come look up with me." He pats the dock beside him.

"I didn't mean to disturb you. . . ." Faith hesitates, and then, at the exasperated scoffing sound he makes, steps onto the dock and walks toward him, her heart giving a frivolous little skip. When she is beside him, she slips off her flip-flops and slides them carefully between herself and Jean Pierre. Then she rolls up her pant legs and hangs her feet into the water. It feels surprisingly warm. Jean Pierre has lit up a cigarette and is lying on his back again, smoking it. The end glows bright when he inhales and then dims, arcing from his lips through the night.

"Not so many stars," Faith says, although, now that she is looking, she can see a blurry band of brightness across the lower half of the sky. The Milky Way, maybe? She would like to think so. It has such an appealing, homey sound, as if the universe is part of a gentle fairy tale.

"But enough, I think."

She darts a glance over at Jean Pierre to see if he is making fun of her, but his face looks smooth and serious in the starlight. She lets the water slip up over her ankles. "How long have you been down here?"

"Maybe half of an hour."

Faith is silent. It seems that in the distance she can see the dark form of the tanker on the water, illuminated by a few tiny white lights. But then, it is not that clear tonight, maybe she is imagining it. Or maybe it is coming closer. "It's warm," she says.

Jean Pierre sits up abruptly, his feet coming out of the water and splashing back down as he pulls himself up. "Shall we make a dip?" he says, tossing the cigarette out into the distance.

"A dip?" Faith cannot see his face now that he is sitting up, turned away from the minimal light of the stars and the lantern on the rocks above.

"A swim in the sea."

"I don't have my suit on."

"Why do you need a suit?" he says. "In the nighttime to swim without clothes in the sea—this is a great thing."

"Oh, no," Faith says, feeling her heart speed up again. "I don't think—"

Jean Pierre is already unbuttoning his shirt; she can hear the rustle of the cotton under his thumbs. When it is off, the skin on his back gleams slightly silver. Faith looks back out at what might or might not be the tanker and sits absolutely still, frozen in the strangeness of the moment, the un-Faithness of the moment, as if she is a passive observer of not just Jean Pierre, but herself. In a removed way, she is curious about what she will do.

Jean Pierre drops his pants and for one second stands naked beside Faith at the edge of the dock, a smooth, dark mass against the paler, less substantial darkness of the night. She is aware of this without looking directly. He disappears for a moment, the surface sealing back up over him, leaving just the night, dark and warm and heavy, punctuated by the lapping of waves, the distant sound of laughter blowing off the rocks. Then his head appears again, a little farther out. "Come on," he says. "It is wonderful."

Faith stares at her feet submerged in the water, as if there is some essential piece of information she can glean from them that will give her the cue for her next move. But there is nothing, just the glimmering black surface where she knows they must be. Almost without thinking she stands up, pulls her polo shirt over her head, unclasps her bra, unzips her pants, and tugs her underwear off awkwardly, kicks it free. With blood rushing against her eardrums, behind her eyes, drowning out all other sounds, she jumps in and down until she feels the sticky softness of the ocean floor against her extended toes. All around her the water feels gentle, but pressing, like a more significant kind of air.

". . . good?" Jean Pierre is saying as she emerges, sputtering, to the surface again.

"Great." Faith strikes out toward the mouth of the cove. It feels delightful not to be wearing Lucy's frumpy, ruffle-skirted suit, which she has had to borrow since lying about her own on that first afternoon here. When she stops, she is about fifty yards beyond the dock, nearly out of the cove. Behind her, Jean Pierre's head is like an inkblot against the glittery black of the water. Lying belly up, she is aware of the eerie paleness of her body, like something not altogether her own but of the ocean—breasts, thighs, and stomach rippling insubstantially in her wake.

"You are a fine swimmer," Jean Pierre says, from only a few yards behind her. Faith brings herself upright and begins treading water.

"I haven't swum at night in forever," Faith says. "I can't even remember the last time."

"I make a swim in the night every time I am here." He is close enough for her to see his face now in the moonlight. Close enough to touch, actually.

Faith is suddenly aware of their invisible nakedness, the long ends of their bodies hanging down into the murky darkness below. "Even when it's cold?" she asks.

"Even so."

It is possible—she does not really want to look, it would be too conspicuous—that Jean Pierre can see her breasts, at least vaguely, just below the surface.

"You are looking very serious," Jean Pierre says.

"What? Oh, no, I—" But then something—Jean Pierre's hand—is touching her face, stopping the words in midair.

"Here," he says, tracing the curve of her cheek gently, almost intangibly, letting the flat of his finger graze the corner of her mouth, pull at her lip, which is still too stunned to tense beneath his touch—and then it is gone. Faith feels her whole body change in the water under her—become soft and fluid, but at the same time more alert. For a moment she forgets to tread water.

"When you are on the water," Jean Pierre says, still looking intently at her, "your face . . ." He lifts one hand out into the air and spreads the fingers.

Faith stares at him, or at his head above the water, like an appendage of the great slippery body they share.

"Come," Jean Pierre says. "We will swim back together."

Almost involuntarily, Faith dives under and swims as far as she can without coming up for air, in the direction of the dock. Somehow she has not pointed herself right, though, so when she comes up, gasping for breath, she is still almost twenty yards away. She can see Jean Pierre pulling himself off, shaking dry. By the time she actually gets to the dock, Jean Pierre is buttoning up his pants over his still-wet skin. Should she just climb out naked beside him? Faith hangs onto the side for a moment, looking up at him. His body, clad in only his khakis, looks quite young and fit. He smiles down at her. "You are like a mermaid," he says, and Faith realizes she is grinning like a girl. "Wait a moment," he says. "I will run in and get a towel and wine."

Once he has disappeared up the dock into the darkness, the sea feels suddenly immense and a little frightening. Faith pulls herself up onto the dock and stands dripping for a moment, wondering what she is supposed to do. Above her, a new streak of stars and night sky has been swept out from under the clouds. Well, it is too cold to just stand here dripping, and besides, she will feel foolish with Jean Pierre watching her dress. She picks up her cotton underwear and uses it to dry herself off, then pulls on her pants and blouse, stuffs her bra into her pocket. Underneath her wrinkled clothes she feels damp and, for the first time in ages, sexy. She balls the sopping underwear up in her fist and hurls it as far as she can out to sea.

Suddenly there are footsteps on the dock behind her. "That was fast," she says, turning around, but then, to her shock, it isn't Jean Pierre but Rock Coughlin, Sr., stumbling slightly on the unsteady dock, glass of bourbon in hand. "Faith," he says. "What are you doing down here?" His eyes have the haggard, glossy look of someone who has been waiting in a hospital overnight.

Disappointment wells up in Faith as acutely as nausea. She can suddenly feel the places where her clothes are sticking to her, the scraggly mass of her hair, the breeze cold against her back. "I just—" she begins.

"I'm glad you're here, though, you know," Rock continues without waiting for her to finish, modulating his own voice to a more serious, slightly pained tone. "I've been wanting to find you alone, because, well . . ." He frowns into his glass and shakes the ice cubes, shoves his left hand more deeply into his pocket. "Because I know as well as anyone just because you're not married to someone doesn't mean you're not still, ahhhh, affected by—their troubles." Here he darts a look back at Faith. So far, he has been aiming this soliloquy off to sea in the general direction of Faith's tanker. "Bottom line—I'm just sorry about this whole mess Jack's in, is really what I've been wanting to say," he says in a lower, less philosophical tone. "If there's anything I can do—you know, besides try to keep Denise out of it, which, believe me, is harder than it should be—I hope you'll let me know."

Faith stares at him, trying to extract some sense from what he has just said. "Mess?"

"The whole—" Rock stops short and stares at her. There is a moment of silence between them in which Faith can hear the chains of the dock tighten and go slack, the water lap at the shore, the faint swell of laughter from the rocks.

"Ahhhhhh." Rock begins making a low lawn mower sound before his voice kicks back into gear. He has turned back out toward the water. "It's not—nothing, really. I shouldn't have . . ."

Faith stands absolutely still, waiting for him to finish. To her alarm, instead of speaking, he thunks himself violently on the forehead with the flat of his fist a few times. "I am such an ass," he says in an almost singsong voice. "*Such* an ass!"

"What kind of mess?" Faith begins, but is thrown off by the sight of Jean Pierre emerging from the darkness with a wine bottle, towel, and bowl of olives in hand.

Rock starts at the sound of Jean Pierre's footsteps on the

dock and then looks back at Faith incredulously. Faith almost feels sorry for him—he looks so upset and startled and she can make no sense of what he is talking about. Somehow Jean Pierre's own look of amused puzzlement gives her a greater sense of calm. Here he has left her naked in the water and comes back to find her soggily clothed, in some incredible conversation with Rock Coughlin. "It's all right, Rock," she says mildly. "I'm used to not knowing what's going on."

Rock looks from Jean Pierre, stopped respectfully some feet down the dock, to Faith. "Pardon me," he says. "I'm just— Pardon me."

Behind Rock, Jean Pierre is raising his eyebrows and making a face. And off to the side, on the surface of the water off the dock, Faith thinks she can see something white floating, which might be her underwear. How ridiculous! She feels a sudden impulse to smile, which she tries to suppress, but this only makes it more acute. In a second, she is laughing—a cracked, hiccupy sort of sound that probably makes her seem like a lunatic, with her wet hair and damp clothes out on a dock in the middle of the night. She can see Rock's face transform from uncomfortable to aghast, which only makes her laugh harder. Here she is, talking with Rock Coughlin about her ex-husband, with a Frenchman bringing her a bowl of olives and her discarded underwear bobbing alongside like a persistent, unwanted dog.

14

ELIOT KNOWS FROM THE MOMENT he wakes up that this will be the day. The sun is bright and insistent, but the air is clear, as if the world has sprung into focus after the blurry heat of yesterday. Outside the window, the lawn is still. No sign of Wheelie or the dogs, just bright, unreal-looking green stretching in an even, almost glowing plane to the edge of the wood. There is a pinging in Eliot's stomach, like a brittle rubber band being flicked, slightly, again, and again, and again. It is not unpleasant, actually.

Seven thirty-three, his watch blinks at him—he has taken to wearing it to sleep. The two threes after the colon have a pleasingly half-finished look that strikes him as auspicious. He has one thing left to accomplish—a simple thing that just requires getting out of the house before Caroline is up to ask questions. Eliot takes the manila folder he has stolen from his father's file cabinet out of the bottom drawer of his desk, opens it once to make sure the white paper with his neatest, blackest, block handwriting is still between its halves, and slides it carefully into his backpack. Then he pulls on his shorts and T-shirt and, careful not to make noise in the hallway, starts down the stairs.

On the threshold of the kitchen Eliot freezes. There is a person standing in front of the sink absolutely still, staring out the window. His father. There is something odd about his pose, arms at his side, shoulders sloping. For a moment Eliot has the absurd but terrifying feeling his father is dead. But dead people fall over; they don't simply freeze. Eliot takes a step onto the cool linoleum of the kitchen floor.

His father turns and looks right at him, but his eyes seem for a moment to be failing, as if they are struggling to make him out through the fogged glass of a windshield. "Eliot," he says, as if the name has just occurred to him.

"Yes," Eliot says.

"You're up early."

Eliot looks at his watch. Seven forty-one. "You're leaving late."

His father's face shifts and hardens and he stands up straighter, looking more like himself. "I'm on my way out." He picks his briefcase up off a chair. "Oh—" He stops when he gets to the door. "Are you—do you have a plan for today?"

Eliot freezes where he stands, one hand on the cornflakes box. "A plan?"

"Now that school is out—I could drive you to a friend's house . . ."

The offer is almost as surprising as the question was.

Eliot can only stare at him. "No," he says finally. "I want to stay here." The idea of his father driving him to a friend's house is preposterous—he can't remember a time when he has ever done such a thing.

"Okay." His father looks relieved. "'Bye, then," he says, and ducks through the door.

As soon as Eliot has finished his cereal, he puts on his sneakers and backpack and heads out of the house, up the driveway, and down Bedford Road toward town. It takes him over half an hour to arrive at Concord Center, but it is not unpleasant to be walking. The town itself, once he reaches it, is still fairly quiet and has a vacant, stage-set-like look—the street is full of commuter traffic, but the sidewalks are empty. A few people bustle in and out of the Colonial Bakery, coffee and newspapers in hand, but the throng of tourists that presses along the sidewalks at midday is blissfully absent.

It is still before nine A.M. Eliot has arrived, actually, a little earlier than he had anticipated and the pharmacy is not even open yet. He sits down on the concrete stoop in front of the store, but then it seems possible that this is a suspicious thing to do. So instead he crosses the street and sits on the shady grass outside Concord Academy in view of the pharmacy door. At five minutes before nine, to Eliot's dismay, the owner of the pharmacy himself, rather than the skinny teenage girl who usually sits at the register in the mornings, lumbers up to the front door. He is a huge, pear-shaped man with the unsettling name of Mr. Person. Eliot knows this from all the trips he has taken to use the pharmacy copy machine with Rosita, to copy the pages of her sister's Spanish workbook. Eliot has never had any sort of friendly feeling toward Mr. Person, though, or vice versa. The man was not kind to Rosita: *One at a time*, he would say warningly as Rosita took out her change purse, as if she would otherwise have jammed a whole fistful of dimes and nickels in at once. *How many copies?* He would demand, sighing and shaking his head. He has a broad, unsmiling face and arms like pale, hairy ham hocks, which leave little steamy marks around them when they rest on the glass counter.

When Eliot walks into the store, Mr. Person is squeezing

through the small gap between the ready-to-wear eyeglasses case and the cash register counter. His behind, enveloped in yards of forest-green khaki, is being severely compressed by the counter's edge, and his face, when it turns at the jingle of the door chime, looks slightly panicked from behind his glasses. Eliot almost backs out in his horror at having caught the man in such a compromised position. But then, with a heroic heave, Mr. Person clears the narrow gap and stands behind the counter, his face restored to its usual grim, impenetrable expression. "Not open yet," he says.

"Oh." Eliot holds out the fistful of dimes he has extracted from his pocket. "I just want to make some copies."

"Machine's not on." Mr. Person pushes his glasses farther up his broad nose with his finger, but doesn't seem to feel inclined toward further conversation. Under his other hand the register is making gurgly sputtering noises like a disgusted CPR recipient.

"Okay." Eliot turns to head back out the door.

"Hold on," Mr. Person barks. "Give me a minute." He says it almost peevishly. So Eliot waits, one hand on the door, the other shoved deep into his pocket, still wrapped around the sweaty dimes. Mr. Person manipulates himself back through the gap, with greater ease this time, and waddles around to the front of the store to punch something into the copy machine, which begins making a gentle whirring sound.

"Not yet," Mr. Person barks as Eliot approaches the machine. "I'll tell you when." Eliot feels almost faint with the desire to get out of the dim, cinnamon-air-freshener-smelling store and into the sun on the street outside. He can see a long, pale blue, old-fashioned-looking car roll to a stop on the street in front of the store and double park. The figure emerging from it looks at first only vaguely familiar—tall, long hair, wearing a white T-shirt. But then Eliot recognizes him: the film-maker from the play.

"Okay," Mr. Person grunts.

Eliot can see the machine's green light blinking READY. He

approaches it quickly, pulls the folder out of his backpack, lines the page up neatly along the ruler the way he has seen Rosita do it. Then he feeds in one of the dimes he has been clutching and pushes the green button—to his relief, the machine spits out a clean black and white copy. Eliot feeds in the dimes and pushes the button carefully, printing out one at a time.

He is so absorbed in the activity, it isn't until the movie-maker says something that Eliot even realizes the man has come in and is standing almost directly beside him.

"What?" Eliot says, feeling the blood rush up over his cheeks.

"Good morning," the man says, smiling. "You Dunlaps certainly are a jumpy family."

Eliot stares at him, uncomprehending. He is without his camera this morning and looks somewhat greasy and dilapidated, but still, there is something out of place about him that, like his camera, seems to bring a certain pressure to the ordinary world around him, like a red spot on a pale blue painting. The tight rubber band feeling picks up again in Eliot, more acutely—as if the rubber band has aged twenty years and is about to snap.

"You're Caroline's little brother, aren't you?"

"Caroline Dunlap?" Eliot asks.

"That's the one." The man laughs.

Eliot does not smile. He has six more copies to make.

"So what are you copying?" the man asks, leaning over as if to get a peek, but the copies come out face down. Even so, a dart of fear runs through Eliot.

"Nothing," he says, and then lies on second thought. "It's for my father."

"*Re*ally." The man emphasizes the first syllable in a way that gives the word an almost heated sound.

Eliot remains silent.

"He has you do his copying? Here?"

"His machine is broken," Eliot mumbles.

"I've got something like it here," Mr. Person wheezes from

one of the aisles, to Eliot's relief. "It's not quite what you're looking for, but it might just fix you."

The man is forced to turn around and face Mr. Person's lightly panting form.

"D-e-r-m-i-t-i-to," Mr. Person is spelling. "I think you'll find it works nicely enough."

Eliot gathers his copies in a cold sweat—he will have to forgo the last few. He opens up his backpack and begins dropping the modest stack into it, but one of the copies slips somehow off the top and drifts, face up, almost directly to the man's feet.

"Great," the man says in Mr. Person's direction, and bends to pick up the paper before Eliot can dive over.

Eliot stands rooted in the position he has lunged into, with the blood pounding in his ears like a contained explosion. The man looks from the page to Eliot, eyebrows raised in genuine surprise. Then he hands it back to him silently. Eliot reaches out and takes it, shoves it hastily into his backpack.

"Let me just ring you up, then," Mr. Person is saying in a high, breathless voice as he squeezes, yet again, through the counter.

Eliot slips his pack on and darts out of the store, through the insipid tinkle of chimes and the man's "Wait a minute— hey—" and out into the relieving non-cinnamon-scented sunshine.

———————

WHEN CAROLINE WAKES UP, her father has left for work already and Eliot's door is closed. Still asleep, probably. Instead of jogging this morning, she will take a swim, she decides. Better for thinking.

Caroline has lost weight over the last few weeks; her bikini feels a little baggy and her skin looks too pale. The usual scattering of freckles across her nose and chest have faded like a leafy shadow under a cloud. Under her bare feet, the grass feels sharp beneath the deceptively soft tips of its blades. The dogs are out; she can see them racing across the back lawn, chasing some poor squirrel or rabbit into the trees. Her father has installed one of those underground electrical fences that gives off a shock when crossed by any animal wearing a matching collar. On the first day the fence was activated, he put on one of the collars and walked over it to see how much the charge it gave off hurt. Apparently, by whatever criteria he was using (painful enough? too painful?), it was satisfactory. Now Caesar and Brutus are free to run around as they please. Caroline opens the fence around the small kidney-shaped pool and shuts it hurriedly behind her.

The pool has not been used yet this year, although Wheelie opened it up almost a month ago. The pebbly concrete around it and the surface of the water are flecked with brown helicopter leaves and dead cicadas, little fuzzy balls of linden blossoms. Caroline brushes off one of the slatted lawn chairs and spreads her towel on it. Then she walks back around to the stairs and steps in, kicking at the surface of the water to send the debris floating off to the edges of the pool. The splash sounds loud and harsh in the morning silence. In its wake, the world feels startlingly empty.

Caroline wades in up to her waist and drops under. She has not swum in ages and it feels good—the pressure of the water rushing in her ears and the smooth muscled effort of moving forward through this thicker substance. After only ten laps, she flips onto her back and floats on the surface. Above her, the sky has a solid, lidlike stillness. She closes her eyes and lets her fingers slip in and out of the gelatinous water.

It is only day three of her job as Stephan's "production liaison" and already she has her doubts about the position. Stephan wants to set up an interview with her father, which, it seems to her, is something of a conflict of interest. The division between production liaison and subject seems to be shrinking. At least in theory; in practice, her father would never agree to such a thing. Stephan may think that since she is his daughter she can persuade him, but this is an enormous misperception. Her father is a man of stubborn and unshakable convictions. He does not bend his own rules on petition.

Poor little Eliot, who has to spend so much time alone with him! She feels a stab of anger toward her mother for leaving him here, in this cold creaky house, to the care of his father. Why couldn't she just have held together until, at least, he was safely away at some boarding school? Caroline drops her feet to the bottom of the swimming pool in a sudden, ungainly movement and pulls herself up onto the rough concrete. She will go see if Eliot would like, maybe, to go out for breakfast. The least she can do while she is stuck here is make Eliot's life a little more pleasant. He is so quiet and remote lately; she can't imagine what is going on in his head. Why, for instance, did he suggest going to Roxbury yesterday?

Inside, Caroline patters barefoot across the kitchen in her towel and wet bikini. "Eliot!" she calls. There is no answer. Maybe, she reminds herself, he is still sleeping. She walks through the dining room, past the long empty table and reproachful-looking form of Sir Percival, through the dim brown reception room and the narrow hallway to the bottom of the stairway.

"Eliot?" she calls again, more gently. Under her bare feet the floor feels cold and an artificial, air-conditioned breeze raises the fine hairs on her clammy thighs. In front of her the broad pine steps are shiny, worn down in the middle by so many years of footsteps. Sold to a different carpenter, on a different day, they could have made a coffin—could lie decomposing in the crowded sod beside St. Bartholomew's. The thought sends an anxious pang up through her.

She climbs the stairs, two at a time, and when she gets to Eliot's door she opens it without knocking. "Eliot?" she whispers, but she can see he is not there. He is already gone, must have left before she even got up or she would have seen him go. But where to this early? For a moment she stands absolutely still next to his papier-mâché sculpture and she can hear everything—the ticking of the clock in the downstairs hall, the steady purr of the air-conditioning, below that, the stiff creaking of the house settling into time.

From down the hall, there is the shrill ring of the telephone. Caroline starts, her heart racing as if it is Eliot calling from wherever he is to tell her to get out of his bedroom. She heads down the hall to her father's room, still clutching the damp towel around her.

"Oh, Caroline," comes her mother's voice from the other end of the phone. "I'm so glad you're there."

"Why?" Caroline says. She does not feel like dealing with her mother right now. "Did something happen?" She sits down on her father's unmade bed and lets her eyes pass over the room, which she has not been in for God knows how long. It looks startlingly chaotic—the shades drawn to different levels, the bed unmade, and T-shirts—how long has he had these up?—hanging over the old family portraits.

"No! No, no! I just wanted to check in—I felt—I've been worrying about Eliot." She does actually sound highly excited, but not in her usual tentative, anxious way.

"How come?" Caroline demands, resisting the chill of the coincidence.

"Oh—I—well, it's silly, I just wanted to check in and see if he was there to say hi to and . . ."

Caroline is not listening anymore, though. Sitting on the edge of her father's bed, she has caught sight of a paper lying on the bedside table. There is a cartoonish image of a little man in a baseball cap flipping hamburgers on a grill in the bottom right-hand corner of the page and a series of blank lines beside Spanish words, filled in with their English counterparts in an unfamiliar neat, curlicued, script. Caroline reaches forward and picks it up to look more closely. *Barbacoa* = *barbeque*, *sopapilla* = *sandwich*, and then down here at the end, two lines filled in with a different, larger, more angular and familiar script. Her father's: *paragua* = *umbrella*, *mustaza* = *not for hamburgers*.

"Is he there?" she hears her mother ask.

"Eliot?"

"Yes, of course Eliot—I'd love to say hello, just—"

"I can't find him," Caroline says blankly, turning the paper over. There is a small coffee stain, a scribble as if someone were trying out a pen, nothing else. *Mustaza = not for hamburgers*: a little private joke. She would have said, two minutes ago, such an exchange could not possibly have emanated from her father.

"In the house?"

"I don't know."

"Know what?"

"I don't know where he is, Mom. Can I—can we call you back later?"

"Is everything all right?" the old panicky sound has crept back into Faith's voice.

"I don't know," Caroline repeats.

"Well, should I—should I come back? And come help you—"

"No, no." Caroline snaps back into focus. The last thing she wants to do is throw her mother into some kind of panic that brings her scampering, nerves raw and exposed, back to Concord. "It's okay," Caroline says. "It'll be fine."

She sits for a minute after she has hung up the phone, holding the vocabulary paper in her hand. Why is this on her father's bedside table next to his boyhood copy of *Gulliver's Travels* and framed photo of his mother?

———————

AT TEN A.M. Jack is settled in his oak-paneled office on the thirty-fourth floor of the Hancock Building trying to review the memo his secretary has placed on his desk for his perusal. The room feels too hot, though. He gets up to pull the blind partway, loosens his tie, takes a deep breath. But he can't shake this unfamiliar asthmatic feeling he has been having since driving down Center Street yesterday.

From his office he can see out over the Boston Common to

the theater district and off over the river into Cambridge to the
north. Anything southward—Roxbury, Dorchester, the South·
End—is obscured by the other half of his own building. Below
him, on the green rise of the monument-topped hill in the
middle of the Common, there are a few tiny figures walking
and sitting on the grass. Who are they? Homeless people?
Tourists? Who can afford to be out in the park at nine-thirty on
a Tuesday morning? Jack strains to make out more about them,
but it is impossible from this distance: they have the same
inscrutable, representative feeling as figures in a diorama. But
what do they represent? Slovenliness, irresponsibility? This isn't
exactly it. Irrelevant. He squeezes his eyes shut to regain focus,
turns back to the desk.

Jack has not slept since yesterday. Has, in fact, spent the
night in the basement dismantling the diorama he was stupid
enough to think he should try to finish. He has taken the
pieces apart and cleaned the studio out from top to bottom,
sorted through his old supply drawers, weeded out hardened
glue cartridges and decrepit bits of plywood. He has even taken
a Dustbuster to the crevices in between cabinets and walls,
along the backs of the dusty shelves. The place is now immaculate, scrubbed clean, no more traces of unfinished projects. It
looks just as it did when he first built it.

And he is not tired this morning; he just has a headache. A
light, persistent knocking, as if something in his brain is clamoring from the inside. He reaches into the top drawer of his
desk, shakes four Advils into his hand, and swallows them without water. He is aware of his throat constricting to press the
pills down into his body, of his whole body working to absorb
them like some soft, elaborately winding, tight-walled cave.

There are four messages on his voice mail. One from an
associate, one from Frank Berucci of Colby Kesson fame, two
from Lilo. *She is perfectly willing to be filmed,* she intones haughtily
from the receiver, *but thinks he should strongly caution Caroline
against involving herself with an artist.* Jack has no idea what she is
referring to. It sounds alarming—an interview with Lilo cannot

be a good thing, but he doesn't have time to think about it this morning. He skips her second message.

Frank Berucci, on the other hand, he will have to deal with. There are young associates he could assign to fire the man, but this is not the way Jack operates. Even under pressure. Put a call through to Frank Berucci, he instructs his secretary, Candice, and a breathless, ingratiating-sounding Frank is on the line in tweny-five seconds flat. How did Jack like "Choices"?— the crowd was a little thinner than usual, of course, but— Jack cuts him off and lays out the facts. Three months' pay, a solid recommendation, and health insurance through October. He has been unusually generous. As he speaks, he finds himself dying to get off the phone. His words seem heavy and inflexible, as if he has to traverse rough, arduous terrain to access them.

There is a pause on the other end when he is finished. Jack braces himself for the usual angry commentary, bitter insults, and hang-ups such conversations inspire. But instead there is just silence.

"I could revise the program," the man says finally, and then adds, "I guess that's not the point."

This time Jack is silent.

"And my family?" The man says.

Jack gets up and walks to the window with the phone. The Harvard crew is out on the Charles, their boats like delicate centipedes skimming the surface of the water. "My wife is pregnant. I'm just—"

"I'm sorry," Jack says. He wants, more than anything, to hang up the phone. And then there is an incredible sound— very faint, but unmistakable. Frank Berucci is crying. Jack holds the receiver away from his ear. The man is a spineless fool. But the sound creates a terrible, grating feeling in Jack's stomach.

"You're just doing your job," the man says. His voice is like a tiny doll's voice, coming from the receiver Jack is holding at arm's length. "I know."

"You can call our Human Resources Department to follow

up with any questions on your package," Jack says into the mouthpiece again, but before he has finished he can hear the receiver on the other end click back into place. Hurriedly he puts his own back into its cradle. Done. He is sweating—the room seems to be getting hotter, pressing in on him with its unsustaining recycled air. Well, he can give the acquisitions team the go-ahead now.

Jack picks the phone back up and calls his secretary to have her cancel his meetings for the rest of the day. He knows what he has to do. He is a responsible man, after all. Contrary to the implications of Rosita's brother-in-law, he has never shirked the consequences of his actions. Not when he knows what they are. He dials his lawyer, George Burt, himself, makes his way past two secretaries, and then waits on hold, an insipid, vaguely familiar melody playing in his ear. He does not relish the prospect of explaining the situation to George, who has not only been Jack's lawyer for the last twenty years, but was in fact his grandfather's estate executor. But he needs advice and there is no better place to get it. George can be trusted to be tight-lipped. He is a circumspect man of the old-fashioned variety—and he is good at his job, a real gentleman's lawyer.

By the time Jack has given the minimal explanation required to arrange a meeting this afternoon, his overheated, short-of-breath feeling has become almost unbearable. In the small private bathroom adjoining his office, Jack splashes water on his face and rubs a towel vigorously over the skin, bringing the blood back to the surface. He looks haggard and unkempt; a rough growth of stubble—gray, it still surprises him—coats his chin and neck. He has forgotten to shave this morning. It doesn't matter, really. He doesn't need to look professional to carry out his plan. But he would like to. It would bring a certain dignity to the situation; he is, after all, acting responsibly.

All things, as his grandfather always said, *happen for a reason.* There was that letter Rosita sent him months ago, which he should have opened. In a way, didn't he suspect what it contained? Didn't he know, in any event, the moment he saw

Rosita at Colby Kesson? Articulating this thought turns the tapping in his head into a monstrous pounding. He is not entirely
to blame. Why didn't she try harder to contact him if she was
indeed pregnant with his baby? He does not want to look into
the answer to this, which his brain already has waiting: She
thinks he is the sort of man who wouldn't care that he has gotten his son's babysitter pregnant. And she has no citizenship,
no papers, no court system to fall back on.

But Jack will show her she was wrong. He will not be called
a delinquent by her brother-in-law when he has not been given
a fair chance to do better—not really. He will show the man
who he is. Because he is a Dunlap, after all, a man who stands
by his actions. *You get a girl in trouble, you get her out of it—whatever it takes.* This was the extent of his grandfather's advice on
carnal matters. He will have George draw up an agreement,
something reasonable and discreet, contingent on proof of
paternity. Which is more than fair play. If the baby is his, he will
subsidize its existence. He chooses clinical terms to form his
thoughts, keeps himself on the safe ground of abstraction.
Twenty thousand a year is a fair amount—generous, really. As
for Rosita herself—

Jack's brain grows hard and blank around the name, like
flesh around a bullet. He will think about her later. One thing
at a time. Jack tightens his tie and puts on his jacket.

When he walks out into the chambered nautilus of cubicles
that lies beyond his office, he can hear a distinct, high-pitched
humming in the air—the whir of electricity through wires or
infrared signals or some other high frequency humans aren't
supposed to tune in to. At her desk, his secretary is inspecting
her long, blood-colored nails, which she plunges guiltily below
her keyboard as he passes.

"Will you—" he can hear her calling something after him,
but he ignores it and keeps going. In a moment he has made
his way out into the elevator lobby, past the row of receptionist
cubicles and the nervous-looking young associates in their uniform of oxford shirts and khakis. Past the potted plants and

antique maps and familiar, trustworthy signs of industry. Now that Colby Kesson is settled, he can call in the Harvard B-school kid, set things in motion. If all goes smoothly with George, he can have something preliminary to deliver this afternoon, can possibly make it back to the office before sundown, even.

FAITH'S BRAIN has been spinning since she hung up the phone with Caroline. Eliot is missing and Caroline sounded strange—tired and unoptimistic. Faith is used to getting Caroline's reassuring voice.

She had to go back and check on the children, she told Lucy, on whose cell phone the call transpired. Not only on account of Eliot's whereabouts, but because of what Rock Coughlin said last night. What was that? Lucy asked, frowning. Well, not much, Faith found herself explaining, something about a mess, whatever that means. . . . Lucy stared at her with the intent look of a parent listening to a child describing something bad he cannot name. In any case, Faith did not expect Lucy to *agree* that she should leave early. She was half suggesting it because after last night the thought of making noncommittal chitchat with Jean Pierre over the lunch table or during the softball game planned for the afternoon had begun to terrify her. But to her surprise, Lucy nodded. It sounded like her children needed her, and Pete was taking the boat in at two, which could get Faith to the four o'clock bus. . . .

So now Faith is leaving this afternoon, a full day early. Which seems both inevitable and slightly tragic. On the one hand, Faith tells herself, it is maybe better this way: Jean Pierre, who has gone fishing with one of the Eintopfs, probably wants nothing more to do with her—he is, after all, a Frenchman. He probably sleeps with women once a month, if not more often. But on the other hand, what if this means she will never see him again, that she will never be kissed again, that she will always wonder what might have happened if she had stayed?

But then she is a terrible person for even thinking about this. Where are her values? Her sense of moral priority? Her own ten-year-old son may be wandering around in the backwoods of Concord, or worse, on his way to California or Las Vegas or wherever it is runaways go! This is what is important. Jean Pierre's hands and brown shoulders, his dry lips and unbashful stare, are not the only things of consequence, not the only things that are real.

Faith tries to shake off the thought of these and begins packing, folding her T-shirts slowly, smoothing them, creasing at the sides, stacking them neatly, just as stern Mrs. Graves taught her to when she was a little girl. She is being careful, holding herself calmly, thinking in a firm, reassuring voice that sounds surprisingly like Lucy's. It isn't working, though—she is shaky with nervousness and excitement. Nauseous, even, her fingers trembling a little, her sweat giving off an acrid, waste-like smell. She has been jolted by so many waves of adrenaline this morning that it feels like she is on drugs—or what she imagines being on drugs would be. She has never actually tried "drugs"—the word conjures up an image of little brightly colored pills—pink, lavender, robin's-egg blue.

The feeling started when she woke up this morning to an unpleasant thrumming sound that turned out to be a bad red wine headache, and a hump under the yellow daisy print sheets that turned out to be Jean Pierre.

She sat frozen at the edge of the bed, trying to think what a person does when waking up beside a near-stranger, what a person says or thinks, whether she takes her clothes and gets dressed in the bathroom or whether she lies back down, shuts her eyes, and—and what? Pretends to sleep and waits for her bed mate to tiptoe out? But then Jean Pierre rolled toward her under the sheets, put one hand on her arm just above the sharp point of her elbow, thumb pointing upward, warm and firm against the slim bone. And he was smiling—not sarcastically, or foolishly, just, well, in a way that answered her question for her—made her lie obediently back down. She resurrects this smile, this pressure of warm hand against her flesh, as she packs up her toilet kit, removes her towel and Lucy's froofy bathing suit from the laundry line. Jean Pierre has a birthmark like a pale coffee stain below his collarbone, and a certain roundness to his body, a compact, yet substantial grace that reminds her of one of those Volkswagen Beetle cars. Remembering the way his knuckles felt grazing her neck, sweeping a half circle out toward her shoulder and then back, stopping just above her heart, she can thrill the skin above her collarbone on command. Through the whole lunatic morning of preparations and assurances, of efforts and missteps, she has felt, under everything, the whirring, trembling, cartwheeling motion of near-cellular change.

Faith drops hold of the zipper she has been tugging at and sits down on the edge of the bed. Her underwear doesn't fit into the suitcase and she has forgotten the green slicker hanging in the closet. Which means she will have to refold the T-shirts, restuff the shoes. She is just packing, she tells herself. It has such a simple, concise sound to it. A basic activity, like breathing, eating, taking a bath. For a moment her heart slows to its normal patter in her chest. It is all so silly—the excitement, the worry, the theater of it all. As if Jean Pierre would even care if she stayed or left! As if her presence in Concord would make one iota of difference to Caroline or Eliot. She is a failure as a mother—as a divorcée, even. She doesn't even know how to conduct an ordinary one-night stand.

Jean Pierre's copper bracelet and package of Marlboros are lying on her bedside table, archaeological evidence of the persistence of that time into this. Faith stares at her underwear, now scattered around her little suitcase on wheels, marketed as "The Smuggler," which suddenly makes sense to her—it has a smug look to it, too small, too precise, too convenient for her life. What made her think she could own a bag like this? Now she will have to start packing all over again to make room for the forgotten slicker.

But instead, she takes one of Jean Pierre's cigarettes out of the crinkly aluminum wrapping and lights it with a match from beside the kerosene lamp. The first puff makes her cough spasmodically, but it gets better. She has forgotten about the exhilarating rush a cigarette can give. She hasn't smoked since—God—since she was pregnant with Caroline; since she was a baby, really, another person altogether. It makes her feel hardened and worldly to be leaning, now, against the windowsill, blowing smoke out over the quiet heathery slope down to the sea. Here she is, smoking her lover's—the word makes her smile sheepishly, but sends a thrill up over her neck as well—her lover's cigarettes, ashing into his abandoned glass of water beside her bed.

When Faith comes downstairs with her suitcase, Jean Pierre is sitting on the porch looking out over the water through his binoculars. His actual presence is incongruous to the one she has created for him over the last two hours in her mind. He looks shorter and paler than she remembered. The binoculars make him less manly.

"Aha," he says, putting the binoculars down on the bench. He stands up and takes the suitcase from where she has deposited it at her feet. "So heavy," he exclaims. "You should have called for help."

"It's not so bad," Faith says, following him around the corner down the steps to the lawn, which he is crossing to bring her suitcase to the dock. She feels shy and suddenly embarrassed. Only ten minutes ago she was using the term *lover* to describe him in her mind. It makes her feel slightly disgusted.

On the dock, there is another suitcase and a bag of golf clubs, blue and gold with an Air France sticker peeling off along the side. "What—?" Faith begins. "Whose suitcases are these?"

"Mine." Jean Pierre drops hers beside them.

"You're leaving?" Faith asks stupidly.

"I will drive you," Jean Pierre says.

"You don't have to do that—" Faith says. "I was going to take the bus—"

"But it is better in the car, no? Not so much worry." Out here, in the sunlight, Jean Pierre looks bigger and browner again.

"It's your vacation, though—you —"

"Shh." Jean Pierre takes Faith's hand and lifts it to his lips. "I would like to."

"Oh." She feels that rush through her insides at the pressure of his touch, the reminder that the human body is ninety percent water. It occurs to her it might be dangerous, all this bodily excitement—she is forty-five, after all, no longer a teenager.

"Okay?" Jean Pierre says. "I will tell Pete you are ready."

The good-byes are awkward, of course. Lucy seems to have alluded to some sort of "situation" and several of the Eintopfs give Faith especially firm hand presses and breathe vaguely reassuring platitudes into her ear.

Rock Coughlin has wound himself up into a state of near-panic with guilt or sorrow or concern, or some combination of all three. "Can I get you anything else, Faith? Water for the road? Aspirin? Another sweater?" He hovers in the background, darting forward every so often with a new query, looking pale and overwrought and strangely like Julia Child. "So long, Farewell, Auf wiedersehen, Good-by-yiy," four of the Eintopfs serenade her from the porch railing as she and Pete and Jean Pierre cross the lawn to the Boston Whaler. Even Lucy looks vaguely embarrassed by this maudlin display.

On the boat, Pete is cheerful as always and assures Faith that when she gets to Concord, Eliot will be sitting at the kitchen table "chomping on a Big Mac like a clown." His own son, Conor, disappeared one time and it turned out he had hitched a ride into New York to see the Schwarzenegger movie Lucy had forbade him from going to—all 45 miles from Greenwich into the city with some balding, off-duty Greyhound driver named Honey. Pete delivers all this as a consolation—Conor and he still "josh" each other over Honey. But for the first time this morning Faith actually pictures Eliot dislodged in the world, standing erect and startlingly pale-haired at the edge of some wide and intimidating highway, in full view of strangers with opaque intentions. It has not actually, in all this commotion, seemed possible that he could be anywhere other than out walking or at a friend's house or involved in any of the dozens of harmless possibilities Lucy and the Eintopfs have presented her with. Now she imagines him in a bus station that smells of old cigarette smoke, beside a fat man with big hands and a gold necklace that spells out HONEY.

"Take good care of my Faith, John John." Pete claps Jean Pierre on the shoulder with a wink. "And you tell that boy of hers to *regardez s'il vous plait!*"

When Pete is gone, Jean Pierre sets off to reclaim his rented Oldsmobile from the parking lot and Faith finds herself alone for what feels like the first time in days—weeks, even— which is ridiculous, of course. She was just alone, up in her room packing, but in retrospect it feels as if there was a great deal of shouting up there—as if there were at least five other people carrying on a stressful, high-stakes argument. Waiting here at the end of this dock, it feels quiet for the first time. In this new calm, Faith fishes out Eliot's map stowed in the inside pocket of her Filofax at the bottom of her cavernous handbag. The delicate lines of streets and driveways, the thicker, darker spine of the Charles River, stare back at her like one of those drawings that can be seen two ways—a goblet or two faces in conversation, a young woman with a hat or an old hag. Try as she might, she can only see the surface of this, though, the roads and hills, not the outline of some truth beneath. She drags the luggage all the way to the other end of the dock where there is a small cluster of pay phones, but there is no answer at 23 Memorial Road, just Jack's curt recorded message on the machine.

ROCK HAS SPENT THE MORNING having his teeth cleaned by a large, sphinxlike woman wearing a full surgical uniform, complete with a clear plastic visor, who pried at his gums in utter silence. A disturbing, no-frills experience of hygiene at its most torturous. Where was the cheery small talk and reassuring use of euphemisms like "the easy chair" and "Mr. Slurpee"? The experience has had the effect of making Rock feel hyperaware of what is really occurring—he has paid someone to use sharp metal instruments to scrape out an intimate cavity of his body. This has only added to the general feeling of unease building in him since his run-in with Denise yesterday. Was all that shit about Jack Dunlap having a baby true? And if so, is it his responsibility to tell Caroline? In his mind, Rock has already covered the pros and cons of broaching the subject with her at least three hundred times. If it isn't true, he will have needlessly upset her and taken part in spreading ridiculous sensational rumors cooked up by a bitter ex-litigator with too much time on her hands. But if it *is* true, she should know, shouldn't she? Especially since it sheds a new light on Mr. Moviemaker's interest in her—didn't Don say the guy had "a few good rumors to follow up on"? Jesus Christ. Rock pounds his forehead. His brain is like a fucking broken record.

Rock parks in front of Don Hammond's and climbs out of the car. He does not want to head back to the "duplex" anytime soon, because if he does, he will have to confront Denise. He has managed, thus far, to avoid her since yesterday, and would like to keep this up as long as possible; that way there will be no opportunities for her to offer some half-assed apology or awkward, unfair rationalization of her behavior. Besides, he has something he would like to ask Don.

Don is home, to Rock's relief, and is even listening to an old Leonard Cohen LP, which, Rock has learned, incongruously indicates he is in excellent spirits. "*An eskimo showed me a movie*," Don sings by way of greeting in an exaggerated imitation of Leonard's sorrowful voice. Rock unwraps the sandwiches he has brought—roast beef for himself and green pepper and cheese for Don, who is a vegetarian and lays into his with half-starved relish.

"The geometer?" Rock asks politely. "She's gone?"

"Hmm?" Don grunts blankly. "Oh, right. *Finite.*"

Rock leans back in his chair, which shrieks under him. "So, you know how we were talking about Stephan—Wendel, whatever?"

Don nods through his vigorous chewing.

"How he told you there were some good rumors or something he was following up on? Did he say what they were? Or, you know, what he meant by 'follow up on'?"

Don cocks his head to the side and looks at Rock inquiringly. "Why?"

"I don't know—I was just thinking he might be after something specific—something I might know about and . . . It's a long story."

"Something about you?"

"No, no—nothing to do with me personally."

Don frowns and puts down his sandwich. "I don't know—I wasn't really listening. He likes to 'uncover things'—whatever." He looks hard at Rock. "It's not worth your time, man. Getting caught up in Wendel's bullshit. Is that what you came over to ask me?"

"Kind of . . ." There is a pause. "But also, actually . . ." Rock shifts uncomfortably in his chair. "Would you mind—would it be all right if I just parked it here this afternoon and you can do whatever you're doing? I'll just sit and read or whatever. I just can't go home right now because of this thing—because of my father's fiancée or whatever." It occurs to Rock as he is speaking that he has not actually brought a book with him and the whole request sounds pathetic.

"Sure," Don says without hesitation. But he narrows his eyes and stares at Rock with an unapologetically evaluative expression. Then he breaks into a fit of loud, almost raucous laughter. "Look at you!"

Rock smiles good-naturedly and waits for Don to finish laughing. But Don keeps on until the smile on Rock's face begins to feel completely foolish.

"What did I tell you yesterday?" Don says. "You got to get out of your father's house—here you are, worrying about Wendel's movie and your father's fiancée—that's no way to live your life."

"I know." Rock crumples the greasy white paper in which the roast beef was wrapped into a ball and brings it over to the garbage.

There is a loud floor-scraping, rustling sound behind him and when he turns Don has left the room. Rock wanders over to the kitchen window and stares out.

"Here," Don's voice comes from behind him.

Rock turns around and Don is holding out two books and a piece of paper. *The Tibetan Book of the Dead,* Rock reads upside down. The other is a grubby, well-thumbed guidebook.

"Peruse this. And this"—Don extends the paper—"is the address and fax number."

"Of . . . ?"

"The monastery."

"They have a fax machine?" Rock accepts the two books reluctantly.

"Sure." Don shrugs. "They're not Druids."

Rock can see himself suddenly in Don's eyes. A grown man, fleeing from his father's house—no, scratch that, his father's *duplex*—to avoid a woman not that much older than himself whom his father is marrying, who has already had a career and is starting a new one, while he himself has been toiling away at a bullshit New Age organic farm, only to be laid off and have nothing better to do than show up here at Don's at a time of day when most people are working, or at least running errands, or being, in some way, *useful.*

"Listen." Don lifts a backpack from one of the kitchen chairs and there is a pungent waft of garlic. "I think all that other shit—your Dad's fiancée and whatever you're worrying about Wendel's movie—you have to get out of it. It's screwing with your karma."

Rock considers this.

"I'm going to the lab. Read that. You can hang out here as long as you want—if you need a place to crash, no problem."

"Thanks," Rock says to the sound of Don's footsteps on the stairs. The thought that his karma has been screwed with actually does seem possible. Isn't there some almost physical revulsion that sweeps over him lately at the thought of Denise and his father's upcoming marriage? Doesn't he find himself adopting their passive sort of joylessness around the house? Calling tomatoes *to-mah-toes* and taking care not to scuff the carpeting on the stairs or leave crumbs in the butter? Is that a sign of his disintegrating karma?

Rock stretches his feet out and leans back on the rickety chair and opens the guidebook. There is a picture of a beautiful white building jutting from a brown hillside. It is, actually, quite breathtaking. He imagines himself there, looking out over the valley below: What the hell would be in it? Rice fields, maybe—or, yes, he turns the page, grazing cattle: the pretty reddish brown kind with long graceful horns. Exotic Tibetan mountain cattle. If he lived there, he could probably help herd them—just walk around all day in the tall grass à la Holden Caulfield, herding cattle. He can't picture exactly what this would entail. A lot of shooing or something—it's not exactly a very manly business. And he'd probably be shat on by all these monks for being new and American and totally ignorant of all things spiritual. And sick from drinking hot yak butter with no Maalox handy. But still. Still, there is something that makes him keep turning the pages.

This place he is looking at actually exists at this moment on this planet. A sign of his deteriorating karma, that this thought should strike him as novel. A sign maybe even that he should go there. What does he have to lose? Wheatgrass-addled e-mails from the animal rights activist he had a free-form relationship with last summer in Mendocino, a free subscription to *The New Yorker*, five guest passes to 24 Hour Nautilus, courtesy of his father.

And Caroline. But maybe—the idea washes over him in a burst of hazy, joyful enthusiasm—just possibly, she would want to come with him? He will have to bone up on the particulars, make a case for it, convince her Eliot will be just fine without her. It is a ridiculous idea—he and Caroline climbing around the Himalayas in long robes herding cattle. And she'd have to give up smoking. But, after all, didn't she say the other night that she wanted to get out of here and go capital *S* Somewhere?

15

By THE TIME JACK LEAVES George Burt's office, it is already late afternoon. The whole process has taken longer than he expected, and given him a hassled, slightly dirty feeling. Watching George Burt's placid, gray face taking in his questions, registering the effort not to look surprised or appalled or whatever must have been his natural instinct to look, has given Jack a greater sense of disgust with himself than any outward gesture of dismay or rebuke the man could possibly have made. Jack walks back through the Common to his car, which is a detour, but he needs the air—he still can't take a deep breath—and has lost something of his sense of urgency. He has an official letter from George, laying out what Rosita must do if, once the baby is born and it proves to be Jack's, she would like support from him. The letter makes him feel oddly conspicuous, which makes no sense. There is certainly no one here who looks even remotely interested in his presence—a homeless man stretched out on a bench, a group of frisky young Spanish tourists, a very thin formal-looking young man reading under a tree, and lots of babysitters, black, brown, white, and Asian, pushing strollers and carriages, unwrapping bottles, speaking in low voices.

An otherworldly calm has come over Jack like that which used to fall on him when he was a young man before important lacrosse games. He feels highly focused in a concentrated, but strangely vacant, way—aware of the muscles moving in his legs, the small tendons in his joints—ankle and knee, the breath entering his lungs and leaving, the swinging of his arms. He walks through the shiny marble lobby of his building, rides the gold-walled elevator to the garage, gets into his car, and navigates his way out to the southeast expressway in this odd, suspended state.

Without full awareness of how he has arrived here, he is soon enough in Roxbury, on Blue Hill Avenue, this time with the Hancock Building behind him. Past the CHECKS CASHED signs and Caribbean Cultural Center, past the dingy murals and fluttering strings of grubby plastic pennants, and then here is Center Street again. The corner deli is open, neon coursing through its Budweiser sign despite the strong late afternoon sunlight. In front of it there is an old woman talking to two little black girls with great cones of hair sticking up off their heads at impossible angles. At the far end of the street, a group of boys are playing a violent-looking game with a red rubber ball—something that could almost be Bombardment, but not quite, it seems quicker and more complex. All of them are wearing ridiculous baggy trousers and baseball caps backward, shouting in a language Jack can't be sure is English. It is oddly jarring; their movements, the trajectory of the ball between them, the cadence of their speech and laughter are so familiar, but then at the same time so utterly foreign. This is the world into which the baby—his baby— The pronoun stops his thought completely.

Jack parks the car and feels for the envelope in his breast pocket. Now that he is here, though, he doesn't know what he had in mind in terms of how to deliver it. To slip it under the door seems best, but is of course completely implausible. Why didn't he send George Burt to deliver the letter? He has been imagining dealing with the brother-in-law, but of course it is equally possible he will ring the doorbell and in fact be greeted by Rosita.

Unlike the other houses on the street, number 37 is absolutely quiet. Despite the freshness of the day, the front windows are closed and behind the shiny picture windowpane on the second floor there is only an opaque rectangle of darkness framed by green- and mustard-colored curtains. He tries to take a deep breath to fill his lungs, but can't quite. Again this tight asthmatic feeling. And in addition, he feels suddenly— what? Dizzy? Ridiculous. A grown man, dizzy. He has not eaten lunch. So he will sit for a moment. Recover himself. He stares at the space between the curtains in the picture window, which remains as blank and unreadable as a closed eye.

He is not sure how much time has elapsed when he is startled by a movement at the door to number 37—a tall, unkempt-looking figure comes out onto the front stoop. It feels as if Jack has just woken from a deep sleep, but his eyes are open already. It has been, he realizes, checking his watch, nearly an hour that he has been sitting here in his car.

The figure jogs down the stoop and looks first toward the boys playing ball and then in Jack's direction. It is, Jack realizes with a powerful jolt, Rock Coughlin, Jr. Jack stares at him, feeling the blood restore itself to his appendages. He is almost, for a moment, convinced he is dreaming. The boy jogs out into the street and, to Jack's increasing amazement, directly toward him. Has he been sent out by someone to inquire what Jack is doing? But by whom? And why is he even here in the first place? Jack considers ducking to avoid notice, but then this

impulse is quashed by his need to know what the hell the kid is
doing. He raises his hand and raps sharply on the car window
with the back of his knuckles. It is the first sound he has made
since he arrived.

Rock, who is now at the driver's-side door of the car parked
in front of Jack's, stops and looks back toward number 37. Jack
raps again, more urgently this time, and Rock's eyes turn and
land on him, pause there, wide and astonished, his face paling
considerably. He does not look as though he is expecting to see
Jack. *Come in*, Jack beckons without unrolling the window. He
leans across to unlock the passenger-side door with an aggressive single-minded grace. This is the flip side of his calm—it
makes Jack feel springy and controlled, predatory as a great cat.

"Mr. Dunlap," Rock says, sticking his head in the door. He
smells of greasy hair and something else, woodsy and vaguely
familiar—it hits Jack—marijuana. He registers this as if from a
great distance. It is not what is important.

"Get in," Jack orders. The open door makes him uneasy.

Rock complies, sliding into the passenger seat and bringing
a puff of warmer, moister air in with him. The temperature of
the car, Jack realizes, has gotten very dry and cold since he
arrived here.

"How's it going?" Rock asks, hazarding a quick, uneasy
glance at Jack, who ignores the question.

"What are you doing here?" Jack asks.

"Me?" Rock blanches. "Visiting a friend."

"In number 37?"

Rock sends another questioning look over at Jack. "The top
floor," he ventures.

"Oh," Jack says. It had not occurred to him the boy could
be coming out of one of the other apartments and he is not
even sure which one is Rosita's. And now he has invited him
into the car, raised questions about what he himself is doing
here. A surge of irritation runs over Jack like a chill. What *is* he
doing here? He should have dropped off the letter and moved
on long ago—the street seems to have some slowing, quicksand-

like effect on him. He has the sudden urge to hurl something at the impenetrable facade of the house—to break the opaque, reflective window on the second floor and hear the satisfying crackle of smashed glass. Instead, he places his hands before him on the steering wheel—equidistant from one another.

"Why? Do you—?" the boy ventures after a pause. "Are you looking for Don?"

Jack stares at the boy. "Don?"

"Oh, all right—no. I didn't know, I just thought you were here, you know, and—"

"Is this"—Jack narrows his eyes—"Don Rodriguez?"

The boy stops fidgeting with the frayed edge of his shorts and looks at Jack with an astonished wide-open expression, which clouds of thought pass over in rapid, transparent succession. "No," he says finally.

"Mmm." Jack ducks his head, looks down at his hands, now on his knees. He has the odd feeling the boy has just come to some conclusion—some awful misunderstanding about him here, in this place, at this time of day.

"Well," the boy says. He looks embarrassed. His eyes shift around the car, avoiding Jack's. And Jack can suddenly see himself clearly in them, sitting here in his Explorer with the engine running, unshaven, loosened tie hanging around his neck, and stubble glinting in the late afternoon sunlight. And he looks all wrong—sleazy, suspicious, like a man who has left his office in the middle of the day to run some desperate, corrupt mission.

"If it's all right, I guess I'll be going," Rock says uncomfortably. "I've got to be—" But Jack isn't listening. There is a movement in the picture window. At first he thinks he has imagined it, just a flicker in the darkness of the pane, but then it is a figure—he can make out shoulders, a body, crossing, disappearing, and then coming back, much closer to the glass this time. Rosita. He can see her face, full on, for the first time since she lived with him. And she is so lovely, in a red shirt without sleeves, her yellowish-brown skin pale against the darkness, one arm lifted, tugging back the ugly curtain, and then coming to rest protectively under her breasts, across the swell of her stomach. Jack can feel the familiar stirring in his gut. Here is a woman who has lived in his home, cared for his son, and cooked his dinners. A woman who once put out a fire that had sprung up in his kitchen curtains and who helped him uproot the mock orange trees behind the garage with nothing more than a shovel and her bare hands. A woman he has slept with, not once, but four times. A woman he dismissed without so much as an explanation.

Seeing her upends Jack, like a yank on a stage wire. In a moment she is gone.

Slowly, gingerly, Jack navigates his way back down onto solid ground. Next to him, this unkempt boy is staring at him expectantly. Jack is aware the car has gone silent, there is nothing but the gentle, rocking wake of words. "All right," he says. His mouth is completely devoid of saliva.

"Is everything— Are you okay to drive, Mr. Dunlap? I can give you a lift if you want."

"No." Jack frowns.

The boy shifts uncomfortably in his seat and another waft of unwashed hair, dust, and the pungent smell of marijuana smoke floats through the car. "Sure?" he asks.

Jack turns to look at him. He does not have a stupid face. It is possible he is in love with Caroline and she will never love him back. Jack feels suddenly sorry. He would like to explain, to find some way to exonerate himself in the boy's eyes. "I'm fine," he says instead, after a pause, enunciating clearly.

"All right. Take care, Mr. Dunlap." The boy opens the door and gives Jack something between a wave and a salute.

Jack watches him climb into the parked car ahead of him, turn the key in the ignition, glance back in the rearview mirror, and for his sake Jack pretends to be fumbling for something in the glove compartment, preparing to drive away. But once the brown Toyota has disappeared around the corner, he turns off the ignition, unrolls the windows. He has a disoriented feeling—as though the orderly drawers and boxes of his mind have been rifled through, their contents dug up and strewn about like the refuse of a robbery.

He is in front of the house of the woman who came back with him after the snowmobile accident to change her clothes, which were, like his own, completely bloody. They drove back to the house in silence, in a kind of shocked awe, seeing still the boy's bloody parka and the stake in the stained snow. Eliot had left the night before, for his first visit to his mother's new home, and the house was empty, ticking with dry heat in the pipes and the occasional groan and shudder of wind against the old boards. And sitting in his car on Center Street, looking up at the dark window, Jack can remember, suddenly—physically, even—coming out of his room with his clean pants still cool against his legs and finding Rosita standing in the hallway, closing her own door behind her. She had turned with a startled expression on her face at his simultaneous appearance there in the dim passage, and there was a moment of awkward, silent proximity. But then she had smiled into this—a small, tenuous, kind smile that seemed more a display of bravery than charm or pleasantry. And Jack was suddenly aware of the smell of lotiony sweetness—and beneath this, the smell of another warm body there in the dim hallway. Her *skin* was so springy and alive-looking, as if its color made it fitter, less sensitive to the ravages of time or weather than a white person's. He had taken two steps toward her, almost without thinking, and touched the smooth line of her neck above the collar of her sweater.

And he can remember, suddenly, the shock of pressing his lips against hers—the strangeness, after so many years, of another mouth—teeth, tongue, and taste, and the feel of her hair pulled back smooth and tight against her skull. And there was the small but amazing feeling of her hand creeping up around his neck, finding the soft skin at the base of his hairline. He had walked the few steps back into her room, one foot after another, one hand lightly steering the base of her spine. He was not drunk, or confused, or irrationally carried away— just precisely, urgently sure. The moment had nothing to do with the sort of hazy delirium in which he has wrapped it up in retrospect. He knew exactly, *wanted* exactly, what he was doing.

And because of this, and the other times like it, Rosita is now having his baby. Jack sits forward and the stiff, suddenly irrelevent envelope sticks into his skin through his breast pocket. At the end of the street a fat black woman has emerged on a stoop and is yelling at one of the boys. There is the shriek of a window opening, sticking in its tracks, and from behind him, the bang and shudder of a bus on Blue Hill. Approaching.

Rock has smoked too much weed since he left Don's and even now, hours later, his nerves feel like the frail white roots that wrap around the edges of a flower pot. Running into Jack Dunlap has startled him—more than startled him, disturbed him, really. What the hell was he doing there? Back at the duplex, Rock has taken a shower, made four cups of slippery elm relaxation tea, and tried to complete the task he left Don's apartment with the intention of completing: preparing for Tibet.

But he is too worked up to get anywhere. He has sorted his clothes into piles labeled, in his own mind, "To Tibet," "To Goodwill," and "To be decided on," which is the biggest, because he has no idea if, for instance, he will need flip-flops or polypropylene underwear in the monastery. The urgent excited feeling he had upon leaving Don's is drifting off like some bright, elusive hot-air balloon. And in its place the image of Jack Dunlap staring out his car window has been burned like a camera flash into the delicate lenses of his eyeballs.

The man is in trouble. Rock can see that much. Sitting there, on that street, at that time of day can only be a bad sign. It seems, somehow, to lend credence to the idea that he has knocked up the babysitter—that his life has entered a real downward spiral. Sitting in his car with that blank look on his face looking for someone named Rodriguez. A coke dealer, maybe. But this seems so bizarre. Jack Dunlap on coke. He is too old for such antics. Or heroin? The idea paralyzes Rock. Absolutely outlandish, but somehow possible. He had that hollow-eyed, desperate look of a user.

Rock rolls another joint to calm down. But this only makes matters worse. His brain feels like a light bulb with shaky wiring; his thoughts come in a series of bright flashes and leave him groping for the contours of meaning. He imagines Jack, in the strange spaced-out state he left him in, being stabbed and left on the sidewalk by some thug who wants his Explorer, or having a heart attack in a crack den. For a moment it seems as if, in fact, this is how Rock left him. Which gives him an uncomfortable, responsible feeling.

Twenty minutes later Rock is on Route 2, making steady forty-mile-an-hour progress toward the Dunlap residence. He has the feeling if he speeds up he will somehow attract too much attention. The objective is to be discreet here. Not alarming. This is the same approach he will take to telling Caroline; he will be discreet, not alarming. Beyond this he has no distinct plan of action.

By the time he arrives at 23 Memorial Road, the sun has sunk behind the gentle rise of the Ponkatawset Golf Course and the evening is full of an eerie purple twilight that looks like it has risen from the ground itself, pushed up through concrete, packed earth, linoleum, bodies of water. It hovers on the lawn, on the white stones of the driveway, on the roof of the garage. The house itself is the only thing that seems impenetrable to it—a solid black hump, no lights on, set against the glowing lavender sky. Rock slams his car door and walks toward it.

He mounts the stairs and rings the doorbell. No one is home and even the dogs are eerily quiet. Rock sits down on the steps for a moment to determine his course—should he leave a note, or wait? But mainly he just feels overwhelmingly tired. Behind him, he can feel the presence of the house like another body—warm and alert and somehow hostile. A strip of skin along Rock's back flinches as if he has just caught sight of it wielding a meat cleaver above his shoulder. He will leave a note, he decides. Just letting Caroline know her father may be involved in something sordid—no, "bad" or "iffy"—this is how he will put it. And—and that he feels in some way he, Rock, can be helpful. This part is less clear to him, but not less true. There is something—he doesn't know what, but he is sure of it; there is something he can do.

As usual, the door to the house is open.

"Hello?" he calls as he steps in, just in case, and gets no answer. The dogs bark wildly from behind the gate in the mudroom. "Shhhhh," Rock says. "It's just me, Rock Coughlin," but this has no effect on them—if anything, it renews their vigor. The trash can is standing in the middle of the room and there is a trail of water on the floor from the refrigerator to the sink. Dishes are strewn across the counter and the tabletop, and in the twilight they glow a vivid, almost animate violet, like debris from another planet. The kitchen looks as if it is on the edge of some metamorphosis—from the center of up-to-date household appliances and domestic industry to the nexus of a significant, all-encompassing chaos.

Rock reaches over to switch the kitchen light on. But then the fact of his present position stops him; as the dogs are making abundantly clear, he is essentially an unwanted intruder. Will turning on the light make his presence in the house more or less invasive? He hesitates for a moment, his hand stretched out before him. The house is trying to intimidate him. He can feel it puffing itself up, gathering its years of righteous, upstanding history, and putting on a fierce, defiant show for his benefit.

With a bold flick of the wrist, he hits the light switch and sends the darkness running like so many frightened roaches into the chinks in the floor, the cracks in the wall, and the space behind the refrigerator. Even the dogs abruptly stop their barking. It gives him an oddly triumphant feeling. Rock walks into the dining room, flicks on the grim little iron chandelier hanging from the ceiling, and watches Sir Percival blink his way back into two dimensions, a flawed arrangement of charcoal and paper. He continues through the living room, into the study, the downstairs hall, the ridiculous brown receiving room, the TV room, and the old greenhouse, sweeping away the darkness and watching Dunlap ancestors withdraw, cowed, into the confines of their portraits, and the shadowy contours of ancient cupboards and footstools resolve themselves into everyday things.

It seems this is actually what he came here to do—to touch all these old rooms and objects and, like a midwife, deliver them into the light. He can feel the insular placenta of dust and darkness fall away, the carefully preserved spirit of the place shift to accept his presence—a person of today, an American of nondescript heritage and standing. When he reaches Jack Dunlap's room he realizes he is actually whistling like some disciple of Julie Andrews.

When he has gone through every room and bright squares of light lie on the grass outside the house like a splintered halo, Rock feels nearly elated, buoyed by the conviction that, for once, without even a moment of deciding or considering, he has done exactly what was needed. He pads through the downstairs to the back of the house—the little butter-churn-chamber-turned-TV-room. Here he stretches out on the sofa and puts his feet up on the coffee table. It feels remarkable to be sitting again, to have the whole world of channels at his disposal. He flips past a sitcom, an old Burt Reynolds movie, the news, and settles on a live national cheerleading competition. There is nothing left to do but wait anyway—for Caroline to come home, for Jack to turn up, for the opportunity to save someone.

CAROLINE IS SITTING across from Stephan in one of the back booths of the Artful Dodger Pub in Concord Center. "Give me some ideas," Stephan is saying. "Quintessential Concord."

Caroline stares at him blankly over her gin and tonic. "Brigham's?" she offers. She is still unclear on whether this is an informal drink—even date—they are on or an official brainstorming session.

"Who're they?"

Caroline swishes her ice cubes. "It's an ice-cream parlor."

"Oh." Stephan nods, but looks disappointed.

"Denise must have some good ideas," Caroline can't resist saying. "I mean, she knows people and stuff." She watches his face for any sign that she has just brought up his lover as opposed to his bossy friend/ex-lawyer.

Stephan shrugs and what looks like a cloud of annoyance passes over his face.

The discussion is not going smoothly. It feels hard to focus, for one thing. The unsettling discoveries of the day—Eliot missing (he is back but has not offered a sufficient excuse as to where he was this morning), her mother freaked out, and a strange Spanish worksheet next to her father's bed—have wrapped themselves around Caroline like a thick, dusty cloud she has to struggle to breathe through. And Stephan seems a little edgy—his movie, he has spent the last twenty minutes telling her, isn't really progressing—or crystallizing, or blossoming, or whatever it is supposed to do.

It's not like a documentary needs to have a plot, does it? Caroline ventured a few minutes ago, and Stephan looked downright exasperated, as if the mere fact of her thinking this were part of the problem. And he was visibly displeased when she told him she didn't think she'd be able to get him an interview with her father.

"There's the golf club," she tries again. "The Summer Swing must be coming up—there's a little cup ceremony and people give speeches and everything."

"Hmm." Stephan raises his eyebrows and picks up his pint glass and drains it. His hands are very brown and long-fingered, with perfect half-moons across the base of his nails. They look capable and clean. There is a familiar stirring in Caroline's gut.

Stephan puts the glass down and looks at her intently, his head inclined slightly backward in a contemplative way. At the table next to them a woman is reading the history of the Louisa May Alcott house aloud to her tired-looking husband and children in a shrilly instructive tone. Caroline can feel herself blushing under Stephan's gaze.

"So did you like growing up here?" he asks finally.

"I don't know—I guess—yeah, there were some things I liked about it."

"Like . . . ?"

"Brigham's," Caroline smiles. "And . . ." She tries to picture her childhood as a collection of distinct parts she can turn over and assess in her mind: carpool, swim practice, the smell of the Drumonds' basement. It is hard to decide whether she actually *liked* these. "Peanut butter and fluff sandwiches," she says.

Stephan smiles, but keeps up his scrutinizing stare. He is very comfortable with prolonged eye contact.

"Does anyone 'like' having grown up anywhere?" she asks, spinning the ice cubes in circles at the bottom of her glass.

"Sure." Stephan shrugs. "My brother says he loved growing up in Cambridge."

"Did you?"

"It was all right." Stephan looks out the window into the twilight and his face takes on a look of self-conscious disinterest that makes her think of the fact that, according to Rock, his real name is Wendel. He probably hated every minute of his adolescence.

"Can I get you another?" Stephan gestures at her empty gin and tonic.

Ordinarily Caroline would feel the need to go through an awkward round of refusal, of getting out her own wallet and getting up herself, or at least offering to—but today she just nods and says thank you. She can feel the gin reaching her knees, light and tingly. For the first time since waking, her body has begun to relax. Maybe it doesn't matter that her father is carrying around condoms in his jacket. Maybe it doesn't matter that Eliot leaves the house before she wakes up on mysterious missions and spends the rest of his time closeted with a giant papier-mâché sculpture. After all, if she were driving across country with Dan, what would she know of all this? The thought seems to somehow absolve her of responsibility; after all, it is just an accident of fate that she is even around to notice anything strange.

Caroline rests her head against the wooden back of the booth. For a pub in Concord Center, the Artful Dodger, with its jukebox full of Bob Seger and its dirty stained-glass lampshades, is not that bad. There is something soothing about its generic outfitting—she could be in Alabama, or Ohio, or anywhere. She could be driving across country to a *real* job, or internship anyway, at the Film Archive, rather than trying to understand if "production liaison" is a euphemism for "jackass."

"Madame," Stephan says, placing a fresh gin and tonic in front of her. There is a spiky-haired older woman staring at him from across the room. He is really so striking. Caroline feels her heart give a little flip-flop of excitement that she is here with him.

"So, I forgot to tell you—I ran into your brother this morning," he says, pushing his hand through his hair. The warm wishy-washy feeling growing in Caroline blows out like a snuffed candle, leaving nothing but a cold wisp of premonition.

"Where?" She puts her drink back down, sloshing a little over the rim onto the table.

"At the pharmacy."

"What was he doing?" Caroline tries to sound casual.

"He was photocopying something," Stephan says, again with the unabashedly watchful stare.

"Photocopying?"

Stephan hesitates significantly. "Does he know someone who was kidnapped?"

"What do you mean?"

"He was copying something that looked like a flyer with a photo of this kid on it—a really young-looking black kid—and underneath, it said 'missing.'"

The faint pull of dread Caroline has felt all day turns into a real force of nature. Eliot is involved in some tragedy. Or he has lost his mind? Or he has gotten tangled up with a cult or something. Her face grows hot and then cold and Stephan's eyes remain on her, inscrutable as a one-way mirror. It feels as though she can't even think under his observation.

"Maybe it was for a school project," he says after a moment.

"Maybe," Caroline says, although she knows it isn't.

"What's he doing this summer? Does he just take care of himself now that there's no babysitter?"

"What?" Caroline says.

Stephan is saying something about latchkey kids in cities, what about the suburbs, but Caroline is stuck a few sentences back. How does he know Eliot has no babysitter? She has never mentioned this. She has the feeling of pieces struggling to place themselves in her mind, of a large exhausting thought pulling itself up out of the darkness. Only she can't quite make it out because here she is, sitting in the Artful Dodger across from Stephan.

"Are you two close?" Stephan asks.

Caroline takes a big swallow of her drink and cocks her head to stare back at him. "Kind of," she says. Behind him, the spiky-haired woman is now smoking, blowing thick yellowish clouds of smoke out of her nostrils. Caroline puts the glass back down. "Would you mind bringing me home now?"

16

ELIOT IS NOT AFRAID of bears, or burglars, derelicts, rabid dogs, ghosts, goblins, Halloween masks, anything you might see in a horror movie. He is not afraid of traffic or heights or snakes or enclosed spaces. He is not like Caroline, whose fears have a certain adaptable logic. In the house alone at night she is afraid of rustling sounds and creaking floorboards; on the ski slopes she is afraid of loose bindings and ice patches and rogue snowmobiles. And he is not like his mother, whose fears spring from unpredictable shifts in her internal weather.

Eliot is afraid of guerrillas. He is afraid of men who come out of the jungle with machetes and machine guns, men who are not afraid to terrorize innocent people in the name of justice, who think nothing of taking a small boy away from his mother to learn to fight and be strong and hard and angry. Men like those who took Roberto.

But they will not come *here,* Rosita would say when Eliot locked the doors or tensed at the sound of unfamiliar wheels on the driveway. Not to this country, or to this neighborhood. This is a protected place, a place of *nice* people. Rosita trusts in greenery, in quiet streets and brand names and money. But Eliot is unconvinced. It is not these men themselves, who he knows are separated by hundreds of miles of desert and jungle and American soil, but the possibility that anyone could become like them—this is what is frightening. They are ordinary men, Rosita says, who have children and parents and favorite television shows and whose lives have been changed by anger. They were not born like this.

Eliot used to think danger belonged to the outlandish—to unfamiliar people and things that donned all the obvious and muscular trappings of death, violence, and hatred. But if it can come from even good men—or at least not really bad men— how is it to be avoided?

Since Rock's car rounded the driveway to the house, Eliot has been in hiding. First in the mudroom closet, then behind the garage, now in the wood at the edge of the golf course. Holding his breath behind the coat rack, he could hear Rock walk in, call out, stand absolutely still for a moment with the dogs barking madly before switching the lights on.

Now it is late enough to get started. In the hour since Rock arrived, the fallen leaves and branches on the ground have been obscured by darkness and the sky has faded from a prescient glowing lavender to a deep, indifferent shade of purple. Eliot feels calm, sluggish almost, from the prolonged effort of anticipation—like one of those elephant seals he has seen on the Nature Channel, whose heartbeat slows to four per minute as they make their way underwater up the icy Canadian coastline. He navigates his way out to the edge of the lawn, which he can skirt protected by shadows, all the way to the break in the bushes that divide the Dunlaps' land from the Dellars'. Once on the softer, more artificial expanse of the Dellars' manicured lawn, he straightens and tugs the straps of his pack tighter. He has what he needs—his copies, his Paul Revere britches, Forester's set of keys.

He imagines for a moment that he is Roberto. He is walk-ing through the patch of uninhabited jungle outside the town his grandmother lives in when he hears gunshots and shouting. Which makes him run, only this time he will run like the wind. He will not let himself be grabbed by some fierce-faced man who wants to make him into a soldier. Eliot will fight back, he will run down the hill he imagines leads out of the lush green jungle. He will run and run—here on the path he breaks into a jog—away from this man and the others. He will make himself disappear into his own life, not the one they have imagined for him. Eliot's legs pound the packed dirt, avoiding roots and fallen branches, staying on the path his flashlight illuminates before him, until he is completely winded. Then he slows back down, shining his flashlight twice behind him to be sure there is no one there, and of course—of course, he reminds him-self—there isn't. There is the rush of cars in the distance and the sweet, bleating sound of the night peepers.

No one has ever looked for Roberto. No one has ever helped Rosita hunt him down and demand he be returned to her. What about the police? Eliot has asked. What about the law? It doesn't work like that there, Rosita says. She does not like to talk about it. Eliot does not understand this. If there are no police, what happens to the thieves and lost children?

At the top of the hill he stops for a moment to adjust his backpack and checks his watch: nearly ten o'clock. The black digits race over the illuminated watch face like industrious car-penter ants—breaking down and building up minutes, expos-ing the machinery of time. His wrist thrums with the motion of recorded instants, sends a buzz up through his shoulder and around the curve of his armpit, all the way back down through his body to his toes.

There is an unfamiliar light to his right, just visible between the slender trunks of a stand of white birches. Eliot takes a few steps toward this, and then looks up to get his bearings. Yes, he is at the rim of the hill that climbs up behind Memorial Road—and it is, yes, his own house, there below him, lit up as if inside it there is some great, all-encompassing fire blazing. He stands spellbound for a moment, all thoughts of Roberto and his father frozen by the bright and unfamiliar definition of his house against the land around it, as if, for the first time in three hundred years, it has decided to stand up.

———

FAITH HAS ALLOWED herself to be lured into eating at Jean Pierre's "most favorite restaurant on the Eastern Seaboard" now that she has managed to reach Eliot from Jean Pierre's cell phone. He was just out walking this morning, he said—or she *thinks* he said. It was not a good connection; his little voice kept cutting out in spaces. He was at home, though. Not missing. Not wandering along the median of a highway somewhere. The knowledge is a huge weight off Faith's shoulders, although she still feels a prickle of unease in her chest. If she could have heard him more clearly, or had the privacy to ask more questions—what the map is for, for instance, and why it was in her pocket—she would be more certain of his safety. More convinced there was nothing to worry about. But it is silly to be so demanding. She has spoken to him. He has assured her everything is all right. She tries to smooth over the stubborn wrinkle of unease with one of Dr. Marcus's positive attitudes.

From their table in the dining room of the Wilford Inn, they can see through the twilight all the way out to the elegant sweep of the Bourne bridge and the rise of Cape Cod on its other side. From here it all looks so basic—dark land and pale water, as simple as the language of ones and zeroes.

"It is a fine view, no?" Jean Pierre asks.

Faith nods appreciatively and takes a sip of her wine. It has been a delicious meal—bluefish and baby parsnips, buttery warm biscuits, and a blueberry cobbler.

"Such an American place," Jean Pierre said when they walked in, gesturing at the furnishings of the tiny front hall: a shaker bench, a braided rug, a whole series of needlepoints hanging behind the desk, one of which was embroidered with *Friends welcome, relatives by appointment.* "You see?" he had said, pointing at this. Faith nodded blankly. Was this really somehow quintessentially American?

"Are you Lucy's only—" Faith stops short and blushes. "French cousin" sounds suddenly like a euphemism—or something derogatory. "Do you have siblings who come to Pea Island also?" she rephrases her question.

"Siblings?" Jean Pierre looks blank. "Ah—brothers and sisters! No, no—I am the only one of my parents' marriage. They were not so—how do you say—much interested in *le bon famie.*"

"Why not?" Faith asks.

Jean Pierre shrugs. "Too much in love for having children."

"Oh," Faith says, taken aback. It has never occurred to her that people who have children could be in love. There is something awfully brave and at the same time foolish about the idea of it. She pictures love as a pond to be stepped into, swum around in, and then climbed out of and toweled off before getting too chilly. Only Jean Pierre's parents have just gone on swimming, defying laws of gravity and resilience, challenging the durability of human skin.

"You were much in love with your husband?" Jean Pierre asks.

"Oh, no—I mean—well, maybe in the beginning," Faith answers. "I guess."

"Hmm." Jean Pierre frowns.

"Why?"

"No reason." He pauses. "You deserve to have been."

It gives her an inadequate, wasted feeling, as if she has

been a coward, someone to be pitied. "Well," she says, feeling in her handbag for her lip gloss.

"You were in love also before you met him?"

Faith considers early boyfriends—Pete Sammuels, and Trick Hudson with those awful braces which had food stuck in them half of the time. But this is embarrassing; to remember possible love affairs she is harkening back to the ninth grade when she was barely even a full-fledged adolescent! Of course, Frank Lawrence was crazy about her, and that was right before Jack, when she was eighteen, but love—the idea never even crossed her mind. He had that ridiculous way of speaking as if he were involved in an amateur performance. . . .

"There were other times." She does not need to sit here and be treated like an old maid. "Excuse me," she says in a formal voice, leaving Jean Pierre sitting with a funny look on his face, staring after her as she walks away from the table.

In the bathroom she reapplies her lipstick and pats her hair, takes some time squirting the lotion from the little white dispenser beside the sink onto her hands. What is she doing here? It feels lonely, suddenly, to be in this place that is neither New York or Boston—where no one knows her whereabouts. She might as well be in some nondescript airport in a connecting city. And meanwhile (there is the prickle again, more uncomfortably this time) her little son is quite possibly all by himself in that big, creaky old house, doing what? What on earth is there for him to be doing? She should have done something to make sure he didn't end up alone there for the weeks until he will go off to that horrible camp Jack insists all his sons go to. She should have made more of a fuss in the custody hearings; she should have tried to have him spend the whole summer with her. Especially if Jack is in some sort of "mess," according to Rock Coughlin.

This stops her short. She has not thought of this, actually, since telling Lucy about it this morning. She doesn't really care what sort of mess Jack is in, but what might it mean for Eliot?

He has possibly been even more than marginally neglected. She could be back in Concord by now, getting to the bottom of things, checking in on her son. She picks her purse up off the bathroom counter and walks out into the dining room with an urgent sense of purpose.

"What is it?" Jean Pierre asks, looking up at her in concern when she has reached the table.

"I think—" Faith is surprised to feel her eyes are hot with tears. "I have a feeling—" She stops, unsure how to continue. "I should go back to Boston right now. I think my son who I called is—maybe is in trouble—"

And already, to her amazement, without any questions or laughter, Jean Pierre has raised his hand to signal for the check from the waiter.

"Eliot," Caroline calls almost before she is through the door once she is back from the Artful Dodger. She tries to keep her voice normal—curious, maybe—but not worried or upset. It sounds strange when it comes out, though—shrill and ineffective, the voice of some tired, hysterical old aunt.

"Eliot?" she repeats as the screen door slams shut behind her. The house is lit up like a Christmas tree. Its ancient windows look stretched out with the pressure of so much brightness from within. Out on the front lawn, Stephan, who has driven her back from the Artful Dodger, is making his way through the purply darkness to the oak with the Revolutionary War bullet in it. She wishes he had just dropped her off and driven home—she is in no mood to give him the tour he has requested.

Caroline crosses the kitchen and the dining room—both fully illuminated and exposed somehow; the dining room in particular looks small, uninteresting, and naked under the bright light of the dusty chandelier. As she walks through the doorway to the gun room, Caroline can hear chaotic clapping and announcing sounds. The television—she breathes out a great sigh of relief. "El?" she calls again, more steadily this time.

But the voice that greets her is not her brother's. "Carol?"

Rock is sitting sprawled out on the sofa, feet up on the coffee table. He has an amazed, wide-eyed look, as if it is five A.M. and he has been up all night.

"What are you doing here, Rocky?" Caroline asks, trying to keep the exasperation out of her voice. "Have you seen Eliot?"

"No—he hasn't—not since I've been here. I just came by— I wanted to—" he is saying, but already Caroline is sprinting up the stairs. "Eliot?" she calls hopefully. Here, too, the lights are blazing—is this Eliot's work or Rock's? There is no sign of Eliot in his bedroom, the bathroom, the maid's room that was Rosita's, the old smoke room with its age-old smell of cured animal fat at the end of the hallway, or anywhere else. Rock is right—he is not home. For the second time today, he is missing.

Caroline walks back down the stairs and stands in the doorway to the TV room, trying not to give in to the heavy feeling of foreboding balanced on her shoulders. On the TV, lots of husky girls in red and white miniskirts and ponytails are leaping around to what sounds like a speeded-up arrangement of "My Country 'Tis of Thee."

"Do you want to sit down Carol?" Rock says, turning to look at her.

"I don't—" Caroline begins. "I just—" She feels overwhelmingly tired suddenly. And the sofa *does* look inviting. She sits down on the arm of it, leans her head against the wall. Onscreen, the troupe of cheerleaders—that is what they are— spin and whirl around some awful gymnasium. Caroline stares at the TV, her mind whirring—or stumbling, really—through possibilities of rational explanation for where Eliot could be. A friend's house (does he even have friends?). Should she call the cops? Would that be hysterical?

"Do you know where your father is?" Rock asks in a strange inversion of her thoughts.

"I have no idea," she says, pronouncing each word clearly. "I have no idea where my father is. I have no idea where my brother is. I have no idea about anything."

Rock looks over at her with a strange look of concern and—is it nervousness? "I just—I actually came over here partly because, I know it sounds weird, but I saw him a few hours ago—"

"Eliot?"

"Your father."

"Oh." Disappointment wells up in her. "Where?"

"Well, that's the weird part." Rock shifts his position to look more fully at her, and he does—he really does—seem nervous. Paler than usual and sort of twitchy. "There's this guy—remember Don Hammond? he worked at Emack's when we were in high school?"

"The drug dealer?" Caroline asks, narrowing her eyes. Rock looks high. He is probably about to launch into some elaborate delusional story. She tries to listen, but her mind has returned to Eliot, who is covertly xeroxing a "missing" poster of some young black boy, according to Stephan. Is he somehow mixed up in a child abuse case? Or has he been converted to some cultish religion?

". . . and he was just sitting there in the car." Caroline forces her attention back on Rock. "I don't know, maybe it's stupid, but I just felt like you should know because he seemed kind of strange—and because—"

Caroline stares at him. Her father sitting in his car outside a drug dealer's house? The image is so incredible it almost makes her want to laugh. Sex and drugs—next he'll be blasting Trent Reznor. It would be funny, except for the condom at Lilo's. This stops her; it seems, for some reason, to lend credence to the idea.

"Because?" she says.

"Because there was this thing Denise was saying—I didn't even know if I should mention it. I'm sure it's not true, but I guess—I guess I thought you'd want to know even if it's just some weird rumor. . . ." Rock's face is flushing uncharacteristically. "That your dad and—that Eliot's old babysitter is pregnant and—it's his baby . . ."

Caroline can feel the blood rush through her veins in an aggressive, possibly dangerous, charge at her head, and then drain away, leaving some cooler, less sustaining substance in its place. *Oh,* she wants to say, but she can only think it. His baby. *His,* meaning her father, and *baby,* meaning his. In the same sentence. She can see this, the phrase, the possessive pronoun and noun, suspended in her mind. So this is why Rosita left.

She is not sure how much time has elapsed since Rock has stopped speaking.

"Caroline?" There is the sound of footsteps and the dogs barking from the kitchen. Stephan—she has completely forgotten him.

From where he is sitting on the sofa, Rock's eyebrows rise in surprise.

"Hi," Caroline says, straightening, pulling herself forward off the wall with what feels like heroic determination. "In here."

"That's an amazing sight," Stephan is saying, ignoring the dogs, whom Caroline has let out from behind the grate and are barking close on his heels. "Shhht. Cut it out," Caroline reprimands them. They seem unusually wound up this evening.

"That bullet hole in the tree," he is saying. "I got it on camera. The contrast isn't any good because it's so dark, but maybe I'll come back tomorrow. . . . Oh—hey, I didn't know you were here," he says seeing Rock from the doorway. "I'm sorry, am I interrupting—?"

"No," Caroline says. "No," she narrows her eyes and stares at him. It must be through Denise that he knew Eliot had no babysitter anymore. "I just feel a little queasy."

"Oh," Stephan says, raising his eyebrows. "Should I come back for the grand tour?"

Outside, there is a faint scratching sound that could possibly be a car turning off the road onto the driveway. "Yes," Caroline says. "I think so." She stops herself. It *is* the sound of wheels crunching over the gravel—she is quite sure. Could it be Eliot? Getting dropped off by someone? She starts across the dining room and through the window she can see the sweep of the headlights, which blink once and then fall into darkness. The Explorer. Her father's Explorer. She breaks into a jog across the rest of the dining room, through the kitchen, out the door onto the steps. There were two people silhouetted in the front seat, she is sure of this. Eliot! Maybe there has been some plan all along for her father to pick him up somewhere at a designated time.

The next few seconds seem enormous—made up of a myriad of complex, independent movements and actions, and at the same time seem very simple and absolute, streamlined almost as if they have been rehearsed. The driver's door opens and then the passenger's, but instead of Eliot, the person who steps out is a young woman in a loose dress and glowingly white sneakers who is unmistakably pregnant. Caroline stops short in her approach, and from behind her she hears the screen door screech wide as Stephan pushes it open and pauses on the threshold between light and darkness, inside and outside. And almost before Caroline sees them, she feels them coming, lets out a little cry, but already the dogs have shot out through the door Stephan is holding open, and in a flash they are running, charging up the driveway with their tails straight out behind them like streamers.

As Caesar approaches the woman—Rosita, Caroline recognizes her now, and she *is* pregnant—she takes a nervous step backward and raises one hand to her head, in a gesture of shock or despair that is almost predictive, an effect preceding its cause, and Caesar slows, lowers his head almost submissively for a moment, but then at once he jumps up and at her, his big paws rising to land on her shoulders. And then for a moment he seems to have subsumed her—his black head obscuring hers and dropping, dropping, until with a breath-stopping thud her head hits the car's rear tire. There is a great deal of shouting—Caroline is not sure if it is coming from her own mouth or her father's or even Rock's; she is dimly aware he, too, has emerged from the house. But the noise attaches itself to nothing, hangs simply overhead, and dissipates into absolute silence. There is no sound from the woman, no bark or growl from the dogs, and no more shouting. In the distance, there is the sound of the rhododendron leaves scraping, like anxious hands, one against the other.

Caroline moves off the flagstone path onto the driveway, as if through some substance thicker than air—thicker, even, than water. Caesar stands off to the side with his head lowered, almost crouching. On the driveway, the woman's body is slung across the pale stones like something roughly used and then abandoned. Her father is kneeling beside it, and Rock, too (how has he gotten there so fast?). Her father is saying something that sounds strange but reassuring, foreign almost, like a comforting word in another language. The dogs stand back a few yards, licking their paws, looking uneasy. One of them is emitting a soft, low-pitched whine.

As Caroline approaches, Rock stands and starts toward the house, but something stops him—his face rearranges itself into an expression of incredulity. Caroline thinks, for a moment, it is she who has somehow surprised him, but then turns and finds herself looking straight into the slick black eye of a camera. It is Stephan, standing not two feet behind her, filming the disaster he has, in a way, created. A tiny green light blinks on as if registering her attention. Something fierce rears up inside her, cutting through the oppressive weight of inaction; she thrusts her hand out over the cold glass lens and yanks it downward, in an age-old gesture of protection.

17

ELIOT HAS IMAGINED this moment often enough that now that it has arrived it feels insubstantial, only possibly more real than it has been the hundreds of times he has thought through it before. He has changed into his Paul Revere knickers, strapped on his backpack (outfitted with water, a sandwich, two apples for Blacksmith, and his leaflets) backward so he can reach into it while he rides. He has saddled Blacksmith and led him out to the muddy ground in front of the stable without a hitch. Above him the night sky seems unusually bright and hollow, scattered with stars. Eliot knocks his hand against the rough-grained wood of the stable door to be sure this time he has his body with him. It grates satisfyingly against his skin, sends the sting of a splinter into the fat of his palm. He is here now, and ready.

Blacksmith sighs and looks patiently into the layered, swaying darkness of the wood as Eliot puts one foot in the stirrup and swings himself up onto his back. It feels somehow higher up than usual; the ground looks faraway and unreliable, but Eliot is not afraid. His body feels firm and indestructible, as if it is made of some solid, uniform substance as durable as Styrofoam. He nudges the horse's warm flanks and Blacksmith starts forward with a swish of his tail over his hindquarters. All around, against Eliot's face and neck and the thin blue nylon of his Paul Revere knickers, he can feel the refreshing cool of evening. There is nothing but the hiss of Blacksmith's footsteps, the chink of the buckles on his stirrups, and the rush of an occasional car on the other side of the trees.

The path that winds into the wood behind the stables will bring them to the first leg of the Revolution Way Bike Trail. Eliot has selected this route carefully. It will take him through Lexington and then Arlington and into Cambridge, where he can then make his way along the river and across to Boston on the Weeks Footbridge. Once he is there, there will be no more bike route. Thinking about this part of the trip makes Eliot nervous. He does not have Rosita's exact address, but when she lived with them she would go to her brother-in-law's on Saturdays, to a place called Roxbury, which he has found on the map—a broad area between a pearlike shape called Olmstead Park and on the other side, the bay. And she must still be there. Eliot has not believed his father for a moment that she moved. She would have told him if she was moving somewhere.

When Eliot is near enough to Concord Center to see the faint forms of the white clapboard buildings of Concord Academy, he slows Blacksmith down to a walk and unzips the backpack, which feels snug and heavy, like a baby against his stomach. He will have to move quickly; it is not quite late enough to be sure there will be no one on the sidewalks even on this sleepy end of Main Street. At the public notice board on the corner he stops and dismounts, loops Blacksmith's reins around his elbow, takes two thumbtacks from the front pocket of his backpack and a flyer from the stack inside. With a quick look over his shoulder, he posts it above an advertisement for typing classes, beside a poster of a band called Thunderhead.

MISSING, it says, ROBERTO RODRIGUEZ. CALL 617 223 4987 IF YOU CAN HELP. It sends a thrill through Eliot—Roberto's dark eyes shining out from the white paper and his own phone number at the bottom of the page. Of course, Rosita will never see this sign here, but it feels important to put it up anyway. Every flyer he puts up will bring Roberto that much more out of the forgotten jungle and into this world of peaceful green lawns and clapboard houses. Once he has reached Roxbury, Eliot will make his way through the tarred wilderness of streets with names like Mansur and Bragoon, which he has picked out because they were the smallest, narrowest gray lines on the map he printed off the Internet in his school library. And he will tack his flyers everywhere—one on every lamppost. He knows when Rosita sees them she will call.

In the beginning, Eliot considered taking the commuter train to find her—the same one she would take to go to her brother-in-law's on Saturday mornings. But the train does not run after ten P.M., and anyway it is better to go on horseback. This way he can make stops in Lexington, Belmont, and Cambridge—he can connect the two worlds with this paper trail of flyers. And until he crosses the river, he can follow in the footsteps of Paul Revere.

Eliot drives the last thumbtack into the post and Blacksmith shifts his weight and snorts, picks up his right foreleg and replaces it on the ground as if in indecision. Two figures have come into view on the other end of Main Street—a man and a woman holding hands under a streetlamp. Eliot swings himself back up onto Blacksmith, crosses the empty street, and makes his way out from under the glare of the streetlights. In front of First Parish Church he posts another flyer, and another again on the mailbox at the corner of Thoreau Street. He had not planned on putting so many up here, but his conviction ripens with each car that passes without stopping to ask what he is doing—a young boy out on a horse in the middle of the night.

At the corner of the Concord Turnpike Eliot finds the second leg of the bike path, which is dirt almost all the way to Lexington—it runs along the road here, obscured from it by a stand of thick pine trees. *A shape in the moonlight a bulk in the dark*—he recites the words to himself as encouragement, because it is dark here, beyond the reach of streetlights. He can see only the outlines of his arms and legs, the bulge of the backpack in front of him. *Beneath, in the churchyard, lay the dead/ In their night-encampment on the hill/ Wrapped in silence so deep and still/ That he could hear, like a sentinel's tread/ The watchful night-wind, as it went/ Creeping along from tent to tent.* He recites bits of the poem to himself and feels the rush of wind through the trees, against his skin, against his eyes, his hair, the insides of his elbows. *A moment only he feels the spell/ Of the place and the hour, and the secret dread,/ Of lonely belfry and the dead.*

It is nearly midnight when Eliot reaches the place where the trail merges with 2A. Blacksmith is hot and sweaty and turns skittish at the feel of the pavement under his feet. "It's okay," Eliot says, patting his neck, and his voice sounds strange to him—inconsequential compared to the suddenly loud clanging of Blacksmith's hooves on the tar. It has taken him longer to get here than he imagined—a full hour, which means the whole trip will be longer than he thought. It is only a quarter of a mile until the trail picks up again on the other side of the road, but there is no sidewalk and not much of a shoulder. He keeps Blacksmith close to the wall of trees along the right. It is just a short way, he reminds himself, no more than a quarter of an inch on the map.

A van rounds the curve ahead of them, and its headlights frighten Blacksmith, who yanks his neck to the side, nearly tearing the reins from Eliot's grasp. The van itself hurtles forward, seeing them only at the last minute and swerving with a dramatic screech of tires to the other side of the road. For a moment its headlights cut a swath of light through the forest Eliot and Blacksmith have emerged from. It looks like a terrifying mess of twisted branches and dead leaves, a confusing and impossible wilderness to have come through. *A shape in the moonlight a bulk in the dark,* Eliot thinks, but the words have lost their inspirational quality. He feels like a vibrant, frightened collection of edges and nerves and bones now, not something strong and solid and bulky, belonging to night. Beneath him Blacksmith feels altogether separate; Eliot's hands seem to be losing their effect on the reins. Another car flies past them and also swerves at the last minute, screeching its tires and leaving a trail of loud music behind. Blacksmith snorts and looks back toward Eliot with a wild eye.

"It's okay," Eliot says aloud and reaches forward to put a hand on the horse's twitching shoulder. "Just a little farther."

But he feels suddenly less convinced that he *can* actually reach Roxbury from Concord, that Rosita's world rests on the same solid ground, in the same state, on the same continent and *planet,* as his. Of course, he knows it does; he understands logically how each street connects to the next. He has even recreated the whole web in papier-mâché. But now that they are out of the woods and on the paved road, there seems to be something wrong with the equation—some lack of correlation to the physical world.

Eliot is aware, only faintly, of the hum of an engine behind him, when there is a tremendous blast, like a gunshot, that issues from its belly. Blacksmith half rears and then shoots off with a stuttering heft of muscles become suddenly fluid, a body determined by grace. And they are sailing over the pavement, past the squat gray houses that have begun to spring up along the road and shiny dark humps of cars parked in driveways, past the modest yards and gas grills and darkened windows with their blissful, quiet safety. Past rows of carefully planted flowers and street signs and spindly, staked saplings like little deer. As he rides, Eliot has the strange, euphoric feeling that he has become Roberto. Become a boy who is missing—a boy who belongs to a world between this one and that of the dead. A boy who has been, for all intents and purposes, forgotten, but still exists, still struggles to mean something in the world. All around him Eliot can feel time opening up and shrugging back the cloak of darkness, softening its shoulders to make room. He can feel it like a wind passing through him, collecting pieces of his anger and sorrow and disappointment and scattering them through the darkness like so many dandelion seeds.

And then suddenly there is the glare of metal—the fender of a pickup truck headed around the curve in front of him—and the heave of Blacksmith's body against the reins—a sort of thump beneath him, and then absolutely nothing, his body coming down into the soft embrace of air rather than Blacksmith's firm haunches. At the same time there is an incredible confluence of sounds: the shriek of brakes and the penetrating blare of a horn, the clatter of Blacksmith's hooves racing away, and the soft crumpling smack of metal against wood. Followed by what sounds at first like an eerie rise of wind swooping toward Eliot—a tornado of sorts, descending on him where he lies now, on his side among the dead leaves in the ditch. A tree falling, slowly at first—a slender aspen felled by the impact of stainless-steel radiator grid against its pliable trunk—and then faster with a whoosh through the snapping branches of other trees and undergrowth, hitting the earth with a dull thud.

Then there is stillness—the dying of the truck's engine like the moment of ending, the TV screen shrinking to a pinpoint and then off.

But not over. Somehow, there is still the slamming of the door, a figure emerging, and the repeated, almost awed whisper, *Oh God Oh my God Oh God*—a large, short-haired woman, rocking herself slightly, hands clasped around her substantial waist, approaching him. Eliot can see her sneakers—dirty, marsh-mallowy-looking shoes and the rolled cuffs of her pants, the stunned fluttering of the aspen leaves against the dirt and underbrush beside him, as if they don't yet know they have been upended—that already the trunk that sustains them is dead.

There is water trickling gently through the ditch and down one side of Eliot's neck. It is uncomfortable. This makes him sit up. *Are you all right? Oh Jesus—are you*—the woman is saying now. She has a wide terrified face. From this upright position, the world slips into a more ordinary focus. There is steam escaping from the hood of the pickup and the headlights are still on, shining into the sad skittery mess of blowing leaves, unnaturally green and bright in the glare. Eliot lifts himself to his knees and tentatively, pressing his hand to the ground, he pushes himself up to stand, mud running down his neck, his shoulder, his right leg. There is a cut on his knee and a pain in his right ankle, but otherwise his body feels whole. In front of him the woman's broad face slackens and, almost as if she has been pushed from behind, she drops, right there in the road, to her knees. *Oh dear Jesus*, he can hear her saying. *Oh sweet Jesus.*

Strapped to the front of him, he still has his backpack, now slick with mud. Staring at it, he feels a pang of some terrible unease rising through him—of what? He looks at the woman, who is asking him a question, at the pickup, at the slender trunk projecting uncannily from the radiator, and then at the dark road, the darkened yards and houses on the other side of the street. There is no Blacksmith. A dark, desperate feeling wells up in Eliot—he can feel it gathering in his stomach and seeping out into his bones. Blacksmith has disappeared. He is alone here on this road with this hysterical woman and his fly-ers, undistributed, miles from Roxbury, no closer to Rosita.

18

WALKING DOWN THE LONG HALL to the window at the end of
the intensive care unit, Jack can see his own reflection on the
floor beneath him—wavery and indistinct, like something a
child might have drawn and then erased. He has an unfamiliar
feeling in his belly—a sort of scraping that accompanies the
squeak of his rubber soles on the linoleum and the whir of air-
conditioning through the complex maze of air ducts overhead.
It feels quiet and empty up here after the mad rush of the
emergency room. No screaming parents and shouting order-
lies, or stretchers being rushed around by frantic interns. No
visitors, just a row of rooms with their doors open, and inside,
vague forms on cots dwarfed by massive electronic life-support

systems. Now and then a plastic drip catches the reflection of the hall light and shimmers like an airborne jellyfish. Who are these people here? Are they unconscious or lying awake and silent in the dark?

Downstairs, Rosita is in labor. This is where the scraping in Jack's belly comes from—something between thrill and dread. It is similar to the feeling of reckless abandon he gets taking jumps on unmarked ski trails, or skydiving—the release of embarking on complete risk. This is not remotely what he felt any of the three times Faith gave birth. He can't remember these with great specificity—they exist in his mind in a sort of smoky blur. The twins, of course, he remembers with a certain vividness because they were the first. He went back to the darkened Park Avenue apartment he and Faith lived in, heated up onion soup and canned brown bread, and sat alone at the dining room table waiting for a phone call. This was before nervous fathers came to the hospital, strapped on surgical masks, and plunged into the childbearing process as if looking on could bring them any closer to the miracle of life. It has always struck him as foolish—the idea of pacing around, or, worse yet, going into the delivery chamber and counting or breathing or whatever it is they do these days.

He has left Rock, who drove after the ambulance with him, downstairs, outside the swinging doors to the obstetrics ward. The boy is young and foolish enough to sit there making conversation, offering words of support to nervous fathers, pacing the room, drinking coffee, and flipping through *People* magazine. For all his simpleminded exuberance, he is, Jack has to admit, a strangely helpful presence. His prattle about the Red Sox, the Yankees, the time his mother had appendicitis, allowed Jack to sit and stare at the institutional carpet—beige, flecked with almost indecipherable bits of turquoise. The work, it occurred to Jack, of some poor frustrated institutional psychologist who must have decided that turquoise, what—calms agitated nerves? Dulls fear?

Jack waited only long enough to hear that Rosita would be

all right; that Caesar's jaws had left only a superficial bite wound, and that she had regained consciousness and was in fact going into labor—the baby would be five weeks early. Did he want to go in? The idea made Jack recoil. It is certainly not his place to see Rosita like this.

The window at the end of the hallway Jack has found himself at looks out over the parking lot, onto the towering lights and incomplete rows of parked cars. There is a print hanging beside it—one of the umpteen washed-out Monet reproductions the hospital has hung on its bleak pale blue walls. Jack has always hated Monet—the soft, euphemistic edges and inexact boundaries, the blurred pastels. But he stares at this painting anyway, taking in its uneven brushstrokes, the sweep of color that changes from orange to yellow to white, the humps of haystacks like tired, shaggy animals. It is exactly right here, among these bodies suspended in between the world of the living and the dead. It makes Jack understand all those cheap prints and posters, Monet umbrellas, breakfast mugs, stationery sets, mouse pads, and tote bags he has always scoffed at. They offer such reassuring visions, miniature images of a world in which borders are unimportant, in which there is no difference between straw and earth, sky and land, life and death. There is something about this that holds him here, staring— that stops the scraping in his stomach for a moment and stills his hands in his pockets. For the first time, Jack understands this longing for such softness—feels it stirring inside him like an uneasy sleeper.

There was a moment, looking at Rosita crumpled on the gravel, when Jack thought she was dead. Thought that in point of fact he had killed her. And it was a vast and shocking feeling like a black wall—the opposite of these vague, forgiving haystacks. She was having his baby and she was dead and he was responsible. And this was absolute and unequivocal and forever. She is not, thankfully, but he is still responsible for what becomes of her and the baby.

Jack has no doubt that the baby is his. He has known, in

fact, through all the writing of the caveats about proof of paternity in George's letter, through all the time spent sitting outside her house, and all the hours spent working on his diorama, through even those first moments of seeing her at Colby Kesson. He can see now that he has held this knowledge, all along, like a photograph waiting for the right light to expose it. And seeing Rosita in the window of her shabby apartment, it was exposed: clear and absolute as day. He is not a man to doubt his instincts. He is the father of her child.

After the baby is born, he will marry Rosita. He has not discussed this with her yet. There has been no appropriate moment between the cacophany of her brother-in-law's rapid Spanish at the doorstep and the violence in his own driveway. But this is what Jack decided, sitting in his car watching her stand and look out through the plate-glass window. The notion of sending discreet yearly payments belongs to the degraded world of divorce and conditional morality, of equivocal notions of responsibility, and indulgence without consequence, profit without labor, expectation without commitment. Which is not the world of the Dunlaps.

And there is something else that makes him sure of this decision—something Jack has no name for, but that he was reminded of, looking at Rosita fold her arms, tilt her head to profile. A kind of wonder and respect he has buried, for the last six months, under the floes of forward movement. She is a woman who can fix leaky pipes herself instead of calling a plumber; who recommends tea and extra sleep to cure Eliot's headaches, not psychological counseling; who unflinchingly steadies a boy's impaled and bloody arm while teaching him to count in Spanish. She is a woman unlike any other he has ever encountered.

Outside the window, five stories below Jack, there is a man walking across the circle of the streetlight toward his car. Jack turns from the painting to watch him from above—he looks so small, nothing more than an outline, really. But for the second time in the last twenty-four hours Jack is seized with an almost

physical realization of the wholeness of a life outside his own—
here is this man walking alone across the dark parking lot,
unlocking the door of his car, pausing for a moment and looking back toward the hospital. He, too, has a life that he is the
only person living. No one else will know of this moment in the
parking lot, standing under the orange streetlight, just as no
one will know of this moment standing at the window in the
intensive care unit. Jack feels suddenly terribly, unreasonably
sad for this solitary shirtsleeved figure in the darkness. How
many moments like this is he taking to his grave? Fifty percent
of his life? Eighty? Even ninety-nine? Jack stares out at the tail-
lights of the car he has climbed into, which blink once and
then steady, the uneven clouds of exhaust streaming up from
under the bumper. In a moment, the car has backed out of the
space and driven to the exit, where it pauses before entering
the traffic on the street.

"Mr. Dunlap." Jack starts and turns to see Rock Coughlin
making his way on squeaky soles down the hall. He looks wild,
with his shaggy hair on end and ragged shorts and long arms—
almost electric, like a charge making its way along a wire.

"It's a boy," he says, when he is a few yards from Jack. "Five
pounds seven ounces."

Five pounds seven ounces. The words have a familiar ring.
This is what Caroline weighed, Jack is amazed to find himself
remembering.

"Healthy," Rock says. He has come to a stop in front of Jack
now. "Ten fingers and ten toes."

Jack can only stand there feeling the blood rushing
through his veins. "And Rosita . . . ?" he asks finally.

"Sleeping. Fine."

Jack turns back to the window—the circle of orange, the
incomplete row of cars.

"Here," Rock says, tapping Jack's arm with the back of his
hand. He is holding something out. "I bummed these off a guy
downstairs."

Jack takes the object Rock is holding out to him and lifts it, casting a light around his stunned brain for the word or meaning—a cigar. Because he has had a baby.

"In honor of the occasion." Rock produces a lighter from his back pocket. He is actually smiling. Jack looks from this oddly exuberant boy in front of him to the cigar in his hand and then tentatively brings it to his lips. Rock reaches forward to light it, and automatically Jack breathes in the rich smoke and feels it pull back into his throat and lungs, fill his brain with a quick, heady burst of tension.

"To beginnings," Rock says, lifting his cigar like a wineglass.

Jack stares at the smoke evaporating into the sterile hospital air, probably—certainly—forbidden. And he nods his head, just a slight inclination, but enough to concede.

At 23 Memorial Road there is the hiss and then slam of the screen door, the screech of the porch boards, the gentle drone of cicadas—Faith feels stunned by the familiar. Here she is, a new person, and here is her old life, exactly the same.

A strange calm has come over Faith on recognizing this. She was right, first of all—Eliot is in trouble. There is no way to explain how she knew this except that she is his mother. *Watch him*, she thinks, *my sweet boy. Please, dear God, take care of my sweet Eliot.* She is not a religious person, but the prayers crop up in her train of thought like weeds. *Dear Eliot*, she finds herself praying oddly to her dead brother, *dear Eliot, watch over your namesake.* The words comfort her. There is just the question of waiting. Thank God Jack is not here.

Faith walks to the area to which Caroline has directed her and bends over, sweeps her hand in a tentative arc through the cold grass. It is nearly one A.M. and pitch-dark out on the front lawn. Darker than she expected away from the bright lights of the house. She squats down and then drops on all fours, pats her hands over the nubbly ground, Caroline has lost her watch here somehow in the chaos. She has described the events of the night at least twice, but Faith still has an indistinct picture of them. It is as if she is surrounded by a whole landscape that is invisible to her—full of dangerous drops and breathtaking valleys which she has to navigate by description. The dogs and the pregnant babysitter and Eliot missing—something about a photograph, the handsome moviemaker, and Rock Coughlin, Jr. And there is the "mess" Rock Coughlin, Sr., referred to, and the image of the woman dropping, as Caroline has described it, falling backward, one white sneaker bouncing upward and then down limp.

Faith is glad to have a task now—something specific, since there is nothing else she can do. She has called the police and the fire department, who refuse to look for Eliot until he has been missing for twenty-four hours. She has even braved calling her sons in Colorado and telling them calmly that Eliot seems to be missing, that she just wanted to tell them, she was sure it would be all right, not to worry. And she has gotten Caroline water and aspirin, made her lie down, told her everything will be fine. They have discussed all the possible normal things Eliot could be doing—remember this morning when he wandered off and came back? Or the time, when he was five, that he hid behind the water fountain? They have not discussed where Jack is now. They have not discussed the fact that this woman, possibly maimed or even dead, was pregnant. They have not discussed the dogs, who have been locked up in the garage. But all the same, there is the long-dormant feeling of closeness between them.

Inside the house, Faith can see Jean Pierre trotting around the kitchen, opening cupboards, pouring water, stirring something on the stove. God knows what he can be putting together from the bare cupboards of her ex-husband's house. "You have had no dinner," he gaped at Caroline's admission. "But you must eat something, with no food in your stomach you can feel no hope." Faith is awed by his sweet, oblivious bustling. He drove the whole way from the Wilford Inn without demanding explanations or asking nosy questions and never once made her feel stupid or hysterical or out of place.

As Faith watches, he looks up and glances out the window, but can't see her out here in the dark. He has put on one of her old aprons and tuned the ancient radio to a classical station, which sends lovely sweet strains of music out into the night. In forty minutes he has dismissed the oppressive, fierce solemnity of the house that Faith couldn't vanquish in twenty years. He has made the kitchen a place to create in, the house look like someone's home. Out in the darkness, Faith feels a swell of gratitude—he is so innocently clueless, so refreshingly out of this world. And he is casting his eyes out across the lawn to see her, Faith Dunlap, scrabbling around in the cold grass on her hands and knees. It makes her feel strong and vindicated—it is as if, in a way, she has finally transcended Jack, even here on his own turf. The blood and the dogs and the ambulance—it was so strange, as Caroline told her, Faith had the feeling she already knew. It is as if all these years she was waiting for it to happen, for Jack's own fierceness to turn on him.

There is a movement at the head of the driveway, a crunch of gravel that, for a moment, Faith thinks must be Jack. But then there is the white nose of a police car rounding the driveway. Faith is not sure whether to be relieved or even more terrified. She stays frozen, kneeling upright, one hand clutched in a fist against her chest. If it is something terrible, she wants to stay here in the darkness deflecting the blow like a lightning rod. But then the car comes to a stop at the end of the driveway and Faith feels herself scrabbling to her feet, almost losing her balance, and there is her son! Her dear sweet child climbing out of the backseat with his awkward, cautious way of moving, standing up and walking across the drive.

"Eliot," she calls, starting toward him. Her knees ache and the ball of her hand smarts from where she has been leaning on it, but she doesn't notice, doesn't even think of this as she runs. In the darkness, she can see him look up, startled, and then alter his course, walk cautiously toward her. He looks tiny and fragile and strange—his thin legs shine in the moonlight and he is covered with dirt—he seems to be wearing something outlandish but oddly familiar. "Eliot," she says again, and she has almost reached him. There is a cut under his eye and dried dirt all over the side of his face. He looks older, more like Jack, she realizes suddenly. "Oh, El—" she says, falling to her knees to wrap her arms around him. "We didn't know where you were."

Eliot stops just beyond her grasp. "I lost Blacksmith," he says.

"You lost . . . ?"

"I lost him."

"Oh, Eliot," she says—straining forward to draw him to her. She does not know what he is talking about—Blacksmith? Her old horse? But she knows, with unusual certainty, what she needs to do. "It's all right," she says, wrapping her arms around him, around this little body that was once part of hers. He smells of mud and sweat and horses and something else, acrid and sweet like burnt sugar or vegetables. "It's all right," she repeats, and as she presses him to her the frail rig of his bones and stiff clutch of his muscles give way, slowly, against her. She can feel his body relax, allow her to reclaim it. And she hugs him fiercely, rocking slightly, just a little bit, back and forth.

"Is he back?" she can hear Caroline call from the doorway. There is a police officer now standing beside the car. Faith doesn't look at him, but she knows he is there, waiting, leaning against the fender. "Is that you, Eliot?" comes Caroline's voice, and from the kitchen there is the clatter of dishes and the slam of the screen door. Caroline starts across the grass toward them, barefoot, in her bathrobe, and Faith realizes the spasms passing through her are coming from Eliot, coming from her little son who is crying, really crying, for what seems like—is it

possible?—the first time in her arms? "Oh, El," she says again—
Dear God, protect this child, make him happy, make him all right. "It's
all right." And she can hear a gentle, faraway thumping, like a
great creature approaching, one foot after the other—the
steady beating of her own heart.

19

THE NEXT MORNING, Rock wakes to what sounds like a large snake hissing, almost rhythmically, somewhere off to his right. He is lying on the sofa in the Dunlaps' butter-churn-turned-TV room. He has on the same clothes he wore yesterday and his whole face feels crusty, as if the top layers of skin have hardened and are starting to crack. He sits bolt upright and casts his eyes over the mahogany end table, magazine basket, and stiff-backed wing chair near the window. No evidence of a snake.

Rock gets up and stretches his stiff back, reaches his arms high above his head like the yoga woman on the late-night show he watches when he can't sleep. There is the buzz of blood in his ears and the crack of his spine, the feeling that something incredible has happened. He has had a baby. No, Jack Dunlap has had a baby. With his Colombian housekeeper. It sends a little skip of a thrill through Rock's body.

There is the sound again—coming from outside the window—a sort of swish and then hiss. Rock walks over and looks out. It is the Dunlaps' gardener, clipping the boxwood bush that hugs this end of the house. In his hands, the long clippers look quite graceful, their blades parting and slicing, the slender ends of brush spraying and tumbling in little cartwheels to the ground. The man's role strikes Rock suddenly as primeval, a quiet, omnipresent maintainer of the Dunlap property.

Rock runs a hand through his hair, puts on his sneakers, leaves the TV room. The house is still quite dark and has the hushed silence of a dimmed theater—a place full of people making no noise. He stands for a moment at the door to the old, formal living room—yes, they are still there, one on each sofa, asleep. It was so late when he and Jack came back last night, he almost thought he had dreamed it. Faith and a Frenchman. Jean Louis? Jean Claude? Rock was too surprised to take in Caroline's whispered explanation. They look sweet in the dim light of morning, like children, lying head to head on the two green-and-white-striped sofas. The man has a placid, innocent-looking face, like a sort of rounder, international version of Jimmy Stewart.

Upstairs, Rock uses the bathroom, splashes water on his face, and borrows someone's sparkly purple toothbrush. It makes him feel fresher and more presentable. Clean on the inside, as his mother used to say. Back out in the hallway, he tiptoes past Eliot's room. The door is open and Rock can see him sprawled across his bed, one arm flung toward the wall, as if reaching for the lion cubs cavorting in the poster tacked up there, the other folded protectively across his chest. He continues down the hall and stops in front of Caroline's room—all quiet. He will just peek in—just check and make sure she is in there. He nudges the door a few inches open over the carpet, careful not to move too abruptly. And yes, there she is—on her side, blond hair spread across the pillow. She looks younger than she does when she is awake, her cheek round and flushed, her lips parted. As he stands looking, her eyes flutter open and come to rest on him.

"I'm just—" he starts to whisper, feeling himself blushing.

She sits up with a strange, slightly frantic motion and then is absolutely still, rising from the waist up out of the tangle of her Laura Ashley sheets like a perplexed, modern-day Aphrodite. "Why didn't you say so?" she says. Her voice sounds raw and childish, pregnant with real longing.

"Say . . . ?" Rock whispers hesitantly.

"I could have changed it." She is still asleep, he realizes. And she looks so lovely and young and confused, with her brow fretted and her T-shirt twisted uncomfortably around her neck.

"No, you couldn't." He says it firmly. Caroline keeps her eyes on him, but her face relaxes. "Go back to sleep."

To his surprise, she lies obediently back down and closes her eyes. Rock watches her hand clasp and unclasp against the bed just below her breast—a sweet, childish gesture. He would like to pull the sheet up over her shoulders, smooth the hair out of her face, cover her fingers with his own. He stands still for a moment, watching her face slip into the calm blankness of sleep, and then closes the door carefully behind him.

Downstairs, Rock walks through the kitchen, which smells uncharacteristically of garlic, and opens the front door to let in fresh air. On the stoop there is a carton of blueberries and a white bag labeled EDNA'S PANCAKES. Rock looks around and sees no one. The morning is beautiful, not too hot, and the grass is still sparkling with dew. As he bends to pick up the mysterious package, there is the familiar hiss and swish sound, more distant this time. When he lifts his head, he can see the gardener rounding the hedge at the far end of the lawn. He holds the bag of mix up and the man nods and raises his clippers. He doesn't seem surprised to see Rock, seems in fact as though he has been expecting him. Rock nods his head in what he hopes looks like a thank-you and the man continues with his clipping. The whole exchange has the oddly profound stamp of silence.

Inside, Rock washes the blueberries and mixes the powdery batter. He has never made pancakes before. There is something nice about the mixing—the simple process of combining water, eggs, and flour, following the printed instructions. Even he, Rock, can provide some sort of nourishment. This is what he liked best at the hospital last night—doling out the squeaky Styrofoam cups of cafeteria coffee, handing out donuts, dispensing the common denominator of waiting.

When the butter is crackling in the pan, Rock drops in, according to the directions, "half dollar"-sized dollops of batter. Who the hell can even picture the size of a half dollar? Rock estimates about the diameter of a golf ball. The first few he fries up come out burnt or doughy and stick to the pan. The second batch goes better. He has two rounds on a plate in the oven by the time the first sleeper, Eliot, awakens and comes down. His bare feet pad across the linoleum and he carries with him the quiet powdery smell of a child's sleep. "More butter," he instructs. "And the flame should be lower." Rock follows his instructions and does not ask him where he disappeared to last night, how he got the purple bruise on his elbow or the cut below his eye. He just stands side by side at the stove with him, flipping odd-shaped pancakes the color of sea lions.

One by one the sleepers drift into the kitchen, with the dazed, newborn look of people who have survived a natural disaster. "There is soup," Jean Pierre (that is the name of the French Jimmy Stewart) offers, pulling a cloudy cellophane-wrapped pot out of the refrigerator.

"For breakfast?" Faith ventures. She looks different to Rock—younger and steadier; the wavery, infinitely flappable look about her is gone.

"Of course," Jean Pierre answers. "This soup is a perfect thing for starting the morning." Rock loves it—Faith's Frenchman offering them soup for breakfast. Eliot, who is, if possible, even quieter than usual this morning, is eyeing Jean Pierre's fringed, ventilated leather shoes suspiciously. Caroline walks around the kitchen silently in her bare feet. She helps Rock serve the pancakes, heats the maple syrup, and clears the table, but looks as caught up in her own mind as someone surrounded by people speaking another language.

When Jack appears in the doorway, they are all seated around the table. Rock has his hand on the jug of water they are drinking, which he sets back down with a splash. Jack's hair is smoothed back and uncharacteristically combed and dampened, which makes it look thinner and grayer. His shirt is tucked in and his shoulders look narrow. In fact, his whole body looks compressed—in twenty-four hours he seems to have become more susceptible to the pull of gravity. Everyone stares down at their pancakes. Even Jean Pierre puts his raised spoon back into his soup.

"Pancakes?" Jack says, and clears his throat, which springs the kitchen into action. Faith makes a garbled, apologetic introduction—*they were on their way back, she had a feeling, Eliot gone, and Caroline alone, the police, it was so late*—and Caroline jumps up to get a chair from the dining room. Rock fills a plate with the last pancakes. Jack listens to Faith earnestly, unblinking; he looks like a man trying to remember Bernoulli's Principle or the Second Law of Thermodynamics. He nods at the end of her explanation, vaguely, impartially, as if he has heard maybe three words out of two hundred. Then he slices into his stack of pancakes and makes no more effort to break through the silence.

"So, is the girl—will she go home from the hospital soon?" Faith asks.

Eliot looks up with surprise. "What girl?" The poor kid has no idea, Rock realizes; he was asleep when they came home last night.

Jack places his knife and fork on the side of his plate and fixes his stare on his little son, who does not look away. "Rosita."

Eliot's face pales and then pinkens—seems literally to stretch with incredulity. "She's in the hospital?" he whispers. Caroline begins coughing uncontrollably, extravagantly, even.

"She's fine." Jack clears his throat. "She is going to come back and live with us here. With the baby."

From outside there is the swish of the clippers, and Brutus thumps into a new position behind the mudroom grate. Rock feels the table spread between them like a vast and shiny ocean, imagines each of them his or her own landmass with its small supply of soup and pancakes and water; with its own language and terrain and natural resources, its own peculiar breed of new and ancient conflicts, folklore and misunderstanding, with its own method of mining iron ore, distilling hops, nurturing hope, and interpreting data, with its own extinct native peoples and thriving breeds of feathered scavengers, weeds, and urbanized wildlife, with its own hampering inefficiencies, corruptions, beachfuls of evolutionary detritus and industrial waste.

"She has a baby?" Eliot asks.

"A boy," Jack says. "Whose last name"—he clears his throat here—"will be Dunlap." It is like a tremor over the water—something that crashes with its own unique sound and meaning, at the same time, on each of their ears. Jack looks around the table as if in challenge.

"It's a good name," Faith says bravely into the clamoring silence, and Jean Pierre picks up his spoon.

20

THE DRIVE TO LOGAN AIRPORT is not a particularly nice one from Concord—first Route 2 and then 60 and then 93. Faith sits in the front seat of Jean Pierre's little white rental car in silence. There is an unreal quality to the bubble they are enclosed in—the gray Pleather seats, the clean floor mats, the flimsy black plastic dashboard. It feels like part of a stage set, a car someone would drive on a third-rate TV show. Faith herself feels like an actress, someone pretending to lead a dramatic, chaotic life. Does Jean Pierre think he has just seen a slice of her everyday existence? Does he think she has a depraved family? Does he think she was a terrible wife? The usual questions play through her brain, but only at low volume, as if actually they emanate from a distant, uninterested source, or are, in fact, intended for someone else.

She glances over at Jean Pierre, who is sitting up very straight beside her. His hands grip the steering wheel firmly, elbows tensed and almost straight. Faith has never driven with a man who looks so ill at ease behind the wheel. It gives her a tender feeling toward him.

"Your husband," he says, keeping his eyes on the highway, "will be happy with this woman?"

"My ex-husband," Faith corrects, without blushing. "I don't know." Outside the window, the Citgo sign triangle lights up and then blinks into a smaller version of itself. "I have no idea." It feels as though she is talking about a stranger, someone even further removed from her than the Jack she was married to. He is now having a baby with another woman. She tries to remember what the girl looks like—she met her once. She had brown skin and a round face; she was slim. Faith can't remember now if she was pretty.

"He will marry her? It is the American way, to get married if there is a child, is it not? If there is intercourse, no matter if there is love?"

"Well, I guess—I don't know," Faith says. "Maybe he loves her."

Jean Pierre glances over at her. "You think?"

"Anything is possible." Faith stretches her feet out as far as they will go under the dashboard. It sounds, actually, like something true rather than the absolving maxim she intended it to be. Her ex-husband is having a child with her son's babysitter, her son has disappeared and returned, and she is now a woman who has had sex out of wedlock.

"So you will see your son next week?" Jean Pierre asks. He is leaning forward slightly now that they have entered the octopus of Logan Airport.

"Next week." It has been settled that Eliot will come stay with Faith for the week before he heads off to Camp Chippewa, as well as the month afterward as originally planned. It will be a good way to ease into the arrangement for next year, in which she will have Eliot for all his vacations. Faith will take him to the Museum of Natural History, and to the restaurant at the boathouse in Central Park, which she has always wanted to go to herself. Of course, she doesn't know if he will think either of interest; the idea of having him all to herself for a whole week sends butterflies through her stomach. But it is also, in some fundamental way, steadying. She is a mother whose son will come see her for a week; a mother who will cook dinner and make plans and offer instructions—these are, after all, things she is capable of.

They have pulled off into the busy, taxi-filled strip in front of the shuttle terminal and Faith realizes Jean Pierre is looking expectantly at her. "What?" she says, and feels a sudden pang of nervousness, and something else, that shivery thrill of desire; she will miss him. He has been by her side for nearly forty-eight hours—he has had breakfast with her ex-husband and children, cooked soup for her daughter, slept on the first matching set of furniture she ever owned.

"I asked when you will come to Paris—the week after?"

Faith stares at him. "To Paris." She can hear herself say it as if it is a new word she is learning.

"What?" Jean Pierre smiles. He looks younger and more at ease now that they are pulled over, although he still has one hand on the wheel. She can't tell if he is being serious. "You thought we would make no plan?"

"No." Faith feels herself smiling—a big, foolish, shy grin. "I don't know."

"The week after next, then. Maybe on Wednesday—we will go to the mountains and eat cassoulet."

"Okay," Faith says, laughing, although it feels almost possible.

Their good-bye hug is awkward, with Faith on the curb and Jean Pierre on the street so that she feels like some giant oafish amazon, wrapping her arm around his dark head. "Faithey," he says, holding her hand for a moment after she has turned,

pressing her four cool fingers into his warm palm. "*Bon voyage.*"
He lifts her hand to his mouth, kissing the flat of her wrist.

Faith blushes and nearly trips over her suitcase, but rights
herself and makes her way through the sliding glass doors without looking back. She recognizes the same posters she saw
when she arrived—Venice, Alaska, Morocco, only this time they
just seem like posters, not escape hatches from her life. People
press past all around her, executives and maintenance men,
midwestern tourists and baseball-cap-wearing teenagers, a
group of veiled Islamic women, an Italian couple, a host of
anonymous travelers on their way from one place to another—
one meaning in the universe to the next. Faith wills herself not
to look back. It is possible she will never see Jean Pierre again.
It is possible he is already at this moment becoming a memory.

But at the foot of the escalator she puts her bag down and
looks anyway—and yes, he is still there, this small dark Frenchman, who, in response to her gaze, lifts his hand in a kind of
salute. Faith feels gratitude well up inside her. Here she is, cast
loose in a great, impersonal world of people, and someone is
waving at her. She lifts her bag and steps onto the escalator.
There is the moment of confusion as her bag is on one step,
and she on another, and then stability—the hum of unseen
machinery, the smooth glide of corrugated metal. It carries her
upward to the world of departures and destinations with the
precision of passing time.

21

THE MORNING AFTER Rosita is released from the hospital, Eliot tiptoes into her room early. It smells of the baby here—of powder and diaper cream and clean linen, and below this, of Rosita herself. The house has been quiet since Rosita and the baby arrived, has had a sort of suspended feeling that Eliot has not yet gotten used to. Eliot breathes in deeply, standing over the bassinet, watching the baby sleep, his translucent fingers curled against the white flannel sheet. With his shut eyes and the soft down of hair on his scalp, the baby has the unfinished quality of a newborn gerbil or hamster; the kind of fragility that is almost disgusting. Last night, when Eliot held him, he was surprised to feel the distinctive weight of flesh and blood.

Eliot knows it is not really his doing that the baby is here, in Concord, or for that matter, that Rosita has returned; his plan was, for all intents and purposes, a failure. He is lucky to still be alive—or, in any case this was the central idea of the pickup truck driver, who must have repeated it at least twenty-five times to the police officer. Often enough that Eliot began to believe it. He knows he got no farther than Lexington, a mere foot away from Concord on the mound of his reproachful papier-mâché project, and that he only put up a total of eight flyers, which Rosita has certainly not seen. Still, there is a piece of him that feels responsible for setting a great wheel in motion, a cause-and-effect chain informed by cosmic rather than earthly logic. Blacksmith is, after all, all right—was found shuffling, saddle askew, through some elderly Lexington resident's peony garden. And Rosita is here, isn't she? The great sense of defeat and despair that Eliot felt upon being delivered by police officers to his mother here at the house has given way to a subtle optimism. A certain confidence in his powers. He could feel something shifting in the way the trees lined up with the sky for that last stretch that Blacksmith bolted—a door to his world creaking open just enough to make room for this new life. And so, in this way, the baby belongs to him. He will teach him how to speak English. He will show him how to climb the fir tree and look over the golf course, how to ride a horse and how to microwave dinner. He will read him stories and plant flowers with him and never allow him to be bored or sad or alone.

"Mijo," Rosita whispers, placing her cool hand on Eliot's head. He has not even heard her come back in. "Your father is wanting you downstairs. You can watch the baby sleeping later—he will still be here."

Eliot looks up at her—in the months since he has last seen her, her face has become thinner and older. She has a purple bruise around her eye and a bandage along the line of her shoulder and the low part of her neck. Her voice sounds exactly the same, though—light and flexible over the English consonants.

"Why?" Eliot whispers back, although he knows she will not

have an answer. They have not spoken about where she has been for the last six months or what has happened to make his father bring her back here. In a way, he understands that the answer to both is the baby. What he understands less is what is going to happen now. Eliot would like to ask Rosita herself, but there is something about the arrangement that makes him shy to ask questions. That makes him feel he has to pretend he doesn't notice that now everything is different.

"I don't know," she says, and then smiles, ruffling his hair. "Go see."

Eliot ducks out from under her hand and goes downstairs, careful to shut the door behind him quietly. He pads down the hall in his slippers, scuffing them slightly along the floorboards. *Shuffle-up-agus*—what was it his mother said she called him when he was very little? He could almost remember—that smooth, kind voice and a cool, thin hand grasping his. A little skip of nervous excitement rises through him at the thought— he is going to visit her, for the first time alone, one week from tomorrow.

Downstairs, in the library, his father is bent over the table under the window. It is dim in here. Even when the drapes are tied back, they keep the sunlight out.

"What?" Eliot says from the doorway, and his father looks up, stares at him for a moment.

"Here." His father slides a paper across the table—white, with a dark photo in the center, their telephone number across the bottom. Eliot is not surprised; he was upstairs when the police came by early this morning. He says nothing, just looks from Roberto's grainy face to the horse and rider sculpture on the mantel.

"You made this?"

"Yes," Eliot says.

His father sits back down and under him the ancient Harvard chair creaks. "He was . . . ?" he begins, and clears his throat. "He is . . . ?"

Eliot stares at his father. Even now, he does not recognize

Roberto. Or does not know him to recognize. It is not exactly that Eliot is surprised by this—but it confirms something. His father may have brought Rosita back here, but he is not the one who knows her best.

"Roberto," Eliot says. "His mother is Rosita."

Jack nods as if he has been expecting this. "He has been missing—" he begins and then stops abruptly for a moment. "For how long?"

"Three years," Eliot says.

His father's face is completely in shadow now. "From Colombia—he was kidnapped?"

Eliot nods. Through the diamond of window framed by the drapes, the world looks bright and sunny; the grass is a brilliant emerald green. Eliot stands very still.

"Why did you do this?"

Eliot shrugs and looks down at his slippers. But then in a way he wants to explain it—and not just the obvious part that he wanted to find Rosita, but everything: Blacksmith and his costume, and the trail linking the two worlds and Roberto himself, and the harsh place he comes from. "Because he's missing and nobody here knows," Eliot says.

He waits, almost without breathing, for his father to respond. It is not a challenge, but a fact he has offered like a flag run up to see if there is enough wind—to see if Jack Dunlap has something that will address the reality that there was this boy in the world who is now gone and no one misses.

"You can't just take off like that," his father says finally, in a gruff voice, and Eliot feels any hope he had of a satisfying response leave his body like a puff of smoke.

But also he feels, in that moment, the absolute presence of Roberto there beside him. And it makes him powerful. He is not alone; he has Roberto. He has this boy who knows more than his own father about the world, who has seen all its events transpire from the other side of the thin, invisible membrane beneath everyone's feet, separating the good from the bad, the safe from the threatened, the living from the dead. And he,

Eliot, knows him and sees him and has him. He is *his*. Behind Eliot the old grandfather clock ticks steadily—in five minutes the ancient springs and interlocking wheels will work themselves up into a series of groaning, creaking gongs.

Jack rises and walks over to the cold fireplace, turns to look at Eliot again.

Eliot says nothing. There is the sound of someone's footsteps on the floor above, Rosita's or Caroline's, and the faint cry of the baby. Outside, Brutus lopes across the lawn. This time the silence persists for long enough that it begins to solidify around them. Eliot wonders if his legs have frozen from standing so still, if he can, in fact, even move them.

"It wasn't completely wrong of you," Jack says finally.

Eliot looks up at his father, standing with his back to the gaping black hole of the fireplace. He looks old and uncertain, smaller than usual. "I know," Eliot says. "It wasn't completely wrong of you, either."

THE GARAGE SMELLS of damp concrete and metal, gasoline, lumber, and now slightly of dog. This is where Caesar has been since the night he attacked Rosita. He has not been neglected: Wheelie has put his L.L. Bean bed in the corner, fed and walked him, and administered his monthly heartworm medication. But all the same, when he approaches Jack there is something wan about him—his coat looks duller than usual and his paws bigger and mangier, like the feet of some clumsy beast. He wags his tail low, with a note of contrition. When Jack leans down to scratch his head, he stands absolutely still, and leans gently against Jack's knees in the greenish fluorescent light.

"Okay," Jack says firmly. "Come." He opens the door and walks out onto the driveway. "Heel." Caesar trots along beside him, the picture of restrained excitement, refusing what must be a slew of nearly overwhelming invitations to his senses after the last few days in the garage. He is well trained, after all; Jack

spent hours practicing commands with him, punishing way-
ward behavior, rewarding his attention. With Caesar at his
heels, Jack makes his way off the gravel onto the grass, across
the lawn toward the little wood he looks at from his bedroom
window every morning. The grass has been cut recently and
smells fresh. Sharp, fragrant little spears cling to the sides of
Jack's shoes. He can see a figure move across the kitchen window—Caroline back from her jog, or Rosita, he can't make out
which from here. Over in the corner next to the table there is a
baby bed Caroline found in the attic, which they have set up for
the baby to lie in when Rosita is downstairs.

In the last four days the house has come to feel unfamiliar
to Jack. There are diapers in the upstairs bathroom, a rocking
chair in the kitchen, and the hushed tones of his own son
singing lullabies. Everywhere there is the warm, claustrophobic
smell of mother and child. Last night Jack was aware of Rosita
lying on the other side of the wall in her old bedroom. He
woke thinking he could hear her breathing, could hear her
shifting her weight on the bed. When they are married, will she
move into his room?

He feels shy around Rosita now, more than he once did,
and especially so in the presence of his children. There is a sort
of awe that has come over him now that he has begun to grasp
the immensity of what he doesn't know about her. She has a
son who is missing. This is a huge and impossible thing—Jack
recognizes this on one level. But it has only strengthened his
conviction that he is doing the right thing, transforming her
life—and his own. It feels wild and reckless and at the same
time predetermined.

Last night, at dusk, Jack caught sight of Rosita out the hall
window, sitting in one of the stiff-backed Adirondack chairs
looking out over the field behind the house into the darkened
wood. The seat was angled away from him, so he could see only
the semi-profile of her face and the slender curve of her arm
along the chair's. There was something so solitary about her, so
absolutely still and contained and unfathomable, it brought an

unfamiliar tightness to Jack's throat. She is strong and good and, in a certain way, old-fashioned, and looking at her fills him with an inexplicable kind of peace or comfort. He is delivering her from poverty and her angry brother-in-law, who would have thrown her out on the street to raise her son in what, Jack shudders to think of it, would surely have been destitute conditions, but here, too—it struck him for the first time—it will not be easy.

Quietly he let himself out the back door and walked toward her. She didn't hear him until he was quite close behind her and shuffled his feet in the grass to give her warning. And she didn't jump, as Faith would have, or exclaim, like Caroline, but just turned, eyebrows slightly raised, to observe him approaching. The white bandage on her neck made a crinkling sound, and in her arms, he realized, the baby was sleeping. He stopped just short of the chair beside her, startled by this second, unexpected presence. "It's okay," she whispered, and smiled—a thin, effortful ghost of the one Jack remembers from that wintry March day in the hallway.

"Do you want anything?" he whispered. "A drink?"

She shook her head, keeping her eyes on his.

"Rosita," he said, dropping onto the broad arm of the chair opposite her. Her name is still uncomfortable for him to say—he has always, even when she lived here before, avoided using it. There was the sound of crickets, a night bird trilling, the creak of the painted boards beneath him. "I think"—he was surprised to find his mouth dry—"we should get married."

There was a stirring at her breast, the baby kicking lightly in his swaddling.

"You want to hold him?" Rosita asked, as if she had not heard him.

Jack stared at her in confusion, drawing back, but then she was already rising a little from her seat, holding the baby out to him. He couldn't think how to accept it—where to put his arms—but then it was in his hands already. He was holding a small, warm body. A terrified, responsible feeling gripped him, but gave way to something else, softer and more incredible—a sense of wonder: out of the chaotic jungle of circumstances and irresponsible actions has come this.

The clear black eyes blinked up at him, struggling to focus, and one tiny, almost transparent hand opened and closed, grasping, finding nothing, grasping again. Jack extended one of his own leathery fingers and the baby closed his little ones around it and blinked with the surprise of having grasped an object where before there was just air. Jack stared at the tiny, perfectly formed hand—at the distillation of hundreds of years of evolution, small amendments to bone density and muscle mass; skin texture, color, thickness, and the proportion of flesh to blood to skeleton. He had brought this little person into the world—this little individual, already marked by something difficult and utterly human, a singularity of being that exceeds all requirements for survival and defies the concise and economical workings of the universe.

There was a creaking of wood—Rosita changing position, leaning forward. "Jack," she said. Yack. It had, in the last moments, become too dark to make out her expression, but he could feel the pressure of—yes, it was—her hand, on his knee. "You are a good man."

And he could only sit and stare, captive to this simple, but utterly unfamiliar assertion.

When he and Caesar have reached the wood, there is the snap of branches under Jack's feet, the swish of ferns against his trousers, and the nostalgic bleat of a bold midafternoon cricket. To the side of the oldest beech tree in the stand, Jack has dug a hole—four feet long and four feet deep. He has been up since early morning working on this; his shirtfront is streaked with dirt and sweat and the shovel he used is still propped against the tree. "Go on," he orders Caesar, who looks up at him with his ears perked in confusion. "Go on," Jack says again, firmly, pointing into the hole. The dog looks into it and

back at Jack, forehead wrinkled and tail quivering. And then—
awkwardly, it seems—he slides down the uneven side of the
embankment and into the darkness.

Once there, he turns and faces Jack, puts his forepaws up
against the incline. From where Jack stands, he looks surprisingly small and very dark, differentiated from the black earth
around him only by the sheen of bluish silver where the dappled sunlight plays over his coat. His eyes, turned up to Jack's,
look deep and inscrutable, a limpid cowlike brown. *A dog that
attacks once will attack again*—Jack can hear his grandfather say
it. This is one of the hazards of good breeding. Jack should
have put Caesar down when he attacked that deliveryman two
years ago. There is something innately aggressive in the dog—
he has more than his genetic share of dingo. Jack tells himself
this, but there is a part of him that suspects it is a makeshift
explanation, that the dog's actions stem in fact from the way he
was raised, from following a precise series of instructions Jack is
not even aware of having given.

Jack pulls the gun out of the case he has been carrying—he
has not fired it for years and it feels heavier, colder than he
remembered. He loads the bullets and then slides and locks
the chamber. *Forgive me*, he thinks, raising his arm. But it
sounds ridiculous—inadequate. Jack does not, he realizes as he
thinks it, believe in forgiveness. Caesar shifts his weight, backs
uneasily farther into the hole.

Good boy, Jack thinks, but this, too, is too trite to say out
loud. He would like to express something firmer and stronger,
but also loving—more like a benediction, but what words are
there in his language to express such a thing? So he is silent.
He breathes in the smell of rotting leaves, live wood, the fresh-
cut grass. Then he fires a bullet cleanly into the smooth strip of
velvety fur between the dog's open eyes. One paw scrabbles
against the dirt and his body falls over, unnaturally—his back
legs twisted, head at an impossible angle. Jack stands absolutely
still, staring, and he has a feeling of being between worlds—
alone with this animal who was just a moment ago living but is

now dead. He is alive and Caesar is dead. And even so, across this most absolute division, he is more connected to this creature than any other living thing he can think of.

Jack stands for a full minute, feet planted in the dry leaves. There is the electric hum of a golf cart on the other side of the fence, the rustle of some small animal in the undergrowth. And below this, there is a dull drone of silence, which seems to repeat the words he has left unsaid in his ears.

Then Jack scrabbles down into the hole and cups a hand around Caesar's nose. It is still wet and cold—but not breathing, there is not even the tiniest stir of air against his palm. Tenderly, he arranges the body, shifts the heavy back legs, adjusts the head, centers it, and climbs back out of the hole. He is sweating and his appendages feel oddly numb. But he picks up the shovel and sinks it into the pile of fresh earth beside him, lifts a shovelful, and holds it suspended over the grave for a moment—soil, small stones, and broken twigs. Then he overturns it, and the clods rain down on the animal's soft body and slide through the smooth fur, which is not yet ready to receive them.

———

THIS EVENING, CAROLINE breaks into a jog almost as soon as her feet hit the gravel. Over the last few days she has developed the smooth, blank feeling of a stone rubbed round and flat in the tumult of a stormy sea. Her father is going to marry Rosita. He informed her of this last night, when she came upon him in the dusky hall, looking out the window at Rosita and the baby. She couldn't tell if it was an announcement or a request for . . . what? Her blessing? "Oh," was the only response she could muster before slipping, almost dizzy, out to the kitchen.

She should, in a way, have seen this coming as soon as he brought Rosita back to Concord. It is, after all, the way his world works: there are rules and precepts he follows like bright lanterns guaranteed to lead even the blindest man across a narrow rope bridge. You get a woman pregnant, she becomes your wife. The problem is, Caroline's mind is still balking at the fact that he slept with her to begin with. It gives Caroline a prickly, nauseous feeling. He had *sex* with her! And she is so young, not so much older than Caroline herself. She was his employee, for Christ's sake! Eliot's babysitter!

What the reality of this marriage will be is nearly unimaginable to Caroline—what will they do, for instance, at Christmas? Or Thanksgiving? She tries to imagine Lilo absorbing the news, or, for that matter, her brothers. They are such fascists she can imagine they will refuse to come home. It would almost make her pity Rosita if she weren't suspicious that on some level maybe all has worked out just as she has planned it. After all, Jack Dunlap is no small catch economically speaking. This thought will certainly be foremost in the minds of Mamie Starks and Gloria Edwards—of that Caroline can be fairly certain. But it was strange the other night, watching her father escort Rosita across the driveway, one hand placed at her elbow and his head bowed beside her. He did not look weary, or resigned, or stoic, but rather protective—even tender. Which doesn't quite fit Caroline's picture. It was at once mysterious and deeply creepy.

And then there is Eliot to be considered. Two days ago, before Rosita came back, he helped Caroline carry the bassinet down from the attic. When it was in place, he hung a photograph of a small brown boy above it. "So he will know his brother," he announced and Caroline could make out suddenly, in stark relief, the gulf of information that had risen up between them—the picture like a plank that he had thrown across. "He is Rosita's . . . ?" she began, making her way tentatively as an acrophobe across the gully. "Where is he?"

"Missing," Eliot said. On his lips, the word had a hollow sound to it—the hiss of wind in an empty canyon.

"Was he—was it—?" Caroline began, realizing she didn't even know what country Rosita came from. "From here, or in Rosita's country?"

Eliot's eyes had rested, almost pityingly, on hers for a moment. "Missing means in both places."

This was an explanation for something larger than the question Caroline had posed; she can see this, although she is not sure how to frame the question it answers.

At the turn along the far side of the golf course, Caroline becomes aware of a car that has slowed down and is driving along behind her. Could it be—her heart gives a momentary jump in her chest. She hasn't yet girded herself to call Stephan and officially renounce her role as "production liaison," although he has probably gathered this is coming. There was a moment, after she knocked down his camera, that she saw in sudden stark clarity what he was doing there beside her: making a movie about the Dunlaps. How stupid she was not to see this! All those questions and conversations and attempts to set up interviews with her father weren't just part of some larger, less centralized project; they were at the heart of what he was after. He probably *knew* about Rosita the whole time. Caroline is almost ready to suspect that he knew what he was doing when he left the door open for the dogs to run through. After all, didn't he say he usually finds whatever it is he sets out to? As long, that is, as he keeps his vision of it simple. And possibly the truth about her family is too complicated to make a good movie. But she has only herself to blame for having served everything up for him to simplify in the eye of the camera.

The car now motoring along beside her is *not* the blue Skylark, though, she realizes with relief. It is, instead, Rock's brown Toyota.

"What's this?" Rock leans out the window. "A New Year's resolution?"

"No." Caroline slows down. "Just me, jogging."

To her surprise, Rock pulls up onto the shoulder of the road, climbs out, and slams the door behind him. In the absence of the car's engine, an ordinary, cheerful silence springs up around them, populated by the sound of crickets, distant traffic, and the buzz of a chain saw on the other side of the hill.

Rock looks different this evening. His hair is still damp from the shower and neatly parted in a way that makes him look boyish. "Walk with me for a minute," he says.

I'm running, Caroline is about to protest, but there is something new and earnest about the way he is acting that stops her. And, she realizes with some surprise, she is actually glad to see him.

"You know how you said you wanted to get out of here?" Rock says falling into step beside her.

"I did?" Caroline says.

"The other day. At the wedding."

"Oh."

"Well, I have an idea." Rock swings around so that he is walking backward, directly in front of her. He is wearing a white button-down shirt above a pair of clean, respectable-looking khakis. There is something alarming about this. Is he—the absurd idea flashes through her—about to propose to her?

"You can come to Tibet with me. We can go live in that monastery I was telling you about—I have a picture of it now and it's amazing—they take "wanderers," women, too, for six months at a time. I mean even outside the religion—forget the religion—you just pitch in at their farm and take turns doing chores and stuff and then you take these amazing hikes and read and learn to meditate. . . ." He is slightly out of breath, still walking rapidly backward in front of her.

Caroline stares at him incredulously. "Rock," she says finally. "My father's going to marry Rosita."

Rock doesn't say anything for a moment and falls back into step beside her. "I know," he says after a pause.

"He told you?"

Rock shrugs. "I just figured—I mean, it's not like he's just going to live with her, right? And, you know"—he looks straight at Caroline—"he likes her."

Caroline says nothing. It stings her that Rock should have seen this.

"Carol," Rock says. "That's all the more reason to come. Your father's on to his own thing, Eliot will be happy to have Rosita around—"

"Rock." Caroline comes to a complete stop. "*You* should go to Tibet. You keep talking about it. You should just *go*." She finds her voice rising in exasperation. "You don't need me, and it's not my thing. It's not what I want to do right now."

"I am." He is smiling, a small, almost wry smile. "I already have my ticket."

"You do?" Caroline stops short and the roof of a barn below catches the setting sun, sends a sharp bolt of light up into her eyes.

"I bought it this morning."

Caroline is surprised to find a little dark space opening up inside her, like the feeling of being the only person left in a room that has cleared out suddenly. She can hear the slam of the door echoing, the dying reverberations of voices.

"It's about time, I figured." He shrugs.

Caroline stares at him.

"Listen, I'll let you keep going," Rock says. "Maybe we can have dinner or something before I go."

"When is that?" Caroline manages to ask.

"Next week—cheap last-minute deal." He says it almost sheepishly.

Caroline raises one hand to shade her eyes from the slanted evening sunlight and looks up at him. The wind has rumpled his neatly brushed hair and he has managed, as they are walking, to roll one of his shirtsleeves up above the elbow. He looks more like the usual Rock again than the one who climbed out of the car. He looks, also, quite handsome. *Maybe I will come,* she wants to say—or, *don't go*—but before she has opened her mouth, he leans forward and kisses her lightly on the forehead. "See you," he says with a little salutelike wave. Then he turns on his heel and walks into the warm wind, which makes cartoonish balloons of his shirt and trousers. Caroline watches him open the car door, settle himself into the seat, and fiddle with the stereo. Then he swings the car into an abrupt U-turn and disappears around the bend.

For a long moment Caroline stands at the crest of the hill, looking back over the valley below. How strange that she, Caroline, seems to be the only one stuck here with no immediate plans for the future. Rock is going off to Tibet, her father is marrying Rosita, her mother has a French lover, and Eliot—well, who knows what Eliot is doing.

As she looks out over the valley, a dark spot separates itself from the small plane that has been hovering just above the hillside, and blossoms into a billowy cloud of red and then a perfect bright half circle with a black speck suspended from it—a sky diver. Some person dropping from a plane to feel the thrill of being alive, the wonder of the universe, and the immense relativity of his existence right here in the unremarkable dip of the Concord Valley. Caroline watches the slow descent at first with something like scorn, but this gives way to a sort of benevolent appreciation of the fact that for this moment, from where he is, this quiet, infinitely tame, set-in-its-ways small town in the heart of New England must be transformed into the archetypal backdrop of life on this planet.

The sight lifts Caroline's spirits enough to pick one foot up again and put it in front of the other. It could be worse, after all, than to be here, in one of the most fortunate spots on the face of the earth. She will have to stay for a while and make sure Eliot is all right. Maybe she should make her own movie about this place and all its obsolete ways and absurd foibles, one that doesn't try to be so clean and simple. Slowly, she presses her stiffening muscles back into action. And step after step she retraces her steps down the hill, back to Memorial Road and the Dellars' field and the whole lot of mixed blessings, lucky circumstances, and defective precepts she comes from.

22

Rosita does not need an alarm—there is the baby to wake her. He cries at one A.M. and then three and then again at five. And anyway she is not really asleep, has not really slept at all. Outside the windows there is still blackness when she wakes to hear him stirring—the elegant, uninteresting blackness of night in this part of the world. Smooth layers of black field, blacker trees, and then the paler black, star-dotted sky above these. No scratch and rustle of chickens waking in their coops; no vague humps of cows or pigs against the grass. There is no uneven shine of abandoned machinery, empty gasoline cans, a shovel, a hoe, a homemade swing, to reflect otherwise unnoticed starlight as there would be in her country. Neither is there the drift of complex shadows under streetlights, behind parked cars, on rotting cluttered porches, or the wail of sirens, screech of tires, occasional shout of laughter or smashed glass that there is at this time of night in Roxbury. Just blank, orderly darkness, as pristine and indifferent as the pane of glass on the window.

The rustling among the clean cotton sheets becomes crying—a thin bleating sound coming from the lungs of the newborn. Rosita rouses herself from the half sleep she has been in and makes her way through the darkness to the bassinet. It is a beautiful carved oak piece, which all the Dunlap children have slept in for two generations. The daughter explained this to Rosita as if there were something funny about it, as if it were ridiculous. Rosita nodded back politely; what could be ridiculous about a sturdy, time-tested bed? She knows the girl less than Jack or Eliot, since she came home only for vacations, or sometimes, once in a great while, for dinner when Rosita lived here.

Rosita reaches down and picks up the baby, brings him to her breast. She would like to sing or pat him on the back and whisper something in Spanish, call him her little *pajarito*, as she used to call Roberto. But then he will learn to love the sound of her voice and she does not want this. He sucks hungrily and with great concentration, as if he is starving—one tiny hand resting on her breastbone. It is good he has such passion for the things that sustain him.

Rosita walks over to the window with the baby still at her breast and looks out into the paling darkness. In the east, over the trees, the sky is turning a faint pinkish gray. *Here is your world*, she thinks to the baby, who does not have a name yet. *Here is what you will know.* He stops sucking for a moment, and blinks up at her almost as if he can hear her through the silence. The little hand flutters on her chest. *Benjamin*, the name pops back into her mind, she read it somewhere, *Benjamin*—it has such a kind, gentle sound. But she is not going to be the one who names him. She is giving up this right.

When he has fallen back asleep, Rosita lays him down on the sheets again and arranges the checked quilt over him—another hand-me-down from his brothers and sister, soft and warm and well made. Then she pulls on the pair of jeans and blouse she has laid out and folds the blanket on her own bed, pulls off the sheets and pillowcase, makes them into a neat bundle, which she will bring downstairs and put on top of the washing machine. Sitting on the bare mattress, she slips into her athletic socks and sneakers, which will be hot in this weather, but she has a long way to travel and they will be more practical than her sandals. In the bassinet, the baby continues sleeping.

She does not really think of him as hers—she would have given him up for adoption if Jack Dunlap had not shown up on her doorstep. She did not want to bring another child into this world after Roberto. She had filled out the forms already: filed them with the woman at the agency, who was not kind when she called to withdraw the application yesterday. It is better that the baby grow up here as a Dunlap than with strangers, though; this way Rosita can know he will have a fine life. She can know he will go to a good school and get a good education and have all the opportunities Roberto never had. He will never have to use ten-year-old out-of-date books in a one-room schoolhouse or get used to the sound of machine gun fire. He will not have to walk eleven miles home from his grandmother's one Thursday through a corner of jungle outside Marquetalia where the FARC guerrilla fighters happen to be training. And he will have enough clothes and food and money to become fat and confident, to assume that goodness is rewarded, that life is full of pleasant surprises, and that God is wise and full of love.

There was a moment when Rosita first came back from the hospital, that she allowed herself to imagine staying, to imagine raising this baby in the safe, protected confines of the Dunlap family, insulated by the reassuring shield of money and history's favor. But there is no real place for her here. She does not know how to raise a child in this world, which is as stark and impenetrable as the manicured darkness outside the win-

dow. It is too closed to enter even with the right key, too full of
unspoken rules and hidden traps for her to ever feel free in it.
And Jack is too much a part and product of its rock-hard heart
to bring her into it, even if he thinks this is what he is doing.

The boy can be a part of it, though, because he is young
and unformed and will never have belonged anywhere but
here. And Jack will be a good father—not because he is one
already, but because he has decided to be. And he is the kind of
man who lives by his decisions. He is a strange man and a
lonely man, and a stubborn man, but he is also good. He is also
the kind of man who picks up litter on the side of the road
when he is walking, and goes to the nursing home once a
month to visit the woman who raised him. He is the kind of
man who asks his son's babysitter to marry him because he is
responsible for her baby.

And the baby will have Eliot, who is such a good, sweet,
quiet boy. It gives Rosita an ache at the back of her throat to
think that she is leaving him, but already he is growing up. In
the last six months Eliot's cheeks have become thinner and a
stubborn hint of manhood has begun to steel itself inside
him—she can smell it in his perspiration and hear it in the
voice he uses when he corrects her English. He would leave her
soon enough himself. She has seen the teenagers her cousin
used to care for. They come by at Christmas with presents and
sit on the sofa smiling too widely and speaking too slowly,
bringing the glasses of supermarket eggnog she serves them
back and forth too often from their lips. Rosita does not want
to stay here to become an obligation to him. Or an embarrassment to her own son. This is not what she came to America for.
She came with her own plans and dreams, and these mean too
much for her to drop them and enter someone else's.

So she will go back to her own country and with the money
she has saved working here she can begin, again, to try to find
Roberto. She will have a good-sized bribe to offer now; she
knows, after all, where to go looking. His father, who is not a
kind or forgiving man, was one of the FARC fighters leading

the training that day outside Marquetalia. This she has never explained to Eliot with his many questions. She can only pray, if she is right about it, that she will be able to track him down and buy her son back—that her son will still be living.

Rosita swings her duffel bag over her shoulder and lifts the bundle of sheets. She stops at the bassinet and looks at the baby. He is still lying as she left him, his tiny face barely outlined in the gray light—round cheek, round forehead, round swells of his eyes under his delicate closed eyelids. *You be good,* she thinks fiercely. *You love this man and this family and this house. You be strong and brave and smart.* Maybe, when she is back at home in her country, she will write to her boy, to explain herself while he is still young enough to forgive her.

Downstairs, Rosita passes through the front hall, the dining room with its unhappy-looking portraits of dead people and huge glossy table, the brown room where she and Jack once made love. It seems now like something that happened in another lifetime. For such a strong man, Jack was so unsure and trembling—not like any other man she has ever been with. It made her want to console him and care for him, it made her feel strong and capable.

Swinging through the door to the kitchen, Rosita hears a jangling of tags. Brutus. She freezes in place—she has forgotten about him. It is not that she is afraid, exactly; she has never been afraid of him. But she was also never afraid of Caesar. Respectful, wary, and cautious, yes, but never frightened. She is suddenly aware of the bandage on her neck, the faint smart of the dissolving stitches. *No barking,* she wills, *please, no barking.* If he begins barking and Jack comes down—Rosita cannot finish the thought. It is not that it will make her change her mind, or that she is afraid Jack will be angry or will try to stop her, just that suddenly there will be so much to be said. And this is a house that depends on the unspoken.

Brutus trots across the kitchen to her and sniffs at her legs, moving in a slow circle around her. Rosita stands absolutely still until he seems satisfied and sits down on the floor looking up at her. She takes a few cautious steps across the room and puts the bundle of sheets on the washing machine. Then she turns to the door, which the dog has parked himself in front of, and approaches slowly. He stares at her with his yellowy brown eyes and Rosita realizes that he has begun whining. He is probably sad that he has lost his brother and is now alone, the single member of his species. Empathy for him rises in Rosita for a moment. But as quickly, its warm tendrils stiffen inside her— here she is, walking off into the night away from her sleeping infant. Roberto is beyond her reach and she is tired and on her own and heading off into the world without anything in her stomach. She hates this dog in front of her for being scared and sorrowful and shut up in this house, when all the comforts and grace of good fortune lie around him in decaying abundance.

She stands still, staring into his eyes until he stops whining and lies down, dropping his head and shoulders with a last desperate sigh and licking his foreleg. Then she walks around him and lets herself out into the fresh almost-morning air, redolent of money—space and tended grass and herbs planted in beds of rich soil. Damp, perfectly cut flagstones. There is a cardinal on a branch outside the kitchen window that flies off as the door clicks shut behind her. Rosita adjusts the bag on her shoulder and starts up over the lawn toward the road, breathing deeply of everything she is leaving.

THE HAZARDS
OF GOOD
BREEDING

Jessica Shattuck

A few summers ago, I was visiting friends at their summer house—a rambling, pedigreed old house on the Massachusetts shore. It was a bright, beautiful, hot July day and it was absolutely quiet—people were napping, or reading on the big old front porch, or lying out on the dock below, listening to the slap of waves. I decided to take a walk.

From this quiet corner of the world I ventured down a dirt road, which turned to pavement, and which brought me to the next town over—home to a whole different New England beach scene. Here the houses were chockablock, lining the street across from the water, their windows decorated with flags and cardboard cutouts of sea shells, their decks full of coolers of beer and collapsible beach chairs. There were people playing radios and games of football, lots of movement, activity, and noise. It was less than a mile away from the house I had come from but it felt like an altogether different, and in many ways more vibrant, world.

There was a melancholy that came with the peace and quiet of the secluded place I was visiting and, in contrast, a frenetic, contagious energy in this less exclusive, more modern place I had walked to. And the contrast was interesting to me. The Waspy old New England house seemed like part of an obsolete story, a vestige of a onetime American dream. This crowded strip of row houses seemed closer to the heart of the new America—a place where people long to be Hollywood celebrities, not members of old families, where the immigrant success story trumps lineage any day.

It made me think of people caught between these two worlds—by choice, by inertia, or by circumstance—people living in an America much larger than the one they were raised to inhabit. And with that came Faith Dunlap, a woman stunted by her lifelong adherence to other people's sense of right and wrong, and her ex-husband, Jack, an arrogant man, resistant to change and isolated by his own stubbornness. And then their children, Caroline and Eliot, both struggling to break out of the claustrophobic and increasingly irrelevant social order their family lives by.

Of course, at the time what happened was more immediate. I imagined Caroline Dunlap, a young woman in some ways like myself at her age, and in other ways not at all, coming home to a house much like the one I had left on that hot summer day. And then her mother, Faith, packing her suitcase—a fragile but resilient woman completely unlike my mother, but yet so familiar to me it was as if I'd known her my whole life. And then Eliot, Rock, and finally Jack Dunlap, who I was a little bit afraid of, but who I knew I would have to give a voice. And the book took off from there. I wrote the first hundred pages at a racing clip and then had to stop and unravel where it was all going: what exactly Eliot was up to, what Jack was going to do, how Caroline and Faith would be affected by the outsiders they had taken up with. I came to love my characters, for all their flaws, and I miss them now that I'm done writing the book.

I think of *The Hazards of Good Breeding* as being about individuals and families and love and frustration more than I think of it as being specifically about WASPs. The Dunlaps, like so many people out there, have hemmed themselves in with their own traditions, sense of propriety, and social insularity—and they are each struggling, in their own ways, to realize essential connections between their lives and the lives of others outside the narrow slice of the world they inhabit. Whether they succeed or not is up to each reader to decide for him- or herself.

DISCUSSION QUESTIONS

1. How does Caroline Dunlap change over the course of the novel? How might her choices for postcollege life have taken a new direction?

2. Jack Dunlap is an inscrutable man to all who know him. How does Shattuck manage to elicit our sympathy for him?

3. *The Hazards of Good Breeding* is a comedy of manners with dark undercurrents. How do these come to the surface over the course of the novel? What do they reveal about the Dunlaps' world?

4. Why is Faith Dunlap attracted to Jean Pierre?

5. The novel is very much about people's public front versus their interior worlds. How does the theme of role-playing manifest itself throughout the novel?

6. *The Hazards of Good Breeding* is told from five different perspectives. How does this shifting point of view (first we see through

Caroline's eyes, then Eliot's, then Rock's, etc.) affect our reading of the book and our understanding of the events that unfold?

7. What does Paul Revere's ride embody for Eliot Dunlap?

8. Is Jack in love with Rosita?

9. Describe the role of humor in Shattuck's society portrait. Given that this is in some ways a story about a fragmented family at a moment of crisis, why didn't she choose a more sober tone?

10. What does Caroline realize from her experiences with Stefan?

11. Caroline is initially dismissive of Rock Coughlin. What accounts for her change of heart by the novel's end?

12. How does Shattuck's story relate to a larger portrait of contemporary America?

13. How does *The Hazards of Good Breeding* fit into the American literary tradition of authors like John Cheever and John Updike? What other writers' work does Shattuck's novel call to mind?

14. What are the "hazards of good breeding" in this book?

MORE NORTON BOOKS WITH
READING GROUP GUIDES AVAILABLE

Abigail De Witt	*Lili*
Jared Diamond	*Guns, Germs, and Steel*
Jack Driscoll	*Lucky Man, Lucky Woman*
Paula Fox	*The Widow's Children*
Judith Freeman	*The Chinchilla Farm*
Betty Friedan	*The Feminine Mystique*
Helon Habila	*Waiting for an Angel*
Sara Hall	*Drawn to the Rhythm*
Patricia Highsmith	*Stranger on a Train*[*]
	Suspension of Mercy[*]
Hannah Hinchman	*A Trail Through Leaves*[*]
Linda Hogan	*Power*
Dara Horn	*In the Image*
Janette Turner Hospital	*The Last Magician*
Helen Humphreys	*The Lost Garden*
Erica Jong	*Fanny*
	Shylock's Daughter
James Lasdun	*The Horned Man*
Don Lee	*Yellow*
Lisa Michaels	*Grand Ambition*
Lydia Minatoya	*The Strangeness of Beauty*
Patrick O'Brian	*The Yellow Admiral*[*]
Jean Rhys	*Wide Sargasso Sea*
Josh Russell	*Yellow Jack*
Kerri Sakamoto	*The Electrical Field*
May Sarton	*Journal of a Solitude*[*]
Susan Fromberg Schaeffer	*Anya*
	Buffalo Afternoon
Frances Sherwood	*The Book of Splendor*
	Vindication

*Available only on the Norton Web site: www.wwnorton.com/guides